George Robert Gleig

The Life of Robert

First Lord Clive

George Robert Gleig

The Life of Robert
First Lord Clive

ISBN/EAN: 9783337333645

Printed in Europe, USA, Canada, Australia, Japan

Cover: Foto ©Raphael Reischuk / pixelio.de

More available books at **www.hansebooks.com**

THE LIFE

OF

ROBERT, FIRST LORD CLIVE.

By REV. G. R. GLEIG, M.A.,

CHAPLAIN-GENERAL OF THE FORCES;
AUTHOR OF 'THE SUBALTERN,' 'LIFE OF SIR THOMAS MUNRO,' ETC.

NEW EDITION.

LONDON:
JOHN MURRAY, ALBEMARLE STREET.
1869.

BY THE SAME AUTHOR.

———◆◇◆———

LIFE OF GENERAL SIR THOMAS MUNRO. Post 8vo.
3*s*. 6*d*.

CAMPAIGNS AT WASHINGTON AND NEW ORLEANS
Post 8vo. 2*s*.

THE STORY OF THE BATTLE OF WATERLOO
Post 8vo. 3*s*. 6*d*.

SIR ROBERT SALE'S BRIGADE IN AFGHANISTAN
AND THE DEFENCE OF JELLALABAD. Post 8vo. 2*s*.

LONDON: PRINTED BY WILLIAM CLOWES AND SONS, LIMITED, STAMFORD STREET
AND CHARING CROSS.

PREFACE.

It has been my object, in the following pages, to treat the individual of whom I write as a strictly historical character I have endeavoured to describe his proceedings fairly ; to assign no other motives to his actions than the circumstances of each separate case should seem to warrant ; to obscure no virtue, to hide no fault, but to paint the man in his life and in his death with the same forgetfulness of all things except the requirements of truth which would actuate me were I dealing with the career of a statesman or a hero who had flourished in some remote age or in a foreign country. Considering that two entire generations have passed away since Lord Clive quitted the stage of life, I hope that I shall not be accused, while following this course, of any want of delicacy towards the feelings of individuals. The time must come, in every instance, when our natural jealousy of the reputation of an ancestor shall yield to the still higher demands of historical verity ; and if the lapse of more than seventy years do not bring matters to this level, I am at a loss to conceive when either the historian or the biographer shall be free to instruct without deceiving the world. Lord Clive was a man far above the common measure in every feature of his character. If his excellences were conspicuous, it cannot be said that his faults shunned the light. It has been my earnest desire neither to overshadow the former nor to explain away the latter, and I hope that I have succeeded.

The sources from which I have sought to collect materials for my work are so numerous and diversified that I abstain from all attempt to particularize them. It is right to state, however, that I did not trouble the family with any application for papers, because I have in my possession a letter from the late lamented Lord Powis, dated so long back as 1831, in which I am informed that the whole of the Clive collection had been intrusted to the care of Sir John Malcolm. I need scarcely add that Sir John Malcolm's volumes have been beside me throughout the progress of my labours, and that I have found them of inestimable value.

London, March, 1848.

(v)

CONTENTS.

LIFE OF LORD CLIVE.

CHAPTER I.

Birth—Early Education—Arrival in India.

THE name of Clive does not appear to have been connected with any historical event of importance, till the exploits of the founder of the British Empire in India achieved for it the eminence to which it latterly attained. A family in Shropshire, of long standing but little note, answered to it throughout many generations. We hear of them first in the reign of Henry II., as proprietors of the small estate of Styche, in the parish of Moreton Say, near Market Drayton; and in the reign of George II. they retain their local habitation and their rank among the minor landed gentry of the county. The father of Lord Clive, whose Christian name was Richard, succeeded to the inheritance on the death of an elder brother, and continued for many years to practise the profession of an attorney, to which he had been bred. He married Miss Rebecca Gaskill, the daughter of a Mr. Gaskill of Manchester, by whom he had a family of six sons and seven daughters, and of these, Robert, the subject of the present memoir, was the eldest, having been born, in the manor-house of Styche, on the 29th of September, 1725.

Without assigning any particular cause for the arrangement, the family records inform us that Mr. and Mrs. Clive sent their eldest son to reside with one of his uncles-in-law before he had arrived at the third year of his age. This gentleman, whose name was Bayley, and who had married a sister of Mrs. Clive in 1717, inhabited a place called Hope Hall, near Manchester. He seems to have behaved with great kindness to the child, who was attacked with a dangerous illness soon after his arrival, and who soon began to exhibit symptoms of that impetuosity and waywardness of temper which distinguished him through life. These facts we learn from certain fragments of Mr. Bayley's early correspondence, which speak of the malady, and the means that were used to remove it; and describe the little patient as meek and gentle under suffering, yet more than ordinarily cross and self-willed as soon as the process of recovery set in. We gather likewise, from the same source, that the organ of combativeness began to develop itself very early in the cranium of the infant hero. Mr. Bayley, writing in 1732, when his charge could not as yet have completed his seventh year, says, " He has just had a new suit of clothes, and promises by his reformation to deserve them. I am satisfied that his fighting (*to which he is out of measure addicted*) gives his temper a fierceness and imperiousness, that he flies out upon every trifling occasion : for this reason I do what I can to suppress the hero, that I may help forward the more valuable qualities of meekness, benevolence, and patience. I assure you, sir, it is a matter of concern to us, as it is of importance to himself, that he may be a good and virtuous man, to which no care of ours shall be wanting."

Young Clive appears to have acquired the rudiments of his education in an exceedingly desultory manner. He was continually changing his schools, the first of which, at Lostock in Cheshire, he entered when very young, and quitted again before he had completed his eleventh year. We are not told how he acquitted himself at Lostock, nor indeed was he celebrated either there or elsewhere for application to his studies ; but one master, Dr. Eaton, was so far struck by him as to predict that, " if his scholar lived to be a man, and opportunity for the exertion of his talents were afforded, he would win for himself a name second to few in history." Next we find him at Market Drayton, under the tutelege of the Rev. Mr. Burslem. From that seminary he removed to Merchant Tailors' school in London, where, however, his residence was not protracted ; and last of all he became one of the pupils of Mr. Sterling, the keeper of a private academy in Hemel Hempstead. In each of these places he established a reputation for daring intrepidity,

and an invincible spirit of command. It is told of him, at
Market Drayton, that, for the purpose of getting a smooth stone
out of a water-spout, with which to make ducks and drakes, he
ascended to the top of the church-tower, and let himself down over
the parapet wall, to the distance of at least three feet. He is
described as putting himself at the head of all the good-for-
nothing lads in the same town, and, after a series of petty outrages on the tradespeople, compelling them to pay a sort of
black-mail as the price of the discontinuance of the nuisance.
Finally, his determination of purpose was shown when, on the
breaking down of a mound of turf by means of which his ban-
ditti were labouring to turn a dirty water-course into the shop-
door of an obnoxious dealer, he threw himself into the gutter,
and filled the breach with his body till his companions were in a
condition more effectually to repair the damage. Such anecdotes, if related of one who lived and died unknown, would
excite as little interest in him who should listen to them as they
would be accepted as creditable to their subject. But Clive rose
to greatness through the display of qualities which fall to the
lot of few; and exploits, which when performed earned for him
the character of "an unlucky boy," came to be regarded as
foreshadowings of that genius which found scope for the exercise
of its powers in nothing less than the conquest of kingdoms.

It had been the design of Mr. Clive to bring up his son
Robert to the profession of which he was himself a member.
The exceeding distaste of the young man, however, for seden-
tary pursuits, and the little progress which he made in scholastic
learning, induced a change of plan, and interest was made, not
unsuccessfully, to procure for him a writership in the service
of the East India Company. Through what particular channel
the appointment was procured I have not been able to ascertain;
but as writerships were in 1743 very different from what they had
become in 1843, it is not necessary to assume that any powerful
interest was necessary to command it. The truth indeed is,
that at the former period the Company was nothing more than
a trading corporation. Its territory consisted of a few square
miles round each of the factories which its agents had established, and for which, as well as for the factories themselves,
rent was paid to the native governments. A handful of troops

sufficed to man, but imperfectly, the ill-constructed forts by which the warehouses were protected ; and the native portion of this force, by far the most numerous, was not only not disciplined after the European fashion, but lacked other arms than the sword and shield, or else a bow and arrows. The civil servants of the Company, too, were neither counsellors nor judges, collectors nor diplomatists, but clerks, whose duty it was to keep accounts, to take stock, to make advances to weavers, to ship cargoes, and to prevent, as much as possible, the interference of interlopers with the monopoly of the India trade, which acts of parliament had secured to them. Moreover, the writers, as they were called, or junior clerks, received such miserable pay that to avoid getting into debt, except by the exercise of extreme self-denial, was impossible. No doubt there were great prizes in store for such as might survive these early hardships. Private trade—that is, the trade of individuals on their own account—was then in the height of its luxuriance ; and large fortunes were made by such as could embark in it at the expense of the interests of their employers. But opportunities of this sort did not come till after long years of residence in the country ; and these were, even under the most favourable circumstances, years of suffering and of drudgery. A writership was not, therefore, considered a hundred years ago in the light of a handsome provision for the younger son of a noble family, or of a Director, and was therefore, much more than it is now, within the reach of persons of far less pretension.

Young Clive received his nomination in the early spring of 1743, and embarked soon afterwards for Madras. He was then in the eighteenth year of his age, and, in spite of an ill-regulated temper, appears to have possessed strong natural affections and a warm heart. His aunt Bayley had died in 1735, but Hope Hall did not cease on that account to be his home ; indeed he retained both then and afterwards a lively recollection of the happy days which he had spent there, and parted from its surviving inmates with great regret. His voyage, besides being tedious and expensive, was not devoid of danger. The ship in which he took his passage put in at Brazil, where it was detained nine months, and suffered a second detention, though not so protracted, at the Cape of Good Hope. The consequence was,

that the autumn of 1744 had set in ere our adventurer reached
the place of his destination. But it tells in Clive's favour that
he did not allow the opportunity which presented itself at
Brazil of acquiring some knowledge of the Portuguese language
to pass unimproved. An accurate Portuguese scholar he never
became; indeed he would appear to have been deficient in that
order of talent which gives to its possessors a facility of acquiring languages; for it is a curious fact that he, who more
than almost any other Englishman understood the character of the
natives of India, and exercised unbounded sway over them, was
never able to hold a lengthened or serious communication with
them, either by writing or in conversation, except through the
medium of an interpreter. But he managed to pick up more
than a smattering of the tongue in which Camoens wrote, and in
after-life his knowledge, imperfect as it might be, was more than
once of use to him.

Two results, both of them of evil consequence to Clive,
arose out of the extraordinary length of his outward passage :
he had expended the whole of his ready money before he
reached Madras; and a gentleman to whom he carried letters of
introduction, and who would have assisted him in the strait,
had already quitted the place and returned to Europe. Under
these circumstances Clive was driven to borrow from the captain
of the ship in which he had come out; and he complains, probably not without reason, of the exorbitant interest which the
lender exacted. He felt himself, likewise, alone as it were in
a new world; for though in those days, not less than now, hospitality was a virtue largely practised by the Company's servants
in the East, Clive, being shy or proud, and destitute of recommendations to any of the residents at Madras, kept aloof from
them all, and was of course in his turn neglected. His irritable
temper did not soften down amid the comparative solitude in
which he lived, and he soon began to experience a depression of
spirits which, as it was constitutional, never afterwards wholly
left him. As a specimen of the manner in which his proud disposition worked, it may be stated that he had not been long at the
desk when he quarrelled with a superior functionary, and gave
such proof of his contempt for the rules of the service that the
Governor, being appealed to, commanded him to apologize.

Clive could not refuse to obey, because any attempt to evade the order would have cost him his place; but he made his submission with a very bad grace, and would never again return to habits of familiar acquaintance with the secretary. When the latter, desirous of burying the dispute in oblivion, asked him one day to dine, he replied, "No, sir; the Governor desired me to apologize, and I have done so; but he did not command me to dine with you."

Besides being wayward and irritable to a degree which rendered him often impatient of control, and not always safe as a companion, Clive began already to labour under occasional fits of low spirits, during the paroxysms of one of which it is said that he twice made an attempt to destroy himself. He had been improvident, it appears, and his pecuniary affairs were involved. The restraints of the office chafed him; and he took in ill part both the advice and the remonstrances of such as prompted him to greater exertion. In this humour he withdrew one day to his own room in Writers' Buildings, and there shut himself up. An hour or two afterwards one of his companions knocked at the door, and was admitted. He found Clive seated in a remote corner of the apartment, with a table near him, on which lay a pistol. "Take it, and fire it over the window," said Clive, pointing to the weapon. His friend did so; and no sooner was the report heard than Clive, springing from his seat, exclaimed, " I feel that I am reserved for some end or another. I twice snapped that pistol at my own head, and it would not go off." Strange as this story may read, it is not unlikely to be true. The explosion of a pistol at last which has previously missed fire is an event of too frequent occurrence to stagger the most sceptical ; and the after-career of the man affords sufficient ground for believing that there were many moments in his life when the thought of self-destruction was not unlikely to be present with him. On the other hand, it is certain that, though often referring to the events of his early Indian career, he was never known to allude to this occurrence. His conversation, on the contrary, when it took that turn, became lively, anecdotical, and replete with good feeling. Every act of kindness done to himself, as well as the persons and names of the parties to whom he had been indebted for it, were brought out pleasantly, as if from the storehouse of a grateful memory; while recollections of a different kind appeared all to have faded away, or to be dismissed. At the same time his correspondence shows that his mind was at this period often ill at ease. He appears to have felt acutely that he was not suited for the occupations of detail and routine to which he had been called. A temperament such as his required strong, if not constant, excitement; his powers of mind languished for want of more congenial objects on which to exercise themselves. He even pined for home, and the endearments of the domestic circle, with an intensity of which his boyhood had given no promise. Writing to one of his cousins, he says, " I have not enjoyed one happy day since I left my native country." In another of his letters we find him declaring, " I must confess, at intervals when I think of my dear native England, it affects me in a very particular manner. If I should be so far blessed as to revisit again my own country, but more especially Manchester, the centre of all my wishes, all that I could hope for or desire would be presented before me in one view." These are touching avowals to come from one who had been noted even in childhood rather for the firmness of his resolves than for the clinging nature of his feelings; but they exhibit a true picture of his sentiments: for Clive had no touch of affectation about him. However, the writer was not without a solace amid his cares more creditable than those upon which functionaries of his standing were for the most part accustomed to fall back. The Governor had a good library, to which he permitted Clive to have free access; and the young man, devoting much of his leisure time to study, acquired in that apartment almost all the knowledge of books of which he seems ever to have been possessed.

CHAPTER II.

Joins the Army—Early Military Services.

SUCH was the manner of Clive's existence when an event befell, which, threatening at the outset to cast a blight over his prospects, proved, in point of fact, to be the turning-point whence his march to eminence began.

The war of the Austrian succession, which had for some years desolated Europe, was extended in 1745 and 1746 to Asia. England and France had taken opposite sides in the quarrel; and, the fleets of the latter obtaining, in the Indian seas, a temporary ascendancy, Labourdonnais, the able and accomplished Governor of Mauritius, determined to make the most of the circumstance. It will be recollected that France had at this time her East India Company, to the full as rich and influential as that of England. She was the mistress, also, of settlements more extensive, and in some respects better placed, than any which flourished under the protection of the British flag; and her local authorities aspired, as is the habit of their countrymen, far more after political influence than increased facilities of trade. Almost all the Spice Islands, including that over the destinies of which Labourdonnais presided, belonged to her. The chief seat of her power was, however, Pondicherry, where Dupleix—a man of greater ambition and almost equal talent with Labourdonnais—held rule; and she was strong in a military point of view—not only because of the number of regular troops which she kept on foot, but because she had already begun to arm and discipline battalions of sepoys after the European fashion, and found them trustworthy.

The possessions of England, on the other hand, though not inconveniently situated for purposes of trade with the interior, were all on the continent of India. On the Malabar side she held Bombay, which had been ceded by Portugal to Charles II. as part of the dowry of Queen Catherine. At the mouth of the

Hoogley, a branch of the river Ganges, Calcutta belonged to her; but Calcutta was as yet so little accounted of, that it had only just ceased to be a dependency on the more important presidency of Madras. Lastly, along the Coromandel coast were scattered Madras, Fort St. David, Cuddalore, and two or three lesser stations, all of which were more or less important on account of the treasures which their storehouses contained, though none were considered capable of being maintained, for a single day, against the power of the native princes, should it be put forth in earnest.

The rival Companies were thus circumstanced when Labourdonnais, after compelling the English fleet to abandon the coast, landed with an army and put Madras in a state of siege. The place, after a weak resistance, capitulated, and the keys of the fort were given into his hands. Whatever property was accumulated in the Company's warehouses became the prey of the conquerors; but it was stipulated that the town should be spared, and that on payment of a ransom, which Labourdonnais pledged himself to fix at a moderate amount, it should be given back to its former proprietors. Meanwhile the English inhabitants were to suffer no molestation; but, considering themselves prisoners of war upon parole, were to abide quietly in their houses.

There had been jealousies between Dupleix and Labourdonnais ever since the nomination of the former to the presidency of Pondicherry. These the success of the expedition against Madras greatly inflamed; and Dupleix, asserting that the Governor of Mauritius had exceeded his powers—inasmuch as all conquests effected on the continent of India were at his own disposal—refused to ratify the capitulation. He even went so far as to threaten that the works of Fort St. George should be blown up; and, despatching one of his own officers to act as Governor, called upon the English residents to renew their parole of honour to him. Indeed he did more: with no other apparent object in view than the indulgence of a small national vanity, he caused the English Governor, with some of the chief members of the factory, to be conveyed, under a guard, to Pondicherry, and marched them, somewhat after the manner of captives in a Roman procession, through the town. So gross a violation on one side of the terms of the treaty was regarded on the other as absolving men from their engagements; and many, among whom Clive was one, no longer considered their parole to be binding. These escaped as they best could from Madras; Clive, with a friend, fleeing in the disguise of Mussulmans, and taking shelter at Fort St. David.

For some time after his arrival in the latter place Clive appears to have led a life of unprofitable idleness. His services were not required in a factory already overstocked with clerks, whom the progress of hostilities compelled, in a great measure, to suspend their commercial undertakings; and he sought sometimes at the gaming-table that escape from dejection which he could not find either in study or the duties of his station. It happened upon a certain occasion that two officers with whom he had been engaged in play were detected in the act of cheating. They had won considerable sums of money from various persons present, and among the rest from Clive; but he, having satisfied himself of the nature of their proceedings, refused to pay. A quarrel ensued, and one of them demanded satisfaction. The combatants met without seconds to settle the dispute, and Clive, having the first fire, delivered it to no purpose, and stood at the mercy of his adversary. The latter, walking up, presented his pistol at Clive's head, and desired him to ask his life. This was done without hesitation; but when the other went on to demand an apology, and the retractation of the charge of cheating, Clive refused to give either. "Then I will shoot you," exclaimed the bully. "Shoot and be d——d!" replied Clive. "I said you cheated, I say so still, and I will never pay you." The officer, declaring the young man to be mad, threw away his weapon, and there the matter ended; for Clive, when urged to bring the whole case under the cognizance of the authorities, declined to do so, and religiously abstained from referring, even in private society, to the behaviour of his late opponent at cards. "I will not do him an injury on any account," was his answer. "I will never pay what he unfairly won; but he has given me my life, and from me he shall take no hurt under any circumstances."

Whether the occurrence just related had any other influence upon Clive's fortunes than to win for him, on account of his desperate bravery, the admiration of his young companions, does not appear; but we find him soon afterwards taking steps to exchange the pen for the sword, and succeeding in obtaining an ensigncy in the Company's army. Doubtless he had, in some measure, earned his commission by the good service which he rendered during the siege of Fort St. David; for when Dupleix, hoping to profit by the consternation which the fall of Madras had occasioned, marched against the latter place, Clive, though a civilian, shouldered a musket, and took his turn of duty with the rest of the garrison. But whatever the immediate occasion of the arrangement may have been, his ensigncy, which bore date in the spring of 1747, did not remove him from the civil service. It enabled him, however, to witness almost all the petty operations in which the autumn of 1747 and the spring of the following year were wasted, and attached him to the force which in 1748 co-operated with Admiral Boscawen's army in the attack upon Pondicherry. The latter enterprise, as is well known, signally failed. It could not indeed do otherwise, for, undertaken at an improper season, it was pushed forward without either energy or skill. Nevertheless, it furnished Mr. Clive with more than one opportunity for the display of that personal coolness and intrepidity which may be described as the groundwork of all other military virtues. It involved him, likewise, in a new quarrel; and would have brought him again into personal conflict with a brother officer, had not the latter, under somewhat peculiar circumstances, declined the challenge. Mr. Clive, it appears, had the command of one of the advanced batteries which were opened against the works of Pondicherry. The fire proving hot, his ammunition expended itself; and he, in his eagerness to renew the fight, ran to the rear for a fresh supply. It is not usual for officers to go in person upon such errands; and the circumstance being noticed by one whose speech seems to have been but imperfectly under the control of his reason, insinuations hurtful to the character of Clive as a soldier were thrown out. The young man lost no time in demanding an explanation, and, the author of the scandal failing to give such as Clive felt that he had a right to expect, a demand for instant satisfaction followed. As the parties were moving to their ground, Clive's opponent, irritated by some circumstance which has not been stated, struck him. Clive drew upon the spot ; but the place being public, the duel was prevented. A judicial inquiry followed, which led to the condemnation of the individual who had given the blow, and imposed upon him the necessity of making a public apology in front of the battalion ; but with this Clive did not rest content. The original ground of quarrel had not been removed, and the fiery young soldier returned to it. His adversary, however, asserting that one apology was enough to wipe out all offences, declined to meet him ; whereupon Clive shook a cane over his head, and told him he was a coward. The result was that Clive came off without the slightest stain on his character, while the originator of the fray was obliged to resign his commission.

I repeat these anecdotes as I find them told, more at length, by the authorities which, in the compilation of the present memoir, it has been necessary to consult ; but I entirely dissent from the opinions of those writers who seem to regard them as creditable to the subject. Brawls and duels, however frequent in the last century, had not the effect even then of elevating men's reputation for courage ; in these days they are regarded both justly and happily as manifestations of bad taste and an ill-regulated mind. Let us not, however, be too severe upon Clive. His duel with the gambler admits of no excuse. It was the last act in a series of indefensible outrages on both morals and manners, and there is nothing to admire about it except the headstrong determination of the man, who would rather submit to be put to death than retract a word which he had once uttered. But the affair beside the lines of Pondicherry is at least more intelligible, though even that can hardly be spoken of except with regret. A quiet remonstrance would have probably gained all the reparation which so palpable and admitted a wrong required ; for Clive's reputation for courage was already such as to render a loose insinuation to the contrary innocuous ; and had the contrary been the case, there was surely no need, after the humiliation to which the other party had been subjected, to force a dormant quarrel upon him. Still here the stories are ; and as I believe them to be authentic, and desire no more than to draw a faithful picture of a very remarkable personage, I cannot refuse to transfer them to these pages. The reader will doubtless find as he goes on other proofs that Clive, however great in the recognised meaning of that term, was by no means, either in his public or private character, a perfect being.

The British army had not long returned from its abortive attempt to reduce Pondicherry when tidings arrived from Europe of the cessation of hostilities. The immediate consequence of this announcement, as regarded public affairs, was the restoration of Madras by Dupleix to the East India Company. Upon the career of Clive it produced this effect, that it restored him for a brief space to his peaceful occupations in Writers' Buildings. But the love of a military life was by this time so rooted in him, that at the first intimation of hostilities, no matter against whom to be conducted, he again volunteered to serve. Accordingly, when in 1749 an expedition was fitted out for the ostensible purpose of restoring an exiled rajah to the throne of Tanjore, Clive joined it. The circumstances of the case were these :—

The district of Tanjore, comprising an extent of seventy or eighty miles in length, and lying within or immediately adjoining to the several mouths of the Cavery, constituted, at the period of which I now write, a Hindoo principality, which the Mahomedans, though nominally establishing their dominion over it, had been content to govern, even in the height of their vigour, through the agency of its native sovereigns. In the reign of Arungzebe, Sivaji, the illustrious founder of the Mahratta confederation, won it with his sword and left it as an inheritance to his children. During four generations these swayed the sceptre, the son succeeding the father without interruption ; but the successor of the last of them, being an infant, was put to death, and then began a scramble for the throne. First Sahujee, the legitimate son of Tuckojee, and as such the uncle of the murdered child, won the prize. He did not keep it long, however, because the same influence which had raised set him aside, and Pritauba Sing, also a son of Tuckojee, though by a concubine, reigned in his stead. It does not appear that the people of Tanjore took any objection to the rajah's title. He made various treaties with the English likewise in the course of several years, which he kept faithfully, and his tenure appeared to be as secure as that of any other of the princes of India. But, soon after the cessation of the war with France, Sahujee, the exile, presented himself at Fort St. David and besought the English to assist him with a portion of their troops in an attempt to recover his kingdom. No doubt his assertion of the justice of his title, and the assurances which he gave of being supported by a majority of the people, had due weight with the English authorities; but there is reason to believe that a promise, in the event of success, of the town and harbour of Dovecotta, at the mouth of the Coleroon, told at least as effectually as either argument. Be this however as it may, a resolution of council was passed to the effect that it would be expedient to assist the rajah in the prosecution of his claim, and a force was ordered to proceed under the command of Captain Cope for that purpose.

Cope's little army, consisting of 430 Europeans, 1000 sepoys, and a few heavy guns, took the field in the month of April. Clive, now promoted to the rank of Lieutenant, went with it, but the issue proved unfortunate; a storm dispersed the squadron in which the guns with the heavy baggage had been sent round to the mouth of the Coleroon, and the infantry either could do or did nothing without the artillery. Cope, therefore, after losing a good many of his fighting-men and almost all his coolies, returned to Fort St. David discomfited. He brought back, indeed, a piece of intelligence which, if it surprised his Government, ought not to have done so; he assured them that their protégé had not a single adherent in the country. But, however mortifying the discovery that they had been imposed upon in regard to this matter, there were cogent reasons in force for persevering in the war for a while. Their arms had sustained a reverse, and the credit which they had lost must be recovered. Accordingly a new expedition was contemplated, of greater force both in men and matériel, and Major Lawrence, an officer of distinguished name in eastern warfare, assumed the command. This time operations were carried on with vigour. After surmounting many difficulties, among which the passage of the Coleroon on a flying-bridge in the face of the enemy deserves to be enumerated, Major Lawrence sat down before Dovecotta, and, his batteries opening with effect, a breach was in due time declared practicable. Mr. Clive solicited and obtained the honour of leading the forlorn hope. He was charged by cavalry while advancing to the bottom of the breach, and not fewer than thirty out of the thirty-four Europeans who accompanied him fell. But the sepoys in support showed a good front, and, Lawrence bringing up the whole of his European battalion, the place was entered sword in hand. A second triumph, at a fortified pagoda about five miles distant from the town, induced the reigning prince to sue for peace, which was granted on condition that Dovecotta should remain in the hands of its captors, and the pretender be pensioned at a rate which would enable him to spend the remainder of his days comfortably in a private station.

Immediately on the ratification of this treaty Major Lawrence, leaving a sufficient garrison in Dovecotta, returned to Fort St. David, whence, in a short time, he proceeded for the settlement of his private affairs to England. Clive likewise, in the persuasion that there would be no further need for him in the field, resumed his civil functions at Madras, where he was admitted to the same rank at which he would have arrived had not the exigencies of the public service withdrawn him for a while from the factory. This was a high but not an unmerited compliment to his talents, of which, however, for the present he was prevented from making any use, for a severe nervous fever attacked him before he could return to habits of business, and he was forced to seek refreshment during the cold season in Bengal. It appears that the effects of this inroad on his constitution were as enduring as they were mischievous. He became more than ever subject to fits of depression of spirits, and, when not occupied with affairs which filled and engrossed his thoughts, was often so miserably low as to shrink from the idea of being left alone. Of what strange materials are the best of us composed! How narrow is the line which separates that which we call genius from insanity! But it is time to look beyond these comparatively trifling details, that we may trace the course of events which were about to give a new aspect to the politics of India, and to call into operation the highest order of talent of which the rival Companies of England and France in that part of the world could boast.

CHAPTER III.

General View of the Affairs of India.

WHEN a handful of English merchants proceeded, in the year 1612, to occupy the countinghouses and stores which were allotted to them for the transaction of business in Surat, their astonishment at the spectacles, moral, political, and financial, which were opened to their view on every side defies description. They found themselves not only without weight or influence in the country, but mere tolerated denizens, and nothing more, of what appeared to them the greatest and wealthiest empire which the world had ever seen. An Emperor, of whom they saw nothing, but who was described as dwelling in luxury and splendour at Delhi, governed the whole extent of the Indian peninsula, from the Himalaya mountains to Cape Comorin. A thousand deputies, rising in degree one above another, managed the affairs of the innumerable provinces into which his empire was divided. These had large bodies of revenue officers and police in their pay, judges and magistrates under them, with standing armies and all the other appliances of sovereign power; and they maintained at their Courts a degree of state which nothing about those of European princes seemed to come near. The habits of the people, likewise, were, as far as strangers could judge of them, civilized in the extreme. The labouring classes might go about well-nigh in a state of nudity, and be content to dwell in earthen huts, without any other furniture than a few mats on which to sleep, and a gourd or a pitcher wherewith to draw water from the wells. But their manners were gentle and polite in the extreme, while their ingenuity as weavers, and their skill in the mechanical and agricultural arts, excited the admiration of persons born in Kent and brought up in Manchester or London. Meanwhile the Indian aristocracy inhabited palaces gorgeously decorated and of vast extent. Their temples, too, and market-places—the

tombs of the dead, and the. monuments erected to commemorate
the virtues of the living—all appeared to the wondering eyes of
our countrymen superb.   In like manner the density of the
population in the cities, and the perfect order which prevailed—
the awe with which rulers seemed to be regarded—and the pomp
and dazzling splendour of their processions—went far to confirm
the impressions which a consideration of other . more shadowy
objects had made.   The letters of our first factors to their
correspondents at home were filled with accounts of the greatness of the princes under whose protection they lived; while
their employers lost no opportunity of urging upon them the
necessity as well as the wisdom of paying implicit obedience to
every mandate which might be issued by these all-powerful
potentates, or their representatives.

The truth, however, is, that this empire, extensive and powerful as it seemed to be, carried in its bosom, from the date of its
first establishment, the seeds of an early dissolution.   Not even
the genius of Baber, nor the extraordinary administrative talents
of Akbar, could give to a machine so constituted the elements of
durability.   An Oriental despotism, tainted with all the vices
that are inseparable from the dominion of race over race, can
never be held together but by the hand of a giant.   The first
symptom of weakness in the chief is sure to operate on his subordinates as a signal of insubordination, which, whether it take
the form of an armed insurrection, or be content to work out its
ends by the process of passive resistance, cannot fail, more or less
speedily, to succeed. This fact, sufficiently demonstrated on various
occasions during the interval which divided the reigns of Akbar
and that of Arungzebe, passed, after the demise of the fallen
prince, into a rule.   Indeed the means adopted by Arungzebe
himself—perhaps the ablest of all the monarchs who derived
their descent from Timour—to obtain the throne, set the seal
to its validity.   The youngest of a family of brothers, he rose,
as is well known, to power after a lengthened struggle with the
other members of his father's house.   It was one of the inevitable
consequences of such a civil war that the chain of connexion
which bound its lieutenants to the Imperial throne should be
weakened.   Opportunity was likewise given to Hindoo tribes,
impatient of a Mussulman yoke, to withhold their tribute; and

C

in the heart of the empire bands of robbers organized themselves, which fell by degrees into political shape, and took rank among the most powerful of the Indian commonwealths. Arungzebe himself, therefore, had through life a part to enact which few princes either of ancient or modern times could have played at all, and which even he played imperfectly. But on the day of his death the foundations of the whole fabric gave way, and the ruin which followed was as complete as it was rapid. The state of India during forty years which followed the demise of this great man has been so admirably described by an eloquent and well-known writer, that I cannot deny myself the gratification of transferring to these pages the whole of the passage.

"The history of the successors of Theodosius bears no small analogy to that of the successors of Arungzebe. But perhaps the fall of the Carlovingians furnishes the nearest parallel to the fall of the Moguls. Charlemagne was scarcely interred when the imbecility and the disputes of his descendants began to bring contempt on themselves and destruction on their subjects. The wide dominion of the Franks was severed into a thousand pieces. Nothing more than a nominal dignity was left to the abject heirs of an illustrious name—Charles the Bald, and Charles the Fat, and Charles the Simple. Fierce invaders, differing from each other in race, language, and religion, flocked, as if by concert, from the farthest corners of the earth, to plunder provinces which the Government could no longer defend. The pirates of the Baltic extended their ravages from the Elbe to the Pyrenees, and at length fixed their seat in the rich valley of the Seine. The Hungarians, in whom the trembling monks fancied that they recognised the Gog and Magog of prophecy, carried back the plunder of the cities of Lombardy to the depth of the Pannonian forest. The Saracen ruled in Sicily, desolated the fertile plains of Campania, and spread terror even to the walls of Rome. In the midst of these sufferings a great internal change passed upon the empire. The corruption of death began to ferment into new forms of life. While the great body as a whole was torpid and passive, every separate member began to feel with a sense and to move with an energy all its own. Just here, in the most barren and dreary part of European history, all feudal privileges, all modern nobility, take their source. To this point we trace the power of those princes who, nominally vassals, but really independent, long governed, with the titles of Dukes, Marquesses, and Counts, almost every part of the dominions which had obeyed Charlemagne.

"Such, or nearly such, was the change which passed over the Mogul empire during the forty years which followed the death of Arungzebe. A series of nominal sovereigns, sunk in indolence and debauchery, sauntered away life in secluded palaces, chewing bang, fondling concubines, and listening to buffoons. A series of ferocious invaders had descended through the western passes to prey on the defenceless wealth of Hindostan. A Persian conqueror crossed the Indus, marched through the gates of Delhi, and bore away in triumph those treasures of which the magnificence had astounded Roe and Bernier; the peacock throne on which the richest jewels of Golconda had been disposed by the most skilful hands of Europe; and the inestimable mountain of light, which, after many strange vicissitudes, lately shone in the bracelet of Runjeet Sing. The Affghan soon followed to complete the work of devastation which the Persian had begun. The warlike tribes of Rajpoots threw off the. Mussulman yoke; a band of mercenary soldiers occupied Rohilcund; the Seiks ruled on the Indus; the Jauts spread terror along the Jumna; the highlands which border on the western sea-coast of India poured forth a still more formidable race—a race which was long the terror of every native power, and which yielded, after many desperate and doubtful struggles, to the fortune and genius of England. It was under the reign of Arungzebe that this wild clan of plunderers first descended from the mountains; and, soon after his death, every corner of his wide empire learned to tremble at the mighty name of the Mahrattas. Many fertile vice-royalties were entirely subdued by them; their dominions extended across the Peninsula from sea to sea. Their captains ruled at Poonah, at Gualior, in Guzzerat, in Berar, and in Tanjore; nor did they, though they had become great sovereigns, therefore cease to be freebooters; they still retained the predatory habits of their forefathers. Every region which was not subject to their rule was wasted by their incursions. Wherever their kettle-drums were heard the peasant threw his bag of rice on his shoulder, hid his small savings in his girdle, and fled with his wife and children to the mountains and the jungles—to the milder neighbourhood of the hyæna and the tiger. Many provinces redeemed their harvests by the payment of an annual ransom ; even the wretched phantom who still bore the imperial title stooped to pay this ignominious ' black-mail.' The camp-fires of one rapacious leader were seen from the walls of the palace of Delhi ; another, at the head of his innumerable cavalry, descended year after year on the rice-fields of Bengal : even the European factors trembled for their magazines. Less than a hundred years ago, it was thought necessary to fortify Calcutta against the horsemen of Berar, and the name of the Mahratta ditch still preserves the memory of the danger."

The eloquence of this description is only exceeded by its remarkable accordance with fact, and the passage in which the author goes on to explain the relative positions of the Emperor and his lieutenants during this interval of anarchy is to the full as trustworthy. " Wherever the viceroys of the Mogul," he says, " retained authority, they became sovereigns. They might still acknowledge in words the superiority of the house of Tamerlane, as a Count of Flanders or a Duke of Burgundy would have acknowledged the superiority of the most helpless driveller among the later Carlovingians ; they might occasionally send to their titular sovereign a complimentary present, or solicit from him a title of honour ; but they were, in truth, no longer lieutenants removable at pleasure, but independent hereditary princes. In this way originated those great Mussulman houses which formerly ruled Bengal and the Carnatic, and those which still, though in a state of vassalage, exercise some of the powers of royalty at Lucknow and Hyderabad."

One of the most important of the greater lieutenancies into which the Mogul empire was divided, is known in history as the Deccan. It included the whole extent of territory which has for its limits the Nerbudda on the north, and on the east, south, and west the Indian Ocean. To the government of that province one of the ablest of his officers, by name Nizam-ul-Mulk, had been appointed by Arungzebe ; and the souhbadar, surviving by many years the emperor to whom he was indebted for his eleva-tion, did not fail, as soon as the opportunity offered, of rendering himself virtually independent of the throne of Delhi.   Nizam-ul-Mulk had, however, difficulties of his own to contend against; the Deccan was under his rule subdivided into lesser lieutenancies as the empire was divided into greater, and of these several were extensive enough to demand cunning as well as force in their management.   The lower Carnatic, or principality of the Nabob of Arcot, formed one; it stretched along the entire Coromandel coast, from the Northern Circars to Cape Comorin; and though narrow, because the ghauts which interpose between it and the territories of Hyderabad and Mysore form its inland boundary, it comprised, nevertheless, all the settlements which both the English and the French had established in that quarter of India. In ancient times the Carnatic had been governed by a cluster of Hindoo princes.   One of these held his court at Arcot, another at Vellore, a third in Trichinopoly; but they had latterly acknowledged their dependence on a common superior, who, like other viceroys of the second order, derived his power, through the souhbadar, from Delhi, and kept his court at Arcot.

In the year 1710, Nizam-ul-Mulk being Souhbadar of the Deccan, Sadat Oolla, Nabob of the Carnatic, died. Having no children of his own, he adopted two nephews, the elder of whom, by name Doost Ali, declared himself successor to the Nabob; while the younger, called Bauker, became governor of the strong fortress of Vellore.   Nizam-ul-Mulk was offended with the presumption of Doost Ali, and took care that his title should receive no confirmation from Delhi.   But Doost Ali retained his place notwithstanding, and married two of his daughters, one to Mortaza Ali, the son of his brother at Vellore, the other to Chunda Sahib, an individual of whom further mention will be made, and who became soon afterwards Dewan or prime minister to his father-in-law.

Time passed, and the Hindoo prince of Trichinopoly, one of the lesser divisions which was held under the Nabob of Arcot, died; and Doost Ali sent his Dewan with an army to demand tribute for the Rana or widow. This was in 1736. But the real object of the Nabob being to possess himself of Trichinopoly, Chunda Sahib received instructions accordingly, and obeyed them.   The Hindoo family were driven into exile, and Chunda

Sahib remained master of the place. Already, however, had dreams of the establishment of political power for his nation in the east entered into the mind of the French governor of Pondicherry.   He had been no inattentive observer of the progress of decay which was going on in the heart of the Mogul Empire; and seems to have made his first move by opening a friendly communication with Chunda Sahib. That personage, it is certain, passed some days at Pondicherry; and the fact of his subsequent refusal to hand over Trichinopoly to his father-in-law leaves little reason to doubt that, whether instigated by M. Dupleix or otherwise, he had already begun to aspire to independence, and probably looked to the dignity of Nabob.

Besides his two daughters, Doost Ali had two sons, one of whom, by name Sufder Ali, had accompanied Chunda Sahib to Trichinopoly. He did not, however, continue there; but, returning to Arcot, found a new Dewan in office beside his father, —and a plan in order of arrangement for the expulsion of his rebellious brother-in-law from the conquest which he had just achieved.

While these things were in progress, a body of ten thousand Mahrattas, led on by a celebrated chief called Ragojee Bhonsela, made an inroad into the Carnatic. They were incited to this partly by the Rajah of Tanjore, one of their own countrymen, partly by the solicitations of the Hindoo family which had been expelled from Trichinopoly ; and in the first encounter with the troops of Doost Ali, they gained a sort of victory, and killed Doost Ali himself. Sufder Ali at once assumed the Nabobship; but, being doubtful of the issue of the war, he removed his family and treasure to Pondicherry, whither also Chudah Sahib had sent his property. At the termination of hostilities Sufder Ali took his family away: not so Chunda Sahib. He had two enemies to fear; the Mahrattas on the one side and the Nabob on the other; and being informed that they were preparing to combine against him, he preferred leaving his children under the protection of Dupleix. He judged wisely. The Mahrattas, invited by Sufder Ali, soon returned. They took Trichinopoly after a siege of three months, and, sparing Chunda Sahib's life, carried him away, and threw him into prison at Sattarah.

Though he had accomplished this purpose, Sufder Ali was by no means at ease. He knew that Nizam-ul-Mulk had been dissatisfied with his father's assumption of power, and he anticipated with alarm the visit from that great man with which he had been threatened. Under these circumstances he sent his son and family to Madras; for the French, in consequence of their patronage of Chunda Sahib, could not be trusted; and giving out that he intended to go on a pilgrimage to Mecca, he shut himself up in Vellore. Meanwhile there was much discontent in the Carnatic on account of the heavy assessment which the Nabob found himself compelled to levy for the purpose of ridding the country of the Mahrattas; and a conspiracy being got up, at the head of which Mortaza Ali, the cousin and brother-in-law of Sufder Ali, placed himself, Sufder Ali was assassinated. The character of Mortaza Ali was not, however, such as to conciliate the people in his favour. It was alleged, also, that in seeking to get the son of Sufder Ali into his power, he meditated another murder; and when the English refused to give the child up, his principal officers revolted from him. He fled in disguise to Vellore, and the infant Mahomed Seid, the son of the deceased Sufder Ali, was proclaimed. Before any steps could be taken, however, to provide a regency or consolidate its power, a new actor had appeared on the stage. Nizam-ul-Mulk, at the head of an enormous army, marched into the Carnatic; and the claims of rival chiefs, whether Nabobs, Rajahs, or by whatever other titles known, dissolved at his presence.

Nizam-ul Mulk was a very old man when he undertook this expedition. He seems to have had, nevertheless, a perfect command of his faculties; and, admitting the son of Sufder Ali into his presence, he treated him kindly, and promised that he should, when of age, become Nabob. He would not, however, permit the youth to return to the protection of the relative who undertook to watch over him, but put him in charge of one of his own officers, whom he nominated to conduct the government during the Nabob's minority. This officer never entered upon the duties of his command. He was found dead in his bed the morning of the day on which he had been appointed to carry the young prince to Arcot, and a soldier of fortune, brave and experienced, of the name of Anwar-u-deen, succeeded to the charge. ·Anwar-u-deen proved to be either very rash or very treacherous. The child, whose guardian he had become, was murdered in his presence, and he himself received from the Souhbadar a confirmation of his right to the vacant principality.

The revolutions which brought Anwar-u-deen, or, as he is called in the correspondence of the day, Alaverdy Khan, to the supreme power in Arcot, and sent Chunda Sahib to prison, occurred just before the breaking out of hostilities between the English and French settlements in India. When the last-mentioned event befell, the French, who at first were weaker by sea than their rivals, applied for and obtained the protection of the new Nabob; but when in a little while they obtained the ascendancy, they denied the right of this prince to interfere between them and their enemies, and attacked, as has already been explained, and made themselves masters of Madras. It was now the turn of the English to ask for protection. The petition was not refused; but partly because they neglected to offer the customary present, and partly that Dupleix worked upon the Nabob's cupidity by promising to make over to him the sovereignty of Madras, no assistance came. By and bye, however, Anwar-u-deen, discovering that Dupleix sought only to deceive, sent ten thousand men under his son to retake Madras. This corps suffered a signal defeat; and for the first time since the arrival of Europeans among them the native generals and chiefs appear to have been awakened to a sense of the superiority of discipline over mere numbers. Then followed the siege of Fort St. David by the French, towards the interruption of which the Nabob contributed with little effect. But time was not afforded for the consolidation of an alliance which Anwar-u-deen seemed at this time disposed to contract with the English against their rivals. The peace of 1748 deprived the belligerents of further excuse for the prosecution of hostilities; and Madras having been restored to its first owners, both parties were content to scheme—the one for the attainment of a small and worthless town at the mouth of a navigable river, the other for the establishment of paramount influence over the whole of the Deccan.

CHAPTER IV.

Gigantic Schemes of Dupleix—Their Progress towards Success.

In the year 1748 died Nizam-ul-Mulk, Souhbadar of the Deccan, one of the most remarkable men whom the Mogul empire in the decadence of its glory had produced. He left behind him a family of six sons to contend among themselves for the succession, as well as a grandson, the child of a favourite daughter, whom he is said to have pronounced to be his heir. The eldest of these sons, by name Nazir Jung, being in possession of his father's capital and treasures, caused himself immediately to be proclaimed. He was acknowledged by his brothers, as well as by the English, between whom and his deceased father he had acted as a medium of communication. He hastened to equip an army wherewith to oppose his nephew, Merzapha Jung, who was at the head of a powerful party. Meanwhile great discontent prevailed in the Carnatic. Anwar-u-deen never overcame the prejudice which the murder of the son of Sufder Ali had raised against him; and partly on this account, partly because the family of Doost Ali had governed well, and were much beloved, a desire arose to set the usurper, as he was called, aside, and to fill his place with some relative or connexion of the old stock. Mortaza Ali was out of the question: his hand had struck the blow which deprived the people of the infant Nabob; and he was well known to be as cowardly as he was cruel; but Chunda Sahib still lived; and, though a prisoner among the Mahrattas, he deserved to be looked to as the legitimate representative of the house of Sadat Oolla. Of this feeling on the part of the people of the Carnatic Dupleix was soon informed; and his fertile imagination concocted out of it, in combination with the civil war which was already begun between the rival branches of the house of Nizam-ul-Mulk, plans as romantic as they were magnificent. What if he should be able to give both a Nabob to the Carnatic and a Nizam or Souhbadar to the Deccan? Was not Chunda Sahib his creature already; and if he could only manage to deliver him from captivity among the Mahrattas, might he not be rendered still more subservient as well as infinitely more useful? The game was a noble one, yet it involved slight risk. Some expense would indeed be incurred; but for that, in the event of success, he should take care to find compensation; and rightly judging that the English would remain neutral during the fray, he could not doubt that success would reward his endeavour. The plan was no sooner matured than he set about its accomplishment. For a while the Mahrattas rejected his proposals to deliver up Chunda Sahib into his hands; but the offer of seven lacs of rupees (70,000*l.* sterling) overcame their scruples, and the rival of Anwar-u-deen for the throne of Arcot obtained his liberty.

Chunda Sahib saw at once that he could succeed in the Carnatic only in the event of the success of Merzapha Jung in the Deccan. He felt also that both Merzapha and himself would be powerless without the aid of Dupleix; nevertheless the pride of a soldier induced him to avoid joining the Nizam in expectancy till he should be able to do so at the head of a respectable body of troops. Money he procured from Pondicherry; and in those days the adventurer who possessed a little money and plenty of courage could never be at a loss in finding retainers who would follow him upon any enterprise in which it should be his pleasure to embark. Chunda Sahib offered his own arm and the arms of his band to a Rajah of Chettledroog in a war which he was waging against the Rana or queen of Bednore, and was so unlucky in the first encounter as to lose his son, who fell by his side, and himself to be made a prisoner. But fortune had not deserted him. He fell into the hands of some Mahomedan officers, whom he persuaded not only to release him, but to join his standard; and hastening to Adoni, where Merzapha Jung lay encamped, he made his obeisance, and was accepted. His next measure was to persuade Merzapha Jung that to march at once into the Carnatic was the wisest step which could be taken. He spoke of the strength of his own party there, and of his influence with the French; and Merzapha Jung, perceiving that there was truth in the argument, acted on his suggestion. Application was immediately made for assistance to Dupleix, who sent four hundred French troops and two thousand disciplined sepoys to the support of the adventurers. They advanced into the Carnatic. Anwar-u-deen marched out to give them battle. The French greatly distinguished themselves, and were the chief causes of the victory which crowned this passage of arms. Anwar-u-deen was slain. His eldest son, Maphuze Khan, fell into the enemy's hands; and his youngest, Mahomed Ali, with difficulty escaped at the head of a handful of fugitives to Trichinopoly.

The result of this decisive victory was to throw the game entirely into the hands of the conquerors, whose object would have doubtless been attained, without further trouble, had they known how to make the most of the opportunity which fortune offered them. This, however, they failed to do. Instead of laying immediate siege to Trichinopoly, which Mahomed Ali was in no plight to maintain, they contented themselves with levying contributions from various Rajahs; and after publishing to the world that the one had become Nizam of the Deccan, the other Nabob of the Carnatic, they began, somewhat prematurely, to act as if the struggle were at an end. It was not so with Nazir Jung. He put his army in motion for the Carnatic, called upon Mahomed Ali to join him with all the force which he could raise, and requiring the support of the English also, in virtue of their theoretical dependence on his authority, was joined by six or eight hundred disciplined troops under Major Lawrence. His rumoured advance induced Merzapha Jung and Chunda Sahib to retreat to Pondicherry. They were cordially received by Dupleix, who, nowise forgetful of the object of the movement, reinforced his European corps in their service till it numbered two thousand men. The hostile armies came into presence, and so convinced was Major Lawrence of the inability of his allies to cope with their enemies, that he besought Nazir Jung to avoid a battle; but that proud though weak prince refused to be guided by the opinion of his counsellor, and drew out his troops for the attack. That which the undisciplined valour of the Patans and Mahrattas in Nazir Jung's service never could have effected was accomplished by the treachery of the French officers. A large number of these gentlemen took the opportu-

nity of a coming battle to mutiny because certain demands of
theirs had not been granted, and time to restore order ere the
shock came failed the commander. The consequence was that he
retired from the field without firing a shot ; and that the native
army, which depended almost entirely upon him, dissolved itself.

Chunda Sahib retreated with his French allies to Pondicherry.
Merzapha Jung, despairing of better things, gave himself up,
on the promise of good treatment, to his uncle. Such promises
are so continually broken in the East that only men of desperate
fortunes pretend to rely upon them ; and on the present occasion
Nazir Jung exhibited no extraordinary respect for the sacredness
of an engagement. He did not put his nephew to death, which
he might have done ; but he transferred him at once from his
own presence to a dungeon. Nor was he more considerate of
the rights of his allies than of the claims of kindred. While
negotiating for their assistance, he had promised to the English
certain tracts of country adjoining to their settlement at Madras.
Now that the victory was in his opinion achieved, he declined to
redeem his pledge. Upon this Major Lawrence marched home,
while Nazir Jung, as if there had been nothing more to do,
relapsed into his customary habits of indolence. Very different
was the conduct of Dupleix and his faithful ally Chunda Sahib.
The mutiny in the French army was soon repressed and the
mutineers punished. The army itself immediately took the field ;
and one stronghold after another in the Carnatic being reduced,
Chunda Sahib's star was again in the ascendant. It was in vain
that Mahomed Ali called upon the English to help him. They
had refused in the beginning of the struggle ; and, though
alarmed, continued the refusal, till by the promise of a large
increase of territory he overcame their scruples ; but the Nabob
having hazarded a battle before they could come up, and suffered
a defeat, they did not consider that they would be justified, unless
paid in advance, to go further. Meanwhile Dupleix opened a
communication with some of the Patan chiefs in Nazir Jung's
army. He easily won them over, and arranged a plan for the
surprise of that weak prince's camp ; and though by some mismanagement the French attack took place prematurely, the
issues of the affair answered all his expectations. Nazir Jung
was assassinated by his Patans while urging them to support the

outposts.   In a moment the fighting ceased, and Merzapha
Jung, the puppet of Dupleix and Chunda Sahib, was brought
forth from his prison and raised to the throne.   Thus, by the
exercise of a wise courage, and through the inexplicable supine-
ness of the Governor of Fort St. David's, Dupleix appeared to
have realised the wildest of his day-dreams.   He had given both
a Nizam to the Deccan and a Nabob to the Carnatic, and he lost
no time in extracting from the circumstances glory to France,
and to himself and his brother officers enormous profit.   The
new Nizam and Nabob paid him a visit at Pondicherry, where
he entertained them with more than oriental pomp, and was
honoured by them as their benefactor.   He was declared Governor, under the Souhbadar, of all India from the Krishnah to
Cape Comorin.   Authority was given to him above that of
Chunda Sahib, and he was appointed to the high honour of being
commander of seven thousand horse.   The only mint henceforth permitted in the Carnatic was to be at Pondicherry.   Of
the treasures which the Viceroys of the Deccan had accumulated,
a large portion was transferred to the coffers of France; and
Dupleix received, as his own share, two hundred thousand
pounds in coined money, besides jewels and robes of silk and
tissue of inestimable value.   In fact there seemed to be no limit to
his gains.   He was the absolute ruler of thirty millions of people.
No favours could be procured from the Government except at
his request; no access could be obtained, by petition or otherwise, to the Nizam unless through his intercession.

Merzapha Jung survived his elevation only a few months.
Having completed the arrangements which were exacted of him
at Pondicherry, he proceeded with his followers towards Hyderabad.   M. Bussy—one of the ablest and most honest men whom
France has ever produced—accompanied him at the head of
three hundred Europeans and two thousand sepoys; a force
which, however numerically small, was deemed sufficient, through
the respect which its valour and discipline commanded, to ensure
at once his safety and his fidelity.   But the same Patan chiefs
who had raised him to the throne took offence at his refusal to
comply with some of their exorbitant demands, and broke out
into a mutiny, during his endeavour to suppress which, the
Nizam was slain.   Ordinary men would have been confounded

by this catastrophe. Bussy knew how to deal with the army, and acted on the suggestions of a sound judgment. He found one of Nizam-ul-Mulk's sons, Salabut Jung, in prison, and, leading him forth to the people, at once declared him Souhbadar of the Deccan. The grateful prince did not hesitate to confirm all the privileges which his predecessor had granted to the French chiefs and nation; and the gigantic schemes of the former, instead of falling into confusion, were not so much as checked for a moment. On the contrary, while Bussy played a bold and victorious game in Hyderabad, Dupleix more and more gratified his own vanity and that of his people by the most extravagant demonstrations of triumph nearer home. These, though they offended the English almost as much as they dazzled the natives and delighted his own countrymen, might perhaps have passed unnoticed had not the exuberance of his folly carried him one step too far. The inhabitants of Fort St. David and Madras, who had noticed nothing out of the way in the vicinity of these settlements over-night, awoke one morning to observe that a number of white flags had been planted close to their bound-hedges, and here and there within them—an unmistakable token that Dupleix claimed as the property of France all the fields which lay on his side of these epitomes of the Bourbon standard. This was indeed to add insult to injury. The authorities of Fort St. David could no longer resist the conviction that the consolidation of French supremacy in the Deccan was incompatible with the continuance of their existence. They had witnessed with alarm the fall of one place after another to Chunda Sahib. They had even attempted to recover Madura, one of the last of Mahomed Ali's strongholds, after his rival had taken possession of it, and suffered a repulse. They knew that Trichinopoly alone remained to their ally; and his continued entreaties that they would come to his assistance warned them that the siege must be close and severe. Still they wavered; their troops on the Coromandel coast were much inferior in point of numbers to those of their rivals. Major Lawrence, the officer on whom they placed their chief reliance, was absent; and having no orders from home which had other than a peaceful tendency, they experienced a great and natural reluctance to engage in war except for the purposes of self-defence. A little calm reflection, however, satisfied the new Governor, Mr. Saunders, that the only chance of escape from ruin for the Company lay in giving assistance to Mahomed Ali against his enemy. He accordingly consented, on Mahomed Ali's undertaking to cede a considerable territory, and to defray the expenses of the contingent, to support him with a body of troops; and five hundred Europeans, a hundred Caffres, and a thousand sepoys were ordered to assemble for the purpose of raising the siege of Trichinopoly. This was in May, 1751, by which time Clive had fully regained his strength, and was engaged in the discharge of new duties, which his nomination, through Major Lawrence's good offices, to the post of commissary to the troops, had imposed upon him. Though his former military rank remained, this new office hindered him, unless distinctly ordered to the contrary, from exercising any military command. It is necessary to state this in order that he may be acquitted of all share in the disgrace which befell the British arms on the present occasion, for he accompanied the force of which Captain Gingen took the command, and witnessed its discomfiture under the walls of Volconda. But he at once separated himself from the fugitives, and returned alone to Fort St. David, while they took shelter in Trichinopoly. There he ceased not to urge upon Mr. Saunders the necessity of taking fresh measures for the relief of the besieged; and when a convoy was sent out for the purpose under charge of a civilian member of council, Clive volunteered to go with it. The troops and stores reached the beleaguered town in safety, and remained there. It was not so with Mr. Pigot and Mr. Clive, who, after delivering over their charge to Captain Gingen, set out, under a slender escort, to return; for being attacked on the march by a cloud of Poligars, they were forced, after expending their last cartridge, to save themselves by flight. Out of twelve sepoys who formed their guard, seven were slain, and Clive and Pigot escaped a similar fate only by the fleetness of their horses.

Clive's conduct during this little affair had been so gallant, and contrasted so remarkably with that of some other officers of a superior rank, that, while they were recommended to quit the service, he was promoted to be a captain. As such he led a second relief party through Tanjore, and, not without a sharp encounter with a French detachment, conveyed it to Trichinopoly.   But the result of his present visit to the scene of hostilities was to convince him that unless some more decisive steps were taken to recall Chunda Sahib from the siege, Trichinopoly must fall, and with it the hopes of the English, which were bound up in the maintenance of Mahomed Ali as Nabob.   He therefore sought out Mr. Saunders immediately on his return to Fort St. David, and proposed to him a plan which, after mature deliberation, was approved, and of which the execution, as good policy as well as justice required, was intrusted by the government to its author.

CHAPTER V.

Capture and Defence of Arcot—General Operations.

Arcot, the capital of the Carnatic at the period when the Carnatic formed a separate province of the Souhbadarry of the Deccan, stands upon the left bank of the river Palar, and, like most other Indian cities of similar importance, consists of a pettah or town and a citadel. The present city is of modern growth, having been built by the Mahomedans in 1716 on or near the site of the Soramundalum of Ptolemy. The citadel, of which the outlines still remain, was accounted, even in the middle of the last century, a place of no great strength. It had the defect, not uncommon in eastern fortresses, of being surrounded on all sides by the town, of which the houses came up to the foot of the glacis, and commanded the ramparts. It was very extensive, too, measuring upwards of a mile in circumference; and of the towers which flanked the defences at intervals, several were in ruins, while the remainder were so circumscribed in their dimensions as not to admit of more than a single piece of ordnance being mounted on each. The walls, badly built at the first, were already loose, and portions had fallen down; the ramparts were too narrow to accommodate even a field-piece in action; a low and slight parapet imperfectly screened them; and the ditch, besides being more or less choked up, had a space of ten feet between it and the bottom of the counterscarp, intended, without doubt, for a *fausse braye*, but left unfinished. Finally, the two gates by which the fortress communicated with the town were placed in clumsy covered ways, which projected at least forty feet beyond the walls, and opened upon causeways or mounds run through the ditch without any cut or opening for the span of a drawbridge having been let into them.

In this place, of which the population might be estimated at a hundred thousand souls, or more, the Nabobs of the Carnatic were accustomed to hold their court. They inhabited a gorgeous palace, and looked round from it upon streets, narrow as those of eastern towns generally are, but built with considerable regularity. The bazaars or market-places were good, and well supplied ; and a manufactory of cloth, besides giving employment to a portion of the inhabitants, brought in a considerable revenue to the vice-regal treasury. All these had fallen into the hands of Chunda Sahib immediately after the battle which had cost Anwar-u-deen his life ; and the place was occupied by a garrison of his troops, of which the strength was represented as amounting to eleven hundred men.

The proposal which Clive made, and to which Mr. Saunders gave a favourable consideration, was this—that, since the English were not strong enough to fight Chunda Sahib and his French allies under the walls of Trichinopoly, they should endeavour to withdraw them from the blockade of that place by making a dash at Arcot. To be sure the amount of force disposable for such a purpose appeared very inadequate ; for, after reducing the garrisons of Fort St. David and Madras — the former to a hundred, the latter to fifty men—only two hundred Europeans with three hundred sepoys could be mustered. But, nowise daunted by the numerical odds that were against him, Clive undertook, at the head of this little band, to enter upon the enterprise ; and the results fully justified the calculations of his own hopes and the expectations of the government which trusted him.

On the 26th of August, 1751, Clive marched from Madras, where his little army had assembled. Three light field-pieces constituted his artillery train, and he had eight European officers to assist him, of whom six had not previously been under fire ; and on the 29th the whole arrived at a place called Conjeveram, forty miles inland. On the 31st, after encountering a furious storm of thunder and rain, he halted within ten miles of Arcot, and, by the mere terror of his presence there, overcame whatever resistance the garrison had been expected to make ; for spies from the town, having seen Clive's column hold on its way in spite of the fury of the elements, made such a report of their movements, that Chunda Sahib's commandant despaired of being able to do anything against such assailants He therefore evacuated the citadel, which was immediately taken possession of by the English.

The prize, though soon won, was not, as Clive easily foresaw, to be retained without a struggle. He at once, therefore, made preparations to resist a siege. He had already sent to Madras for a couple of 18-pounders; and, finding eight cannon of different calibres in the place, he lost no time in arming both the towers and the curtains. Store of provisions was laid in; and to the people who inhabited the fortress, in number about three or four thousand, the utmost kindness was shown. No private property was either seized or injured: indeed the discipline which he maintained was so strict that merchants from the town committed their stocks of goods to his keeping. And the consequence was that the whole multitude preserved both then and afterwards a perfect neutrality, except when, by the promise of reward or the offer of pay, they were prevailed upon to assist in repairing the dilapidated portions of the walls.

The first blow in this memorable siege was struck by Clive himself, who, ascertaining that the fugitive garrison was encamped near Fort Timery, about six miles from Arcot, marched out on the 4th of September to give them battle. They stood till the English arrived within the range of musketry, and exchanged some cannon-shot with Clive's gunners, but they avoided a close contest by fleeing to the hills. A second sally on the 6th brought Clive into collision with the same people, now increased to two thousand, and a sharp affair took place. But though he defeated them in the field, Clive, having no battering guns, could not reduce the fort into which they threw themselves, and he therefore returned to Arcot. During the ten subsequent days his operations were strictly defensive, which so emboldened the enemy that they approached with three thousand men within three miles of the glacis; but a sortie at midnight, on the 14th, totally routed them without the loss to the English of a single life.

Soon after this Clive learned that the 18-pounders for which he had sent were on their way; and that the enemy, hoping to intercept them, had occupied Conjeveram in force. Reserving only thirty Europeans and fifty sepoys to guard the fort, he sent out the whole of his garrison to the succour of the convoy, of which the enemy were no sooner informed than they hurried back, and endeavoured to carry the citadel by assault. But, in spite of the numerical weakness of his garrison, Clive offered such a stout resistance that no entrance could be effected, and at dawn the following day he had the satisfaction to receive within the gates both the troops which had been sent out and the guns and stores which they were employed to escort.

The occupation of Arcot produced the effect which Clive had expected from it. Chunda Sahib detached largely from the corps with which he was blockading Trichinopoly; and the fugitives from the late battle coming in, Rajah Sahib, the son of Chunda Sahib, sat down before Arcot with ten thousand men, of whom one hundred and fifty were Europeans. For fifty days he pressed the siege with all the vigour of which an Indian general was capable. A constant fire of musketry from the houses on the glacis swept the ramparts. Heavy guns battered in breach till they brought down a wide extent of wall; and the utmost vigilance was exercised in order to prevent supplies of provisions from being conveyed into the place. Clive, on his part, was indefatigable, and the devoted courage of his handful of troops passes all praise. Indeed, here, as in our own time in the noble defence of Jellalabad, European and native rivalled each other in heroism and endurance. It was during the height of this siege that an instance of self-devotion on the part of the native soldiers occurred, of which the memory can never fade away. The stock of rice beginning to fail, the sepoys waited upon Clive, and besought him that he would restrict his issues to their European comrades. All that they desired, or indeed would accept, was the water in which the grain had been boiled; and upon this thin gruel they sustained the labours of the siege for many days.

Aware of the importance of recovering his father's capital, Rajah Sahib tried every expedient of negotiation, threat, and the offer of a bribe, to induce a surrender; but Clive was deaf to his arguments. He spurned the offered bribe, derided the threats, and refused to enter into any negotiation with the enemy. Nor was his defence altogether passive. He made repeated sallies, of which one or two were supposed to be at least as bold as they were judicious; and, though sacrificing some lives, he well kept up the spirits of the survivors by the proceeding. An attempt was made to relieve him from Madras, but it failed; and Lieutenant Innis, with the party of which he was in command, retreated to a fort about fifteen miles from the place whence he had set out. At last Clive managed to communicate with Morari Row, a Mahratta chief who had been hired, with his corps of six thousand men, to assist Mahomed Ali, but who up to this period had lain inactive on the frontiers of the Carnatic, as if waiting the issue of the siege of Trichinopoly, that he might take part with the victor. This robber-chief, admiring the bravery of Clive and his people, agreed to come to their assistance, and on the 9th of November his advanced parties were seen in the neighbourhood of Arcot. Now the Rajah Sahib felt that he must strike a decisive blow, or relinquish his undertaking. Having again failed to overcome Clive's firmness by promises of reward and threats of vengeance, he issued his orders and made ready to hazard a general assault.

The 14th of November is a day kept holy by the worshippers of Mohamed, in honour of the murder of the brothers Hassan and Hosseen, two of the most illustrious of the saints and martyrs in their calendar. The festival is observed in Hindostan with exceeding fervour, the devotees deepening the sentiment by the free use of bang, an intoxicating drug, of which one of the effects is either to stupify altogether, or to inflame the individual who is under its influence into madness. Rajah Sahib fixed this day for his final assault on the citadel of Arcot, in the well-grounded conviction that numbers who, under ordinary circumstances, might have done their duty and no more, would, when inspired by the combined influence of religious zeal and intoxication, force their way through all opposition, or perish in the attempt. He could not, however, conceal his purpose from Clive, who made every necessary disposition to thwart it, and who lay down to rest only after he had seen that all was in readiness for the storm. It came with the dawn of the morning, and lasted in its fury about an hour. Four columns advanced to the attack of four different points—two assailing the breaches, two endeavouring to force open the gates. The latter process they attempted by driving before them elephants having their foreheads covered with plates of iron; the former they executed

—some by passing over the ruins that choked the ditch, others endeavouring to cross where the water was deep upon a raft. The elephants, galled by the musketry fire of the garrison, turned round and trampled upon their own people. The assailants who endeavoured to clamber over the fallen masses of rubbish were cut down by discharges from behind the parapet; and Clive, directing with his own hand a field-piece at the raft, cleared it in a moment. In a word, the enemy was repulsed at every point, in spite of the frantic attempts of those who led them on;—and drew off, leaving not fewer than four hundred dead bodies in the ditch, or scattered over the piece of ground which interposed between it and the bottom of the wall.

Clive's loss in this encounter was very trifling. It amounted to no more than five or six men; and well was it for him that the casualties did not prove more serious. His corps, originally small, had become so reduced by hard service, that there remained to meet this final assault no more than eighty European and one hundred and twenty sepoy soldiers; while the whole of his officers, with a solitary exception, were placed *hors de combat*. Perhaps, too, he had reason to be thankful that the enemy, discouraged by the extent of their losses, and fearful of an attack from the Mahrattas in their rear, did not renew the attempt. They continued, however, throughout the day, and till the night was far advanced, to harass him with a constant musketry fire from the houses, which they intermitted only for an hour or two in order to bury their dead. But this suddenly ceased about one or two o'clock on the morning of the 15th, when intelligence came in that they had retreated, and a patrol sent out to ascertain whether the case were so, brought back a report that not a man remained in the town.

A valuable booty in treasure, guns, and military stores fell into the hands of the victor, who however did not permit success to lull him into indolence. He was no sooner joined by a reinforcement from Madras than he took the field, and, carrying a portion of Morari Row's warriors along with him, made himself master of the fort of Timery, and fell upon a corps which had been despatched from Trichinopoly to Rajah Sahib's assistance, which he destroyed. He next accepted the surrender of Arnee, and with it seven hundred disciplined natives, whom he took into the English service; and, after a short cannonade, re-duced Conjeveram, into which the French had thrown a garrison. This done, he proceeded to Fort St. David, as well to report to Government the particulars of his services as to arrange a plan for further and more important operations.

The effect produced on the natives by Clive's successful con-duct of the war was marvellous. Many who had declared for Chunda Sahib abandoned him, and not a few of the waverers gave in their adhesion to the cause of his rival. But the same thing happened here which occurs on almost all other theatres of war, whatever be their scale. Only one master-mind was pre-sent ; and, wherever that happened not to be, affairs went wrong. Mahomed Ali and Captain Gingen continued to be cooped up in Trichinopoly, and made no effort to free themselves. Mean-while Rajah Sahib gathered together a new army, which the addition of four hundred Frenchmen rendered very formidable; and, after laying waste the districts which adhered to Mahomed Ali, fell upon Poonamalee, and destroyed both it and the country residences of the English gentlemen at St. Thomas's fort. This was in January, 1752, and Clive was at once sent out to put a stop to the annoyance. Though greatly superior both in numbers and artillery, the enemy retreated as he advanced; and it was not without difficulty that he forced them to give battle at a place called Coverspak. But to bring an enemy to action and to overthrow him were with Clive events of never-failing sequence. Nine pieces of cannon fell on this occasion into his hands, as well as sixty European prisoners, and the bodies of fifty French-men and three hundred of Rajah Sahib's sepoys were counted on the field. Nor was Clive's loss trifling: it amounted in killed to forty Europeans and thirty sepoys, with a much larger number of both classes wounded.

Having accomplished the object for which he had been sent out, Clive marched back with his victorious army towards Fort St. David, on his way to which he passed a town which Dupleix, in the pride of his first successes, had founded and called after his own name. It was built round about a monumental column, the four fronts of which were designed to sustain tablets on which, in four different languages, the exploits of the founder of the French empire in the East were about to be inscribed,

Clive, justly regarding this as much more than a display of mere personal vanity, caused both town and column to be levelled with the earth. He knew too well the susceptible nature of the Indian temperament not to perceive that such a memorial was as likely to bind the native princes to French interests as victory itself; and he resolved that they should never have it in their power to say that an English general and his army saw yet passed it by untouched. This done, he continued his progress to Fort St. David; but he had not rested there many days ere a summons called him to Madras, where the seat of the English Government in this part of India was now established.

Affairs were not going well at Trichinopoly. Captain Gingen confined himself to the castle; and Mahomed Ali, whose palace was protected by the guns of the fort, remained with his troops in the town. It was determined to force the enemy's lines from without; and to the command of the troops about to be employed on this service Clive was nominated; but before he had time to organize his corps and commence his march Major Lawrence arrived from England, and the command, as was fitting, devolved at once upon him. Clive, however, took his own share, and played a very conspicuous part in the operations which followed. It was the object of Lawrence to force his way into Trichinopoly; it was the obvious business of the besiegers to prevent this; and a smart affair occurred, of which the brunt fell on Clive's division, and of which the results were unfavourable to the enemy. Lawrence made good his entrance into the beleaguered city, and began at once to change the whole order of the war. His force, if somewhat inferior in point of numbers to that of the enemy, was better organised and far better commanded; indeed Dupleix complained, and not without reason, that there was nobody at his disposal to execute the plans which he formed; and if they in their turn charged Dupleix with personal cowardice, his exceeding carefulness never to bring himself under fire seems to indicate that they too had justice on their side. But however this may be, the movements of M. Law, to whom the blockade of Trinchinopoly had been intrusted, both dissatisfied his superior and indicated on his own part a grievous lack of military talent. He suffered himself, with all his army, to be shut up in the island of Seringham: he made a false move under the idea of helping M. d'Auteuil, whom Dupleix despatched at the head of a separate corps to relieve him; and in a night action, rashly brought on, sustained a heavy loss. As the part played by Clive in this latter affair was a remarkable one, it is necessary that I should describe it more at length.

The island of Seringham is formed by the severance of the river Coleroon into two branches, which would again unite at no great distance from Trichinopoly, but that an artificial bar has been created by the erection there of a huge earthen mound. The island is holy ground in the eyes of the Hindoos, and contains one of the most celebrated pagodas of which southern India can boast. There M. Law established his head-quarters, Chunda Sahib inhabiting a separate wing of the pile. Clive suggested that between the passages of the Coleroon and the roads which lead to Pondicherry a strong post should be established; and Lawrence consenting, the author of the design was put at the head of the detached corps and took up his ground at the village of Samiaveram, which, with its two pagodas, he proceeded to fortify. He was in this position—very strong, and commanding with his heavy guns all the approaches to the island—when the advance of M. d'Auteuil was reported to him. He determined to attack the enemy on his march; but D'Auteuil, having received tidings of Clive's intention, hastily retreated to Utatore; and Clive, not finding his enemy where he expected him to be, returned to his lines. Meanwhile M. Law had been informed of Clive's manœuvre. He calculated, fairly enough, that the English camp would be left in charge of a weak guard, and he resolved to strike at it. With this view he sent a corps across the river as soon as it became dark, which arrived about midnight at the English piquets. The corps in question consisted of seven hundred sepoys and eighty Europeans —of whom forty were deserters from the English army. These being in front answered the challenge of the English sentries, and the column was permitted to pass. The scene which followed baffles all attempt at minute description. Not aware that Clive with his main body was returned, the officer in command of the French detachment moved on as far as the lesser pagoda, and might have done almost what he liked, had not his Europeans opened their fire too soon. Clive sprang from his bed, a musket-ball having broken a chest on which his head was supported. He ran to the greater pagoda, where the European part of his force lay, and found them already under arms. Neither party seemed to be aware for a considerable length of time of the real nature of their respective positions. Clive, running among the French sepoys, scolded and struck at them as if they had been his own men, till he received from one of them a wound in the thigh. He pursued his assailant, who took to his heels, as far as the lesser pagoda, and there for the first time discovered that an enemy was in the heart of his camp: but his presence of mind never forsook him. He told the French sentinel who stood at the door that he came to offer terms, and, several soldiers of that nation throwing down their arms, Clive gave them into the charge of a guard of sepoys. The sepoys carried their prisoners to what they assumed to be their own stronghold, and handed them over to a French sergeant who was in possession of it, and who in his turn was so completely confused, that he permitted the sepoys to depart unhurt. By degrees, however, things took some form. Clive, divining all that had happened, kept his troops in hand till daylight came in, and then, attacking the enemy on all sides, cut them to pieces. He had a narrow escape, however, ere the business ended: for one of the deserters, while parleying about submission, fired at him, and killed two non-commissioned officers on whose shoulders he leant, loss of blood having rendered him unable to stand upright.

Of all that followed Lawrence, and not Clive, was the chief director; it may therefore be epitomised in few words. Chunda Sahib, seeing that his affairs were become desperate, requested his followers to shift for themselves, and, entering into a secret negotiation with the leader of the Tanjorean contingent in the camp of the besiegers, put himself into his hand for the purpose of being passed, in disguise, beyond the lines. The Tanjorean, according to the usage of his nation, proved false. He threw Chunda Sahib into chains, and made a boast of the value of the prize which he had won; but he gained little by this proceeding. The English, Mahomed Ali, and the Mahrattas all claimed the captive; whereupon the Tanjorean, rather than submit to the humiliation of giving him up, put the unfortunate Nabob to death. Meanwhile the operations against M. Law had not been

suspended for a moment. Post after post was wrested from him,
till in the end he shut himself up in the pagoda, and there waited
till relief should come; but it never came at all. A second
attempt by M. d'Auteuil to reach him was intercepted by Clive,
the French detachment dispersed, and the castle of Volcondah
taken. M. Law now felt that his case was desperate; and, after
the endurance of great suffering for lack of provisions, he laid
down his arms on capitulation.

The destruction of this army was a heavy blow to Dupleix,
yet he did not sink under it. On the contrary, he threatened,
bribed, intrigued, and expended his private fortune in stirring
up dissensions among the allies of the English, and, the
elements of discord being rife, he fully succeeded. He could
not, however, prevent Major Lawrence from winning a decided
victory over his nephew under the walls of Gingee, nor stay
the progress of Clive, who, at the head of such an army as probably no officer except himself would have trusted, reduced in
succession the two strong fortresses of Chingliput and Covelong.
The force which was set apart for the performance of this service
comprised five hundred newly-raised sepoys and two hundred
recruits from London, the sweepings of the streets and of the
jails. So entirely unsoldierlike were these people in all their
habits, that, when their new commander first brought them into
the field, they ran away at the sound of their own fire; and once,
when a cannon-shot struck a rock near them, and, by the splin-
ters which flew off, killed and wounded a few, the panic became
such as even Clive could with difficulty arrest; indeed, one of the
heroes disappeared altogether, and was not found till next day,
when they discovered him hidden at the bottom of a well.
Still, by judiciously accustoming them to danger, and bringing
them little by little under fire, Clive raised their spirit in the end
to such a height that he took one castle by assault, and, after
destroying in an ambuscade a party sent out from the other,
compelled it to surrender. But he had overworked himself by
these gigantic exertions, and found it necessary to seek repose.

CHAPTER VI.

Marriage—Goes to England—Brief career there—Return to India—
Fall of Calcutta.

WORN out with the great exertions which he had made, and re-
joicing in the consciousness of a well-merited renown, Clive
returned, towards the end of 1752, to Madras, where he soon
afterwards married Miss Margaret Maskelyne, a lady to whom he
was much attached, and who is described as possessing many
attractions, mental as well as personal. She was the sister of one
of his earliest and most intimate friends, and stood in the same
relation towards Dr. Nevil Maskelyne, the celebrated mathema-
tician, who at a subsequent period became Astromomer Royal. It
was a union productive to Clive of almost all the real happiness
which he seems to have enjoyed through life; for his love for
his wife never fell away, and she repaid it by sustaining when
she could not cheer, and bearing with him through many a season
of anguish of which the world never heard. Moreover, the condition of public affairs in the Carnatic was by this time so
flourishing, that he did not hesitate to apply for leave to return
to England. It was readily granted, and in February, 1753, he
embarked with his bride at Madras.

Clive's reception in London was such as rarely falls to the lot
of any one who, however prosperous, has not yet reached the
twenty-eighth year of his age. His name had been before the
public ever since the siege of Arcot; and each new report or
hostilities tended more and more to raise it in general estimation.
The Court of Directors had already noticed him in their communications with the Governor at Fort St. David by expressing, to use their own words, "the great regard we have for
the merit of Captain Clive, to whose courage and conduct the
late turn in our affairs has been mainly owing: he may be assured
of our having a just sense of his services." They were now prepared to greet him with all the marks of respect to which a

career so brilliant entitled him.   He was the honoured guest at one of their great public dinners : he received from them a diamond-hilted sword of the value of five hundred guineas, which, it is worthy of remark, he declined to accept till Lawrence, his old commander, had been voted a similar mark of their good will. Moreover, the plaudits which they heaped upon him gave a strong impulse to that current of popularity which in this country runs with the strength of a spring-tide in such cases, and for the most part ebbs again as rapidly as it rose.   Nor were his personal friends and relatives backward in making a display of their sense of his merits.   His father, who appears to have looked upon him at the period of his departure for India as a confirmed dunce, could not find words in which adequately to express his pride.   When the first tidings of "Bobby's" triumphs reached him, he smiled and said that " the booby had some sense after all."   He was now beside himself at the thought of his son's greatness, and spoke and wrote as an elated father is apt to do whose feelings are too powerful for his judgment.   Mrs. Clive bore herself differently.   She was a sensible, discreet, and right-minded woman, of whom her son invariably spoke as having done more for him in his childhood than all the tutors under whom he was placed, and now, in the day of his first exaltation, she took care to add her praise to that of the world in a tone which, without casting a shade over his honest triumphs, had a tendency to keep him from being carried away with them.   And in truth no man ever stood more in need than Clive of this sort of counsel, judiciously applied.   Naturally headstrong, and embued with violent passions, he was much better calculated to fight his way through difficulties than to bear with equanimity the burden of success; and his weakness in this respect soon began to show itself by the somewhat ostentatious manner in which he met the advances of society.   He had realized a handsome but not an extravagant fortune during his ten years' residence in India, and used it well, in so far as he applied a portion of it to redeem the debt with which his paternal estate was encumbered, and to render the latter days of his father and mother comfortable.   But the moment he began to aim at making a figure in fashionable circles he committed an error.   He was not rich enough to bear the expense of the brilliant equipage

and costly liveries by which his presence or that of his wife in
the different resorts of the gay world socn began to be noticed;
and the gay world repaid this attempt to dazzle and eclipse with
affected contempt and real envy. But the culminating point of
his weakness was not reached till he permitted himself to be
involved in the expense of a contested election. The matter
befell thus:—

Clive returned to England at a period when the Government
was in a state more anomalous than had affected it since the
accession of the House of Hanover. There was no ostensible
opposition in either house of parliament. The Jacobites, broken
down by the recent failure of Charles Edward's expedition, held
aloof from public life, or disguised their sentiments when forced
to mix in it. The Tories, having no leader, nor indeed any
definite rallying point, lay as it were upon their arms, and left
the affairs of the nation to be managed by a cabinet compounded
of the most discordant materials that ever came together. On
one side stood the Duke of Newcastle, trusted by none, personally loved by few, yet maintained in his place through apprehensions of his rival. On the other was Lord Sandwich,
dependant mainly on Henry Fox, a bold, able, and most unscrupulous politician, who, though he held but a subordinate place
in the administration, exercised immense influence over the
House of Commons. Through some inducement or another—it
does not exactly appear what—Clive was persuaded to throw in
his lot with this latter or ultra-Whig party; and hence, when
the Duke of Newcastle, at the general election of 1754, set up
his two candidates for the borough of St. Michael, in Cornwall,
Clive took the field against one of them. Thanks to a lavish expenditure of his private means, and the free use of the Sandwich
interest, Clive was returned, but a petition was immediately got
up against him. Now, whatever we may think of the manner
of appointing the committees which in our own day try the
merits of disputed returns, during the half-century which succeeded the accession of the first George there was not so much
as a pretence of impartiality about them. Disputes about
seats were mere battles of party, and the prevailing party in the
House packed its juries as regularly as juries were called for. A
fierce struggle took place on the present occasion—for the

strength of the Newcastle and Sandwich cliques was nearly balanced—in which Sandwich prevailed. Fox was a member of the committee, and no head could be made against his eloquence. But it was necessary that the House should confirm the decision; and here Newcastle turned the scale. The Tories, who, disliking both, preferred the Duke to the friend of the victor at Culloden, threw their weight into his scale, and Clive was unseated. The decision operated as a severe disappointment to an ambitious young man, and seriously affected him in another quarter. His pecuniary circumstances became embarrassed; and, all hope of winning a way to eminence in political life being set aside, he felt himself compelled to look about for honourable employment elsewhere.

It chanced that at this time the relations between England and France were again become unsettled. Leading men in both countries anticipated a speedy rupture; and nobody could doubt that war once begun in Europe would not be slow in extending its ravages to India. Besides, though the English had so far prevailed as to give a Nabob to Arcot, at Hyderabad Bussy was still all-powerful, and, so long as French influence guided the policy of the Soubahdar, the tenure by which Mahomed Ali held his seat must be insecure. The Court of Directors therefore felt that the sooner their army on the Coromandel coast was put upon a respectable footing the better chance there would be of success in a contest which must come sooner or later, and would probably be a decisive one. Under these circumstances they gladly availed themselves of Clive's offer to serve again in the field of his recent fame; and, the better to fit him for playing his part with vigour, as well as to guard against the evil effects of a jealousy which prevailed then to a ridiculous extent between the officers of the King's and those of the Company's army, they obtained for him a lieutenant-colonel's commission from the Crown. A higher compliment to his merits could not have been paid; and Clive, justly gratified by it, hurried forward his preparations, and quitted England for the second time in 1755.

Clive carried with him on the present occasion three companies of royal artillery, and three hundred European infantry. His directions were to conduct them to Bombay, whence, after being reinforced by all the disposable troops in that Presidency, he was, in conjunction with the Mahrattas, to attack the French and their allies in the Deccan. But the jealousy of which mention has just been made interposed to frustrate this arrangement. Colonel Scott, an officer brought up in the service of the Crown, who had come to India the preceding season in the capacity of chief engineer, was, at the instance of the Duke of Cumberland, nominated from home to command the expedition; and Clive, whose permanent position was that of Governor of Fort St. David, with a contingent right of succession to the government of Madras, applied for permission to proceed at once to the proper scene of his labours. This, however, the Directors refused to grant. They believed him to be the only officer in the service who by a combination of natural talent and local experience was qualified to conduct such a war as they anticipated, and they made a point of his directing his course to Bombay, in the hope that some lucky accident might throw the chief power into his hands. By a strange coincidence their dream received, to a certain extent, its fulfilment. When Clive reached Bombay he found that Colonel Scott was dead, and at once he assumed the command of the little army. But he could not march into the Deccan: a convention had been entered into between Mr. Saunders, Governor of Madras, and M. Godeheu, Dupleix's successor at Pondicherry, which barred both the French and the English Companies from interfering in the quarrels of the native princes; and, there being no other excuse for the meditated inroad than the necessity of supporting the Mahrattas against the Soubahdar, the project was abandoned.

The harbour of Bombay constituted at this time a rendezvous for the English fleet in the Indian seas, and the town was full of troops. Admiral Watson, a brave, rough seaman of the old school, commanded the squadron, and, feeling not less than Clive that such a brilliant armament ought not to be broken up without accomplishing some useful end, he agreed to co-operate with Clive in an attack upon Gheriah, a rocky fortress, where a pirate chief called Angria resided. This rover—who boasted of a lineal descent from the celebrated leader of the Mahratta fleet which during the height of the contest between that people and the Mogul wrought such harm to the latter—had long been the scourge of the Malabar coast. His barques swept the narrow seas, making prizes of the traders of all nations; while from time to time his men would land, burn and plunder a town on the beach, and escape again to their ships ere an alarm was given. Clive and Admiral Watson, having received the sanction of the autnorities in Bombay, determined to extirpate such a noxious swarm of outlaws; and it is characteristic both of the men and of the theatre on which they operated, that a council of war was held previously to the departure of the expedition, in order to fix the proportions according to which the spoil which they counted on securing was to be divided. For this it is which casts its darkest shadow over the entire series of events which led forward the East India Company from its original state to that in which we now find it. Plunder seems to have been the one great object sought by leaders of armies and of fleets throughout the whole of our earlier wars in the East; and it not unfrequently came to pass, that, having achieved conquests and gained honour in the field, they ran some risk of losing at least the latter in squabbles over the booty. On the present occasion the grand question mooted was said, in some way or other, to touch the honour of the sister services. The army claimed for Clive as its leader a share equal to that which should be given to the leader of the fleet. The navy insisted that Clive should pocket no more than the amount to which his professional rank entitled him; in other words, the same amount of rupees which were given to a naval captain under three years' standing. Let justice be done both to Admiral Watson and Colonel Clive. The former would not abate one jot of the rights of his profession, but he offered to make up Clive's share out of his own to the same amount with that of Rear-Admiral Pococke. Clive, on the other hand, would not disturb the unity without which combined expeditions never end successfully. He pressed his claim without quarrelling about it; and when it was refused, he declined to take advantage of Admiral Watson's liberality.

At last the expedition sailed, and Gheriah, after offering a stout resistance for a couple of days, was taken and razed to the ground. The capture of other fortresses followed, as well as the entire destruction of the pirate fleet; but the Mahrattas, who were to have assisted in the operations and shared in the spoil, were shut out from both. This done, Clive pursued his voyage westward, and reached Fort St. David on the 20th of June, 1756. It was the very day that witnessed the capture of Calcutta and the suppression of the Company's settlement on that side of India ; and in two months subsequently Clive was summoned to give his counsel in Madras in regard to the measures which it would be necessary to adopt for the purpose of repairing so grave an evil. It may be well to give, in a few words, an outline of some of the principal events which exercised so remarkable an influence over the fortunes of the English in India.

The provinces of Bengal, Bahar, and Orissa, constituting the most fertile and populous of the viceroyalties into which the Mogul empire was divided, had been for fifteen years subject to the active and able government of Aliverdy Khan. His death in the month of April, 1756, made way for the accession of his grand-nephew, Suraj-u-Dowlah, a young man conspicuous even amongst the princes of the East for cruelty, rapacity, and avarice ;—whose hatred of the English had been concealed during the reign of Aliverdy Khan, but now broke forth with irresistible fury. He scarcely felt himself secure in his seat when he made preparations for expelling the obnoxious settlers from the kingdom. Apprehending a war with France, the chiefs of the English settlement on the Hooghly had taken steps to strengthen the works of Fort William. He commanded them to desist, and threatened, in the event of disobedience, to level Calcutta with the earth. By and by he sent to require that they would deliver up to him one of his subjects, whom he charged with having robbed the public treasury and fled with his booty to Calcutta. His messengers were assured that the English would reserve the person of the accused for his Highness's pleasure, while at the same time proof was given that he had brought no treasure with him. Suraj-u-Dowlah would listen to no excuses. He assembled a numerous army, enticed Mr. Watts, the chief of the factory at Cossimbazar, into his power, cast him into prison, and marched to the attack of the factory itself. This he soon reduced, after which he moved towards Calcutta ; and on the 18th of June drove in the piquets, and took possession of the outworks. Meanwhile the alarm and confusion within the walls were extreme. Nobody appeared to have the slightest confidence either in himself or others. In this quarter of India there still existed that dread of native prowess and numbers which the experience of better things had destroyed in the Carnatic ; and hence, when the face of the country was seen to be covered with the Nabob's troops, governor, commanding officer, and men in the fort felt their hearts sink within them. A hasty resolution to abandon the place was come to ; yet such was the effect of terror on men's minds, that no measures were taken to concert even an orderly retreat. On the contrary, the Governor, Mr. Drake, set the example of flight by jumping into a boat, and pushing off for the ships. Captain Minchen, who commanded the troops, acted in a similar manner ; and then all who could, ran, without thinking of anything except their own personal safety, to the beach. About one hundred and fifty Europeans, among whom Mr. Holwell was one, found themselves without the means of escape. The last boat had pushed off; and its crew, in spite of the cries of the deserted, refused to turn back. Nothing therefore remained for this unhappy company but to try the effect of a negotiation, during the progress of which the Nabob's troops rushed through the gates, and the fort, with all its inhabitants, became their prey.

The fate which overtook these miserable captives is well known. Carried before Suraj-u-Dowlah, they are said to have been spoken to kindly—at all events it is certain that Mr. Holwell's hands were unbound, and that hopes were held out to him of protection ; but the means taken to guard against an attempt at escape effectually marred them. The guard to whose care the Europeans were intrusted, in sheer wantonness, or because they could not discover in the place a more convenient prison, thrust the whole into the common jail. It was a filthy, low-roofed, underground apartment, measuring in space about twenty feet square, and ventilated through several air-holes, narrow, and made secure by the insertion of iron bars into the mullions. When told to enter there, the prisoners laughed at the suggestion as a joke ; but they soon discovered their mistake. Forced through the aperture, and having the door closed and bolted upon them, their sufferings became in a few moments such as no language can describe ; and their shrieks and cries for mercy were not only disregarded, but seemed to afford great amusement to the guard. But it is useless to go on with the

horrible description. Let it suffice to state, that, after strug-
gling to burst open the door, and treading one another down in
their agony, one after another died raving mad; so that when
morning came, and the Nabob issued his order to bring them
forth, there were but twenty-three living men left to profit by it.
The rest lay where they had sunk, and the process of decomposi-
tion was already begun upon many of them.

It is not clear that this hideous massacre was perpetrated by
the command or even with the cognizance of Suraj-u-Dowlah.
It seems, on the contrary, to have arisen out of the indifference
of his soldiers to the sufferings of their European captives, and
their fear of disturbing the Nabob in his sleep; for the guards,
though offered large sums of money, refused to awaken their
sovereign. But the tyrant's behaviour to the few survivors
when brought before him next day showed that he cared as
little for the past as he experienced anxiety about the future.
They were cast into more airy prisons, and fed upon grain and
water. This done, he wrote a pompous letter to his nominal
sovereign at Delhi, in which he boasted of having extirpated the
English out of Bengal; and, leaving a garrison in Fort William,
with strict orders that no European should be permitted to settle
in the neighbourhood, he gave up the town of Calcutta to plunder, and marched back with the bulk of his forces to his own
capital.

CHAPTER VII.

Proceeds to Bengal—Recovery of Calcutta—Attack of the Nabob's Camp—
Peace with the Nabob.

Tidings of the fall of Calcutta reached Madras on the 16th of August. They created the greatest consternation and resentment everywhere, and on the 18th a despatch was sent off to Fort St. David requiring Clive's immediate presence at the seat of government. It was determined to retake the captured factory, and to punish the tyrant who had so cruelly abused his power; and General Lawrence being an invalid, Clive was at once selected as the fittest person to command the troops which should be employed on that service. There was at this time at Madras a Colonel Adlercron in command of a King's regiment, whom the authorities did not judge it expedient to employ, partly because he refused to be at their disposal in regard to the period of his return, partly because he would not pledge himself to reimburse the Company's losses out of the booty, whatever it might be, which the army might acquire. This gentleman forthwith set himself to baffle, as far as he could, the preparations that were making, and went so far as to insist upon the relanding of a train of royal artillery after it had been put on board, and the transports were on the point of sailing. But neither Colonel Adlercron's opposition, nor the apprehensions which were entertained of a French war, prevented Mr. Saunders and his council from devoting the whole strength of the Presidency to one purpose. Admiral Watson lay in the roads with five King's ships—one of which, the "Cumberland," was a 74. These gave accommodation to as many officers and men as could be conveniently stowed; and, five of the Company's vessels being fitted up as transports, nine hundred European infantry, fifteen hundred sepoys, and a few field-pieces, were embarked. The whole sailed from Madras on the 11th of October, and on the 22nd of December the head-quarters of the expedition reached Fulta.

Here, in a village on the left bank of the Hooghly, about twenty miles below Fort William, the fugitives from Calcutta were assembled, their small military force being under the orders of Major Kilpatrick, an excellent officer, who had arrived in the Ganges some weeks after the fall of the place, and looked anxiously for the coming of such reinforcements from the coast as should justify him in attempting its recovery.

Though two of the ships of the squadron had been separated from the rest in a gale of wind, and two hundred and fifty Europeans, four hundred sepoys, the greater part of the guns, and almost all his military stores were missing, Clive did not delay the commencement of operations one hour. Having failed to procure boats for the transport of his men, he marched through the jungle upon Budge-Budge, before reaching which he encountered a strong body of the enemy at a disadvantage, and overthrew them. Budge-Budge immediately opened its gates, whereupon he continued his progress to Fort William; and, while the fleet battered it from the river side, he occupied all the approaches from the land. On the 2nd of January, 1757, it submitted. And here again the jealousies of service towards service showed themselves. Admiral Watson refused at first to permit a Company's officer or soldier to come within the walls, and was with difficulty prevailed upon to make over the military command to Clive, though aware that the latter held a Lieutenant-Colonel's commission in the service of the King. Nor was it in this quarter alone that Clive had many prejudices to surmount. Ever since the evacuation of Calcutta the affairs of the Company in that part of India had been managed by a committee of merchants, who, thinking more of their own losses than of the blow which had been struck at the influence of their employers, objected to the plenary powers with which Clive appeared to be vested, and did their best to resist them. But Clive was made to contend against difficulties and to overcome them. His correspondence both with the Admiral and with the committee, though couched in language sufficiently respectful, was uniformly firm; and so well was his character understood, even at this early stage of his career, that none ventured to contest a point which he showed himself determined to carry.

Meanwhile the Nabob was beginning to effect the discovery that the expulsion of the English from his dominions would be no gain to him. The revenue fell off from day to day so remarkably that he was prepared to make with the fugitives fresh treaties, when intelligence of the arrival of the squadron in the Hooghly reached him. He had never calculated on any such occurrence as this. In the plenitude of his ignorance he used to assert that there were not ten thousand men in all Europe, and the possibility of an attempt being made by Europeans to retaliate such injuries as he might inflict on them seems never to have struck him. Indignation, not unmixed with fear, took possession of him now. He ordered all his disposable troops to assemble at Moorshedabad ; and began, as soon as a sufficient force had been collected, his march upon Calcutta.

But Clive and Watson were not idle. Having ascertained that the town of Hooghly, situated above Fort William, on the same branch of the Ganges, was full of rich merchandize and slenderly garrisoned, they determined to surprise it. With this view one hundred and fifty Europeans and two hundred sepoys were placed under the command of Major Kilpatrick and Captain Eyre Coote, and directed, with a light squadron of armed ships, to move up the stream. One of the armed vessels happened to get aground on a shoal, and the expedition was delayed so long that Suraj-u-Dowlah found time to throw considerable reinforcements into the fort ; but the fort itself was not placed thereby out of the reach of danger. On the contrary, some hours of cannonading from the water having beaten down a wide extent of wall, the land-forces at early dawn on the 11th gave the assault, and after a feeble resistance the British flag floated in triumph over that of the Nabob. An inconsiderable booty, not more, it is said, than 15,000*l.*, rewarded the captors for their exertions. This they secured. and. after destroying some stores of rice which had been laid up in an open village about three miles distant, the troops were re-embarked, and the expedition returned to Calcutta.

The attack on Hooghly was undertaken rather with a view to alarm than to inflict any serious injury on the Nabob. To a certain extent this object was served ; but anger more than kept pace with the growth of fear : and, while the negotiations continued, the march upon Calcutta suffered no delay. It was not judged prudent, even by Clive, to impede or interrupt it. On the contrary, he permitted the Bengalese army to pass more than one defile which it was competent to him effectually to block, and encouraged the committee to use every legitimate argument of conciliation. And in truth there were many circumstances which combined to render a policy of peace in Bengal a wise policy for the English at this moment. The long-expected breach with France had occurred, and the authorities at Madras, in daily expectation of being attacked, were without the means of offering a steady resistance should the enemy approach them in force. Again M. Bussy, after having been driven to defend himself with the strong hand in Hyderabad, was become so powerful in the Deccan that he was able, with a thousand Europeans and a large army of well-disciplined natives, to threaten the English factory at Vizagapatam. Moreover, there was a French settlement in Bengal itself which created a good deal of uneasiness, and not without reason, in men's minds. Chandernagore had always been an eyesore to the Company's representatives on the Ganges. It absorbed a considerable portion of the inland trade, and, being better supplied with troops than Calcutta, its political position, however apparently isolated, could not be regarded as a feeble one. It would have convicted the English authorities of absolute infatuation had they not, under such circumstances, been earnestly desirous of peace with the Nabob. But the character of the Nabob inspired no confidence. They could not trust to his promises, far less to his generosity ; they were, therefore, driven to treat with arms in their hands, even while they abstained from using them. It is just to the character of Clive—a man sufficiently open to censure, and seldom spared either in his own day or subsequently—to state, that such were precisely the views which he took of public affairs at this crisis. He counselled peace, yet ceased not to anticipate war, and made the best disposition of his force which circumstances would warrant, to meet either emergency. It was becoming that there should be no open exhibition of distrust in the Nabob. Clive therefore disentangled his field force from the town and its suburbs, and, encamping just so far apart as that he might be able, in case of need, to come to the assistance of the regular garrison, he there awaited the development of plans which the Nabob seemed either to keep immature, or to be at a loss how best to execute.

There was constant intercourse all this while by accredited agents between Suraj-u-Dowlah and Mr. Drake; nevertheless the march of the Nabob's army was not suspended. With forty thousand men he marched upon Calcutta till he placed it virtually in a state of siege. He interposed likewise between Clive's camp and the town, and pushed some of his people into the very streets. It was clear to all reflecting persons that forbearance on the part of the English would soon reach its limits. On the 4th of February Clive sent to remonstrate against these encroachments, and to desire that the Nabob would fall back; but the Nabob scarcely condescended to admit the English messengers into his presence, and treated them so roughly when there, that they were glad to escape with their lives. This was enough. Having ascertained that the Nabob's battering-train lay in an enclosure called Omichund's Garden, beside the Mahratta ditch, in the hostile camp which was established there, Clive resolved to capture it if he could. With this view he applied for a reinforcement of seamen, which, to the extent of six hundred men, was afforded, and at three o'clock in the morning of the 5th he led out one thousand three hundred Europeans and eight hundred sepoys to the attack.

The affair that followed, though not free from military errors, as well in the plan of the operation as in its execution, seems so entirely characteristic of the genius of him who devised it, and produced so strong a moral effect upon his own mind, and upon the minds of others, that it well deserves to be narrated at length. And as I have given in another publication what I believe to be an accurate sketch of the encounter—as accurate, that is to say, as any account of a military operation can be which is compiled from the disjointed narratives of others—I shall take the liberty, on the present occasion, of quoting my own words:—

"About an hour before dawn—about three or four o'clock in the morning—the English army, consisting of six hundred and fifty European soldiers of the line, one hundred artillery-men, eight hundred sepoys, and six hundred seamen, formed in a single column facing towards the south. One wing of the sepoy battalion led; this was followed by the European infantry; the other sepoy wing came next; the artillery, six field-pieces, drawn partly by seamen, partly by Lascars, succeeded; and the rear was brought up by a party of small armed men from the fleet; their especial business was to guard a party of coolies on whose shoulders loads of spare ammunition were laid. Clive himself took post beside the European battalion, and, like the rest of the European officers, marched that day on foot.

"It was yet dark when the head of the column fell upon the enemy's outposts, which, after discharging a few matchlocks and rockets, retreated; though not till, by the explosion of a sepoy's cartouch-box, on which one of these missiles fell, some confusion had been created in the English ranks. Order, however, was soon restored, and the column passed on, a fog overspreading them like a canopy as the day broke, and rendering objects quite invisible at a yard's distance from the eye. By and by they came opposite to Omichund's garden, where, in the interior of the Mahratta ditch, the Nabob had fixed his head-quarters; and here, for the first time since the advance began, they became aware of a threatened attack. The sound of horses in movement was heard. It approached rapidly from the direction of the ditch: and the fog opening, as it were, for an instant, a well-mounted line of horsemen was seen within twenty yards of their flank. The column halted, gave its fire with terrible effect, and swept the enemy away as dust is swept aside by the wind when it suddenly rises. Once more the men resumed their march, moving slowly, and firing at random by platoons; while the artillery from time to time discharged round-shot obliquely, as if with a view to clear the course of the column, and protect its progress.

"The troops had now reached a causeway, which, being elevated by several feet above the level of the surrounding country, led through some swampy rice-fields, across the Mahratta ditch, and so into the Company's territory. The causeway was understood to be entrenched, and it formed part of Clive's plan first to carry this barricade by assault, and then, countermarching on the inner side of the Mahratta ditch, to double back upon Omichund's garden, and enter it from the rear. The leading sections accordingly clambered up the ascent, and, facing to the right, prepared to make the rush. But the artillery, now in the rear, not being aware of this change of front, continued to fire as here-tofore; and the shot, striking full among their own people, forced them to seek shelter by leaping down into a ditch on the opposite side of the causeway. Great confusion ensued. Each new company, as it arrived, followed the example of that which went before, till by and by the whole were thrown into a shapeless mass together, quite out of the direction which their leader had proposed to follow. Nor did the mischief end here. A couple of heavy guns from a small bastion on the ditch opened with canister-shot at a short distance, and the first discharge killed or disabled twenty-two Europeans. Clive saw that it was useless to think of rallying in such a position. He therefore gave the word to push on, and made for another elevated mound or causeway a full mile and a quarter to the south, and by so much out of the line of his proposed attack.

" The execution of this movement was much retarded by the damp nature of the soil, over which, interrupted by numerous gaps or channels of irrigation, it was necessary to drag the guns. By nine o'clock, moroever, the fog dispersed, and, the false position of the English becoming evident, the enemy's horse repeatedly endeavoured to charge. And now was seen the obstinate courage of the men, who kept up such a steady and well directed fire that not a horseman ventured to face it. On, therefore, they marched, till, having reached the second causeway, they made a face to the right, and were by and by carried beyond the Mahratta ditch. Clive had it now in his power either to attempt, at a palpable disadvantage, his original design, by marching upon Omichund's garden, or to avail himself of the communication with Calcutta which he had opened, and to lead his people into the town. He preferred the latter course, to which, indeed, the exhausted condition of his people strongly urged him : and about noon, or a little later, jaded and footsore, though not disgraced, the column penetrated within the walls."

Clive's loss on this occasion was, considering the extent of his resources, very severe. It amounted to 120 Europeans, 100 sepoys, and 2 pieces of cannon, while the object for which the movement had been avowedly made was not attained. Nevertheless, the Nabob was so much astonished at the boldness of the attempt, that he hastily evacuated that portion of the town which he had seized, and encamped some space without on the open plain. Here he renewed his overtures of peace; and Clive, in spite of Admiral Watson's reasoning to the contrary, conceived that he was not in a condition to reject the proffered terms. He therefore ratified a treaty which bound the Nabob not only to restore the English to all the rights which the Imperial charter conferred upon them, but to give back their villages, to make compensation for all losses incurred during the war, private as well as public, to pass their merchandize through his territories duty-free, and to sanction the setting up of a mint in Calcutta. In return for these concessions, the English agreed to consider the Nabob's enemies, wherever situated, as their own, and to furnish such aid in troops as their means would allow whenever he should see fit to call for it.

We need not now affect to be ignorant that both parties, when they signed this treaty, counted little, if at all, upon its observance one moment longer than should suit the convenience of the strongest. Clive, in a letter informing the Chairman of the Court of Directors that hostilities were ended, urged the keeping up of a respectable force in Bengal on this plea, " that it cannot be expected that the princes of this country, whose fidelity is always to be suspected, will remain firm to their promises and engagements from principle only." In like manner Suraj-u-Dowlah, ere the seal was appended which testified to his acceptance of an English alliance, had begun to correspond with M. Bussy and M. Law on the subject of the expulsion of these allies from Bengal. Still, according to Clive's judgment—and surely none could be more impartial—the arrangement was in every respect advantageous to his countrymen. " If I had only consulted the interest and reputation of a soldier," he says, " the conclusion of this peace might easily have been suspended. I know at the same time there are many who think I have been too precipitate in the conclusion of it; but surely those who are of this opinion never knew that the delay of a day or two might have ruined the Company's affairs by the junction of the French with the Nabob, which was on the point of being carried into execution: they never considered the situation of affairs on the coast, and the positive orders sent me by the gentlemen there to return with the major part of the forces at all events: they never considered that, with a war upon the coast and in the province of Bengal at the same time, a trading company could not exist without a great assistance from the Government: and, last of all, they never considered that a long war, attended through the whole course of it with success and many great actions, ended at last with the expense of more than fifty lacs of rupees to the Company." These arguments, however strange they may sound in our ears, who have seen " The Company " lavish, without appearing to feel the expenditure, not fifty lacs of rupees, but fifty millions of pounds sterling, upon its wars, were founded, at the period when Clive lived and wrote, upon the soundest view of the state of public affairs.   We were but traders and adventurers then in the land where our rule is now absolute; we could not fight, or were supposed to be incapable of fighting, a Nabob of Bengal, except at a disadvantage.   We shall see, as we proceed, with what a sure yet rapid pace new and bolder conceptions entered into men's minds.

CHAPTER VIII.

Up to the period in his history at which we have now arrived, Clive deserves to be considered only in one point of view. He had acted hitherto as a soldier with equal bravery and skill. Whatever instructions he received from the Government under which he served he had accomplished with consummate ability. But a new page in his public life is now turned; success in war would seem to have sharpened his faculties and inspired him with greater confidence in his own perceptions and judgment than in those of his political superiors. He began to think for himself, and gave indications of a will not easy to be controlled, by first evading and then positively refusing obedience to the orders which were transmitted to him from the coast; for, ever since they received official information of war between England and France, the Madras Government had been urgent in their demands for Clive's return, and Clive had repeatedly promised that, as soon as matters could be arranged, he would obey them. But other views of what would best promote the interests of the Company began gradually to open upon him. He resolved not to leave behind him such a formidable nucleus of evil as the French settlement at Chandernagore; and, remembering that its reduction had been suggested to him ere he sailed from Madras, he made up his mind to effect the conquest now. He informed his friends on the Coromandel coast of this design; and added, that till it should have been accomplished it would be idle for them to expect that he or any portion of his army would come among them.

The moment for entering upon this enterprise was not unfavourable. In the hour of his own weakness Clive had proposed to the French Governor of Chandernagore that a treaty of neutrality between that settlement and Calcutta should be formed,

and the French Governor appeared nowise disinclined to accede
to the proposition. But Bussy's success in the Deccan, and, as
Clive had good reason to believe, the intrigues of Suraj-u-
Dowlah, led to procrastination and something like a change of
mind on the subject. It was obviously as unsafe as it would
be impolitic to leave matters in so unsettled a state, and Clive
pressed the representative of the French Company to give him
a decided answer. The answer came, and amounted to this—
that the writer was very willing to enter into an armistice in the
province of Bengal, but that he had no power to pledge himself
for its observance by the Governor of Pondicherry, or by those
acting under his orders. There was no mistaking the real
purport of such a communication, and Clive took his measures
accordingly.

Ever since the capture of Cossimbazar, Mr. Watts, who when
Suraj-u-Dowlah fell upon the factory happened to be its chief,
had resided in a sort of honourable captivity at Moorshedabad.
The Nabob put no restraint upon his movements, and often
admitted him into his presence; indeed Mr. Watts came at last
to execute functions not dissimilar to those which used to be discharged by English residents half a century ago at the courts of
native princes; but he was interdicted from returning to Calcutta. He managed, however, chiefly through the instrumentality of an individual of whom further notice will be taken
presently, to keep up a regular and even a confidential correspondence all the while with his own Government. This gentleman was employed by Clive to solicit the Nabob's sanction
for an attack by the English on Chandernagore. He met for a
while with no encouragement; but by and by the dread of an
Affghan invasion caused the Nabob to hesitate, and hopes were
held out that the request would be acceded to. Still the Nabob
was very unwilling to sacrifice the French. He looked to them
as to the only power which was capable of counterbalancing the
influence of the English; and, with the fickleness of a barbarian,
not unfrequently anticipated that the time would come when he
should be able, through their assistance, to expel the obnoxious
race from his dominions. But he was equally unwilling to offend
a power which recent experience had taught him to respect,
especially at a moment when the value of their alliance, offensive

and defensive, was about to be tested. He made a demand for an English corps to help him against the Affghans. It was readily furnished; and the English army began its march; but Clive, who went with it, saw his opportunity, and took advantage of it. On the 7th of March he addressed a letter to the Nabob, in which he represented the danger to which his countrymen would be exposed were he to leave an enemy's settlement between them and the force which he was conducting to his Highness's support. He further stated his purpose of halting in the vicinity of Chandernagore till his Highness should have given a decisive answer to the proposal already made to him through Mr. Watts. Meanwhile Admiral Watson had written in strong terms, and to the same effect; but the tone of the sailor served rather to irritate than to persuade; for, instead of acceding to the demand, Suraj-u-Dowlah marched an army to Hooghly. A good deal of uneasiness in Calcutta and elsewhere followed this movement. The Committee declared against a breach with the Nabob, and Admiral Watson inclined to their opinion. But Clive's resolution was fixed, and he adhered to it. He moved on; and no sooner was the Nabob made acquainted with this advance than he recalled his troops from Hooghly. Mr. Watts immediately informed Clive of all that had occurred, adding an assurance that the Nabob had given a verbal assent to the proposed attack on Chandernagore; and Clive, whom no considerations of delicacy were ever known to bend from a purpose previously considered and fully determined on, was content with the assurance. He invested Chandernagore from the land on the 12th; and, the fleet moving up as fast as the wind and current would allow, the operations of the siege began. They were conducted with great vigour. On the 23rd of March Chandernagore capitulated; and the whole of the European garrison, with the exception of about one hundred persons who were permitted to depart on their parole, became prisoners of war.

It is impossible to over-estimate the value of this conquest to the English East India Company. The time had arrived when their continued existence, even as a trading corporation, was clearly incompatible with the success of the schemes to which the French had committed themselves; and the utter overthrow of one or other of these rival communities became a mere matter of calculation. It was a great point to have extinguished on the side of Bengal such an important settlement as that which had just fallen ; and it now remained to follow up the blow with vigour, and to take away from the enemy all hope of recovering his lost ground. At the same time, Clive was unable to hide from himself that an active prosecution of the French war in this part of India would inevitably involve the Presidency in a war with the Nabob; for the Affghans had not persevered in their threatened invasion. A considerable money-bribe had prevailed upon them to return to their own country ; and now Mr. Watts reported that Suraj-u-Dowlah, furious at the fall of Chanderna-gore, was in constant and active communication with M. Law and M. Bussy. Indeed the former of these officers had arrived with a small corps within the principality, and many fugitives from the garrison of Chandernagore had broken their parole to join him. The latter was understood to be at Cuttack, whence a march of two hundred miles or less would carry him to the banks of the Hooghly. Clive at once determined to play the bold game. The letters of recall which began to pour in upon him from Madras he answered by stating, that to quit his present sphere of action at such a moment was impossible. Neither would he fall back upon Calcutta, though repeatedly urged to do so by the Nabob. He was aware of the entangled state of that wretched man's affairs, and soon took a prominent part in hur-rying forward their crisis.

No attentive reader of Oriental history need be told that the dominion of the Moguls in India was everywhere, and at all stages of its continuance, a government of the sword. The power of life and death, of imposing taxes, of commanding armies, and, to a certain extent, of dispensing criminal justice, the Mussulmans kept in their own hands ; but all the details of finance and of accounts, from the management of the public treasury down to the stamping and assaying of money, they com-mitted, as in some sort beneath their care, to the more subtle and effeminate Hindoos. The bankers in large cities, the money-lenders in little villages, had always been Hindoos These men, though attended by less parade and state than their Mussulman neighbours, exercised extensive influence in the country, and were on that account treated, in the ordinary course of things, with some consideration by their rulers. At the same time, neither Emperor nor Viceroy hesitated to fleece a Hindoo subject whenever the wealth of the latter appeared to have accumulated too much, or his own exigencies required it ; and the Hindoo, well aware of the fact, though he might discountenance insurrection for its own sake, was ready at any moment to conspire against his prince, provided it could be shown that he would personally benefit by the measure. " I prefer Hindoos as managers and renters to those of my own religion," said Ameer-ul-Omra, the second son and able minister of Mahomed Ali, Nabob of the Carnatic, " because a Mahomedan is like a sieve and a Hindoo like a sponge. Whatever you put into the one runs through ; the other retains it all, and you may recover it at any moment by the application of a little pressure." On the same principle the thrifty Hindoo lent all the aid which cunning and the influence of wealth could command to keep men faithful to the supreme ruler so long as he left his renter or manager unmolested. But, at the first appearance of a coming storm, the renter prepared to work against it, and was just as ready to use his wealth in raising an enemy to the throne as in keeping upon it the prince through whose favour he had grown rich. In such a state of society there could be very little confidence, and no sentiment of honour, on either side. The ruler would oppress the subject as often as it suited his convenience to do so ; the subject would cheat the ruler habitually if he could, and had no scruple about destroying him if necessary for his own purposes.

Suraj-u-Dowlah succeeded to a full treasury by the same event which placed him on the viceregal throne of Bengal. His capital likewise could boast of several wealthy bankers, all of whom, being Hindoos, were open, as a matter of course, to be dealt with according to the Nabob's pleasure, provided he should exercise but a little discretion in the use of it. Suraj u-Dowlah, however, had no discretion. He squandered upon mean pleasures the wealth which his predecessor had painfully accumulated, and suffered no consideration of justice or ordinary prudence to restrain him in seeking to replace it. His exactions from the great Hindoo bankers of the capital were horrible. Now, though a patient race, the Hindoos are both avaricious and vindictive, and in the present instance they had not even the principle of fear to restrain them. They knew that the man who oppressed them had no hold upon the country. His troops, mutinous for want of pay, were ready to rise against him, and all his great officers of state his cruelty or his pride had alienated. They entered, therefore, into conspiracies which might or might not have led to serious results, but which were brought to a point mainly through the instrumentality of one to whom I had occasion to allude a short time ago, and of whom a few words will give all the account which the purpose of the present narrative seems to require.

Among the money-getting, money-loving, and intriguing Hindoos of that day there was none more noted for his avarice and his talents than Omichund. He had carried on the business of a merchant in Calcutta, and been useful to the English in procuring for them good investments, and in helping them, ere yet the fury of Suraj-u-Dowlah overtook them, in evading the Nabob's taxes. By the fall of Calcutta he had been a sufferer to a considerable extent, and could therefore lay claim to a share of the compensation which the Nabob had promised. On the return of peace this man had removed to Moorshedabad, where, by dint of cunning and a ready adaptation of his own views to those of the Nabob, he managed to ingratiate himself into the favour of Suraj-u-Dowlah. He kept up, at the same time, a good understanding with his co-religionists, and soon took a forward place in the conspiracy to which they were committed. It is worthy of note that in all their plotting these men never entertained the most distant idea of substituting a Hindoo for a Mussulman government. They desired only to exchange one Mahomedan master for another, and cared for few other qualities in their candidate than a respectable name, high station, and so much strength of character as should justify their hopes of success. The object of their first choice was one Khuda Yar Khan Lattee, a man powerfully connected, and high in the service of the Nabob. With him Omichund happened to be on familiar terms, and, being admitted into his confidence, he played his game for him. But, for some reason or another which has never been fully explained, the conspirators in a short time threw their first favourite aside, and, without consulting Omichund, made overtures to Meer Jaffier, the Nabob's commander-in-chief. The wily merchant of Calcutta, though offended at this slight. loved the wages of iniquity too well to make a public exhibition of his sentiments. When the pressure of circumstances forced the party to offer him a renewal of their confidence, he did not decline it, though he seems even at this stage in the business to have determined that they should pay for the indignity which they had put upon him.

It was natural that men so circumstanced should look round in every quarter for support; and the conspirators were not slow in determining that in the English they would find allies at once zealous and powerful. They opened a communication with Mr. Watts as soon as their plans were matured, and employed Omichund to conduct it. Omichund was too ambitious to be content with the humble part that was at first assigned him. He got all their secrets out of them, and forthwith placed himself in the first rank of the conspiracy. His object was to convince Mr. Watts and Colonel Clive that nothing could be done without him; and up to a certain point in the transaction he appears to have succeeded. Nor would it be fair even to his bad memory were we to deny that he had a great deal from first to last in his power. By making himself useful to the Nabob in various ways, he contrived to have free access to his person, and was therefore in a position not only to betray him to his enemies, but to betray his enemies to the Nabob. Moreover, it is very certain that, up to the critical moment, the intelligence which he communicated was of vast importance. Mr. Watts, indeed, was personally a witness to many outbursts of temper; but Omichund saw more; for the secret, and, as far as such a man could deliberate calmly, the calm deliberations of the Nabob for the destruction of the English were not kept back from him. These he took care to describe in glowing terms both to Mr. Watts and Colonel Clive; and the consequence was, that they came by degrees to consider him, what he certainly was not, the moving spring in the great revolution which they had resolved to bring about.

Time passed, and this game of plot and counterplot went forward bravely. The Nabob, profligate, cruel, and avaricious, though he had no hold at all upon his native subjects, yet resolved at all hazards to get rid of his English allies. Towards

the end of March, just after the fall of Chandernagore, he wrote
to M. Bussy in these terms :—"This news" (the news of the
advance of the French army towards his position) "gives me
pleasure. The sooner you come here, the greater satisfaction I
shall have in meeting you. What can I write of the perfidy of
these English ! They have, without ground, picked a quarrel
with M. Renault, and taken by force his factory * * * *
When you come to Pallasore I will then send M. Law to your
assistance, unless you forbid his setting out. Rest assured of my
good will towards you and your Company ; and, to convince you
of my sincerity, I now send perwaunahs to Deedar Ali and Ram-
majee Punjet, and to Rajaram Singh, that, as soon as you enter
their province, they meet and render you all possible assistance."
In the same spirit he loaded M. Law and the fugitives from
Chandernagore with favours, and positively refused to deliver
them up to the English. Meanwhile he expressed himself in
terms of strong indignation on the subject of Clive's continuance with his army at Chandernagore. It was an act, he said,
of exceeding audacity to capture that place without his sanction ;
but to persist in keeping an army so far in advance of the Company's territory was a thousand times worse. Accordingly he
directed Meer Jaffier to proceed to Plassey at the head of fifteen
thousand men, and to reinforce the division which was already
there under the orders of another of his officers, while at the
same time he did his best to close the navigation of the Ganges,
and spoke openly of marching upon Calcutta. The most unguarded of these expressions were retailed to the parties affected
by them with elaborate minuteness. Clive was told that the letters which he wrote were torn by the Nabob and trampled under
foot. The next post brought the Nabob's answers to these very
letters couched in the most fulsome style of Oriental rhetoric.
Mr. Watts complained that one day he was driven from the
durbar with a threat of being impaled—that the next, he was
sent for in order to listen to an abject apology. In a word, it
was evident that hatred and fear strove against each other in the
mind of this weak and wicked man, and that as soon as the latter
feeling could be overmastered the English in Bengal would
experience the effects of the former to their utmost conceivable
limits.

Under all these circumstances, Clive gave it as his opinion that no terms could any longer be kept with Suraj-u-Dowlah. It was a game of life and death between him and the English; and to play such a game timidly would be to lose it. He therefore threw himself with all the vigour of his nature into the schemes of the conspirators, and urged his colleagues in the committee to adopt a similar course. They wavered long, but at last yielded to the combination of the influences which assailed them. It was agreed that, on certain conditions, they should assist Meer Jaffier in his attempt to wrest the sceptre from the unworthy hand which held it; and it must be confessed that, with whomsoever originating, the conditions were marvellously favourable to themselves. They pledged the Nabob in expectancy to all manner of pecuniary obligations. Now in the shape of compensation for losses already sustained, now under the head of gratuities to the army, to the navy, to the members of Committee—indeed to every European or native functionary connected with the Company—Meer Jaffier undertook to pay, as the price of his elevation, much more than the resources of his principality could produce; but the native princes were in those days as reckless of their promises as the European settlers were exorbitant in their demands: and the results are, that they and the parties bribed by them have long ago changed places.

Matters had proceeded thus far when three events befel, any one of which would have deterred a man of less iron nerve than Clive from pushing them further. In the first place, the Committee of Government took fright at the threatening attitude assumed by the Nabob, and wrote to Clive not only to caution him against committing himself in his correspondence with Mr. Watts, but to entreat that he would return with all his forces to Calcutta. As timid men are apt to do, however, they rested their argument for the latter course on a fictitious ground, and spoke of the cost to the Company of keeping the troops in the field. Clive's answer is too characteristic to be given in any other words than his own. After turning into ridicule their cautions in respect to his correspondence, he goes on to say,— " By your manner of expressing yourselves with regard to putting the troops into garrison, it somewhat appears as if I had unnecessarily kept them in the field. Give me leave to say, gentlemen, I am equally desirous with you of saving every possible expense to the Honourable Company, and that it is long that I have waited for an opportunity of going into quarters; but let me ask you whether the situation of affairs has admitted of it hitherto? I fully intend in a day or two to put the coast troops into garrison at Chandernagore, and to send the rest to Calcutta, if nothing very material occurs to prevent it. The former are entirely under my command, and you may be assured that, as I shall never make use of the power vested in me to the injury of the Honourable Company's affairs, I shall be as far from suffering you to take away any part of it. I say thus much to prevent further disagreeable intimations, which can tend to no good end."

The second obstacle which presented itself at this stage in the business came in the shape of a positive refusal on the Admiral's part to share in the responsibility of the undertaking. He expressed himself willing and ready to give all the aid which the fleet could afford in men and in the means of transport; but, anticipating an unfavourable result, he would not be a party to an enterprise so pregnant with danger to the Company's interest by professing to approve of it. Clive was annoyed, but did not therefore abandon his purpose. He treated the Admiral's communication as if it had been all that he desired, and persevered in his career. A little more of caution, perhaps, he found it necessary to exercise; and his letters to the Nabob became in consequence more and more conciliatory every day. But these might have failed in accomplishing their object had not circumstances enabled him to make a display of magnanimity which proved as effective in its results as in design it was hollow. Clive received at this moment letters from a Mahratta chief, which, after denouncing the conduct of the Nabob, proposed, in co-operation with the English, to invade Bengal; and engaged not only to cover all the losses of the Company twice over, but to secure to them the exclusive commerce of the Ganges. Now, nobody knew better than Clive that from a Mahratta alliance, even if the offer were genuine, nothing but evil could come; and his own mind, fruitful in expedients, led him to suspect that the whole might be neither more nor less than a stratagem of

Suraj-u-Dowlah for the purpose of throwing upon the English the odium of a rupture. He therefore sent the despatch to Moorshedabad, and the effect more than realized his expectations. The Nabob, pleased with such a signal exhibition of good faith, not only spoke but acted for a brief space as if his confidence in the English had returned, and the conspirators were enabled to push forward their preparations with increased facility and boldness.

The plan agreed upon by the confederates amounted to this: that, as soon as he should be informed of the maturity of his friends' preparations, Clive would advance to Plassey; that Meer Jaffier, instead of giving him battle, should join him with his whole corps; and that the allied armies, marching upon Moorshedabad, should seize Suraj-u-Dowlah in his palace, and raise Meer Jaffier to the throne. Meanwhile, the better to deceive the object of their plot, Clive, towards the end of April, announced his intention of putting his troops into quarters. He entreated Suraj-u-Dowlah to imitate his example by withdrawing his people from Plassey, and received in return promises which were never accomplished. Here, then, was a fair excuse for throwing off the mask; and an ill-advised attack on a boat which was proceeding with a supply of arms and ammunition from Calcutta to Cossimbazar added to its weight. Clive's tone immediately changed. He wrote to Mr. Watts that "the Nabob was a villain." He desired that Meer Jaffier would be secured by a prompt ratification of the treaty that was between them, and then went on as follows:—

"To-morrow we decamp: part of our forces go to Calcutta, the other will go into garrison here" (at Chandernagore); "and, to take away all suspicion, I have ordered all the artillery and tumbrils to be embarked in boats and sent to Calcutta. I have wrote the Nabob a soothing letter; this accompanies another of the same kind, and one to Mohun Lal" (a creature of Suraj-u-Dowlah), "agreeable to your desire. Enter into business with Meer Jaffier as soon as you please. I am ready, and will engage to be at Nusary in twelve hours after I receive your letter, which place is to be the rendezvous of the whole army. The Major who commands at Calcutta has all ready to embark at a moment's warning, and has boats sufficient to carry artillery and stores to

Nusary. I will march by land and join him there; we will
then proceed to Moorshedabad, or the place we are to be joined
at, directly. Tell Meer Jaffier to fear nothing; that I will
join him with 5000 men who never turned their backs; and that,
if he fails seizing him, we shall be strong enough to drive
him out of the country. Assure him I will march night and
day to his assistance, and stand by him while I have a man
left."

It is impossible, perhaps, to carry on political intrigues of any
sort without doing more or less of violence to the laws of integrity
and honour. Indeed, the duplicity of statesmen and diplomatists
has passed, even in Europe, into a proverb, less just, probably,
in its application now than it was a century or two ago, and
growing, we are willing to hope, more and more inapplicable
every day. But to the web of deceit in the weaving of which Clive
took the part which has been here imperfectly described, there
is not, as far as I know, any parallel even in Eastern story. No
doubt our countrymen had this to say for themselves, that their
wits were in duel with the cunning of one to whom the very
meaning of the term truth was unknown; and that, unless they
stooped to fight him with his own weapons, their destruction
and the ruin of the affairs of their masters were inevitable;
and perhaps the conventional morality which sets life and goods
above honour may force us to accept their excuse. But for
the crowning act of wrong in which Clive, in his own person,
involved them, no apology can be admitted. I have spoken
elsewhere of Omichund, and of the unworthy part which he
played in the course of these most discreditable transactions.
In heart and soul a villain, this man, after bringing matters to a
point whence there could be no retreat, suddenly turned round
upon his employers. It had already been agreed that, in
addition to the fullest compensation for the losses which he had
sustained in the capture of Fort William, he should receive
a handsome reward for services performed in the course of the
present negotiation. He had, besides, by awakening the Nabob's
fears, though in a wrong direction, obtained from him a grant
of 40,000*l*. He now waited upon Mr. Watts, and told him
that, unless he were assured of receiving 300,000*l*. sterling, as
the recompense of his agency, over and above the enormous

sum already promised, he should inform Suraj-u-Dowlah of all that was in progress, and cause the conspirators, English as well as native, to be arrested on the spot. The communication of this fact to Clive constituted the third of those obstacles to success of which I have spoken as scarcely to be surmounted by any other individual than himself. It did not stand in Clive's way for a moment: " Promise all that he seeks," was the tenor of his reply, " and draw up any form of engagement which shall satisfy him and make us secure against his treachery." This was done ; and, articles of agreement being drawn up were sent back to Clive for ratification. The rest of the story, as far as concerns this portion of it, cannot be better told than in Clive's own words :—

" I have your last letter," he writes to Mr. Watts, " including the articles of agreement. I must confess the tenor of them surprised me much. I immediately repaired to Calcutta, and, at a committee held, both the Admiral and gentlemen agree that Omichund is the greatest villain upon earth, and that now he appears in the strongest light, what he was always suspected to be, a villain in grain. However, to counterplot this scoundrel, and at the same time to give him no room to suspect our intentions, enclosed you will receive two forms of agreement—the one real, to be strictly kept by us, the other fictitious. In short, this affair concluded, Omichund shall be treated as he deserves. This you will acquaint Meer Jaffier with."

Enough is stated in this extract to show that, if Omichund was capable of extreme baseness, he was no match in duplicity for the European statesmen with whom he had to deal; but the writer is not quite so explicit as he might have been in giving credit where it was due. The Committee had many scruples in adopting this device, and do not seem to have been persuaded into an acquiescence in it till there were spread out before them two treaties—one upon white paper, from which Omichund's name was omitted ; the other upon red, where all that he had stipulated for was granted. It would scarcely be fair to assume that the hesitation of these gentlemen had its root in any misgivings respecting the practicability of the device which was suggested to them. They could not surely be so innocent as to believe that the preparation of a two-fold treaty was impossible.

But, whatever the ground of their doubts might be, they seem to have yielded to the exhibition of the red and white documents as soon as they were placed before them. The Admiral was less plastic: he had condemned the scheme from the first; he would have no concern in it now; and when reminded that the absence of his signature would rouse suspicion and might mar all, he still refused to sign. What was to be done? Clive took upon himself the ultimate arrangement of the affair: he forged the Admiral's name, and sent off both deeds duly executed, at least in form.

CHAPTER IX.

Advance of Clive—Battle of Plassey.

I HAVE recorded these facts—for facts they unfortunately are—with deep regret—with more of regret than of indignation. It would be vain to offer for them any apology; they will admit of nothing of the sort; yet is it certain that never to the end of his days could Clive be brought to see that he had committed the slightest outrage upon principle. When charged with these acts as a crime, he denied the criminality while he admitted that he had performed them. His manner of reasoning is certainly hard to follow, but there can be no doubt that it was consistent with itself. We can scarcely suppose that any circumstances would have led him to falsify his own solemn engagements in Eng'and, far more to forge the name of another; nevertheless he appears to have thought nothing of the guilt of such proceedings in Bengal, as if moral right were as contingent as the complexions of men upon climate; and that transactions which in Europe would cover the actors with infamy, might in Asia be consummated with impunity. At the same time, justice compels us to add, that, if such were really his sentiments, he was not the only person of his own age, and on his own scene of busy life, who seemed to be guided by them. His colleagues in office, the gentlemen of the Committee, and even the Admiral, however squeamish at the outset, soon got rid of their scruples. The most rigid had no objection to praise the deceiver when his deed was done, and to become partakers in the benefits arising out of the deceit.

All these preliminaries having been settled, and Mr. Watts fully instructed in the course which he was expected to follow, Clive set himself, with his usual industry, to prepare for action. The accounts from Moorshedabad continued to be unsatisfactory. Meer Jaffier either feared to commit himself, or wavered in his faith. Omichund was just as likely to prove a traitor at the eleventh hour as at the ninth; but things had gone too far to admit of further procrastination, and to procrastinate unnecessarily was not Clive's humour. On the 12th of June all the troops stationed in Calcutta, together with one hundred and fifty armed seamen from the fleet, proceeded to Chandernagore. Here a junction was formed with that portion of the army which a short time previously had been distributed in quarters through the town; and the whole, leaving behind them an hundred seamen to guard the place, resumed their march on the morrow. The better to keep the Europeans fresh, they, with the artillery and stores, moved up the river in boats: the sepoys moved in a parallel column by land, and were always within sight of their comrades; and so the whole proceeded. On the 14th they arrived at Culna, where Mr. Watts, who had escaped the preceding day from Moorshedabad, found them. The 16th carried them to Patlee; and on the 17th Major Coote made himself master, after a brief resistance, of the fortress of Cutwa. There, on the plain by which the castle is surrounded, they pitched their tents; but on the 19th the weather broke with unexpected violence, and, in order to escape the fury of the storm, the troops were forced to shelter themselves among the huts and villages near.

Meanwhile Suraj-u-Dowlah was in a state of the greatest indignation and alarm. He had for some days entertained a suspicion that all was not as he desired it to be, and on the 14th sent to require Mr. Watts' presence at court. To his amazement he found that the bird was flown. Omichund was next summoned; but Omichund also, though he had been with him at a late hour on the preceding day, was gone. By and by a messenger arrived laden with a packet from Clive, which, when the Nabob had opened and read, removed from his mind whatever doubt might have still lingered there. In a letter which he despatched from Chandernagore the day previous to the advance of the army, Clive spoke out without reserve or equivocation. He reproached the Nabob with his French connexion—upbraided him on account of the non-fulfilment of his engagements—charged him with meditating an attack on Calcutta as soon as Admiral Watson and himself should have quitted the Ganges—and made a formal recapitulation of all the injuries which he had already inflicted on the Company. " For these reasons," continued the letter, "I have determined, with the approbation of all who are charged with the Comany's affairs, to proceed immediately to Cossimbazar, and to submit there our disputes to the arbitration of Meer Jaffier, Roydullub, Juggeit Seit, and others of your Highness's great men. If these decide that I have deviated from the treaty, I swear to give up all further claims upon your Highness ; but if it should appear that your Highness has broken faith, then I shall demand satisfaction for all the losses sustained by the English, and all the charges of the army and navy." This remarkable epistle, of which the object could not be mistaken, concluded with an announcement at least as startling as any of the clauses which preceded it—that, " as the rains were now near at hand, and it required many days to receive an answer, the writer would not linger where he was, but would wait upon his Highness immediately in his capital."

The Nabob read this letter with feelings of mingled indignation and alarm. He saw that the crisis to which he seems for some time to have looked forward had arrived, and gave orders for the immediate advance of his army to Plassey. The whole moved without the slightest hesitation, and took up its ground as directed ; for though it had been agreed between Clive and Meer Jaffier that the latter should pass over to the English with his division, the fears of the conspirator prevailed over his ambition, and in the hour of difficulty he stood fast. Meanwhile Clive suffered much from anxiety and doubt. His entire force numbered only three thousand men, of whom less than one thousand were Europeans, and his artillery train did not exceed eight six-pounders and a howitzer. It seemed little short of madness to risk, with a handful of troops, however good, a battle in the open plain against fifty thousand adversaries—and at less than fifty thousand nobody rated the host which lay between him and the accomplishment of his wishes. Accordingly his letter to the Committee of Government, dated from Cutwa, on June 19. 1757, says—" I feel the greatest anxiety at the little intelligence I receive from Meer Jaffier, and, if he is not treacherous, his sang-froid or want of strength will, I fear, overset the expedition. I am trying a last effort, by means of a Brahmin, to prevail upon him to march out and join us. I have appointed Plassey as the place of rendezvous, and have told him at the same time that, unless he gives this or some other sufficient proof of the sincerity of his intentions, I will not cross the river. This, I hope, will meet with your approbation. I shall act with such caution as not to risk the loss of our forces; and whilst we have them we may always have it in our power to bring about a revolution, should the present not succeed. They say there is a considerable quantity of grain in and about this place. If we can collect eight or ten thousand maunds" (eight or ten hundred thousand pounds), "we may maintain our situation during the rains, which will greatly distress the Nabob, and either reduce him to terms which may be depended upon, or give us time to bring in the Beer-Boom Rajah, the Mahrattas, or Ghazee-u-Deen.* I desire you will give your sentiments freely how you think I should act if Meer Jaffier can give us no assistance."

The danger could not be trifling which was capable of wringing from a man of Clive's nerve such avowals as these—nor indeed was it trifling. There he stood, isolated as it were, with a handful of men, the slightest disaster falling upon whom must lead not only to their destruction, and the disgrace of their leader, but to the entire ruin of the Company's affairs in India. Between him and the enemy ran that branch of the Ganges which flanks on one side the island of Cossimbazar, across which, in its present state, it would be easy to march, but which a few days' rain would render impassable. Below him, no doubt, the country was open, and he had supplies enough within reach to avert all hazard of famine. But delay, now that the mask was thrown aside, would operate, as he well knew, far more favourably for the Nabob than for him. Plassey was distant not more than ten days' march from the scene of operations; and on the Coromandel coast the greatest alarm was felt lest an expedition, long looked for from Europe, should arrive and attack Madras while yet unprepared. The tone of composure, therefore, in which he wrote of maintaining himself at Cutwa during the rains could not be other than assumed; and the measure to which he resorted on the 21st testifies that it was not enduring. On that day, for the first and last time in his life, he assembled a council of war, and proposed to it the question—" Whether, in our present

* Native powers, who were equally willing to assist in tearing the Nabob of Bengal in pieces.

situation, without assistance, and on our own bottom, 't would be prudent to attack the Nabob; or whether we should wait till joined by some country power?" Of the sixteen officers com-posing this court nine voted for delay and seven for an immediate attack. Among the majority were Clive himself, and Major Kilpatrick, his second in command; Major Eyre Coote, afterwards so celebrated in Indian warfare, took his place with the minority. The conclusion was accepted by all as definitive, and the conclave broke up.

But Clive, though he had been the first to give his advice in favour of timid counsels, was not satisfied with the decision. He wandered away alone from the camp; he sat down under a clump of trees, and continued in deep thought for more than an hour. He rose at the termination of that space of time impressed with a conviction that the policy of delay was unwise. Meeting Major Coote on his way back to camp, he told him that he had changed his mind; and orders were forthwith issued to prepare for crossing the river on the morrow. It is said that just at this moment letters from Meer Jaffier reached him which removed in some degree his doubts of that officer's good faith: but, besides that the rumour in question rests on no very sure foundation, it is certain that his resolution to advance could not possibly have been formed in consequence of such communication. The fact is, that Clive saw then what we clearly understand now, that any appearance of misgiving on his part would prove as serious as a defeat itself. He could not permit the decision of a council of war, or his own personal responsibility in acting against it, to weigh for a moment where so much was at stake. He therefore treated the vote of the morning as if it had not been given, and looked to the final issues for a justification.

At dawn of day on the 22nd the army began to cross the river; by four in the afternoon the last division was safely across. No halt ensued. The boats being towed against the stream with great labour, the infantry and guns pushed forward; and after a march of fifteen miles the whole bivouacked about three in the morning of the 23rd in a grove or small wood not far from Plassey.

Clive's intelligence had led him to expect that the enemy were in position at Cossimbazar. A rapid march had, however carried them on to Plassey, where they occupied the lines or entrenched camp which, during the siege of Chandernagore, Roydullub had thrown up; and scarcely were the British troops lain down ere the sound of drums, clarions, and cymbals warned them of the proximity of danger. Piquets were immediately pushed forward, and sentries planted, and for an hour or two longer the weary soldiers and camp followers were permitted to rest.

Day broke at last; and forth from their intrenched camp the hosts of Suraj-u-Dowlah were seen to pour. 40,000 foot, armed, some with matchlocks, others with spears, swords, and bows, overspread the plain; 50 pieces of cannon moved with them, each mounted upon a sort of wheeled platform, which a long team of white oxen dragged, and an elephant pushed onwards, from the rear. The cavalry numbered 15,000; and it was observed that, in respect both to their horses and equipment, they were very superior to any which Clive and the soldiers of the Carnatic had seen on their own side of India. The fact was, that this force consisted almost entirely of Rajpoots, or Patans, soldiers from their childhood, and individually brave and skilful with their weapons. But among them, not less than among the infantry, the bond of discipline was wanting; and, placing no reliance one upon another, their very multitude became to them a source of weakness. On the other hand, Clive's small but most pliable army stood silent as the grave. It consisted of about 1000 Europeans, inured to toil and indifferent to danger; and of 2000 sepoys. who, trained in the same school, had imbibed no small share of the same spirit. Of these Europeans a portion of Adlercron's regiment constituted, perhaps, the flower. The name of Adlercron has long since ceased to be had in remembrance; but the gallant 39th still carry with them. wherever they go, a memorial of that day—the word " Plassey," and the proud motto " *Primus in Indis*," standing emblazoned upon their colours, beside many a similar record of good service performed in Spain and in the south of France.

The battle of Plassey began at daybreak. and was continued for many hours with a heavy cannonade on the part of the enemy, to which the guns of the English warmly replied. The fire of the latter told at every round; that of the former was much more noisy than destructive, partly because Clive sheltered his men behind a mud fence which surrounded the grove, partly because the Nabob's artillerists were as unskilful as their weapons were cumbrous. No decisive movement was, however, made on either side, for Clive felt himself too weak in numbers to act on the offensive. Besides, he still expected that Meer Jaffier would come over to him, and, till some indication of the anticipated move were given, he did not consider that he would be justified in quitting his ground. The Nabob's troops, on the other hand, were such as the ablest general could not pretend to manœuvre under fire, and able generals were wholly wanting to them. Under these circumstances Clive, whom excessive fatigue had worn out, lay down and slept, though not till he had given directions that, in the event of any change occurring, he should be immediately called. Accordingly, about noon, one of his people awoke him and said that the enemy were retiring. He started·up : the day, it appeared, being overcast, a heavy shower had fallen, which so damaged the enemy's powder that their artillery became in a great degree useless ; and, as they trusted entirely to their superiority in that arm, they no longer ventured to keep the field. In a moment Clive gave the word to advance. There was one little band attached to the Nabob's force which served him in good stead that day. It consisted of about 40 French soldiers, European and native, the remains of the garrison of Chandernagore, with four light field-pieces. Against these Clive first directed an attack to be made, and, though they resisted stoutly, he drove them from a redoubt in which they were established, and seized their guns. With the apparent design of preventing this, the Nabob's people again sallied forth ; but they came on, this time, in a confused mass, and a well-directed fire from the English guns first checked and then turned them. Advantage was promptly taken of the panic ; no respite was given to the fugitives, for the victors, entering with them pell-mell into their camp, soon converted the retreat into a flight. In an hour from the first movement of the English beyond the exterior of the grove, a battle, on which may be said to have hung the destinies of India, was decided.

Military operations, such as that which has just been described, as they set all the rules of calculation and probability at defiance, so they are placed out of the pale of sober criticism. Proceedings which in any other quarter of the world, and in the face of any other enemy, would have convicted a leader of sheer insanity, were shown by the result to have been in Clive's case as judicious as they were bold. No doubt he was encouraged to place himself in contact with the Nabob by assurances from Meer Jaffier of support; and Jaffier, though he did not fulfil his promise as he ought to have done, unquestionably held aloof in spite of repeated orders to the contrary. Indeed, there seems no cause to doubt that apprehensions of treason within the camp operated as powerfully as terror of the English army to take away from Suraj-u-Dowlah the slender share of courage and presence of mind which nature had bestowed upon him. But be the causes what they might, never was a victory so important in its political consequences gained at such a trifling loss of human life. Of the conquerors there fell that day 22 killed and about 50 wounded, chiefly sepoys. Not more than 500, out of the rabble of 60,000 or 70,000 men that marched under the Nabob's standard, died in the battle. Their dispersion was, however, complete, and guns, tents, baggage, with an enormous booty of every sort, became the prey of the conquerors.

CHAPTER X.

WHILE the fighting, such as it was, went on, Clive observed a large. body of troops on the left of the enemy's line gradually withdraw from communication with their comrades, and move obliquely round his own right. They sent no messenger to communicate with him, nor endeavoured by any other process to explain their intentions; they were therefore fired upon more than once when their eccentric evolutions threatened to bring them nearer to the grove than seemed desirable. No sooner was the battle ended, however, than horsemen came in to announce that the suspicious column consisted of Meer Jaffier's corps, and that Meer Jaffier heartily congratulated his friend on the results of the struggle. That night the two armies encamped close to one another, and early on the following day Meer Jaffier visited Clive in his tent. Whether conscious that appearances, if not facts, were against him, or being moved by the common feeling of his countrymen on such occasions, he exhibited strong symptoms of uneasiness when a guard turned out to receive him; but these Clive made haste to dispel. He went forth to meet him, embraced him in the presence of his people, saluted him as Nabob of Bengal, Bahar, and Orissa, and ushered him into his tent. There Meer Jaffier explained the circumstances which had prevented an earlier fulfilment of his engagements; and described the Nabob as having laboured for many days under a degree of excitement which came little short of insanity. The last act of this miserable man had indeed something very touching about it. After upbraiding and threatening Meer Jaffier up to the morning of the attack, he sent for him, just as the columns were filing out of their entrenchments, and, pulling off his turban, cast it in the general's lap, and implored him to do his duty. To pull off the turban and lay it in the lap of another is the last act of humiliation and confidence which a Mussulman can perform ; and Meer Jaffier, probably moved by the proceeding, swore to defend the turban and its wearer to the death. But the oaths of Orientals are not often more binding than the promises to pay of traders in a state of bankruptcy ; and Meer Jaffier no sooner quitted the presence than he forgot the scene which he had witnessed there. How he bore himself throughout the contest has already been explained.

While Clive and his protégé were discussing the events of the past and plans for the future, Suraj-u-Dowlah fled, well-nigh unattended, to Moorshedabad. He shut himself up in his palace, and listened for a while to the advices of such of his friends as accompanied him from the field or joined him from the city. Now he determined to give himself up to the English, being persuaded to believe that with them his life at least would be safe ; now he resolved to try again the fortune of war, and to prevail or perish in the defence of his capital. But he had not courage enough to sustain him in the accomplishment of either purpose. As soon as darkness set in he disguised himself in the dress of a mechanic, and, taking a casket full of valuable jewels in his hands, let himself down from a window in the palace and got into a boat, which he desired might carry him towards Patna. He did not, however, succeed in making his escape. Though his flight was not discovered for some days after it had occurred, a vigilant search was immediately made in all directions, and, being found or betrayed in the neighbourhood of Rajahmahal, he was seized, carried back to Moorshedabad, and there beheaded.

Meanwhile Clive and Meer Jaffier, having arranged their plans of operation, proceeded without an hour's delay to carry them into execution. Meer Jaffier pushed on at once to Moorshedabad, where he arrived some hours before Suraj-u-Dowlah quitted it. Clive, directing the main body of his troops to follow, marched in the same direction at the head of two hundred European and three hundred sepoy infantry. Not a sword was drawn, not a spear levelled, to oppose the progress of the successful conspirator towards the palace. But the ceremony of instalment he would not permit to go on till Clive had come up to take part in it. It was the Englishman's hand which led the new

Nabob to his throne; and amid the stupefaction occasioned by such a rapid succession of marvellous events, neither Mahomedan Nabobs nor Hindoo bankers appeared to look with surprise on the proceeding. This lull in feelings which were as acute, a century ago, among the native aristocracy of India as they are now among ourselves, could not, however, be expected long to continue. Their pride, if not their patriotism, soon awoke. They could not bear to have the conviction forced on them that adventurers whom, till now, they had never beheld in their presence except as petitioners for commercial advantages or protection against danger, should enter the halls of their princes armed to the teeth, and give a ruler to their country. And if, in due time, even Meer Jaffier began to think more of the degradation to which his race was subjected than of the benefits conferred personally on himself, he must take but a limited view of human nature, and the springs of action which stir it, who can affect either surprise or indignation at the circumstance.

Regret and indignation rarely find scope to exercise themselves amid the excitement of a successful revolution. Whatever he came by and by to feel, Meer Jaffier was for the present full of gratitude; and the satisfaction which he experienced was shared with him by the leading men who had been his advisers and friends during the progress of the conspiracy. Whatever terms Clive proposed they urged the new sovereign to accept, and he did accept them. That these were extravagantly severe will not, it is presumed, be in our days disputed. Clive and the gentlemen who had the largest share in his confidence did not so regard them; because they laboured under a mistaken belief that there were no limits to the wealth of the native princes. Indeed, Messrs. Watts and Walsh, whom Clive, to use his own words, "sent forward to inquire into the state of the treasury, and to watch proceedings in the palace," gave such an exaggerated account of the riches accumulated by the Nabobs of Bengal, that there can be no wonder if both they and he should have overshot the mark. The consequence was, that, when the final treaty came to be arranged, it promised to the Company advantages which went as far beyond their wildest expectations as they exceeded the power of Meer Jaffier to confer without ruin to himself and

to his provinces. The following details I extract from Clive's
official letter to the Secret Committee of the Court of Directors,
dated at Moorshedabad on the 26th of July, 1758 :—

" The substance of the treaty with the present Nabob is as
follows :—

" 1. Confirmation of the mint, and all other grants and privileges in the treaty with the late Nabob.

" 2. An alliance, offensive and defensive, against all enemies
whatever.

" 3. The French factories and effects to be delivered up, and
they never permitted to resettle in any of the provinces.   ·

" 4. One hundred lacs of rupees to be paid to the Company in
consideration of the loss at Calcutta and the expenses of the
campaign.

" 5. Fifty lacs to be given to the English sufferers at the loss
of Calcutta.

" 6. Twenty lacs to Gentoos, Moors, and black sufferers at
the loss of Calcutta.

" 7. Seven lacs to the Armenian sufferers. These three last
donations to be distributed at the pleasure of the Admiral and
gentlemen of Council, including me.

" 8. The entire property of all lands within the Mahratta
ditch, which runs round Calcutta, to be vested in the Company ;
also six hundred yards all round without the said ditch.

" 9. The Company to have the Zemindarry of the country to
the south of Calcutta lying between the lake and the river, and
reaching as far as Culpee, they paying the customary rents paid
by the former Zemindars to the Government.

" 10. Whenever the assistance of the English troops shall be
wanted, their extraordinary charge to be paid by the Nabob.

" 11. No forts to be erected by the Government on the river-
side from Hooghly downwards.

" 12. The foregoing articles to be performed without delay,
as soon as Meer Jaffier becomes Soubahdar."

It is impossible for us, who are accustomed to think of the
East India Company as sovereigns of the whole extent of territory
which lies between Cape Comorin and the Himalaya Mountains,
to conceive the importance of such an arrangement as this to the
same Company, being as yet traders and merchants in the land.

Comparatively small as the Zemindarry conceded to them might be, it established them in the country as a substantive power—bound, indeed, to pay to the Nabob a stipulated tribute, but absolute masters, after this should have been discharged, of all the revenues, from whatever source arising, which they could collect throughout their territory. The value of these Clive, in the letter from which I have just quoted, calculates at ten lacs, or 100,000*l.* sterling. The expulsion of the French, also, and the entire disarming of the river, ensured to the Lords of Fort William and its dependencies the monopoly of the trade of all the districts through which the Ganges held its course: and the pledge taken that English troops should be liberally paid for as often as the Nabob might require their services amounted well-nigh to an engagement that the Company's army would be maintained at the expense of the sovereign of Moorshedabad. In like manner the pecuniary grants made, in the shape of compensation for damages received, fell not short of 1,770,000*l.* But, enormous as this outlay seems, we have not yet completed our list of payments. The army and navy both expected to share in the riches that seemed to descend from heaven in a shower, and one million more of sterling money was thus added to the Nabob's debt, which went on accumulating as members of Council, political agents, and I know not how many other functionaries besides, put in claims, and had them agreed to. Meanwhile Omichund flattered himself that 650.000*l.* were secured to him, and Clive was already in possession of 160,000*l.* which Meer Jaffier, in the first burst of his gratitude, had presented to him. And now came the question—How were all these pecuniary obligations to be discharged? The treasury, which Mr. Watts had described as crammed with 4,000.000*l.* in bullion, besides jewels of inestimable value, was found, on examination, to contain in all 1,500,000*l.* The obligations given, without taking into account Omichund's claim, the claims of the Committee, or the gift already accepted and received by Clive, amounted to 2,700.000*l.*—if the two latter sums be added, to upwards of 3,500,000*l.* Whence were the means of liquidating so prodigious a debt to be derived, and how was the Nabob to keep his own army in a state of subordination by paying up even a portion of the arrears which were already due to them? The question was full of difficulties, and could not have been answered at all, had not Roydullub, the finance minister, and Juggeit Seit, the wealthy Hindoo banker, come to the assistance of the unfortunate Meer Jaffier. By the assistance of these persons the Nabob proposed to pay one half of the amount immediately—two-thirds of this portion in coined money, the other third in plate, jewels, and goods ; while the other half he engaged to liquidate in the course of two years by equal instalments. Clive writes of this arrangement so early as the month of July in the following terms :—" The part to be paid in money is received, and safely arrived at Calcutta ; and the goods, jewels, &c., are now delivered over to us, the major part of which will be bought back by the Nabob for ready money, and in the remaining there will be little or no loss. A large proportion was proposed to be paid us in jewels ; but as these are not a very saleable article, we got the amount reduced one-half, and the difference to be made up in money."

It is not pleasant to put upon record the memorial of such transactions as these. The glory of conquest seems to be obscured by them, and patriotism and high emprise degenerate, as we read, into sordid impulses and the mere lust of gain. Let us not, however, bear too hardly upon the individuals who thus cared for their own interests. They acted in the spirit of the age in which they lived. India appeared then to the people of England pretty much what Mexico and Peru were held by the Spaniards to be when they first discovered them—a mine of wealth which could not be exhausted ; and if Clive and his friends considered that they were justified in gathering as large a portion of the produce as circumstances would allow, perhaps they took a view of their own case not different from that which most men so situated would have taken. But there is a darker shadow on their fame which I must not shrink from describing. Of the double agreement with Omichund notice has already been taken. That, as well as the subscription of the Admiral's name by a strange hand, both the Committee and the officer most deeply affected by the transaction had forgiven ; and it now only remained to inform the Hindoo of the extent to which he had been duped. On the morning of the day when Clive met Meer Jaffier and his counsellors in order to arrange for the payment of the new

Nabob's debts, Omichund joined the conclave. He suspected no fraud: not an act or word of Clive or any of his colleagues had ever led him to harbour a suspicion of their double dealing; and, after hearing the white treaty read, he waited, expecting that the red document would in its turn be produced. Clive felt that the time was come for putting an end to the delusion. " It is now proper," said he in English to Mr. Scrafton, one of the Company's servants who was present, " to undeceive Omichund. You may tell him how the case stands." Mr. Scrafton at once undertook the office of interpreter. " Omichund," he quietly observed in the language of the country, " the red treaty is a sham : you are to have nothing." The wretched man fell, as if shot, insensible, into the arms of an attendant. He was carried out into the air and revived ; but the blow proved more severe than his faculties could sustain. He never uttered a complaint, but passed by rapid degrees into a state of idiotcy. It is said that Clive pitied and spoke kindly to him, advising him to go upon a pilgrimage to some holy shrine, and offering to pay his expenses. It is even hinted that, in spite of all that had occurred, he entertained serious thoughts of again employing the Hindoo in the public service ; but the Hindoo did not comprehend the nature of either proposition. After surviving a few months, in the course of which he squandered the residue of his fortune in trinkets and jewels and rich garments, he died ; and, amid the busy scenes of that busy stage in Indian history, ceased, at least for a while, to be remembered.

As it seems desirable to get rid of so painful a portion of my narrative, I may be permitted, perhaps, to give in this place an outline of the proceedings which occurred when the plunder of the new Nabob came to be divided among his allies, even though I be compelled somewhat to anticipate, in so doing, the chronological order of events. With respect to the presents bestowed upon the Committee, there seems to have been no remarkable difference of opinion anywhere. Clive, as president of the body, received by common consent a larger share than any of the rest. It amounted to two hundred and eighty thousand rupees, or 28,000*l.* sterling. The members were satisfied each with two hundred and forty thousand rupees, or 24,000*l.* sterling ; while subordinate agents—such as Messrs. Watts, Walsh, and suchlike, came in for their douceurs. One name, and only one —that of Warren Hastings—does not appear in the list of recipients of the Nabob's bounty. Yet Hastings played his part, though of course a subordinate one, in the money-making drama.

Again, the spirit by which the whole body of these adventurers was animated showed itself in the exhibition of a mean jealousy of the army against the navy, and of the officers in the service of the Crown and of the Company—one class towards the other. It makes one blush to read, even at this distance of time, how councils of war assembled that they might wrangle and fight over the distribution of the spoil of one for whom they professed to have drawn the sword. Among other disgraceful resolutions, there was one which decided that the seamen who accompanied the expedition, and helped to drag the guns, should receive, not as soldiers, but only as sailors belonging to the fleet. This, of course, reduced their share much below that of men whose dangers and hardships they had shared ; and, though Clive seems to have severely censured this resolution, even he had not influence enough to compel a reversal of it. But another outrageous proposition he did curb ere it could be carried into effect. The officers composing this council demanded to be put at once in possession of the sums granted to both services, in order that they might distribute them without the intervention of prize-agents, and protested against Clive's refusal to yield the point. The Colonel must tell his own story on this occasion, for rapacity must have gone beyond all limits of toleration when it drew from Clive such declarations as the following :—

"I took the first opportunity," he says in a letter to Admiral Watson, "of a little spare time to call a council of war for the division of that share of the prize-money which belongs to the army. I am sorry to say that several warm and selfish debates arose ; and I cannot help thinking that the officers belonging to the navy with the expedition here have had injustice done them in not being allowed to share agreeable to the land division, which was carried against them by a great majority. Enclosed I send you the proceedings of the council of war. The last article, after having been in a manner agreed to, was again brought upon the carpet ; and, notwithstanding that I represented to the gentlemen in the strongest terms that the money could not be divided till it was shroffed, and the agents of both parties present, without the greatest. injustice to the navy, they still persisted in giving their opinions for an immediate division of the money; upon which I overruled the votes and broke up the council of war."

Clive overruled the votes of his officers, but did not overcome so easily the spirit in which they originated. A protest was sent in against his decision; to which he replied, first, by putting in arrest the individuals who presented it, and then by addressing to the body for whom they acted the following note:—

" Gentlemen,—I have received both your remonstrance and protest. Had you consulted the dictates of your own reason, those of justice, or the respect due to your commanding officer, I am persuaded such a paper, so highly injurious to your own honour as officers, could never have escaped you.

" You say you were assembled at a council to give your opinion upon a matter of property. Pray, gentlemen, how comes it that a promise of a sum of money from the Nabob, entirely negotiated by me, can be deemed a matter of right and property? So far from it, it is now in my power to return to the Nabob the money already advanced, and leave it to his decision whether he will perform his promise or not. You have stormed no town and found the money there; neither did you find it in the plains of Plassey after the defeat of the Nabob. In short, gentlemen, it pains me to remind you, that what you are to receive is entirely owing to the care which I took of your interest. Had I not interfered greatly in it, you would have been left to the Company's generosity, who perhaps would have thought you sufficiently rewarded in receiving a present of six months' pay; in return for which I have been treated with the greatest disrespect and ingratitude, and, what is still worse, you have flown in the face of my authority, for overruling an opinion which, if passed, would have been highly injurious to your own reputation, being attended with injustice to the navy, and been of the worst consequences to the cause of the nation and the Company.

" I shall therefore send the money down to Calcutta, give

directions to the agents of both parties to have it shroffed ; and when the Nabob signifies his pleasure (on whom it solely depends) that the money be paid you, you shall then receive it, and not before.

"Your behaviour has been such that you cannot expect I should interest myself any further in your concerns. I therefore retract the promise I made the other day, of negotiating either the rest of the Nabob's promise, or the one-third which was to be received in the same manner as the rest of the public money, at three yearly equal payments.

"I am, Gentlemen,

"Your most obedient, humble servant,

(Signed)   "Rob. Clive.

" *Moorshedabad,*
     5th July, 1757."

This sharp rebuke produced the full effect that was desired. The officers knew better than to hold out against a chief of Clive's temper, and withdrew their protest, offering at the same time an ample apology for having presented it. Much gratitude was likewise expressed by the Admiral for the care which was taken of the seamen's interests ; and all sourness on account of the forged signature, if indeed any such feeling ever existed, died out. "The Admiral," wrote Captain Latham, his confidential aide-de-camp, "drinks every day a bumper to your health "—the surest token, a hundred years ago, of friendship on the part of the drinker. Nevertheless, Clive, though seeming to prosper in all to which he put his hand, was not without his causes of anxiety. The authorities at Madras had repeatedly recalled him, and each new letter brought with it proofs more strong than another that impatience was deepening among them into discontent. The Committee of Government at Bengal, with Mr. Drake at its head. began in like manner to discover that they were likely to find in the commander of their armies more of a master than of a colleague. They, too, harassed him with their communications, and spoke of the necessity of providing for the defence of Fort William on the very day when he gained for them the decisive battle of Plassey. Clive had no hesitation in treating such remonstrants with the contempt which they merited. He told them, in point of fact, that he was a better judge than they of what would best conduce to the well-being of the settlement, and pursued his own course. But with the Madras Government his game was more delicate; he played, however, with boldness, and he won. He assured them that his presence in Bengal was of more importance now to the Company's interests than it had ever been, and declined sending back a man till the negotiations on which he had entered should be complete. Posterity has never blamed him for this. He had made a move from which there was no retracting: he had brought the affairs of his employers into such a state that there was no alternative for him or for them except complete success or entire ruin. The degree of responsibility which he was bold enough to assume would have crushed, by the bare thought of it, almost any other man than himself. Yet the results justified his measures; and, as public men have in all ages been tried rather by the issues than the strict propriety of their plans, so he won for himself a proud name by a process which might have subjected him to the last penalty of the law. Out of such materials are heroes and conquerors formed.

CHAPTER XI.

Fresh troubles in Bengal—Colonel Forde's expedition to the Northern Circars—Clive's Jaghire or Feof.

Having placed the affairs of Moorshedabad in such a train as promised to lead to a satisfactory settlement, and engaged a powerful interest to obtain for Meer Jaffier a formal acknowledgment from the Emperor of his title as Nabob, Clive, whose presence in Calcutta seems to have been much required, returned to that city. He found it, as settlements are wont to be on which unlooked-for prosperity has fallen with a strong tide, filled with people who could not sufficiently rejoice, but neglected by its rulers, who, equally with the inhabitants, appeared to imagine that reverses could never come again. Not a step had been taken to repair or enlarge the fortifications, though the right to do so was accounted one of the most important of the articles included in the treaty. Nobody knew or had adopted measures to ascertain the geographical limits of the Zemindarry of which the Company had become possessed; and a great influx of wealth had produced its usual consequences in those days, by relaxing the bonds of discipline among the military classes, and lowering the tone of morals—already low enough—in every other. Clive set himself to remedy these abuses with the vigour which appertained to his character, and did not permit the death of Admiral Watson, though he deeply and sincerely lamented it—for the time at least required in doing honour to the funeral —to interfere with his public duties. But his measures of reform were yet very incomplete when pressing calls in other quarters carried him again to a distance. It soon became apparent that neither by natural talent nor yet on account of the embarrassment of his circumstances was Meer Jaffier suited for the station to which accident had raised him. His treasury being exhausted, and his troops clamorous for pay, he could devise no better means of replenishing the one or satisfying the other than by plundering the more wealthy of his subjects. This was an old game, for which the Hindoo bankers and the governors of provinces could scarcely be unprepared; and they consequently assumed, as with one accord, the attitude of men who were determined to play it out. Roydullub, who had much befriended him while conspiring against his master, withdrew from attendance on Meer Jaffier, and fenced himself round with friends. The Rajah of Purneah, the Manager of Midnapore, and the Ruler of Patna, all went into rebellion; and, to complete the difficulties of the Nabob's position, Sujah-u-Dowlah, the Viceroy of Oude, assisted, as was believed, by the latter of these nobles, made preparations to invade the provinces. Moreover, the Viceroy of Oude, who was doubly formidable because of his well-known connexion with the French party, had at his own disposal resources not inferior to those which in his palmiest days the Nabob of Bengal could command. Thus threatened on every side, Meer Jaffier sent repeated entreaties that Clive would hasten to his assistance. The latter could not refuse to comply, though the disposable force which he was able to muster amounted to no more than 500 Europeans and 2000 sepoys. Nevertheless, as he well understood the causes of these disorders, and had the best reason to believe that the Hindoo chiefs were far more disposed to look to him as their protector than to the Nabob as their enemy, he entertained no misgivings about the result. His reasoning proved to be as sound in this case as it usually was. No sooner was it known that Clive came to mediate between parties, than first one and then another of the malcontents threw themselves upon his protection. He did not reject them, while at the same time he spared, as far as it was possible so to do, the feelings of the Nabob; and the result was, first, a progress by Meer Jaffier and the English leader and his troops through the disaffected provinces, and, by and by, the full re-establishment of that Hindoo influence at court which the Nabob had hoped, by the assistance of the English, to overthrow. There is no doubt that, by the part which he took in these domestic quarrels, Clive wrought the Nabob good service. It is equally certain that he did not forget either the Company or its servants. He unquestionably extricated the former out of

perplexities from which he never could have extricated himself;
—but he did so on his own terms. He caused Meer Jaffier to
make an assignment of the revenues of certain districts for the
purpose of liquidating the residue of the debt still due to the
Company and to individuals ; and he obtained, over and above, a
grant of the monopoly of saltpetre, which is produced to a considerable extent in the province of Patna. Finally, the necessary forms for investing the Government of Calcutta with the
Zemindarry were made out. In a word, " We may pronounce,"
as he himself expresses it, " that this expedition, without blood-
shed, was crowned with all the advantages that could be expected
or wished, both to the Nabob and the Company."

Clive patched up the affairs of the Nabob's government on
the present occasion as well as he could. He seems to have felt
that his own personal honour was in some measure pledged to
the maintenance of Meer Jaffier on the throne ; and he probably
conceived that the time was not yet fully come for playing
a bolder game: nevertheless, there is good reason to assume
that he had already begun to look further, and that plans for
the substitution of a direct in the room of an indirect sovereignty
in the Company which he served were maturing themselves in
his mind. This is shown as well by various expressions in his
letters, as by the line of policy which he counselled and enforced
on more than one delicate occasion. For example: a report
of the speedy arrival of a French armament in the Ganges was
about this time spread. The Committee of Government took
the alarm, and wrote to Clive, begging that he would enforce
the terms of his alliance with Meer Jaffier, and prevail upon the
latter to send an army to their assistance. Clive refused to do
anything of the sort ; he pointed out, in his answer to the Committee's application, that the relative positions of the Company
and the Nabob were changed in Bengal. The Nabob owed to
them his throne ; he depended upon them for support, or believed that he did so, and hated, in consequence, the very power
without which his sovereignty, as then conducted, was not worth
an hour's purchase. So long as they held towards him an attitude of superiority things would thus continue ; but the moment
they became suppliants—especially suppliants for protection
against a foreign enemy—a revulsion of feeling on his part

would arise. Promising whatever should be sought, without so much as intending to keep the promise, he would assume the same air of superiority which his predecessors used to wear, and, either with or without the assistance of the French, would do his best to govern alone. Clive's reasoning prevailed; no application was made to the Nabob for aid. Indeed, an encounter at sea between the English and French squadrons soon afterwards taking place, of which the issues were doubtful, if indeed they did not tell rather against than in favour of the former, furnished him with an occasion, which he took good care to improve, of boasting about the resistless power of his country by sea as well as by land. The Nabob, accepting his testimony, could only congratulate himself on having secured the friendship of such a people; and certain advances which Bussy had begun to make were repulsed without ceremony.

Clive remained but a few days subsequently to these transactions at Moorshedabad. Early in June he returned to Calcutta, and began to make arrangements for carrying help to the Presidency of Fort St. George. He was thus employed, when the arrival of the "Hardwicke" East Indiaman, with despatches from the Court of Directors, paralysed, for a moment, the whole machine of government. The despatches in question contained the Honourable Court's plan for the management of the affairs of their settlements on the Hooghly, of which it is not too much to say, that arrangements more ridiculously incapable of working, except for harm, could not have been devised. By some curious perversity of intellect or purpose, too, the plan was not simple, but complex. One document, signed in August, and drawn up immediately on receipt of disastrous intelligence from Fort William, appointed a Committee of five to conduct the government, of which Clive should be president. Another, dated in the month of November following, when the re-capture of the fort seems to have been known, dismissed Mr. Drake, of whose incompetency there could be no doubt, and nominated a council of ten. From the names of the gentlemen appointed to this charge that of Clive was omitted; and it was directed that the office of president should be held in a rotation of three months respectively by the four senior members. Of the policy which could thus, with malice prepense, subject the executive to certain feebleness, if not to a worse end, it is not worth while to speak. Only men in their dotage, or else so blinded by suspicion as not to see an inch before them, could have adopted it ; but the omission from the list of rulers of the name of that particular person whom the Court acknowledged to be the ablest among their servants could not have occurred except designedly. It is said, and I believe with truth, that already had that jealousy which waited upon Clive at every stage in his extraordinary advancement begun to show itself. Whether reports of his contumacy from Fort St. George operated to his hurt, or that mediocrity waged war in Leadenhall-street, as it does everywhere else against genius, the result was the same. Though all felt that they could not do without him, the majority of the Directors would appear to have decided that it would be prudent to keep such an aspiring soldier as far as possible in the background. But whatever the policy of the Court might be, the state of public feeling in Calcutta, as well as the real exigences of the settlement, interposed an insuperable bar to its accomplishment. The ten gentlemen named as counsellors, with the four presidents elect at their head, passed a resolution that a form of government such as that dictated in London would never work at Bengal. They further decided that Clive, and only Clive, was capable of conducting matters under existing circumstances to a triumphant issue ; and they drew up a paper in which they entreated him to accept at their hands the office of president, and to discharge its duties till time should be afforded for communicating further with the Court of Directors. Clive, indignant at the slight which seemed to be put upon him in London, refused at first to accede to this proposition ; but the feeling in favour of the arrangement ran so high in Calcutta, that he was constrained to yield. In a handsome reply to a very handsome address, he expressed his readiness to undertake the charge, and entered immediately upon the government with as much courage as if the authority which he wielded had come to him from Leadenhall-street, or the Court of St. James's itself.

I must not pass on from the consideration of this subject without observing that there was one member of the Court of Directors—Mr. Payne, the chairman—who seems to have escaped the contamination of the feeling, whatever it might be, which arrayed his colleagues at the present juncture against Clive. His letters to the hero of Plassey are in existence, and they show that he entertained for his correspondent equal respect and regard. He says, indeed, that the "almost unlimited powers with which the select committee of Fort St. George" had armed Clive on first proceeding to the Ganges, as they had alarmed others, so they had staggered even himself; and expresses an opinion that Clive, in taking advantage of them, though it were even for the public good, had stirred the jealousy of the home authorities. But he so delivers his views as to leave a decided impression on the mind that he, at least, would have been glad to see Clive where Clive's coadjutors in the local government placed him. Indeed Clive himself, when referring to the circumstances in after-life, declared that Mr. Payne's letters went no inconsiderable way to induce his acceptance of the presidency which the local Council pressed upon him. There can be no doubt now that it was this arrangement, and nothing else, which laid the foundation of a British empire in India; and both they who waived their own rights, and he who did not shrink from governing without a commission, deserve honourable remembrance. Moreover, the event proved that, in taking so decisive a step, Clive and his friends only anticipated the wishes of their superiors. The next despatches which arrived, having been drawn up with a knowledge of the battle of Plassey and of its results, did full justice to the character and services of the victor in that fight. Clive became, by virtue of a commission from Leadenhall-street, Governor of Bengal, with powers more ample than had ever been conferred before on any of the Company's representatives in India.

Meanwhile matters were not going on very prosperously either in the Carnatic or elsewhere. The French, having received a considerable accession to their strength, advanced against Fort St. David and took it. They made preparations next to invest Madras itself, which Lawrence, now less vigorous than he once was, found much difficulty in counterworking; and the demands for Clive's return, or at all events for a return of the coast division of troops, became very urgent. Clive was not inattentive either to these matters or to the proceedings of the enemy in other quarters. He had seen with regret and alarm the pro-

gress which Bussy had made in those provinces which lie between
Madras and the mouths of the Ganges, and which are known as the
Northern Circars; and it now occurred to him that the best mode
of succouring Madras would be to invade these conquests from
Bengal. Even this proposal, when he made it, however, met with
strong opposition in the Council. The arrival of a French fleet
in the Hooghly was anticipated from day to day. Fresh causes
of uneasiness, of which I shall speak presently, were springing
up at Moorshedabad; and M. Law, who after the defeat of Suraj-
u Dowlah, had escaped into Oude, was reported to be organizing
a force wherewith to take advantage of them. The Council
therefore opposed themselves to a plan which, though it might
not carry any portion of the army beyond the reach of recall,
would undoubtedly cripple the military resources of the province
to an extent which they could not contemplate with equanimity.
But Clive had made up his mind, and, according to usage in
such cases, prevailed. Not blind to the weakness, perhaps
natural in persons circumstanced as they were, which led the
rulers of each province to think of the Company's interests as
absolutely bound up in the safety of their own settlement, he
agreed with the Council in refusing to detach a man to Madras;
and he gave as his reason a belief that the authorities there
would do as he had done—keep the troops after they had got
them, let the wants of Bengal become as urgent as they might.
At the same time he felt that the Bengal Government was bound,
on every account, to succour the sister presidency to the utmost;
and he came to the conclusion that the safest mode of doing so
would be to attack the enemy in their newly-acquired possessions
in the Northern Circars. Accordingly, having selected Lieutenant-Colonel Forde, an officer of promise, though as yet untried
in the field, to command the expedition, he caused five hundred
European infantry, two thousand sepoys, with six field-pieces, and
as many heavy guns, to be told off;—and sent them by sea to
co-operate with the native ruler of Vizagapatam in the defence
of that province against the French. This left him with barely
two thousand four hundred available men of all arms, of whom
four hundred and fifty, and no more, were Europeans. Nevertheless, he abated not an inch of his attitude of command; and,
while he wrote cheerfully to Mr. Pigot, the Governor of Madras,

advising him how to wield his military resources, and encouraging him to look for success, he himself entered, without hesitation, into a by-play, of which the aspect was at one time disagreeable, and the issues well-nigh to the last uncertain.

The reconciliation which Clive had brought about between Meer Jaffier and his Hindoo bankers, his minister of finance, and subordinate chiefs, lasted only till the presence of the irresistible pacificator was withdrawn. Almost immediately on being left to himself, Meer Jaffier began again to form plans for the plunder of these functionaries. Roydullub was the first to experience the pressure—of which, indeed, the Nabob's son, a tyrannical and capricious man, was the chief cause ; and it was only through the vigilance of Warren Hastings, now Mr. Watts's substitute at the court of Moorshedabad, that the unfortunate man escaped with his life. Juggeit Seit, and other wealthy bankers, were next threatened ; and in due time the Nabobs or rulers of Purneah, Midnapore, and Patna were, or believed themselves to be, threatened as before. Indeed there were chiefs nearer to the person of the Nabob who began to act as if their safety were compromised ; and how the matter might have ended had the Nabob been left to shift for himself it is hard to say. But Clive, who honestly desired to keep things as they were for the present, interfered. He invited the Nabob to visit him at Calcutta, and prevailed to obtain leave for Roydullub to bear him company. Indeed he went further. After reminding Meer Jaffier of the services which the Minister had rendered to him during the conspiracy, and assuring him that the English never deserted those to whom their faith was once plighted, he caused the wives and children of that functionary to be released from the restraint which the Nabob's son had put upon them, and they also made their way to Calcutta. This done, he so wrought upon the Nabob's fears, as well as upon whatever sense of right might belong to him, that, when the latter set out on his return to his own capital, it was with an expressed determination to govern on a principle of equity, and to fulfil his engagements to his benefactors. But no great while elapsed ere a storm-cloud began to collect in a new quarter.

The sceptre of Arungzebe, divested of all except the shadow of its former lustre, was wielded at this time by the Emperor

Alumjeer the Second, a weak prince, over whom the vizier or minister, Ghazee-u-Deen, the grandson of the celebrated Nizam-ul-Mulk, exercised sway. The latter used no moderation in his dealings with any one, and by his misconduct drove the Emperor's eldest son, the Shah Zada, or, as he is more generally called by English writers, Shah Alum, into exile. This young man, fleeing from Delhi, soon gathered about him a band of adventurers, whom he was persuaded to lead towards the frontier of Bengal, with the avowed purpose of displacing Meer Jaffier, and establishing himself upon the throne of that kingdom. The province of Bahar, of which Patna is the capital, lies between Delhi and Bengal Proper, and upon it the fury of the invasion first fell. This inroad was encouraged, with little attempt at concealment, by the Viceroy of Oude; and the young prince, declaring that he fought in his father's name, Meer Jaffier, not without good cause, became alarmed lest his discontented chiefs would fall off from him. He wrote urgent letters to Clive, entreating that he would come to his support. He charged Ramnarrain, Rajah of Bahar, with harbouring treasonable designs, and with being ready to deliver up Patna as soon as Shah Alum should appear before it. Clive, though loth to credit this report of Ramnarrain, was a good deal shaken by an evasive answer which that chief sent back to one of his communications; and, perceiving that the crisis was a serious one, ordered the remains of his army into the field, and put himself at its head. He marched upon Moorshedabad, where his presence soon restored discipline in the Nabob's troops—the most discontented of the native leaders being satisfied with his assurance of redress, the most timid being encouraged to repose implicit trust in his protection; for Clive's authority over the minds of all classes was by this time more absolute than appertained to any native prince of which the annals of Bengal make mention. To be sure, it was the individual, and not the system, of which the natives stood in awe. They could not, in those days, understand that power, as Europeans, or at least Englishmen, wield it is a concrete and not a special essence. To the name of Clive they all looked as to the cause and sole support of European influence in Bengal: and more than once, it is said, they entered into conspiracies to cut him off, in the full assurance that with

him would fall the strange dominion which he had erected.
But matters had not yet come to this. On the contrary, Meer
Jaffier still looked to him as to a being of a superior order.
"Are you yet to learn," said he one day to one of his nobles,
whose people had engaged in a brawl with some of Clive's
soldiers, "who this Colonel Clive is, and what station God
has given him? How can you venture to affront one so
favoured? "I.!" replied the chief, "I affront the Colonel ! I,
who never get up in the morning without making three low
bows to his jackass !" Accordingly, the determination of Clive,
while he supported the Nabob, to protect all good subjects
from wrong, and all rich ones from robbery, was no sooner
made known than confidence took the place of distrust about the
royal person, and the march of the combined forces for the
relief of Patna was as amicable and as orderly as such movements generally are.

Ramnarrain was not a traitor at heart ; he merely respected,
as all Indians still did, the Emperor's name ; and not knowing how
far even Clive would take part with Meer Jaffier in a war
against Shah Alum, he wished to provide a loophole of escape
for himself in every emergency. No sooner was he made aware,
however, of the advance of the English, than he took his line.
He resisted Shah Alum's attacks with the utmost vigour of
which he was capable, and received, as he deserved, warm praise
from the English leader for having done so. The consequence
was, that, when Clive's advance touched the outposts of Shah
Alum's army, Patna still held out, and the descendant of
Arungzebe, not venturing to risk a battle against 3500 disciplined troops, with their famous leader at their head, raised the
siege and retreated.

The sequel of this story may be told in few words. Shah
Alum, deserted by the Nabob of Oude, and seeing troop after
troop fall off from his standard, at last applied to Clive for the
help which he could not find elsewhere. Clive, though determined to sustain Meer Jaffier against all enemies, was not
sorry to receive at this time a communication from Ghazee-u-
Deen, which informed him that Shah Alum was acting contrary
to the Emperor's wishes, and desired that he might be seized and
delivered over to be dealt with as the Emperor might judge

expedient. This Clive had no desire to do ; but when the young man subsequently entreated for leave to seek an asylum in Calcutta, it was refused. Clive contented himself with sending the fugitive about one thousand pounds in money, by which the son of an emperor was enabled to keep a few followers near him, and to escape from the fury of the vizier.

Clive did Meer Jaffier excellent service at this time. He saved not only his sovereignty but his purse ; for when the frightened Nabob proposed to purchase the retreat of Shah Alum with a large sum of money, Clive withstood him, and argued against the arrangement with as much wisdom as effect. "If you do this," he wrote, "you will have the Nabob of Oude, the Mahrattas, and many more, come from all parts of the confines of your country, who will bully you out of your money till you have none left in your treasury. I beg your Excellency will rely on the fidelity of the English and of those troops which are attached to you." His Excellency did so trust, and was very grateful for the result. While the Emperor marked his sense of Clive's forbearance to espouse the cause of Shah Alum by raising him to the rank of an Omra, and the commander of 5000 horse and 7000 foot, Meer Jaffier determined that a jaghire or grant—not of land, for land is never granted in India, but of the government share of the produce or the rent—should be made to him, that he might support in a becoming manner the expenses incident to his new dignity. After casting about for such an arrangement as might best agree with the convenience of all parties, he resolved that Clive should receive the rent of the Zemindarry which he had not long previously conferred upon the East India Company. Clive did not, of course, decline to accept what Meer Jaffier had the fullest right to bestow—for Meer Jaffier was by this time confirmed in his position as Nabob by firman from Delhi—and thus became possessed of an income from his estates in Bengal of not less than 30,000*l.* per annum.

CHAPTER XII.

Colonel Forde's expedition to the Northern Circars—Operations in the Carnatic—Destruction of the Dutch force in the Ganges.

It will be necessary, in order to understand aright the policy which guided Clive at this juncture to support the Madras Government by a diversion rather than by detaching largely from his own force, that the reader should be put in possession of a general view of the state of affairs south of the Nerbudda, as these arranged themselves subsequently to the renewal of hostilities between England and France. Of the successful operations of Bussy, and the influence which he established for his country in the Deccan, sufficient notice has been taken elsewhere. An attempt, on the part of some native chiefs to shake off the yoke, which he signally defeated, served but the more to render the Souhbadar dependent upon him ; and with such exceeding judgment was his influence wielded, that the native Government and people, not less than the French East India Company, largely benefited by it. Among other services which he rendered about the period of Clive's expedition to the Hooghly, the reduction of the Northern Circars to the dominion of the Nizam deserves especial mention ; for though this fertile district had from time immemorial been included among the provinces over which the Viceroy of the Deccan held sway, it was a sway which, in the eyes of many of its chiefs, was already more nominal than real, and had ceased, amid the confusions consequent upon civil war, to be acknowledged at all. Bussy obtained leave from the Souhbadar, though not without difficulty, to march with the main strength of his army against the malcontents. He overthrew them one after another, attacked and took their towns, and was in the full career of conquest when letters reached him from Suraj-u-Dowlah and from his countrymen in Bengal, urging an advance into that province. He proceeded as far as the frontier, expecting that Suraj-u-Dowlah's agents would meet him there, and that arrangements would be made for securing to him a safe passage through Cuttack; but instead of these came intelligence of the fall of Chandernagore—a blow from which Bussy was too clear-sighted not to perceive that the French interests in Bengal would never recover. Then followed the revolution, which he could only watch from afar, without interfering in the most remote degree to prevent it. Next, he saw the throne filled by Meer Jaffier, on whose feeble mind he strove indeed to work, though covertly, but from whom he was all along certain that assistance against the English was not to be expected except in the event of such an invasion from Europe as would give to the invaders a decided superiority without him. Under these circumstances, Bussy returned to his operations in the Circars, and, after a sharp siege, compelled Vizagapatam, with its English factory, to surrender. He marched thence upon Rajamundry, whence tidings of a new conspiracy at Hyderabad recalled him to that capital. Here his presence restored order, though two of the Nizam's brothers were engaged in the plot; and he was on his way to Golconda, Salabut Jung attending him, when the Marquis de Conflans arrived in his camp, and presented to him a despatch which imposed an immediate and most ungracious term upon his career of glory. The uth is, that Bussy had become an object of envy, and therefore of dislike, to the worthless Court and the contemptible Company which he served. These, in sending out M. Lally to be at the head of their affairs in the East, placed power in the hands of one who was not likely to use it discreetly, and whose first act was to deprive of his command the only officer in the French army who knew what Eastern politics were, and was capable of bending them to his own purposes.

Bussy obeyed the orders of his superior at once. He resigned his trust to M. Conflans, and marched as directed with the bulk of his troops to join Lally. He left, indeed, a handful of men with the new general in Hyderabad, and placed a garrison in Masulapatam; but the Circars were well-nigh denuded of troops, and Vizagapatam was but slenderly provided for. Now, the Northern Circars were kept quiet only by the terror of Bussy's name and army; and no sooner were these removed than its chiefs began to communicate with Clive in Bengal. It was in consequence of these communications, and because he found a ready ally in Nizam Ali Khan, one of the Souhbadar's brothers, that Clive resolved upon making a diversion in favour of Madras by sending an expedition into the Circars; and Lieutenant-Colonel Forde, an officer of much promise and some experience, was selected to direct the operations of the little army.

While Clive was thus arranging matters, Lally opened the campaign in the Carnatic with great apparent energy. He invested Fort St. David the evening of the day of his landing : and that place, though recently strengthened and well supplied with men, surrendered after two days of open trenches. Lally razed the fortifications to the ground and burnt the town, after which he proceeded, first to Tanjore, where he met with a repulse, and next to Arcot, of which he made himself master. But Lally did not care merely to harass: his object was to root out the English name from the Carnatic, and with this view he determined to lay siege to Madras itself. In order to have at his disposal means sufficient to press that operation with vigour, he exhausted the public treasury in hiring Mahratta horsemen and infantry from Mysore: he even advanced large sums from his private resources for a like purpose; and when he found that there was still a deficiency of funds wherewith to provide beasts of burden, and that coolies were wanting, he recklessly endeavoured to accomplish by violence what he found himself unable otherwise to effect. He issued orders to press, without regard to caste or station, all the country-people and their cattle into the service of the commissariat. It was a grievous error, from the consequences of which Lally never recovered. Death is far less dreaded by a Brahmin and a man of the military caste than that he shall be compelled to do the work of a pariah ; and the individual or the power which seeks thus to degrade him becomes to him an object of unmitigated abhorrence. Every village along the line of Lally's march was deserted as he approached ; and he sat down in consequence before Madras with a good army, indeed, of nearly three thousand Europeans and four thousand sepoy troops, but comparatively destitute of means of transport, and dependent for all his supplies upon Admiral d'Ache's squadron.

To raise his force to this amount, Lally had called in all his detachments, including the bulk of the corps which Bussy had commanded in the Deccan, with Bussy himself at its head. The English, in like manner, concentrated their troops at Madras; and had now, with the force in Fort George, about eighteen hundred European and four thousand native soldiers. Now, five thousand eight hundred disciplined men, under the command of such a leader as Colonel Lawrence, were more than sufficient for the defence of Fort St. George; and Clive, being convinced of that fact, steadily refused to risk the safety of Bengal by either coming in person or detaching largely to the assistance of Madras. He knew, moreover, that a powerful expedition must shortly arrive from England, which, including the 84th King's regiment, of which Eyre Coote, now promoted to the rank of Lieutenant-Colonel, was at the head, would give to his countrymen a decided preponderancy in the Carnatic. But, while he adhered to this policy so long as circumstances seemed to recommend it, he was not unprepared to act contrary to his own wishes should an emergency arise. His final directions to Colonel Forde were, that he should make himself master of Vizagapatam and as much of the Northern Circars as possible, in the first place, and then, in the event of pressing instances from Madras, march to the relief of that presidency. The result showed that Clive's views were as sound as his energy in the execution of them was untiring. The garrison of Madras stood its ground, not without obtaining many brilliant successes in the sorties which were occasionally hazarded, till the arrival of Admiral Pococke on the coast compelled the French squadron to withdraw, and deprived M. Lally of all hope of success. On the night of the 16th of February, 1749, he raised the siege as abruptly as he had formed it; and, leaving all his sick and wounded, together with his battering train, fifty pieces, and a large store of ammunition, to be taken possession of by the garrison, retreated towards Pondicherry.

Meanwhile Forde was justifying, by the skill and vigour of his operations, the wisdom of the choice which had put him at the head of the expedition into the Circars. He soon confirmed the Rajah of Vizagapatam in possession of that place. He marched thence to Rajamundry, where, in a sharp affair, he defeated M. Conflans, taking almost all his artillery and the whole of his camp equipage. His next proceeding was to invest Masulipatam, of which the garrison greatly exceeded in numbers the army that sat down before it; and he pressed the siege with so much vigour that three practicable breaches were soon effected. M. Conflans, who had thrown himself into the place, was invited to capitulate, but refused. He trusted to the promised support of Salabut Jung, and looked daily for the arrival of a French force from Pondicherry: he therefore treated Forde's overtures with disdain. Upon this, the English commander, whose position was critical in the extreme, resolved to hazard an assault. He attacked the whole of the breaches at midnight, forced his way into the town, and found, when the morning broke, that three thousand and thirty-seven men, of whom five hundred were Europeans, had laid down their arms to nine hundred. Moreover, Forde stormed Masulipatam with a timid, perhaps a treacherous, ally, the Rajah of Vizagapatam in his own camp, Salabut Jung being distant only fifteen miles;—and M. Moracin, from Pondicherry, arrived with three hundred men within a day's sail of the harbour. The effect was miraculous. M. Moracin did not so much as land, but sailed towards the north; Salabut Jung hastened to propose a treaty; the French were finally expelled from the Deccan; and Masulipatam, with eight valuable districts adjacent to it, became the property of the English.

The delight of Clive at the success of Colonel Forde's operations was such as every great mind experiences in witnessing the fulfilment of hopes which it had cherished of individuals, and finding that its plans for the advancement of the public good are advancing. His letters both to Mr. Pigot at Madras, and to the Chairman of the Court of Directors in London, are filled with praises of the successful soldier. Nevertheless he did not relax an iota in his exertions. Having settled the Circars, he instructed Forde to detach a portion of his army to the Carnatic, and to return himself with as many of the residue as could be spared to Bengal, where, indeed, on several accounts, his presence was needed, and at which place he arrived with the regularity which marked all his public proceedings.

A disinclination to interrupt the thread of the principal narrative has caused me as yet to pass by, without notice, certain minor transactions, in the management of which, however, Clive's characteristic firmness was not less clearly shown than in the conduct of points of far more perceptible importance. For example, he had scarcely put down that spirit of captiousness which was exhibited in the proceedings of the councils of war that sat upon the distribution of the Moorshedabad prize-money, ere fresh cause of uneasiness appeared in a struggle for precedency among the officers belonging to the different services of which his army was composed. At this period in Anglo-Indian history the highest rank to which an officer actually in the service of the East India Company could attain was that of captain. Captains, however, commanded battalions, and the European subalterns serving under them were few in number; so that the privation to which these gentlemen were subjected deserved to be accounted more nominal than real, and told painfully only when they were brought immediately into contact with officers bearing commissions from the Crown. There were, however, three distinct presidencies then as there are now; and it did not often occur that the troops of all these were or could be associated together on the same service. It happened, however, that, during the campaigns of Fort William and Plassey, Madras troops came to the succour of the troops of Bengal, and that both were reinforced by a detachment from Bombay. Clive was too much of a soldier not to perceive that the three little armies would become much more handy when blended into one : he therefore issued orders that the distinctions of presidency should cease, and that the officers should take rank according to the dates of their commissions, no matter at what station subscribed. Strange to say, there was murmuring at this; indeed, to so great a height did the feeling of discontent arise, that the Bengal officers ventured to remonstrate against the arrangement as unjust. Clive made very short work with such a temper. A sharp reprimand, accompanied by a threat of further proceedings, soon brought the dissentients to their senses, and the army was remodelled, without further opposition, according to his wish.

This matter had been settled some time, and Colonel Forde was returned, though in bad health, from Masulipatam, when fresh ground of alarm arose in a quarter from which Clive, at least, was slow to believe that danger to the interests of the English at Bengal could threaten. Though the nature of my subject has hitherto led me to speak only of the French and of the English as settlers in India, and rivals both for its commerce and for influence at the courts of its princes, the reader of history will not need to be told that the Dutch, the Portuguese, and even the Danes, had their factories and trading stations at various points along the shores of the Indian peninsula. The Dutch, indeed, besides having established a firm footing in Batavia and Ceylon, were masters of more than one depôt on the continent, among which Chinchura, a town situated on the Ganges, though considerably higher up than Fort William, or even than Chandernagore, was the chief. Here they had a governor with a considerable garrison, who seems personally to have lived on the best terms with Clive, but who could not, of course, refuse to adopt, in his official capacity, whatever line of proceeding might be dictated to him by his superiors. It was whispered in many circles that this gentleman, Mr. Bisdom, had much communication with Meer Jaffier, and that the tone of their correspondence was the reverse of friendly to the English. But that either had conceived a design for the extermination of a power which had just raised the one to his throne, and offered to the other no molestation, the most invidious appear to have discredited, till rumours of the approach of a Dutch armament to the Ganges began to circulate. Then, indeed, a good deal of alarm was felt. Men remembered that the latest accounts from Europe referred to differences between the Cabinets of St. James's and the Hague ; and, nothing doubting that war had either been declared, or was looked upon as certain, they came to the conclusion that a blow was about to be struck in Bengal. Clive alone discredited, or affected to discredit, these stories. He professed to believe that the armament which was preparing in Batavia would be employed against the native princes of Ceylon ; and he gave the best evidence of the sincerity of this persuasion by purchasing bills to a large amount on the Dutch East India Company, and sending them to be cashed and remitted to England in a Dutch trader.

It is worthy of remark that for some time after the accession of Meer Jaffier to the throne the Dutch refused to recognise his title by paying to him the compliments which they had been accustomed to pay to his predecessors. This necessarily involved them in disputes, which led, among other annoyances, to the stoppage of their trade, and caused them to apply to Clive for his intercession to have the embargo removed. It was readily granted, notwithstanding that their chief ground of offence with the Nabob took its rise from his having granted to the English a monopoly of the saltpetre-mines in Patna. But, though expressing themselves grateful for the moment, the majority in the Council no sooner discovered that Meer Jaffier and his son were chafed than they did their best to aggravate the feeling. They seem, indeed, to have gone so far as to hold out hopes of aid from Batavia, in case he should require it ; and they unquestionably put matters in such a light before the Government of that island that the latter counted on little else than the ascendancy of Dutch influence at the Court of the Nabob. With a view to promote this, they embarked about seven or eight hundred European soldiers, with as many Asiatics, and a train of artillery, in a squadron of five large ships, of which three were armed like men-of-war, and sent them, without assigning any reason for their movement, into the Ganges. This was in the month of October, 1758, when the force at Clive's disposal happened to be unusually small, some of his troops having been left in Masulipatam, part being detached at Patna, and others sent on to assist Colonel Coote in his brilliant campaign on the Coromandel coast. But Clive, feeling how necessary it was to prevent the junction of the new-comers with the original garrison at Chinchura, applied for and obtained an order from the Nabob prohibiting the Dutch ships from ascending higher up the stream than Fulda. The better to enforce obedience to this mandate, he equipped all the little forts which had been established on the banks of the river with heavy guns, placed the militiamen of Calcutta under arms, and ordered back the detachment from Patna, while at the same time his guard-boats stopped every small craft which showed itself, and would allow nothing to pass on board of which were either troops or military stores. The Dutch remonstrated, complained, and were vehement in their professions of meaning no harm ; but Clive adhered to his purpose, and got the Nabob at last to issue an injunction for the immediate departure of the strangers from his territories.

The Dutch would not move. On the contrary, it was ascertained that they had agents at various places, who had raised recruits for their service, and sent them by twos and threes either to Fulda or Chinchura. It was manifest to Clive that evil must shortly come, either upon his own Government or upon these strangers; and he was not slow in resolving that his own Government should not be the sufferer. To be sure there was no war as yet between England and Holland; neither, in strict justice, was it competent to him to determine how many or how few troops the Dutch East India Company should maintain at their settlement of Chinchura. But the game was one of policy, not of justice, on both sides; and Clive, prevailing to have the Nabob as his partner, played it without fear. He assembled a force of 300 or 400 Europeans and 800 sepoys, which, with six pieces of cannon, he sent, under Forde's orders, to cut off the communication, by land, between Chinchura and the Dutch anchorage. Forde conducted the enterprise very ably; he crossed the river, received a skirmish in the outskirts of Chandernagore, and drove back a party from the garrison into Chinchura. He had hardly done so when intelligence reached him that the Dutch had landed from the vessels, and were marching towards him. He wrote himself to inform Clive, adding this hint, "that, if he had only an order of Council, he would attack the Dutch, and had a fair prospect of destroying them." Clive happened to be engaged in a rubber of whist when this important communication reached him. He did not so much as rise from the table, but wrote with a pencil on a slip of paper, " Dear Forde, fight them immediately, and I will send you the order of Council to-morrow."

Forde, trained in a school which had no overweening dread of responsibility, acted without hesitation on these instructions. He attacked the Dutch at a place called Bridona, defeated them with great slaughter, made prisoners of fifteen officers, among whom was the chief in command, and forthwith placed Chinchura itself in a state of siege. Of these memorable transactions, and of the circumstances which led to them, Clive gave a detailed account to the Court of Directors in a document which is still extant. He there states that the Dutch had left him no alternative; that first upon a small scale, and in the commencement of hostilities, they forced him to appeal to the sword; and that, having drawn it, his duty to the Company required that he should use it effectually. Accordingly, he equipped and armed three merchant-vessels which lay near Fort William, and, sending them against the Dutch squadron, fought a naval battle almost simultaneously with Forde's action at Bridona. It ended in the perfect triumph of the English arms; whereupon the Dutch, thoroughly cowed, prayed for pardon, and obtained from his clemency the deliverance of Chinchura from destruction.

Perhaps there is no series of transactions in Clive's eventful life which redounded more to his honour as a soldier and a citizen than those of which I have just spoken. Whatever he did was done from the purest patriotism; for he risked both good name and a large amount of private property in the adventure. Had he failed, there is no telling how the Company or the English Government would have taken it; and success itself, considering the relations in which England and Holland stood, was full of hazard. Yet he preferred running all these hazards, and put in jeopardy his large investments, of which the Dutch had charge, rather than expose the interests of those whom he served to the perils with which they seemed to be threatened. Fortune favoured the brave in this as she does in most instances. The Dutch, too conscious of their own evil designs to affect indignation, made no remonstrance on account of their losses. On the contrary, they apologised for the misconduct, as they termed it, of their officers, and proposed to defray the expenses of the war, provided the English would be satisfied. It is hardly worth while to add, that the proposals were willingly acceded to.

CHAPTER XIII.

Clive proposes to return to England—His views for the future management
of British India.

The affairs of British India (if I may be permitted to anticipate
a term) were now in a state of great prosperity and still brighter
promise. Bengal, elevated by the genius of one man to be the
chief of the Company's settlements, took well-nigh a distinct
place among the substantive powers of Hindostan. On the Coromandel coast a series of gallant exploits had turned the scale so
entirely against the French, that rivalry between them and the
English nation at any future period was become, in that part of
the world, next to impossible. The battle of Wadewash destroyed
the last hope of Lally, and, by leaving Bussy a prisoner in the
hands of the victors, deprived him of the only officer in his army
who was capable, had circumstances favoured him, to retrieve
the fallen fortunes of his country. Then followed the siege and
capture of Pondicherry itself, which, being razed to the ground,
ceased to hold rank even as a second-rate town in the Carnatic.
Meanwhile the tide of fortune flowed with equal steadiness and
force on the side of Bombay. Not only was the commerce of
that important station daily enlarging itself, but the state of the
adjacent districts encouraged the Governor to undertake military
operations ; from one, at least, of which he derived very sub-
stantial profits.

The ancient town of Surat stands at no great distance from
Bombay. It had been the seat of the earliest settlement which
the English had formed on the shores of the Indian seas, and
was much valued by the Mahomedans as the port where pil-
grims annually assembled on their way to worship at the tomb
of the prophet. The Court of Delhi was in the habit of equip-
ping here a vessel which should convey the devout to the Red
Sea ; .and the ship in question, as well as the commerce of the

place, had been for some time committed to the care of a neighbouring chief, who was honoured with the title of Admiral to the Emperor. The Admirals of the Emperor, however, had their stipulated remuneration, namely, an assignment of three lacs, or thirty thousand pounds, per annum, on the revenues of the town; and, on the plea that it was not regularly paid, one of them seized the castle, and gave law to the town. The consequence was, that Surat and its commerce soon became profitless to the Emperor. One-third of the revenues was appropriated by the Seedee or Admiral; another third went to bribe the Mahrattas into the maintenance of peace; and the remainder was divided among the officers who governed in the Emperor's name. This division of authority, together with the intrigues and disputes to which it gave rise, proved as troublesome to the English residents as it was ruinous to the town and its inhabitants. The Council of the factory therefore applied to their countrymen for help; and the principal native merchants and local authorities undertaking, on their suggestion, to pay two lacs of rupees annually as the price of English protection, the Government of Bombay readily undertook to interfere. An expedition was fitted out against the Seedee, which proved successful; and the Emperor, looking favourably upon the enterprise, confirmed by firman the right of the English to this revenue, and appointed them governors of the castle and admirals of the imperial fleet.

Having largely contributed to bring matters to this issue, and conceiving that he could render better service to the cause which he had much at heart in London than at Calcutta, Clive began at this time to meditate a return to Europe. The announcement of this design created much alarm both among the Company's servants and at the court of Meer Jaffier; for the former were fully alive to the importance of having such a man at their head, and the latter believed that, were Clive to abandon him, he could not sit upon the throne for a year by himself. Indeed, his pecuniary circumstances had become so involved, and so many difficulties beset him both from within and from without, that, even with Clive to counsel, and, if need be, to protect him, his seat was the reverse of a firm one. In the first place, he was driven, by the engagements into which he had entered with the English, to part with his revenues almost as soon as he had collected them ; and not possessing either the firmness or the power which were needed to enforce a system of economy at home, he fell day by day more into arrear with the payments of his own troops and with his civil functionaries. In the next place, the growing dissatisfaction of the native gentry with the vassalage to which the European connexion had reduced them could neither be concealed nor explained away. They saw that all real power was passing rapidly into the hands of strangers; and, though too little united among themselves to arrange a plan for arresting the progress of the evil, they complained of the Nabob for failing to do that which it would have been ruinous to him, unless assured of their hearty co-operation, so much as to attempt. In the next place, there had sprung up among the Company's agents, as well Asiatic as European, wherever scattered through the provinces, a spirit of domineering and a desire to take undue advantage of the privileges which their situations afforded them which was quite intolerable. So offensive, indeed, was their conduct in some cases, that Clive found himself under the necessity of interfering to put a stop to it; and in many of his letters, public as well as private, he complained bitterly of the seeds of mischief which they were sowing. Nor was this all. The Shah Zada, or eldest son of the Emperor, had again gathered retainers about him ; and, encouraged by promises of support from the Viceroy of Oude, was reported to be upon his march for the invasion of Bahar. All these circumstances rendered the Nabob uneasy, and were not without their effect upon the mind of Clive himself. Nevertheless, after looking attentively at all sides of the question, the latter came to the conclusion that the aspect of the immediate future was not such as could justify the abandonment of the plans which he was devising, and which he could hardly expect to put in progress towards execution except by personal communication with the home authorities. What these plans were will be best understood after I shall have given a slight sketch of the constitution of that body under whose direction the affairs of the English in India were in those days managed.

The history of the rise and progress of the East India Company has been too often told, and is now too generally known, to demand from me in this place more than a very brief allusion to it. Stirred to emulation by the successful adventures of the Dutch and the Portuguese, and distrusting the ability of individuals to enter into competition with them, a body of enterprising men applied for and obtained, in the year 1600, a charter of incorporation from Queen Elizabeth; and, under the title of the London Company of Merchants trading to the East Indies, undertook to extend the commerce and navigation of their country in the seas and among the islands and continents east of the Cape of Good Hope. They enjoyed the monopoly precisely a hundred years, at the expiration of which period a second company arose, which, like the first, obtained a charter, and between which and the old Company a rivalry, at once mischievous to themselves, and, as was then believed, hurtful to the mother country, arose. William the Third, who incorporated the latter body, interfered to put a stop to this state of things. The two firms were persuaded to come to an understanding with one another; and a new charter raised them into the corporate body which still exists as "The United Company of Merchants of England trading to the East Indies."

The objects for which these gentlemen were associated being purely commercial, they gave to the Company and to its Directors, or managing body, such forms and powers as promised to facilitate the ends of a successful trade, and were not, perhaps, calculated for much beyond it. The Company consisted of individual subscribers of capital to the amount of 500*l.* or upwards, each of whom, whether male or female, was entitled to vote and take part in such discussions as might arise at general meetings—or, as the charter called them, " General Courts of Proprietors." The Court of Directors, on the other hand, consisted of twenty-four members, elected by the proprietors out of their own body. Those only were qualified whose stock amounted to to 2000*l.* at the least, and their tenure of office did not go beyond twelve months, for they were elected annually. Thirteen Directors formed a quorum, and, when assembled, became a Court. It was necessary that a General Court—or Court of Proprietors— should be held once in every quarter of a year; and a Committee was empowered to frame by-laws, which, so far as the Company and its servants were concerned, were declared by the charter to have the same force as Acts of Parliament, so long as they did not contradict statutes already in existence.

It is clear that, in framing such a constitution as this, neither the merchants, nor the Crown, which conferred upon them their privileges, could have looked to any other results than those which the title of the incorporated body pointed out. That they had leave to purchase lands in India wherever the exigences of the trade might require is indeed true; and their factories and settlements soon began to spring up in various provinces. But these were simply what they professed to be—depôts or stores, in which the goods brought down from the interior might be laid up and kept till the ships intended to transport them to Europe should arrive. Hence all their transactions, both at home and abroad, were entered upon and followed up in the spirit of barter, which looks for gain on mercantile speculations, not for territorial aggrandisement; and, however well calculated to maintain discipline in counting-rooms and shops, is not exactly fitted to administer the affairs of a great empire.

As commerce gradually merged in political operations abroad, the Courts of Proprietors and Directors at home seemed in some sort to alter their character. At first alarm, and nothing but alarm, prevailed in Leadenhall-street. But when the victories of Clive and of Coote opened out before them larger prospects, the bearing of the Courts to which Clive and Coote were servants underwent a change. Some members rejoiced honestly in the results of the military operations, especially in Bengal. Others were overwhelmed with terror, expecting to hear by every fresh ship that the whole power of the Mogul Empire had combined to expel their agents, and that their trade was ruined. A third party took a middle line; and, while they praised the valour of the soldiers who had fought for them, deprecated a continuance in the policy of aggrandisement. A fourth, envious both of the renown and of the large fortunes which their foreign representatives were acquiring, seemed to care for little else than that they should be plundered, and their property thrown into the common heap. It was owing to the struggles of these seve- ral parties in the Direction that so many contradictory orders reached Calcutta in regard to the management of that Presidency. When the timid or envious sections of the Court happened to be in the ascendant, such instructions as those which set the Rotation Government on foot went forth; as soon as the more sanguine, and, perhaps, the more generous, parties prevailed, justice was done to the claims of individuals, and a practicable scheme of management devised. But though all parties conceded the first place to Clive, there was a steady disposition among the Directors to fall back, in the event of his refusing the Government, on the Rotation system. Mr. Holwell, who returned home after his deliverance out of Suraj-u-Dowlah's hands, seems to have been the chief adviser of this project: Mr. Payne, at that time Chairman of the Court, gave it his steady support. These were opposed by Mr. Lawrence Sulivan, Deputy-Chairman, and Mr. Stephen Law, both men of considerable talent; and Mr. Sulivan secured in consequence the friendship of Clive for a season. But Clive was not slow to discover that such a constitution as that which admitted of factions in the supreme governing power was not capable of being made applicable to the state of things which he had already begun to anticipate. He knew the weakness of the native powers, and considered that the advance of the English to political supremacy in India was a mere question of time; he therefore turned over in his own mind the possibility of connecting the soil of British India with the British nation, and establishing a more intimate relation than as yet existed between its civil and military government and the supreme government at home. His views on these heads are so well and so fully set forth in a letter addressed by him at this time to the Prime Minister, that a sense of justice to his memory urges me to transcribe the document entire :—

> *" To the Right Hon. William Pitt, one of His Majesty's Principal*
> *Secretaries of State.*

" Sir—Suffer an admirer of yours at this distance to congratulate himself on the glory and advantage which are likely to accrue to the nation by your being at its head, and at the same time to return his most grateful thanks for the distinguished manner you have been pleased to speak of his successes in these parts, far indeed beyond his deservings.

" The close attention you bestow on the affairs of the British nation in general has induced me to trouble you with a few particulars relative to India, and to lay before you an exact account of the revenues of this country, the genuineness whereof you may depend upon, as it has been faithfully extracted from the minister's books.

"The great revolution that has been effected here by the success of the English arms, and the vast advantages gained to the Company by a treaty concluded in consequence thereof, have, I observe, in some measure, engaged the public attention; but much more may yet in time be done, if the Company will exert themselves in the manner the importance of their present possessions and future prospects deserves. I have represented to them in the strongest terms the expediency of sending out and keeping up constantly such a force as will enable them to embrace the first opportunity of further aggrandising themselves; and I dare pronounce, from a thorough knowledge of this country government,* and of the genius of the people, acquired by two years' application and experience, that such an opportunity will soon offer. The reigning Subah, whom the victory at Plassey invested with the sovereignty of these provinces, still, it is true, retains his attachment to us, and probably, while he has no other support, will continue to do so; but Mussulmans are so little influenced by gratitude, that, should he ever think it his interest to break with us, the obligations he owes us would prove no restraint: and this is very evident from his having lately removed his Prime Minister, and cut off two or three principal officers, all attached to our interest, and who had a share in his elevation. Moreover, he is advanced in years; and his son is so cruel, worthless a young fellow, and so apparently an enemy to the English, that it will be almost unsafe trusting him with the succession. So small a body as two thousand Europeans will secure us against any apprehensions from either the one or the other; and, in case of their daring to be troublesome, enable the Company to take the sovereignty upon themselves.

"There will be the less difficulty in bringing about such an event, as the natives themselves have no attachment whatever to particular princes; and as, under the present Government, they

---

* The application is here limited to the government of Bengal.

have no security for their lives or properties, they would rejoice in so happy an exchange as that of a mild for a despotic government: and there is little room to doubt our easily obtaining the Mogul's sunnud (or grant) in confirmation thereof, provided we agreed to pay him the stipulated allotment out of the revenues, viz. fifty lacs annually. This has, of late years, been very ill paid, owing to the distractions in the heart of the Mogul Empire, which have disabled that court from attending to their concerns in the distant provinces: and the Vizier has actually wrote to me, desiring I would engage the Nabob to make the payments agreeable to the former usage; nay, further; application has been made to me from the Court of Delhi, to take charge of collecting this payment, the person intrusted with which is styled the King's Dewan, and is the next person both in dignity and power to the Subah. But this high office I have been obliged to decline for the present, as I am unwilling to occasion any jealousy on the part of the Subah; especially as I see no likelihood of the Company's providing us with a sufficient force to support properly so considerable an employ, and which would open a way for securing the Subahship to ourselves. That this would be agreeable to the Mogul can hardly be questioned, as it would be so much to his interest to have these countries under the dominion of a nation famed for their good faith, rather than in the hands of people who, a long experience has convinced him, never will pay him his proportion of the revenues, unless awed into it by the fear of the Imperial army marching to force them thereto.

" But so large a sovereignty may possibly be an object too extensive for a mercantile company; and it is to be feared they are not of themselves able, without the nation's assistance, to maintain so wide a dominion. I have therefore presumed, Sir, to represent this matter to you, and submit it to your consideration, whether the execution of a design, that may hereafter be still carried to greater lengths, be worthy of the Government's taking it into hand. I flatter myself I have made it pretty clear to you that there will be little or no difficulty in obtaining the absolute possession of these rich kingdoms, and that with the Mogul's own consent, on condition of paying him less than a fifth of the revenues thereof. Now I leave you to judge whether an income yearly of upwards of two millions sterling, with the possession of three provinces abounding in the most valuable productions of nature and of art, be an object deserving the public attention ; and whether it be worth the nation's while to take the proper measures to secure such an acquisition,—an acquisition which, under the management of so able and disinterested a minister, would prove a source of immense wealth to the kingdom, and might in time be appropriated in part as a fund towards diminishing the heavy load of debt under which we at present labour.   Add to these advantages the influence we shall thereby acquire over the several European nations engaged in the commerce here, which these could no longer carry on but through our indulgence, and under such limitations as we should think fit to prescribe.   It is well worthy consideration that this project may be brought about without draining the mother country, as has been too much the case with our possessions in America.   A small force from home will be sufficient, as we always make sure of any number we please of black troops, who, being both much better paid and treated by us than by the country powers, will very readily enter into our service.   Mr. Walsh, who will have the honour of delivering you this, having been my secretary during the late fortunate expedition, is a thorough master of the subject, and will be able to explain to you the whole design, and the facility with which it may be executed, much more to your satisfaction, and with greater perspicuity, than can possibly be done in a letter.   I shall therefore only further remark, that I have communicated it to no other person but yourself; nor should I have troubled you, Sir, but from a conviction that you will give a favourable reception to any proposal intended for the public good.

" The greatest part of the troops belonging to this establishment are now employed in an expedition against the French in the Deccan ; and, by the accounts lately received from thence, I have great hopes we shall succeed in extirpating them from the province of Golconda, where they have reigned lords paramount so long, and from whence they have drawn their principal resources during the troubles upon the coast.

" Notwithstanding the extraordinary effort made by the French in sending out M. Lally with a considerable force the last year, I am confident, before the end of this, they will be near their last gasp in the Carnatic,* unless some very unforeseen event interpose in their favour. The superiority of our squadron, and the plenty of money and supplies of all kinds which our friends on the coast will be furnished with from this province, while the enemy are in total want of everything, without any visible means of redress, are such advantages as, if properly attended to, cannot fail of wholly effecting their ruin in that as well as in every other part of India.

"May the zeal and the vigorous measures projected for the service of the nation, which have so eminently distinguished your ministry, be crowned with all the success they deserve, is the most fervent wish of him who is, with the greatest respect, Sir, your most devoted humble servant,

(Signed)   " Rob. Clive.

" *Calcutta,*
" *7th January,* 1759."

The above is a very remarkable document. It shows that the views of the writer extended a great way beyond the circumstances by which he was surrounded, and exhibits him in the light of a far-seeing and deep-thinking politician. Doubtless the constitution of the government under which he immediately acted has undergone many important modifications since the letter was drawn up. The establishment of a Board of Control has given power to the Crown through its ministers—if not to originate, certainly to modify and direct, all measures of regulation intended for the management of the affairs of India : while at each renewal of the charter Parliament has more and more broken in upon the monopolies secured to the Company by previous grants. But let it not be forgotten that in 1759 there was no Board of Control in existence, and that the Directors were as independent both of the Crown and of the Houses of Parliament as if they had belonged to a foreign state, and were intrusted with its government. Now, no man possessed of Clive's knowledge in Indian affairs could look upon such a state of things with complacency. Anticipating, as he did, constant accessions

* Clive's prediction of the result of affairs in the Carnatic proved, as has been shown, true to the very letter.

of territorial empire to his country, and foreseeing that this must inevitably lead to an entanglement more and more complicated in Asiatic policy, he was desirous that the mainspring of action should be established where it was likely to move with a vigorous and a consistent impetus : and being without experience of any other source of political power than the Crown, he desired to place at once the territories won by the valour of the King's subjects under the protection, and of course under the control, of the Crown and its Ministers.   There is no knowing what the consequences might have been had Mr. Pitt listened favourably to the proposition.   But Pitt, though he acknowledged the practicability of the plan, was deterred from adopting it by a consideration, at that time exaggerated, of the difficulties which seemed to beset both its principle and its details.   Clive's project thus fell to the ground.   But Clive's views are so rooted in wisdom and common sense, that sooner or later we may calculate on their adoption ; and it is more than probable that a late exercise of power by the Court of Directors, in the recall of a Governor-General without any reason assigned, or any reference made to the wishes of the Queen's Ministers, will tend to accelerate the issue.

CHAPTER XIV.

HAVING waited till the few clouds which hung in the political horizon were dispersed—having fully instructed Major Carnac and Colonel Forde how to deal with Shah Zada should he not be induced by the defeat of the Dutch armament to abandon his design upon Patna, Clive, after taking formal leave of the Nabob at Moorshedabad, returned to Calcutta, and began to make preparations for an immediate departure for Europe. He was thus engaged when a despatch arrived from the Court of Directors, of which both the style and the substance gave serious and on the whole just offence to the chiefs of the local government. Such a communication was not calculated to remove the convictions on which Clive's letter to the first Minister of the Crown had been founded; and in the reply, which he is understood mainly to have dictated, no disguise was put upon the sentiments of the parties wronged. I have thought it necessary to refer to this circumstance, because the entire transaction, from its first stage to its last, is eminently characteristic of the body which took the lead in it. To Clive, indeed, neither the folly nor the insolence of the Directors was now of any moment. He had made his fortune; and it was a princely one. He had earned a name second only to that of Wolfe—if second even to his—in the estimation of his countrymen; and being on the point of quitting their service, it mattered little to him how they might receive that reproof which their servants conveyed to them. But on the fate of India it told seriously; for, the wrath of the Honourable Court being excited, they forthwith dismissed from their employ the ablest and most trustworthy of Clive's colleagues. Of their intention to act in a manner so well calculated to involve their own affairs in confusion he knew nothing, when, after handing over the government to Mr. Holwell, he took final leave of his colleagues and of the inhabitants of Fort William. On the 5th of February, 1760, he embarked with his family on board of ship, and the following day was making head with a favourable wind and current down the Ganges.

There are few instances on record of such success in life as that to which Clive had by this time attained. Beginning the world without a shilling in his purse, he was now, at the age of four-and-thirty, one of the wealthiest subjects of the British Crown. In hard cash he had received, partly as gifts from the Nabob, partly as his legitimate share of prize-money, about 300,000*l.* To this must be added no trivial amount of accumulations arising out of the interest of moneys invested, and savings on his regular pay; while the returns of the jaghire or feof are put down by himself as averaging full 27,000*l.* annually. They whose wish to state his income at the lowest admit that he must have been in the receipt of at least 40,000*l.* a-year. Others, probably as well informed, and who have no apparent motive to deviate from the truth, rate it at 60,000*l.* In either case the amount would be enormous now; in the middle of the last century it had few parallels even among the revenues of princes. It is due to the memory of this remarkable man to state that he made, upon the whole, an excellent use of his wealth. His liberality to his parents, and indeed to all who by the ties of blood or of friendship had the most distant claim upon his kindness, was unbounded. Hearing that his old commander, General Lawrence, was but indifferently provided for in the world, he settled upon him an annuity of 500*l.* He paid his father's debts, which seem to have amounted to more than 9000*l.*, and allowed him an income more than handsome for his station in life, and desired a coach to be kept for his use. He presented to each of his five sisters a portion of 2000*l.*, and was generous even to his aunts, to his cousins, and to the cousins and aunts of his wife. Still, when all was done, he remained the richest commoner of his day. Clive, however, was rich only because money came to him more quickly than he was able to spend it. He was not only not of a niggard disposition, but his personal habits ran into the opposite extreme. It is amusing to read the orders for fine dresses and rich wines which he sent home to his agents in England:—"I must trouble you," he writes to Mr.

Orme on the 1st of August, 1757, "with a few commissions concerning family affairs. *Imprimis*, what you can provide must be of the best and finest you can get for love or money :— two hundred shirts, the wristbands worked, some of the ruffles worked with a border either in squares or points, and the rest plain ; stocks, neckcloths, and handkerchiefs in proportion : three corse (sixty pairs) of the finest stockings ; several pieces of plain and spotted muslin, two yards wide, for aprons ; book-muslins ; cambrics ; a few pieces of the finest dimity ; and a complete set of table-linen of Fort St. David diaper made for the purpose." In the same spirit his friend, Captain Latham of the Royal Navy, whom he appears to have employed among the tailors, writes to inform him that he, the Captain, had prepared for the Governor a court-suit — namely, a fine scarlet cloth coat, with handsome gold lace, " which he preferred to the common wear of velvet," and a rich brocade waistcoat to match. The gallant commissioner adds—" It is my design to line the coat with parchment, that it may not wrinkle." Nor must I forget to add, while referring to this subject, that, a wig being then indispensable to the equipment of a gentleman, Clive had a whole boxfull of this species of head-gear sent out to him. The individual who could thus care for his own dress and outward appearance was not likely to stint his wife in her wardrobe, or to shut his doors against friends, or indeed against any who were entitled by their rank in the service to visit him. Clive's hospitality was unbounded ; and though he never appears himself to have exceeded in wine, he placed at the disposal of his guests ample means of indulging a taste which was then more prevalent than it happily has become since. In like manner he betted freely at cards and in the cock-pit—the latter amusement (a most brutal one) being much in vogue among the gentlemen of India in those days ; and his horses, equipages, &c., were as numerous and as brilliant as " love or money could procure." It must not be supposed, however, that such subjects as these occupied his thoughts for one moment to the exclusion of graver matters. Clive's ruling passion was ambition. He never won a step in the ladder of fame or of social position without immediately seeking to ascend beyond it. Being Governor of Bengal, he desired his father to ascertain by inquiring among his friends

whether or not it might be practicable to obtain an appointment
as Governor-General of British India. When satisfied that the
time was not yet come for such an arrangement, he avowed his
determination, as soon as he should return home, to obtain a seat
in the House of Commons, and to go with the Ministry. The
same spirit it was which urged him to correspond with many of
the leading men of the day, among whom may be enumerated
Lord Chancellor Northampton, the Archbishop of Canterbury,
Lord Barrington, and Mr. Henry Fox. And yet he, who
evidently desired to keep well with the great, and had, perhaps,
too much courted them during his first sojourn in England, never
forgot the companions of his youth, or persons who might have
been kind to him while in obscurity. His old friend and brother-
in-law, Captain Maskelyne, seems to have made no figure as a
soldier; yet Clive, though he would not promote him to places
of trust which he was unequal to fill, added 10,000l. to his
savings, and sent him home with a competency. To Mr.
Chauncy, a gentleman of no note, who, having been connected
with the India Company, was instrumental in procuring for
Clive his writership, the letters of this successful commander
are uniformly grateful and generous: "If I have been any way
instrumental in the late revolution," he says, writing to this
worthy man about the overthrow of Suraj-u-Dowlah, "the merit
is entirely owing to you, who countenanced, favoured, and protected me, and was the chief cause of my coming to India in a
station which rendered me capable of serving the Company.
Accept, sir, of my gratitude and sincerest wishes for your welfare. May you enjoy the blessings of peace and retirement, and
may success and every other happiness in this life forsake me
when I forget how much I am obliged to you."
 Meanwhile the fame of Clive's great exploits, and of the important services he had rendered to his country, was filling
every circle in the empire. His own relatives and personal
friends were of course loud and incessant in his praises ; indeed,
the anxiety of his worthy father, that the shadow of a shade
should nowhere be permitted to obscure his son's merits, was as
apt at times to place the object of the good man's adulation in a
false point of view, as it jarred against both the policy and the
better taste of Clive himself. The truth, however, is, that Clive

stood in no need of such blowers of bubbles to render his name illustrious. It was in everybody's mouth; at Court; and everywhere else; and the most forward to load him with praise seems to have been George the Second himself. In the year 1758, when disaster attended all the military operations of England by land and sea, and the Duke of Cumberland was forced, by public opinion, to retire from the office of commander-in-chief, Lord Ligonier, who succeeded him, took occasion one day to ask the King's permission for the young Lord Dunmore to serve as a volunteer in the army of the King of Prussia. Leave was refused, upon which the Commander-in-chief went on to say, " May he not join the Duke of Brunswick, then?" " Pshaw!" replied the King, " what can he get by attending the Duke of Brunswick? If he desire to learn the art of war, let him go to Clive." But higher renown befell him than this when the illustrious Pitt spoke of him as a heaven-born general*—as the only officer who by land or sea had sustained the reputation of the country and added to its glory. All these anecdotes, and many more which the limits of the present work compel me to omit, were repeated to Clive in the letters which he received from home. But it is not in the nature of things that so much good should come upon any man unalloyed by evil. There is a degree of renown and an extent of prosperity which command the admiration of all without stirring in any the feelings of envy; but no sooner are these exceeded than a host of enemies hang, as it were, upon the skirts of the prosperous, and endeavour to pull him down. Had Themistocles done less good service to Athens, he would not have died in exile; George Canning might have retained the political friendships of his youth to old age had he been content to play a subordinate part to men who soon went a thousand miles beyond him in the career of liberalism. In like manner, Clive, whom all men had welcomed with applause on his return from the defence of Arcot, became, as victor of Plassey, and the arbiter of the destinies of crowned heads in the East, an object of undisguised jealousy to many. Among the Directors of the India Company in particular, this bad feeling seems to have

* This remarkable expression of the father, when speaking of Lord Clive, came to be applied in after years to the son as a minister. The late Mr. Pitt was called "a heaven-born minister" in his youth, for the purpose of travestying Lord Chatham's adulation of the victor of Plassey.

struck root; and Clive's father, who delighted in nothing so much as retailing gossip of every sort to his son, took care that the latter should not be ignorant of the fact.

Clive's nature was not so framed as to take any very deep or painful impression from the exertions of the envious. He loved praise, and was open to flattery; but detraction only roused him to deal out blows at least as heavy as the enemies of his good name endeavoured to inflict upon him. He was, however, a man of the world; and, knowing how apt injudicious laudation is to stand in the way of the party praised, he did his best to restrain the zeal of the friends who vied with one another in fighting what they conceived to be his battles in his absence. In a letter to one of his agents, in which he discusses at length his own past career and future prospects, this point is strongly pressed. "As this good news," he says, "may set my father upon exerting himself too much, and paying too many visits to the Duke of Newcastle, Mr. Fox, and other great men, I desire you will endeavour to moderate his expectations; for although I intend getting into Parliament, and have hopes of being taken notice of by his Majesty, yet you know the merit of all actions is greatly lessened by being too much boasted of. I know my father's disposition leads this way, which proceeds from his affection for me."

Besides these embarrassments, which may be considered to a certain extent as inseparable from the career which he had run, Clive was subjected at this time to trials of a different description, which he felt acutely. I have elsewhere explained that he was very happy in his marriage. There was not much uxoriousness about him, to be sure, neither was his taste of such a nature as led him particularly to delight in the prattle of babes or the sports of very young people; but he was sincerely attached to Mrs. Clive, as indeed it well became him to be, and had a father's honest affection for the children whom she brought him. One of these, an infant boy, died just as he was about to depart the second time for India. Another, also a boy, was so ill at the period of his embarkation to return home in 1760, that it was found necessary to leave the little fellow behind. Mr. Fullerton, a friend of the father, took charge of the invalid, and laid him in his grave soon after the ship which bore the rest of the family to England had begun her voyage. Clive's letters show that these visitations, and especially the latter, were not unfelt by him: nevertheless, the tone of his correspondence upon private affairs is generally cheerful ; giving proof that his home was a happy one—so far, at least, as a man of his temperament can be said to find sources of real happiness anywhere. His own health, however, was not good ; he had suffered much during the latter months of his stay in Bengal from rheumatism, and feared at one time that it would end in gout. His apprehension on that score soon vanished, it is true, and he describes himself, at the period of his departure from Calcutta, as being in excellent health. But he had not been in England many weeks ere another and a more alarming illness overtook him. He appears on this occasion to have suffered greatly from that depression of spirits to which he had been liable from boyhood. The malady was not, however, on the mind, but in the body ; and for some months his medical attendants entertained serious misgivings as to the issue. But it may be well to devote a separate chapter to a sketch of his manner of life from the autumn of 1760, when he reached London for the second time, to the early summer of 1764, when for the last time he quitted it to return to the scene of his early glories.

CHAPTER XV.

Clive's public career in England—His private habits.

I HAVE not been able to ascertain the exact date of Clive's landing in England. It seems to have been some time in the month of September or of October 1760, and enough remains on record to show that his first reception both at Court and in the India House was very flattering. Clive himself, indeed, never affected to hide his disappointment at the limited extent to which honours were conferred upon him by the Crown. In a letter to Major Carnac, dated the 27th of February, 1762, he more than insinuates that he had expected to receive the red ribbon, and to be raised at once to the British peerage; instead of which an Irish peerage only was offered, though it was accompanied by a sort of assurance that his Majesty had higher things in store for so distinguished a subject. But in attributing the circumstance to the severe illness with which, as I have just explained, he was attacked almost immediately on landing, he probably judged aright. Out of sight out of mind is a form of speech which may be applied as freely in cases like this as in the more vulgar affairs of visiting and acquaintance. The gratitude of men in power, like the hospitalities of the gay and wealthy, seldom seeks out for objects on which to expend itself. They who desire to take advantage of either must, at all events, keep themselves in the way not to be overlooked.

Though not a member of the House of Lords, Clive soon established for himself a large share of influence in society. He fought his own way into the House of Commons, and surrounded himself there with a phalanx of friends, who, owing their seats to him, were devoted to his interests. His first essay in political life had attached him to the party of which Fox was at the head. The commanding genius of Pitt in a short time won him over; but his true devotion was to George Grenville, whom he continued to support, whether in office or out of it, with all the strength which he could command. Accordingly, when Lord Bute prevailed upon the young King to separate himself from Pitt, and by and by to throw the Duke of Newcastle and his section of the Cabinet overboard, Clive, though requested in some sort to name his own terms, refused to support the new Administration. "Now that we are to have peace abroad," he writes in November, 1762, "war is commencing at home among ourselves. There is to be a most violent combat at the meeting of Parliament whether Bute or Newcastle is to govern this kingdom; and the times are so critical that every member has an opportunity of fixing a price upon his services. I still continue to be one of those unfashionable kind of people who think very highly of independency, and to bless my stars indulgent fortune has enabled me to act according to my conscience. Being very lately asked by authority if I had any honour to ask from my Sovereign, my answer was, that I thought it dishonourable to take advantage of the times; but that, when these Parliamentary disputes were at an end, if his Majesty should then approve of my conduct by rewarding it, I should think myself highly honoured in receiving any marks of the royal favour."

Refusing to co-operate with the Government of the day, Clive was, of course, treated by it with coldness. He was not even consulted while negotiations with France were pending respecting the terms on which it would be proper to insist in order to protect the interests of the English in Bengal; his case thus offering a remarkable contrast to that of Bussy, who no sooner returned on parole to his own country than he became the chief adviser of the French minister on all points relating to Indian politics. But Clive resembled the Duke of Wellington in this, that, wherever he conceived that by volunteering advice he could effect a public good, he did not hesitate to state his views, even to a hostile Administration. Accordingly, he drew up a paper or memorial, which he forwarded to Lord Bute, setting forth, in clear and forcible terms, the outlines of the political systems of France and England in the East, and explaining in detail the extent to which, and no further, concessions might be made, in the event of peace, by the latter power to the former. He is particularly urgent in this document on two points—namely, that in the Carnatic the French shall be limited as to the number of troops which they are permitted to keep on foot, and that they shall not, on any account whatever, be re-admitted into Bengal except in the character of merchants.

Lord Bute could not but see the force of his correspondent's reasoning, and expressed himself much obliged by it. He adopted Lord Clive's project, likewise, so far, that the French Government, in the treaty of 1763, agreed not to maintain any troops either in Bengal or in the Northern Circars. But, at the suggestion of an influential member of the Court of Directors who had long ceased to be on a friendly footing with Clive, the Minister had well-nigh marred his own work by stipulating for the recognition of Mahomed Ali Khan as Nabob of the Carnatic, and agreeing consequently to acknowledge the right of Salabut Jung to the Souhbadarry of the Deccan. By mere accident Clive learned what was in progress, and did not scruple to expose the absurdity of mixing up questions so entirely extraneous with matters which concerned the French and English nations, and these only. The clauses were withdrawn, and the treaty, thus amended, received the sanction of both Courts.

I have alluded to the change of feeling which had arisen between Clive and an influential member of the Court of Directors with whom he had formerly been on terms of amity. The individual in question was Mr. Lawrence Sulivan, a man of undeniable talent, and of clear though somewhat limited views, but of a disposition so peculiar that he could not bear to be either thwarted in his purposes or helped to the accomplishment of them by any hand except his own. Having spent some time in India, he brought into the Direction, when called to a seat in that Court, a qualification which was possessed by few, if any, of his colleagues—namely, a practical acquaintance with the wants and circumstances of the country which he assisted to govern. Admiring Clive while at a distance, he had given him a general support, which Clive repaid by throwing the whole of his influence among the proprietors into Mr. Sulivan's scale. And chiefly through their exertions Mr. Sulivan was placed in the chair, where he soon succeeded in establishing a moral supremacy over the body. No sooner, however, was the fact of Clive's intended return to England made known than Mr.

Sulivan took the alarm. He foresaw that, should Clive's ambition point in the direction of the India House, his own influence there would soon be cast into the shade, and he determined, by every means in his power, to avert the catastrophe. His course of action was obvious enough, and he followed it. The offensive letter from Bengal served as a peg on which to hang a general charge of pride and insubordination. Nobody brought this openly forward, it is true, because the object of it was beyond the limits of the Court's jurisdiction; but it was cautiously infused by one mind into another till the whole became conscious of its power, and of the angry feelings which it stirred. Again, Clive had become too rich. The Company, and not the individual, ought to have reaped the reward of the Company's exertions; and, above all, this jaghire, which their servant had accepted, was intolerable. It ought not to be permitted to continue—and it should not. At the same time, neither Mr. Sulivan nor any other member of the Court could deny, that whatever it was competent to Meer Jaffier to give, it was competent to Lord Clive to accept; and the necessity of acting with caution and delicacy was admitted. Mr. Sulivan does not appear, at this stage in the business, to have desired to go further. By alarming Clive for the continuance of his jaghire, he hoped to keep him out of the vortex of Leadenhall-street politics, and for a time he succeeded. Clive accepted the warning which Sulivan gave in good part, and for a while held aloof from interference with the proceedings of a body which tacitly pledged itself, through its chairman, to abstain on these terms from interfering with him.

Clive was willing to purchase the quiet enjoyment of his jaghire by leaving to others the general management of affairs at the India House; but it was not in his nature to forget old friendships, nor perhaps to suffer old antipathies to die out. As most men in high command are apt to do, he desired to promote the interests of those who had served immediately under his own eye, and made their merits conspicuous to him. Others, whose claims might be of equal weight, though differently established, he overlooked; and in one memorable case, at least, he carried the principle to an inexcusable extent. Colonel Forde was an especial favourite with Clive, as indeed he deserved to be; so was Major Carnac; so was Captain Calliaud; and so was a Captain Knox—of one of whose exploits I shall have occasion to speak in another portion of this memoir. But Colonel Coote had not even his friendship, and he scarcely did justice to that gentleman's services on the Coromandel coast in his eagerness to advance Forde at Coote's expense. It happened that Mr. Sulivan and he took different views of this subject. Many of those whom Lord Clive recommended to the Court's protection Mr. Sulivan disliked; almost all whom Clive disliked Mr. Sulivan was anxious to patronize. Collision on points like this necessarily leads to estrangement and mutual distrust; and the step from distrust to hostility, in tempers like that of Clive, is never a wide one. In November, 1762, I find his Lordship writing to his old friend Mr. Vansittart in the following terms :—

" There is a terrible storm brewing against the next general election. Sulivan, who is one of the Directors this year, is strongly opposed by Rous and his party, and by part, if not all, of the East Indians (particularly the Bengallese), and matters are carried to such lengths that either Sulivan or Rous must give way. I must acknowledge that in my heart I am a wellwisher for the cause of Rous, although, considering the great stake I have in India, it is probable I shall remain neuter. Sulivan might have attached me to his interest if he had pleased; but he could never forgive the Bengal letter, and never has reposed that confidence in me which my services to the East India Company entitled me to. The consequence has been, that we have all along behaved to one another like shy cocks—at times outwardly expressing great regard and friendship for each other."

Time passed, and the daily recurrence of contrarieties, for I cannot call them bickerings, more and more embittered the feelings of these two gentlemen towards one another. Mr. Sulivan was a protégé and firm supporter of Lord Bute; Lord Clive took the side of Granville, having despaired of the return of Pitt to office. He disapproved of the peace of 1763, and voted with the minority in the House of Commons which condemned it. Lord Bute was much annoyed; and, seeking about for some means of diminishing Clive's influence, he found in Mr. Sulivan a willing instrument wherewith to work ;—for Sulivan had become doubly jealous of his rival, as he now considered him, in consequence of the credit which the latter received among the proprietors for having guarded their interests by the amendments which he had introduced into the treaty of peace with France. As a matter of course, hostility on one side begat indignation and the wish to retaliate on the other, till at last Clive threw himself, with all his might, into the arena. It was clear to him either that he himself must cease to have weight in the councils of India, or that Mr. Sulivan's authority must be absolutely struck down. He determined to aim at the latter alternative. With this view he set himself, at the election of 1763, to resist the return of that gentleman to the Directory. He left no means untried to effect his object. He purchased 100,000*l.* worth of stock, and, dividing it among friends on whom he could rely, into 500*l.* shares, he commanded such a retinue of voters as had never before followed one man to the India House. All on whom he had or was believed to have a claim were solicited to go with him likewise; and at the show of hands the majority in his favour was prodigious. Writing to Mr. Vansittart on the 19th of March, 1763, he says—"The tremendous day is over. I need not be particular about it. You will have it from many hands. I should imagine there were present not less than eight hundred proprietors. Numbers of neutral parties went off; and no small number of our friends, thinking our majority so great that there was no occasion for their presence. Indeed, upon the holding up of hands, I thought we were at least two to one. This is really a great victory, considering we had the united strength of the whole Ministry against us."

If gigantic exertions, and the risk of much pecuniary loss, deserved to secure a victory of this sort, Clive ought clearly to have come off a conqueror. He availed himself to its utmost limits of the iniquitous law which sanctioned—or rather of the absence of the law which ought to have prevented—the creation of fictitious votes. Of the two hundred proprietors who, for the purposes of the election had each his 500*l.* stock, probably one hundred and ninety were pledged, as soon as the contest was over, to restore their qualifications to him from whom they had borrowed them. But Clive's opponents were neither less diligent nor more scrupulous than he; and above all, there was the test of the ballot-box to be sustained. It decided against Clive, and he was soon made to feel that not to prevail in such a contest was to expose himself to trouble and mortification. One of the first acts of the new Court was to address a letter to the Governor of Bengal, in which he was commanded not only to pay into the Company's treasury the amount of Clive's jaghire for the current year, but to make out a statement of the sums paid to Clive since the jaghire was first granted, with a view to compel restitution to be made. Clive's indignation, when the fact of such orders having gone forth first reached him, was extreme; nevertheless he bore himself with greater appearance of composure than might have been expected in a man of his naturally impetuous temper. He wrote to his friends in India, urging them to delay compliance with the Court's instructions in case the slightest loop-hole should be afforded of escape from prompt compliance with them. His next step was to apply to the Court of Directors for a copy of the proceedings on which a measure so deeply affecting his interests was founded ; and on their refusal to furnish the information sought, he filed a bill against them in Chancery. There could be little doubt as to the issue of the trial, had it come on. All the most eminent lawyers of the day, including Mr. Yorke, then Attorney-General, and Mr. Fletcher Norton, the Solicitor-General, had given their opinion that the Court of Directors had no case; indeed, that their own tenure of the Zemindarry rested on the same ground which assured to Clive his rents or reserved revenue arising out of such Zemindarry. But before matters could be brought to an issue, circumstances arose which threw both the Court of Directors and the Company itself in some sense at Clive's feet. There had been mismanagement and confusion in the province of Bengal ever since Clive resigned his seat as President of the governing body. Without a head to direct, or an arm vigorous enough to restrain them, the Company's servants, as well European as native, had been guilty of all manner of abuses. Revolutions had been brought about at Moorshedabad by processes and with a view to the accomplishment of objects which were alike unjustifiable; and the consequence was, an interruption of the Company's trade, and the entire cessation of means wherewith to pay the dividends. Now, to hit the proprietors here was to wound these gentlemen in vital parts. They were not very careful to investigate the claims of rival Indian princes to their thrones; whether the subjects of these princes throve or went to ruin was a question with which they took little concern; and the peculations of their own friends and relatives, so long as they were confined within moderate limits, afflicted them not: but to touch the dividends was to dry up the current of their blood at its fountain-head. The wildest alarm pervaded the whole body. They demanded inquiry; and the more the case was investigated the less were they satisfied with the results. What was to be done? As if actuated by one feeling, the proprietors met in full Court, and determined that Clive alone could save them from ruin. They entreated him to return to Bengal, and assume once more the management of their affairs in that quarter. Indeed, they went further. If he accepted the trust which they pressed upon him, he was to go, not as President of the Governing Council of Calcutta, but as Governor-General and Commander in-Chief over the whole of the Company's possessions in the East. And that there might be no plea for declining the offer because of the unsettled state of his dispute with the Court of Directors, the Court of Proprietors proposed that the jaghire should be at once restored, and Clive's right to its continued possession officially recognised. This was indeed the triumph of talent and genius over envy. But Clive declined to avail himself of the Court's enthusiasm. He said that he had his own proposal relative to the jaghire to make, on the compliance of the Court of Directors with which one obstacle to his acceptance of the important trust offered to him by the proprietors would be removed. This he briefly stated; and, when the Court accepted it by acclamation, he went on to say that there was yet another point which they must concede to him, otherwise he must decline entering again into their service. He differed, he said, so much from Mr. Sulivan in opinion of the measures necessary to be taken for the good of the Company, that he could not consider that gentleman as a proper Chairman of the Court of Directors; that it would be in vain for him to exert himself as he ought, in the office of Governor and Commander-in-Chief of their forces, if his measures were to be thwarted and condemned at home, as they probably would be, by a Court of Directors under the influence of a Chairman whose conduct, upon many occasions, had evinced his ignorance of East India affairs, and who was also known to be his personal and inveterate enemy; that it was a matter totally indifferent to him who filled the chair, if Mr. Sulivan did not; but that he could not, consistently with the regard he had for his own reputation, and the advantages he should be emulous of establishing for the Company, proceed in the appointments with which they had honoured him, if that gentleman continued to have the lead at home.

Mr. Sulivan seems to have been ill prepared for this direct attack. He knew his man too well to hope, that, having made the move, Clive would ever withdraw from it; and, fearing lest his influence should be utterly destroyed, he endeavoured to protect himself by a display of zeal in the cause of others. After expressing his concurrence in the opinion of the General Court as to the talents of Lord Clive, with whom he could conceive no reason why he should be at variance, Mr. Sulivan proceeded to represent the impropriety of superseding (by the civil and military powers proposed to be granted to his Lordship) Mr. Vansittart, Governor of Bengal, and Major-General Lawrence, who had lately been induced to return to Madras. He also stated the disappointment which the nomination of Lord Clive would occasion to Mr. Spencer, a Bombay servant lately nominated to the head of affairs at Bengal. But the General Court were in no temper to listen to such reasoning, and with one voice insisted upon the Directors making the appointment. The Directors, as a last resource, desired to try the question by ballot; but the by-laws of the Company establish that no ballot shall take place except by a requisition of nine proprietors. Though upwards of three hundred were present, this number could not be found to sign their names to such a requisition; and the Court, in consequence, adjourned.

The Court of Directors, thus compelled to attend to the wish of the Court of Proprietors, nominated Lord Clive Governor and Commander-in-Chief of Bengal. There was some hesitation about the military commission interfering with that of Major-General Lawrence, who, though advanced in years, and infirm, had accompanied his near relative, Mr. Palk, when that gentleman was appointed Governor of Madras. But Clive intimated that it was far from his wish to supersede his old commander: all he required was, that neither Major-General Lawrence nor any other officer should have the power of interfering with his command in Bengal.

Lord Clive received his appointment* within a month of the general election ; and the Directors hurried their preparations for his departure, from a desire that he should leave England before that event took place ; conceiving, no doubt, that his doing so would evince a confidence in their support, and prevent that opposition which several of them expected on the ground of their known hostility to the popular Governor. A letter was, in consequence, written to Lord Clive by the Secretary, informing him that a ship was ready to receive him. He replied, that, for reasons he had assigned at the General Court, he could not think of embarking till he knew the result of the election of Directors, which was to take place in the ensuing month. The Directors, when they received this answer, declared that they considered it as a resignation of the government. They therefore summoned a General Court, at which one of the proprietors in their interest moved, that, as Lord Clive declined the government of Bengal, they should proceed to a new nomination; but his Lordship's declaration at the late Court had made too deep an impression to be easily erased. The proprietors saw nothing in his conduct but manly consistency with the sentiments which he had previously avowed ; and, viewing the conduct of the Directors as an unworthy artifice to evade compliance with their wishes, they threw out the proposition with violence and clamour.

Strong in the support of the Proprietors, and firm in his purpose of excluding from the Direction the individual against whom he now cherished a feeling more bitter, perhaps, than even his conduct merited, Clive remained in England till the election of the 25th of April 1764 was over. It did not give to him a triumph so decided as he had hoped for. Mr. Sulivan was still a popular man with the East India body, and therefore, though no longer supported by ministerial influence (for Lord Bute was by this time out of office), he contrived to carry twelve

* March, 1764.

out of twenty-four seats, his own being one of the number. The remaining twelve were filled by Clive's friends; and when the struggle for the Chair arose, they prevailed. Mr. Rous became Chairman, and Mr. Bolton, a member of the same party, was appointed to be Deputy.

A Court so constituted was not likely to resist any reasonable proposition on the subject of his jaghire which Clive might make. His right of possession was confirmed for ten years, should he live so long, and the Zemindarry still remain in the Company's hands; whilst the ultimate disposal of the property was passed by as an arrangement which would be most conveniently settled when the occasion arose. Neither were his plans for the better management of the province assigned to him in any degree thwarted. The emergency which had caused his nomination to office led to his being intrusted with very extensive powers. He was permitted to name his own Committee of Council. His recommendations of different military officers were also attended to. The King's troops being at this period recalled, all officers in his Majesty's service were ordered to England. Major Calliaud, promoted to the rank of Brigadier-General, had been appointed to Madras; Major Carnac's services were rewarded with a similar commission, and the command of the troops in Bengal; Sir Robert Barker was appointed to command the artillery; Majors Richard Smyth and Preston were nominated Lieutenant-Colonels of the European corps; and Major Knox advanced to the rank of Lieutenant-Colonel, to command the sepoys.

The victory which Lord Clive obtained at the India House was followed up by his friends, who, on the next general election (1765), strengthened their party among the Directors very considerably; and Mr. Sulivan, notwithstanding the active exertions of his adherents, was again defeated. This success gave Clive the support which he required during his short but important administration of the affairs of Bengal. It laid, however, the foundation of the future troubles of his life; for those over whom he now triumphed cherished their resentments;* and their ranks

* Mr. Sulivan was not defeated without an active struggle. Mr. Walsh, in a letter to Lord Clive of the 5th April, 1765, speaking of the contest, observes—" Lord Bute joined him (Mr. Sulivan) very strenuously, and got

were early recruited by numerous malcontents from India, whom
Clive's reforms had either deprived of the means of accumulating wealth, or exposed to obloquy. The efforts of his confe-
derated enemies will be noticed hereafter: the subject is mentioned here merely as a consequence of his engaging personally
in the politics of Leadenhall-street. How far that step was one
of wisdom, or of necessity, it is very difficult to determine.

Having thus described the public life of Lord Clive during
the interval between his second return to England and his departure for the last time to the scene of his early labours, it
seems necessary, in order to fill up the outlines of the portrait,
that some notice, at least, should be taken of his personal habits,
and the state of his affairs as a domestic man, and a member of
general society. Clive was enormously rich, and he indulged
the passion for display which was natural to him without reserve.
His horses were the finest, his equipages the most brilliant, of all
that appeared at Court. He was a good deal about the palace
likewise, and was greatly flattered when the Queen proposed to
stand godmother for one of his children. He made rich presents
to multitudes of people, and did not forget either the King or
the Queen. An anecdote is told of him in reference to this
weakness which seems to me to deserve repetition. George the
Third had a great fancy at this time for strange animals,—and
elephants, antelopes, hog-deer, and such like, were not then so
common in Europe as the zoological societies of various countries have since caused them to be. Clive wrote to several of
his friends in India, requesting that they would send him " curiosities " of the sort, which he might present to the King. For a
good while no " curiosities " came ; but at last he got a letter
from Mr. Vansittart, in which that gentleman informed him that
he had sent home two elephants, a rhinoceros, and a Persian
mare, and requested that his Lordship would, with the writer's
brother, Mr. Arthur Vansittart, present them to his Majesty.
Clive did not quite understand the meaning of this communication till the animals had actually arrived. But when Mr. A.
Vansittart requested that his Lordship would accompany him to

the Duke of Northumberland to do the same. This change may appear
extraordinary ; but abject submissions on the one part, and tender solicitations on the other, are said to have brought it about !"

Court in order to fulfil his brother's wishes, the wrath of the great man burst forth. He sat down and answered the note of his correspondent in a tirade, of which I subjoin a short specimen :—

" Upon the receipt of your letter, enclosing a copy of a paragraph from your brother, I can plainly perceive that Mr. Vansittart, declining to comply with the request I made him, of purchasing and sending home, on my account, an elephant to be presented to his Majesty by me, has taken that hint to send one home on his own. This unkind treatment I neither deserved nor expected from Mr. Vansittart. I am persuaded his Majesty will not think I am wanting in that respect which is due to him, if I decline presenting, in another person's name, an elephant which I intended to present in my own. At the same time, I shall take care that his Majesty be informed of the cause of my desiring to be excused attending you to his Majesty with Mr. Vansittart's presents."

This sharp rebuke, as subsequent explanations proved, had really not been deserved. But the captain of the ship in which the animals were brought home had blundered in describing the designs of Mr. Vansittart in embarking them. And it may serve to illustrate the state of Clive's feelings when I add, that he never could be persuaded out of the belief that Mr. Sulivan put the unlucky seaman on this method of giving annoyance to his enemy.

If Clive was ostentatious in some of his proceedings, he was eminently generous in others. I say nothing of the expenditure of 60,000*l.* in electioneering within the space of eighteen months. He had the purposes of party and personal ambition to serve in this : but his presents to poor relatives and friends continued to be princely. He settled 2000*l.* additional on each of his sisters, and rendered his brothers independent. He encouraged Major Carnac to continue in the service in spite of the neglect which he had suffered, by assuring him that he had done what he could for him, besides leaving him in his will 500*l.* a-year. Styche had long become his. He caused the old house to be fitted up and enlarged ; but, finding it still too small, he purchased the estate of Walcot, and built upon it a palace after the design and under the superintendence of Sir Robert Chambers, one of the most celebrated architects of his day. The spacious house in Berkeley-square, in which, till very lately, his descendants continued to reside, he purchased on a lease of ninety years, and fitted it up in a style of oriental magnificence. But it was not in such channels as these exclusively that Clive sought for and found a fair share of happiness. His letters betoken a mind, morbid, indeed, and restless, but capable of strong domestic affections ; and we cannot doubt that the indulgence of these operated beneficially on his temper. Moreover, he had some friends, as well as a host of enemies, and was gratified by the assurance that a statue would be raised to him in the India House as a mark of the Company's sense of his services ;—and a medal was actually struck to commemorate the great victory of Plassey. We cannot know all this without assuming that, if it be within the compass of honour and prosperity in this life to fill up the measure of man's longings, Lord Clive had little to desire. That they did not satisfy him is, however, certain : have they ever satisfied any man's mind, which had the power, whether exercised or not, of raising itself for an instant above the things of sense ?

CHAPTER XVI.

Retrospect of the course of affairs in Bengal.

I MUST crave the reader's indulgence for a brief space while I
endeavour, at this stage in my narrative, to sketch the outlines
of the more important of the events which occurred in Bengal
between Colonel Clive's resignation of the government of that
province in 1759 and his return as Lord Clive in 1765, with
powers largely increased, to the scene of his early glory. The
task, though the reverse of agreeable, is imposed upon me by
the necessity of accounting for that sudden burst of popular enthusiasm which, as already described, lifted the subject of it in
one moment above the malice of his enemies; while of the
revulsion of feeling which began ere long to manifest itself, and
which led in due time to proceedings both in Parliament and
elsewhere, it is impossible to speak, with a knowledge of the
facts which we now possess, except in terms of strong reproba-
tion. If ever Clive served the Company and the country well,
it was during his last administration of the affairs of Bengal.
If ever he had a right to count upon receiving marks of his
employers' gratitude, and honours from the Crown, it was when
for the last time he had rendered up the trust which the Court
of Proprietors had in some measure forced him to undertake.
But as the motives which induced the Company to put itself and
its affairs absolutely into his hands were not of the most exalted
kind, so his efforts to do justice to the native population of
Bengal, as well as to the proprietors of stock and their European
representatives, minds inferior to his own had no power to
appreciate. Far be it from me to stand forward as the indis-
criminating advocate of Lord Clive's good name. Few men
filling so large a space in the public eye have committed
graver offences against moral right. His faults of temper and
taste, and perhaps of something more important than either,

seem to have been innumerable. But the offences to which I allude had been at least forgiven, if indeed the seal of public approval was not put upon them in 1762; and for errors of another sort he was surely not accountable to the tribunal before which he was arraigned.

For some time previously to the meeting of the Court which declared that Clive, provided he would accept the government of Bengal, should be allowed to dictate his own terms, all the accounts received from British India had been of the most unsatisfactory nature. From Bengal, especially, tidings arrived with every ship of decaying commerce, foreign wars, anarchy in the ruling body, and, as a necessary consequence, misgovernment everywhere. Mr. Vansittart, who had been nominated to succeed Clive, was a Madras servant, and therefore unpopular with his colleagues. Though a well-meaning and in some respects an able man, he was not possessed of sufficient energy of character to grapple with the difficulties in which he became immediately involved. He was greatly misled likewise by Mr. Holwell, who, as senior member of Council, occupied in his absence the President's chair, and who, though by and by removed from the service, continued long enough after Mr. Vansittart's arrival to embue that gentleman with some of his own worst prejudices. Among other points which he laboured too successfully to accomplish, Mr. Holwell succeeded in establishing in the mind of the President a rooted antipathy to Meer Jaffier. Doubtless, that wretched man had many faults. He had earned the character of a good soldier while serving as commander-in-chief under Suraj-u-Dowlah ; but his unfitness to administer the affairs of a kingdom became manifest almost immediately on his accession to the throne. Still Meer Jaffier's difficulties had been gigantic from the outset. He promised more, as the price of his elevation, than he found himself able to perform, and, in order to gain time and conciliate the forbearance of his benefactors, he was forced to connive at endless abuses by their agents and servants. I have elsewhere alluded to the steps which Clive took with a view to check, if he could not wholly put a stop to, these abuses. As long as he remained the evil was at least endurable ; but no sooner was the master-mind withdrawn than the English community in Bengal, like a watch of which the mainspring is broken, became utterly confused.   Everybody thought of enriching himself; nobody cared to inquire whether to the native sovereign or his people, or to the interests of the Company, damage was likely to arise from his efforts to accomplish this purpose.   The system of private trade, which I shall take occasion to describe by and by, was pushed to a large extent.   Meer Jaffier, cut off by it from the ordinary channels of his revenue, fell into arrear in his payments to the English, to his civil functionaries, and to his troops.   The Shah Zada, known as Shah Alum, now raised by the murder of his father to the throne of the Moguls, was marching to the attack of Patna; and the Rajah of Purneah, with the Viceroy of Oude, the latter being just appointed Vizier of the empire, had espoused his cause.   Had Mr. Holwell been left under such an accumulation of unfavourable circumstances to fight his own battle, the chances are that he would have fought it unsuccessfully.   But Clive, who foresaw the gathering of the cloud in the north, had provided for the consequence of it previously to his departure.   Colonel Calliaud marched to support Ramnarrain. This faithful friend of the English risked a battle previously to Calliaud's arrival, and was defeated, but he shut himself up in Patna, and maintained it against the Emperor with great resolution.   The junction of his European allies gave him, as a matter of course, the superiority.   Another battle was fought unfavourably for the invader; when, after a vain attempt to surprise Moorshedabad, and a second attempt, equally fruitless, to make himself master of Patna, he was compelled to retreat towards Delhi, and to leave the provinces for a little while unmolested.

Meanwhile Meer Jaffier, and his son the Prince Meeran, were making preparations to operate against the rebel Rajah of Purneah.   In these they were anticipated by the activity of Captain King, who pushed at the head of his detachment to meet the enemy, and overthrew him in a decisive battle ere the Nabob had time to make a couple of marches from his capital.   But the satisfaction arising from this victory was a good deal diminished by an event of which the consequences proved far more serious than any one could have anticipated Prince Meeran. Meer Jaffier's son, was killed by lightning while resting in his tent.   Though cruel and very ill-disposed towards the English, Meeran possessed courage and energy, and, for an Indian prince, good faith.   Whatever he promised to do he at least strove to perform ; and the army, of which he was at the head, reposed great confidence in him.   It was his assurance that they would sooner or later receive their pay which kept the troops quiet in spite of the heavy balance due to them ; and his undisguised abhorrence of the state of debasement to which strangers had reduced their country gave him much influence among the nobility and gentry of the kingdom.   His death seemed to bring about at once a dissolution of all the bonds which held society together.   The army, in a state of mutiny, surrounded the Nabob's palace, and clamoured for their wages.   The heads of the police and revenue departments declared that they would act no longer.   It was now that Meer Jaffier felt what it was to have lost the friend on whom he was accustomed, on every emergency, to rely.   There was no longer a Clive at Fort William.   Nevertheless, Clive's successor was there, and the Nabob fondly flattered himself that the promises made by one representative of the Company would be regarded as sacred by another.   He entreated Mr. Vansittart therefore to come to his aid ; and Mr. Vansittart, with the entire approbation of his otherwise intractable Council, determined to get rid of him.

The revolution which set aside Suraj-u-Dowlah and raised Meer Jaffier to the throne of Bengal was, I believe, inevitable. It was dictated to the English by the strongest of all instincts— self-preservation ; and, had it been managed with more moderation in regard to the sums of money extracted from Meer Jaffier as the price of his elevation, it might have proved as fortunate for the native population as it was advantageous to the Company.   It was an experiment, likewise, which with all the drawbacks attending it, the Bengal Government was justified in making for once ; and it undoubtedly met with the approval of the leading men of the provinces.   But Meer Jaffier had done nothing to incur the penalty of deposition.   He was in debt, doubtless ; so was almost every other native sovereign of India at that time ; and if his debts rested upon him with greater weight than theirs, it was because the English claimed a right to interfere with the collection of his revenues.   Surely he was no object of legitimate censure on that account ; surely the English, and not he, were to blame? But Mr. Vansittart and his colleagues viewed the matter in a different light. The then Governor or President of Bengal compiled, as is well known, a narrative of his administration, in which the circumstances which led to the dethronement of Meer Jaffier are explained ; and the event itself is elaborately, if not very successfully, defended. The following extract from his work will show with what sort of logic the king-makers of the last century were in the habit of satisfying their own consciences :—

"The season had now begun," says Mr. Vansittart, "when our forces were to take the field against a powerful enemy, whilst we had scarce a rupee in our treasury to enable us to put them in motion. The easy channel in which the Company's affairs ran whilst the sums stipulated by the treaty (with Meer Jaffier) lasted had diverted their attention from the distresses which must unavoidably fall on them whenever that fund should be exhausted ; and, continuing to act on the same extensive plan in which they set out, they now found themselves surrounded by numerous difficulties, which were heightened by the particular circumstances of the country at this period, and weighed down with the very advantages which they had acquired,—that is, an establishment which had lost the foundation on which it was built ; a military force proportioned to their connections and influence in the country without the means of subsistence ; a fortification begun upon the same extensive plan, at a vast expense ; and an alliance with a power unable to support itself, and threatening to involve them in the same ruin." Mr. Vansittart adds, that, had indolence and weakness been the Nabob's only faults, destructive as they were to the welfare of the country and of the Company, he would have lamented more the necessity of measures the tendency of which was to dissolve the engagements between him and the Company ; but that, in addition to this, he found a general dissatisfaction to his Highness's government, and detestation of his person and principles, in all ranks of people. This statement hardly deserves the degree of credit which we give to Mr. Vansittart's previous argument. But if it were as fully established as the fact that Meer Jaffier lived and died, I cannot see that the case is at all altered by it. That stands exactly where it was, and well merits the judgment which was given against it—that the measure "of not only breaking a solemn treaty without previous warning and negotiation with the prince with whom it was contracted, but even of dethroning that prince, without attempting to remedy by some convention the temporary evils complained of, was a rash and unjustifiable measure, particularly where the change and all the articles of the new treaty were so obviously for the advantage of one of the parties only."

Having arrived at the conviction that Meer Jaffier ought no longer to reign in Moorshedabad, the first step taken by Mr. Vansittart and his friends was to look about for an individual ambitious enough to seek the Crown, and sufficiently eager for it to accede to the terms, whatever they might be, which the English Government should propose. They were not long in finding their man. Cossim Ali, the son-in-law of Meer Jaffier, though sure of the succession at his father-in-law's death, was too impatient to wait the ordinary course of nature; and, with the improvidence of his race, came at once into the terms of those who offered to raise him to the throne. These implied the fulfilment of all the engagements into which Meer Jaffier had entered, and the surrender to them besides of the fertile provinces of Burdwan, Midnapore, and Chittagong, while the interests of individuals were not overlooked, nor the example set by Clive and his coadjutors in the former revolution forgotten. The Nabob elect undertook to pay to eight individuals the sum of 200,000*l.*, of which 58,000*l.* were to go to Mr. Vansittart; and would have pledged himself to double the amount, had not a minority in the Council disapproved of the whole arrangement, and therefore declined to accept any share of the booty.

When these arrangements were all complete, Mr. Vansittart proceeded to Moorshedabad, carrying with him two hundred European soldiers, six hundred sepoys, and four pieces of cannon. He went, as he himself has told us, in the hope of being able to persuade Meer Jaffier of the fitness of the proposed change— in other words, he was desirous, if possible, to cajole the Nabob into a resignation of his dignities, and thus avoid the scandal of a forcible deposition. That he was not unprepared, however, for any extremity, the narrative of an eye-witness explains. Mr.

Lushington, who accompanied the troops as interpreter, after describing their entry into Moorshedabad, and the preliminary negotiations which followed, goes on to say,—

" We waited all the next day; but, no answer coming, the Governor thought it proper not to lose any time, and therefore ordered Colonel Calliaud to go by water with his detachment so early that he might surround the palace at daybreak ; sending at the same time a letter, acquainting the Nabob that he had sent the Colonel to settle those affairs which he had conferred with him about, and to which he had promised to give an answer, but none was brought. The Nabob sent word to the Colonel he would give no answer until the troops returned to Moraudbaug, as he never expected such treatment from the English. Some few conferences were afterwards held by Mr. Hastings and myself with several of the Nabob's ministers ; but as nothing could be agreed on, I was sent back to Moraudbaug, to give an account of our proceedings to the Governor, and to have his final order whether we should storm the palace in case the Nabob refused to comply. He answered he wished not to spill the blood of a man whom he had raised to such dignities, but that the affair must be finished before sunset. With this I returned ; and found, to my great surprise, Cossim Ali Khan's standards, and the nobits* beating in his name. Colonel Calliaud now told me that the Nabob had sent out the seals to his son-in-law, and offered to resign the government if the English would be security for his life. This was immediately agreed to, and a meeting was held between the Colonel and the Nabob, who made the following speech, as well as I can remember :—'The English placed me on the musnud ; you may depose me if you please. You have thought proper to break your engagements. I would not mine. Had I such designs, I could have raised twenty thousand men, and fought you if I pleased. My son, the Chuta Nabob (Meeran), forewarned me of all this. I desire you will either send me to Sabut Jung (Lord Clive), for he will do me justice, or let me go to Mecca; if not, let me go to Calcutta, for I will not stay in this place. You will, I suppose, let me have my women and children ; therefore, let me have budgerows and be carried

---

* Large drums.

immediately to Moraudbaug.'   The Governor saw him soon
after this, and he made much the same speech to him, adding, he
could be nowhere safe but under the English protection."

That Mr. Lushington did not concur very cordially in the
measures described, may be inferred from his concluding observations. " The Company," he observes, " are to receive the
countries of Burdwan, Midnapore, and Chittagong, for this service. I therefore should be glad to know how this Nabob will
be any more able to pay his people than the old man, after having given away a third part of his revenues."

There can be but one opinion in regard to the moral turpitude
of this transaction, which brought with it, however, its own
punishment, and was very soon felt to be as impolitic as it had
been iniquitous. Meer Jaffier was not indeed put to death :
that would have been a climax too atrocious under the circumstances. On the contrary, he was removed with his women and
children to Calcutta, where, upon a pension granted to him out
of the revenues of the ceded provinces, he dwelt in retirement.
But the golden age to which the promoters of this scheme professed to look never came at all. They had much mistaken the
character of their puppet. Willing he might be to fulfil his public
engagements ; at least he rigidly redeemed the pledges which he
gave to individuals ; but, as Mr. Lushington has well observed,
the power was wanting to him. And then, instead of dealing
fairly by him in his straits, they who raised him to the throne
began immediately to talk of further changes. But Cossim Ali
was not the sort of man to be set aside without a struggle. He
conducted it fiercely, no doubt, as Indian princes generally do,
and became, on account of the atrocities which he committed, an
object of abhorrence to the English. But let it not be forgotten
that he was driven to madness by the conduct of individuals of
that nation. He was first raised to power rashly by one faction in
the Council, which proved too weak to support him in its exercise, and then, in the pursuit of its own interests, and the promotion of its own political views, it considered all means justifiable
that promised to accelerate his downfall.

The first year of the new Nabob's reign was marked by success against his foreign enemies. Major Carnac, who now commanded the English troops in Bengal, defeated the Emperor in

person; and a rebellion of the Chief of Beerboom and Burdwan was suppressed with the aid of a detachment under Major York. In the former of these engagements M. Law, the last representative in India of the band of heroes who had fought for supremacy there, and well-nigh won it, fell into the hands of the victor. He was treated by Major Carnac as the brave in success are in the habit of treating the brave in misfortune, as indeed was the Emperor himself, on whom, after his defeat, Major Carnac waited, that he might show him all the marks of respect that were due to his high station. Such conduct to the fallen, however rare among semi-barbarous chiefs and natives, is not lost upon them. The Emperor made peace with Cossim Ali, and the same year granted him investiture as Soubahdar of Bengal, Bahar, and Orissa, on condition that the new Soubahdar should pay into the imperial treasury an annual tribute of 240,000*l.*

It is characteristic of the sort of faith which Indian princes keep with one another, that the Emperor, at the same time that he was confirming Cossim Ali in the Soubahdarry of Bengal, offered to the English, as the price of their assistance in establishing himself on his father's throne, to confer upon them the Dewanee, or chief management, of the whole of the financial affairs of the three provinces of which Cossim Ali had become supreme ruler. I state this fact, because it seems to prove that the policy subsequently pursued by Clive was no wanton outrage on the rights of any one—at all events, that the Court of Delhi, with which in theory if not in fact the right of determining all questions of the highest import rested, was not opposed to it; but for the present the proposition could not be entertained. The Bengal Government had no funds at its disposal wherewith to enter upon so remote an expedition; and the fear of increasing the alarm and embarrassments of the Company added weight to the objection. Accordingly, the financial management, not less than the judicial and military control of the kingdom, devolved upon the new Nabob; and he was not slow in convincing both his allies and his native subjects that, if the exchequer was doomed to remain empty, it would not be for the lack of endeavours on his part to fill it.

One of the first acts of Cossim Ali, after he felt himself secure in his seat, was to crush Ramnarrain, the Nabob or Governor of Patna, who, through evil report and through good, had remained true to his faith with the English ever since, in the arrangement of Suraj-u-Dowlah's deposition, he had pledged it. This was done in the belief that there would be found at Patna treasure enough to discharge his many obligations; and, to the disgrace of Mr. Vansittart's administration, it met with no opposition from that quarter. To be sure Major Carnac first, and afterwards Colonel Coote, being successively in command of the troops, refused to take any part in the transaction—a proceeding for which, as military men, they were without excuse, however sound we may feel their views of abstract justice and even policy to have been. But the only result of their disobedience of orders was, that they were both superseded, and that Ramnarrain, falling into the hands of the Nabob, was first imprisoned and then put to death. Never had judicial murder, more wanton and more unproductive, been perpetrated in India. The unfortunate Hindoo was found to possess no hoarded treasure; and the ignominy attending a gross breach of faith was all that resulted from his death both to Cossim Ali and to the English.

Meanwhile the abuses of private trade, to which I have referred as disturbing the whole course of Meer Jaffier's reign, grew to a height which could no longer be tolerated. They had their origin in the short-sighted policy of the Court of Directors, which, sending gentlemen to India with salaries so small that it was quite impossible to provide out of them the commonest necessaries of life, left their servants at liberty to rush into commercial speculations on their own account, and to make of such adventures what profit they could. It cannot be said, in extenuation of this error, that it was committed unadvisedly. So early as the reign of James the First, Sir Thomas Roe had warned the Company against sanctioning so mischievous a practice. "Absolutely prohibit the private trade," he says; "for your business will be better done. I know this is harsh. Men profess they come not for low wages. But you will take away this plea if you give great wages to their content; and then you know what you pay for."

This excellent advice was not followed. From age to age the Company adhered to the old system, paying low salaries and conniving at the by-gains of its servants.   The pay of a member of Council, at the period of which I now write, was barely 300*l.* a-year; and it was notorious that such a functionary could not exist in India upon less than ten times that amount.   As to laying by, with a view to spend his latter days at home, that was out of the question, unless, indeed, he took large advantage of the facilities of making a fortune which the customs of the service afforded.   Now no man went to India then—no man goes to India now—except in the hope of earning a competency there on which he may ultimately retire.   That, therefore, which the Company's servants seek now by competing honourably for situations of responsibility and profit, they sought eighty or ninety years ago by trade; and the enormous fortunes which most of them realised proved that they seldom sought in vain.   For a while this system wrought harm only to the body which sanctioned it.   The Company's dividends were diminished in proportion to the amount of profits realised by individuals; and the servants grew rich while the masters complained of being in difficulties.   But as soon as the Company began to change its character, and to stand forth in the light of a governing body, the case was altered.   Its servants might retain their old titles of factors, junior merchants, and senior merchants; but they wielded the powers of proconsuls, proprietors, and procurators of extensive provinces.   They would have been more than human, receiving the salaries which they did, had they not abused their powers.   Henceforth the system of private trade became the fruitful source of oppression to the native, and constant pecuniary embarrassment to the English governments.   And the cause was this:—

From time immemorial customs had been collected all over India on the transit of goods from one kingdom or province to another through the interior of the country.   The practice prevailed in Bengal, as well as everywhere else; and, as the importance of the Company's dealings increased, it produced much annoyance and led to many quarrels in consequence of the many tolls and inspections to which the merchandize was liable when in progress to and from the marts of purchase and of sale.   To obviate these inconveniences, it was arranged with the Nabobs, in explanation of the Emperor's firman, that the Com-

pany's flag and dustuck (or written permit) covering its boats
or other conveyances should secure the goods contained in them
from search; and as the Company's trade consisted solely of
goods from foreign parts for sale in the country, or of country
goods for foreign exportation, the privilege only partially interfered with the trade of the interior. So long as the Nabobs and
their officers were in full power, any abuse of this privilege was
easily checked. But when, after the accession of Meer Jaffier,
the English had become all-powerful, and it was dangerous to
interfere with their acts, or to question their proceedings, the
Company's servants, who had still the privilege of trading on
their own account, not only covered their private adventures
by passports under the Company's name, but all their servants
and dependents claimed an exemption from internal duties on
the same plea, and entered into the internal trade of the country
to an extent which was quite unjustifiable. During the vigorous
administration of Clive such attempts had been rare; but when
all fear of correction was lost in the increasing weakness of his
successors, men set no limits to their efforts to enrich themselves.
The Nabob's revenue was injured, and his authority insulted,
in every quarter of his dominions, by the exemptions claimed for
the trade of European agents, and the respect demanded for the
persons of the lowest of their servants. Against the pretensions
and excesses of these parties the Nabob made most forcible remonstrances, but in vain. Many of the persons of whom he
complained were members of Council; and complaints against
members of Council, when Clive was not present to receive
them, obtained no hearing. Cossim Ali became impatient of
delay; and finding his representations produce no effect, and that
the orders of the Government were either evaded or disobeyed,
he himself took and authorised measures of violence to be taken
that increased the discontent and hostility of the party opposed
to Mr. Vansittart; for, many of them being the persons chiefly
benefited by the abuses complained of, they of course charged
their obnoxious President with leaving British subjects and
public servants of the Company at the will and mercy of a
capricious tyrant whom he had unjustly raised to the throne.

To remedy these evils, Mr. Vansittart negotiated a treaty by
which, while some advantages were secured for the servants of

the Company, many of the privileges hitherto claimed by them were done away. This treaty, though exceptionable in some of its clauses, might have operated well enough had Mr. Vansittart's Council been disposed to listen to reason, and Cossim Ali been more temperate. But the Council was not reasonable, neither was Cossim Ali temperate. The latter trusted to his judicious and active administration of the customs as one of the sources out of which he was to discharge the heavy pecuniary obligations under which he had come to the English; and as he adopted the strictest measures for enforcing their collection, the adjudication and enforcement of all fiscal demands had (unfortunately as affairs stood) been left in his hands, and numerous collisions instantly ensued. " In truth," says Mr. Verelst,* a dispassionate observer, " it soon became a personal quarrel. Meer Cossim, in the orders issued to his officers, distinguished between the trade of his friends and of those who opposed him, treating individuals with indecent reproach." This was undoubtedly true to a certain extent; but the fault did not rest wholly with the Nabob. The English traders were as extravagant in their demands as he was fierce in his measures to resist them; and the opponents of Mr. Vansittart, who thought their interests injured, and who now formed the majority of Council, combined in measures which soon led to an open rupture.

Meantime the claims set up by the English and their native servants, for carrying their goods free from the duties paid by the Nabob's own subjects, became excessive and unbearable. The whole commerce of the country was thrown, indeed, into confusion, and ruin was threatened to the Nabob's finances. As a measure of justice to his own subjects, and to prevent the daily breaches of the peace which occurred, he saw no remedy left but to abolish all customs throughout his dominions. An order was accordingly issued to this effect; and the English private traders, whom it deprived of their iniquitous monopoly, became furious. The Council took the matter up, exclaimed against the arrangement as an infraction of the treaty, and sent two agents, Messrs. Hall and Amyatt, to demand its annulment. Neither were they content to abide the issue of their own re-

---

* Verelst's View, p. 47.

monstrance. Having called in most of the heads of factories from the out-stations, and largely increased thereby their majority over the Governor's party, they began to debate the propriety of a third revolution, and instructed their people to arrest the Nabob's revenue officers because they ventured to obey the orders given to them by the government which they served. The Nabob became, as might be expected, exceedingly angry. His indignation was increased by the overbearing tone which Mr. Ellis, the chief of the Company's establishment in Patna, assumed towards him ; and he adopted measures which his enemies in the Council were not slow to accept as a virtual declaration of war. Two boats, laden with arms, which had been despatched from Calcutta for the use of the detachment at Patna, he seized upon the river. He next required that Mr. Ellis and his armed force should be withdrawn from the city ; and when Mr. Amyatt proceeded to remonstrate with him on the proceeding, he broke out into loud complaints of the injustice which the English had done him. Mr. Ellis, who had already obtained permission from the Council to act vigorously in case of need, seized the citadel. He was instantly attacked there, and, with the whole of his force, made prisoner ; whereupon a series of outrages began, which caused every other feeling to merge at Calcutta in that of horror and indignation towards the perpetrator of them. Mr. Ellis, Mr. Amyatt, and about 150 British subjects more, of whom 50 were officers in the civil or military service of the Company, were put to death : after which the Nabob, evacuating his capital, retired as the British army advanced, and took refuge at last within the territories of the Viceroy of Oude.

CHAPTER XVII.

War with Cossim Ali—Restoration of Meer Jaffier—Plans of Clive for a
Reform of the Government of Bengal.

It was at this unfortunate moment, when Mr. Vansittart was
already opposed by a majority of his council, that the Court's
reply to the offensive letter of 1759 reached Calcutta, and that
the four senior members—of whom three were his supporters—
received intimation that they were no longer in the service of
the East India Company. Feeble before, the President became
henceforth powerless; and a tyrant majority pursued its own
plans to the utmost. It was proposed and carried by vote in
Council that Cossim Ali, having violated his engagements, had
ceased to reign. Measures were then taken to provide an occu-
pant of the throne of Bengal; and the unanimous choice of the
Company's representatives fell upon Meer Jaffier. The price
paid by that weak man for leave to resume the trappings of
royalty was, to be sure, sufficiently high. He made presents to
individuals, confirmed the Company's title to the provinces of
Burdwan, Midnapore, and Chittagong, and restored the trade
of the kingdom to its former footing—yielding to the English
whatever they demanded, though not unaware of the ruinous
consequences both to the native merchants and to himself. But
Meer Jaffier seems never to have abandoned the hope that Clive
would yet return to Bengal: and when rumours of the event
began to circulate, he took courage to dare everything. He did
not live to witness the realisation of these hopes. After a short
and uneasy reign he died, though not till he had marked his
sense of Clive's merits and of his own esteem and regard for that
great man by bequeathing to him a legacy of not less than
70.000*l.* sterling.

Meer Jaffier died in February, 1765; and the question was
immediately mooted at Calcutta on whom the succession ought

to devolve. There were two representatives of the family of the deceased Nabob whose claims were supposed to be pretty equally balanced. Nujeem-ud-Dowlah, the son of Meer Jaffier, had attained to his twentieth year, and was therefore assumed to be competent to discharge the functions of royalty in person; the grandson of the deceased, being the son of Prince Meeran, was an infant of only six years of age. After some deliberation the Council decided that it was better that the son of the late Nabob should succeed his father; and the terms on which he was to be maintained on the throne were proposed, and, as a matter of course, accepted. They included all the privileges which by former governments had been secured to the English—that is to say, presents, trade on advantageous terms, the revenues derived from provinces, and such like; and they laid the new Nabob under other restrictions such as had never been thought of by his predecessors. Distrusting either his will or his power so to manage the financial affairs of the kingdom as that they should suffice to meet the many demands that would be made upon the royal exchequer, the Council stipulated, first, that the military defence of the country should devolve wholly on the English, the Nabob keeping no more troops in pay than might be necessary for purposes of show; and next, that he should appoint as his minister or vicegerent an individual of whom they, the members of Council, might approve. It is right to observe, however, that this latter article of treaty was not quite new at the elevation of Nujeem-ud-Dowlah. Meer Jaffier had been obliged, as part of the price of his restoration, to accept a similar dry-nurse; and in defiance of the protest of Mr. Vansittart, was encouraged by the majority to nominate Nundcomar, a Hindoo of the worst character. But Mr. Vansittart had quitted Bengal previously to the demise of Meer Jaffier; upon which the Council, as if to make the whole world aware of the real nature of the principle on which they acted, cast their own worthless instrument aside. Nujeem-ud-Dowlah was advised to take into his service Mahommed Reza Khan, a Mahommedan nobleman of talent and reputed integrity; and Mahommed Reza Khan became in consequence Naib Subah or minister to the new Nabob.

Meanwhile the spirit of insubordination and rapacity which

prevailed among the civil servants of the Company was not slow
in gaining an ascendancy over the military classes in like manner.
I have already had occasion to speak of the refusal both of Colonel Calliaud and Colonel Coote to obey the instructions conveyed to them by the supreme government. They set an example
in this which their inferiors were not slow to follow, till by and
by orders came to be either obeyed or disregarded, according as
they happened to fall in with the humours or supposed interests
of the parties receiving them, or the reverse. Both officers and
men likewise learned to regard their pay as a very inconsiderable
portion of the remuneration to which they were entitled. At
each change in the person of the Nabob or his minister they
claimed and received their share in the presents that were going;
while the idea of taking the field, except upon the assurance of
a good douceur at the end of the campaign, would have been
scouted. It was a necessary consequence of this state of feeling,
that the bands of discipline were everywhere relaxed. Desertions
from the ranks became frequent; indeed to such a height was
the matter carried, that from the force which Major Munro commanded at Patna, and with which he operated against Cossim
Ali, a whole battalion endeavoured to pass over, with its arms
and accoutrements, to the enemy. Major Munro acted with great
decision in the case. The battalion was intercepted and brought
back; the ringleaders in the mutiny were tried upon the spot,
and 24 persons received sentence of death, which was to be carried into execution by blowing them away from the mouths of
cannon. Four grenadiers who happened to be among the parties
doomed claimed as their right the privilege of leading the way in
this march into eternity. Their courage and the spirit which
dictated such an unusual request were much admired, but the
executions went forward notwithstanding. The mutiny was suppressed, and the troops behaved ever afterwards with their customary valour.

Into the details of the military operations which followed I am
not called upon to enter. They resulted in the entire defeat of
Cossim Ali and his ally Sujah-u-Dowlah, who, being driven out
of Oude, was forced to take refuge among the Rohillas. The
contest was, however, more severe than any in which the English
had as yet been engaged with native troops; for Cossim Ali had

paid great attention to his army, and brought it to a state of very respectable discipline. But the final issues were so decisive as to leave the victors little to desire except the discovery of some fund whence their exhausted treasury might be supplied. At Madras likewise, as well as in the direction of Bombay, the foreign politics of the Company prospered, though not without well-grounded charges against the former Presidency of forgetting old friends and services of former years, in the anxiety of its rulers to extend their power and increase their revenues. But of the issues of the contest into which the Bengal government had entered nothing was yet known in London, when Lord Clive, at the urgent request of the Court of Proprietors, consented to undertake the difficult task of reducing chaos into order. I am not friendly to the habit of introducing into such narratives as this long extracts from official correspondence, provided it be possible, by another and a shorter process, to set the views of the subject of a memoir on important subjects in a clear light. But Lord Clive's letter to the Court of Directors, bearing date the 27th of April, 1764, seems to me so important, that it would be not more unjust to the character of the writer than unfair towards my readers were I to withhold it. It is a masterly production, embracing every difficult point of Indian policy, as well for the time being as in reference to the future; for neither the exigencies of the military service nor the evils resulting from the transfer of officials with superior rule from one Presidency to another are overlooked in it. And serving, as it will be found to do, as the sort of text according to which his Lordship's subsequent proceedings when in power were framed and fashioned, I conceive that, upon the whole, the purpose of my present work will not be accomplished, unless it be enriched by something more than a meagre outline of the contents of this important document.

" In obedience to your commands," he writes, immediately before joining the ship which was to convey him to the scene of his labours, " I now transmit the purport of what I had the honour to represent to you by word of mouth at the last Court of Directors, with some other particulars which slipped my memory at that time.

" Having taken into consideration your letter sent me by the

Secretary, as also the request of the General Court of Proprietors, I think myself bound in honour to accept the charge of your affairs in Bengal, provided you will co-operate with, and assist me in such a manner that I may be able to answer the expectations and intentions of the General Court.

" As an individual, I can have no temptation to undertake this arduous task, and nothing but the desire I have to be useful to my country, and to manifest my gratitude to this Company, could make me embark in this service, attended as it is with so many inconveniences to myself and my family. I cannot avoid acknowledging that I quit my native country with some degree of regret and diffidence, on leaving behind me (as I certainly do) a very divided and distracted Direction, at a time, too, when unanimity is more than ever requisite for the carrying into execution such plans as are absolutely necessary to the well-being of the Company.

" I shall now enter into a short discussion of your political, commercial, and military affairs in Bengal. Without searching into the causes of the unhappy revolution in favour of Cossim Ali Khan, I shall only remark, that if the same plan of politics had been pursued, after he was placed upon the throne, as that which I had observed towards his predecessor, he might with great ease have remained there to this day, without having it in his power to injure either himself or the Company in the manner he has lately done. Indeed, Mr. Vansittart's ideas in politics have differed so widely from mine, that either the one or the other must have been totally in the wrong. Soon after Cossim Ali Khan was raised to his new dignity, he was suffered to retire to a very great distance from his capital, that our influence might be felt and dreaded as little as possible by him :—he was suffered to dismiss all those old officers who had any connexion with, or dependence upon us ; and, what was the worst of all, our faithful friend and ally, Ram Narrain, the Nabob of Patna, was given up ; the doctrine of the Subadar's independency was adopted, and every method was put in practice to confirm him in it. We need seek for no other causes of the war ; for it is now some time that things have been carried to such lengths abroad, that either the princes of the country must in a great measure be dependent on us, or we totally so on them. That the public and continued disapprobation of Cossim Ali Khan's advancement to the government, expressed by the gentlemen of Calcutta, increased the Nabob's jealousy, is most true; and that it was the duty of every one, after the revolution was once effected, to concur heartily in every measure to support it, cannot be denied. It is likewise true, that the encroachments made upon the Nabob's prescriptive rights by the Governor and Council, and the rest of the servants trading in the articles of salt, beetle, and tobacco, together with the power given by Mr. Vansittart to subject our gomastahs (or agents) to the jurisdiction and inspection of the country government, all concurred to hasten and bring on the late troubles; but still the groundwork of the whole was the Nabob's independency. It is impossible to rely on the moderation and justice of Mussulmen. Strict and impartial justice should ever be observed; but let that justice come from ourselves. The trade, therefore, of salt, beetle, and tobacco having been one cause of the present disputes, I hope these articles will be restored to the Nabob, and your servants absolutely forbid to trade in them. This will be striking at the root of the evil. The prohibition of dustucks to your junior servants will, I hope, tend to restore that economy which is so necessary in your service. Indeed, if some method be not thought of, and your Council do not heartily co-operate with your Governor to prevent the sudden acquisition of fortunes, which has taken place of late, the Company's affairs must greatly suffer. What power it may be proper to vest me with, to remedy those great and growing evils, will merit your serious consideration. As a means to alleviate in some measure the dissatisfaction that such restrictions upon the commercial advantages of your servants may occasion in them, it is my full intention not to engage in any kind of trade myself; so that they will divide amongst them what used to be the Governor's portion of commercial advantages, which was always very considerable."

The next subject to which Lord Clive refers is the state of the Company's military affairs in Bengal, of which, while he does full justice to the gallantry of the native troops, he points out all the defects. He says, what every other officer of experience has said since his day, that, however efficient as a supplementary force the sepoys might be, they were not, except when acting side by side with Europeans, altogether to be relied on. "For the good of the Company, therefore," he continues, "I would propose that you should always have in Bengal 4000 or at least 3000 Europeans, to consist of three battlions of 700 each, four companies of artillery of 100 each, and 500 light horse." Moreover, as the King's troops had all been withdrawn, he recommends that, in order to establish a more effective system of subordination in the Company's battalions, there should be an immediate increase of European officers, and that three field-officers should be given to each of them. "I would recommend," he says, "the appointing three field-officers to every battalion, a colonel, lieutenant-colonel, and major, and the officers I would choose to command the battalions should be Majors Carnac, Richard Smith, and Preston. You have already done justice to Major Carnac's character by reinstating him in the command of your forces in Bengal, and by acknowledging his services in the most public manner. This gentleman will, I flatter myself, stand as high in your esteem as Brigadier-General Calliaud; and will, I hope, have the same rank and appointments. The military merits of the other two gentlemen you are likewise well acquainted with, having both received from the Court marks of approbation for their distinguished services. To command your artillery I would recommend Sir Robert Barker, whose abilities in that department have been exceeded by no officer that ever was in your service. Your sepoys are already commanded by Major Knox, whose merits I could wish to have rewarded with a lieutenant-colonel's commission. Your horse, when raised, should be commanded by a lieutenant-colonel, or major.

"I have very strong reasons to wish this idea of regimenting your troops may take place; for without such a subordination I shall not be able to enforce your orders for the reduction of your military expenses, which have been a constant dead-weight, and have swallowed up your revenues. I could wish, that whatever emoluments are unavoidable may fall to those few who, having been long, are high in your service, whether civil or military. Thus will the expense be scarce felt by the Company, in comparison to what it is at present, when, for want of due subordination, every one thinks himself entitled to every advantage; and the juniors in your service be excited to exert themselves, from a certain knowledge that application and abilities only can restore them to their native country with fortunes honourably acquired."

These are explicit and statesmanlike suggestions. Neither are Lord Clive's views of the best manner of recruiting for the Indian army unworthy of being placed upon record, especially at a time when the wants and wishes of the British soldier are attracting the degree of public attention which has been too long withheld from them. Lord Clive, like every other officer of experience and strong mind, condemns the crimping system which prevailed in his day, and has not, we are afraid, as yet altogether ceased to be acted upon. His project was to obtain permission of the Crown to keep on foot in England two battalions of Company's troops, each 500 strong, with its due proportion of officers, which might serve as a nucleus round which volunteers might gather, in order to be taught, ere they should be sent to India, some knowledge of their drill, and the rudiments, at least, of soldier-like habits. He further advised that the services of Colonel Coote and Colonel Forde should be rewarded by placing them at the head of these battalions respectively.

Last of all, he notices the distracted state of the Government Councils at Calcutta, and accounts for them. " The heart-burnings and disputes, which seem to have spread and overrun your settlement of Calcutta, arose, I must fear, originally from your appointment of Mr. Vansittart to the government of Bengal from another settlement, although his promotion was the effect of my recommendation. The appointment, therefore, of Mr. Spencer from Bombay, can only tend to inflame these dissensions, and to destroy all those advantages which the Company only can expect from harmony and unanimity abroad. The resignation of Messrs. Verelst, Cartier, and many other of the senior servants, which must be the consequence of Mr. Spencer's appointment, will deprive me of those very gentlemen on whose assistance I depend for re-establishing your affairs in Bengal."

Lord Clive was not, however, satisfied with pointing out defects: he avowed his determination, if rightly supported from home, to provide a remedy for them. After deprecating all attempts at extending too far the territorial dominion of the Company, and advising such a course of general policy as should convince the Nabob, whoever he might be, and his principal officers, that the Company had both the power and the will to protect them, not only against foreign enemies, but each against the unjust aggressions of the other, he thus expresses himself:—

" To carry this balance with an even hand, the strictest integrity will be necessary in every one who shall have a vote in your councils abroad. I found myself every day assaulted by large offers of presents, from the principal men of the province, not to support the Nabob in resolutions contrary to their interests; and from the Nabob, to sacrifice them to his capricious resentments.

" But even this conduct alone will not be sufficient to keep us from giving umbrage. During Mr. Vansittart's government, all your servants thought themselves entitled to take large shares in the monopolies of salt, beetle, and tobacco, the three articles, next to grain, of greatest consumption in the empire. The odium of seeing such monopolies in the hands of foreigners need not be insisted on; but this is not the only inconvenience : it is productive of another, equally, if not more prejudicial to the Company's interests ; it enables many of your servants to obtain, very suddenly, fortunes greater than those which in former times were thought a sufficient reward for a long continuance in your service. Hence these gentlemen, thus suddenly enriched, think of nothing but of returning to enjoy their fortunes in England, and leave your affairs in the hands of young men, whose sanguine expectations are inflamed by the examples of those who have just left them.

" This, therefore, will be the greatest difficulty which I shall have to encounter; to persuade, or, if necessary, to oblige your servants to be content with advantages much inferior to those which, by the prescription of some years, they may think themselves entitled to. Yet if this is not done, your affairs can never be settled on a judicious and permanent plan. My fortunes, my family, and the other advantages I may be possessed of, will naturally make me wish to accomplish my intentions for the Company's service abroad as soon as possible, that I may return to my native country, which, it cannot be imagined, that I quit without some regrets ; but if I should meet in your councils abroad men whom private interest may render averse to my maxims, I shall, perhaps, instead of settling your affairs as may be expected from me, find myself harassed and over-ruled in every measure by a majority against me in council.

" It therefore rests with the Court of Directors to consider, seriously, whether they should not intrust me with a dispensing power in the civil and political affairs; so that whensoever I may think proper to take any resolution entirely upon myself that resolution is to take place. The French Company gave Mr. Godeheu sole and absolute control over all their settlements to the east of the Cape of Good Hope, at a time when their affairs were not in a worse condition than ours are at present. In India we ourselves have had examples of supervisors. I myself was intrusted with great powers by the gentlemen of Madras, when I went down to Bengal against Suraj-u-Dowlah; the use which I made of these powers will, I hope, justify my opinion, that I may, without danger, be intrusted with an authority so highly necessary at present. The occasions of exerting it will rarely happen, but will certainly happen at times, when all may be lost for want of it. Moderation, I will venture to say, was always a part of my character in political concerns; and as a means to induce the gentlemen abroad to contract their views of private advantage within the bounds essentially necessary to the interests of the Company, the first step I shall take will be, to give up to them every commercial advantage, as I did during my last residence in Bengal. I need not mention that these advantages are, to a Governor, great, and adequate to his station.

" To prevent dissensions, I am willing to receive a military commission inferior to General Lawrence's; but that gentleman has received from the Court of Directors so very extensive a power over all their forces in India, that the presidency at which he resides, is, in fact, little less than the residence of a Governor-General over all your settlements in India. If ever the appointment of such an officer as Governor-general should become necessary, it is evident that he ought to be established in Bengal, as the greatest weight of your civil, commercial, political, and military affairs will always be in that province. It cannot, therefore, be expected that I should be subject to have any part of the military forces allotted for that province recalled or withheld from me at the will of an officer in another part of India; or that even the presence of that officer in Bengal should, in any way, interfere with my military authority in that province. It will likewise be necessary (at least until affairs in Bengal are restored to perfect tranquillity) that whatever troops, treasures, or other consignments may be destined from England to that presidency, shall not, as usual, be stopped and employed by any of the other presidencies at which they may chance to arrive in their passage towards the Ganges."

With the dictatorial powers here applied for, the Court of Directors did not judge it expedient to intrust Lord Clive; but they took a course which, for all practical purposes, gave promise of a happy result. A select committee was appointed at home, with power to supersede the authority of the President and Council; and such gentlemen being nominated to serve as were understood to be both personally and on principle attached to Clive, and steady advocates of his opinions, no serious opposition to his views could well be anticipated. The committee in question consisted of Lord Clive, General Carnac, Mr. Verelst, Mr. Sumner, Mr. Sykes,—of whom the two latter accompanied Lord Clive from England, and gave him, from first to last, an unwavering support.

CHAPTER XVIII.

Clive reaches Calcutta—Proceedings in Council.

THERE were one or two points which Clive was very desirous to settle previously to his departure for India. Foremost among these may be accounted the arrangement of a plan for the entire depression of the individual whom he hated with no ordinary rancour; and who, to do him justice, returned the feeling, if with less ostentation of bitterness, with at least as much of its reality. Clive had succeeded in excluding Mr. Sulivan from the chair by making such exclusion one of the terms on which alone he would consent to re-enter the service of the Company. He now besought his friends to use every possible exertion to shut him out from the direction altogether. In this he did not succeed; for Mr. Vansittart, immediately on his return to Eng land, took Mr. Sulivan's part, and inflamed, by so doing, into hostility the estrangement which had already begun between himself and Lord Clive. Clive's next proceeding—which proved more easy of accomplishment—was to separate himself from all political connexion with the parties in Parliament. His personal regard for Mr. Grenville continued unabated; and he desired the seven members whom he returned to the House of Commons to vote on all subjects as he himself would have done —that is, so as to strengthen the hands of his friend. But neither the Administration as such, nor Lord Bute and his partisans, exercised, at this time, any influence upon his sympathies. He was therefore well pleased to be set free from all ties except those of personal predilection, and acted with great judgment in the matter. Finally, his more private and family concerns, in some measure, arranged themselves. Lady Clive remained at home to superintend the education of his children; and of his estates, houses, and money—agents in whom he reposed confidence took charge. Thus relieved from anxiety in regard to matters in Europe, he turned his thoughts earnestly and exclusively to the East, whither he was proceeding, with no view to make additions to his already princely fortune, but simply and solely in order to accomplish great public good, and to encounter both obloquy and opposition in the process.

On the 4th of June, 1764, Lord Clive, attended by Messrs. Sumner and Sykes, embarked at Portsmouth on board the Kent, and just before sun-set the same evening the ship got under weigh. They had the satisfaction of knowing that preparations were in some measure made for the course of stern yet necessary reform on which they were about to enter. The Directors, convinced that the great moving cause of all the revolutions which had succeeded the first in the kingdom of Bengal was the expectation, encouraged by members of Council and others, of growing rich upon the plunder of newly-made Nabobs, had already issued an order that no more presents should on any account whatever be accepted by their servants from native princes or their ministers. They had followed up this regulation by transmitting a form of engagement, which all persons acting under their authority were required to ratify, and of which the effect was to bind the parties so signing to pay into the Company's treasury, on pain of dismissal, the full amount of such gifts as, subsequently to the receipt of the Court's order, might have been forced upon them. These facts were well known to Clive and his colleagues, who had besides ample time to discuss the defects of the existing system of management, and consider the means of remedy which presented themselves. And, as the best understanding subsisted among them, they were strengthened to undertake the task by the reflection, that, so long as they should act honestly and vigorously together, it was always in their power, by commanding a majority of votes, to command at the same time success, at least at the outset.

The outward voyage of the Kent, without being attended with any positive danger, was tedious and disagreeable. It occupied eleven months; and the ship, either compelled by stress of weather, or being forced to seek a supply of water and fresh provisions, put in at Rio Janeiro. It is well known that at this time the alliance between England and Portugal was, for obvious reasons, close and strict. Portugal having everything to fear from her nearest neighbour, could not look, except with extreme jealousy, at the family compact, which, whatever might be its object in other directions, exposed her independence to be assailed at any moment by the united forces of France and Spain. She therefore clung to England with a confiding tenacity, of which the stronger power took no undue advantage, and enlisted, by so doing, the sympathies of English statesmen of every party in her favour. Among others, Lord Clive seems to have bestowed upon her ticklish concerns some small share of his parliamentary care; and now, being brought into personal contact with the most important of her transatlantic settlements, he examined it with a soldier's eye, and made a report of its helpless state to the King's government. The report, which was conveyed in a private letter to Mr. Grenville, is eminently characteristic of the man :— " I should think myself," he says, " deserving of everlasting infamy if I did not, with a single battalion of infantry, make myself master of Rio Janeiro in 24 hours." Lord Clive, it will be observed, wrote and spoke on all occasions as he always felt, and generally acted, in extremes. IIis judgment in regard to the worthlessness of the defences of Rio Janeiro seems, however, to have been correct; and the IIome Government advertising the Cabinet of Lisbon of the fact, the works were put in a better state, and armed with guns less " unserviceable and honeycombed."

It was towards the end of April, 1765, ere the vessel in which Lord Clive had taken his passage entered the Hooghly. On the morning of the 3rd of May he himself reached Calcutta, and the same afternoon began to study the Minutes of Council, in order, as he expresses it, that " by seeing what had been done he might be able to form a clearer opinion of the plan of operations on which it would be necessary to act." IIe was not slow in discovering that a gross and flagrant breach had been committed of the Company's orders on a point concerning which no evasions or subterfuges could any longer be admitted. The Lapwing packet conveying the covenant, of which I have elsewhere spoken, as well as the Court's explanation of the same, had arrived at Calcutta on the 24th of January. From that day forth, therefore, practices heretofore connived at, because nowhere forbidden, became illegal; and parties falling into them lay open to the penalties which in the Court's letter were threatened. It further appeared that the letter in question had been read, criticised, and partially acted upon. It conveyed instructions for the regulation of the private trade, as well as urgent notes concerning the issue of batta, or field-allowances to the troops, and to these the Council paid some attention. But a third subject, more important than either of which the despatch treated, seemed to have been passed over in silence. Meer Jaffier died on the 6th of February, that is to say, thirteen days subsequently to the receipt of the communication which prohibited the Company's servants from accepting presents. Within a day or two of the decease of his father, Nujeem-ud-Dowlah was communicated with, and a bargain struck, whereby, on his engaging to pay to the Governor and Council the sum of 200,000*l.* sterling, his succession to the vacant throne was secured to him. Nothing could exceed the indignation of Clive when this atrocious fact forced itself on his notice. He saw that no terms could be kept with men who were capable of thus setting the declared will of their superiors at nought; and he took the earliest opportunity of convincing them that the powers which he had received from their common masters in London he was prepared to wield unflinchingly. On the 5th of May a meeting of Council was held; of the remarkable proceedings at which Clive, and Clive alone, must give an account. Having described in a letter to General Carnac how the different commands in the army were distributed, and corresponding rank bestowed upon its principal officers, he goes on to say :—

"After this matter was settled, I desired the Board would order those paragraphs relative to the power of the committee to be transmitted to the chiefs and council of the subordinate settlements, to the Commander-in-chief of the army, and to the two presidencies of Madras and Bombay, that they might know what powers the committee were invested with. I then acquainted the Board, that the committee was determined to make use of the power invested in them, to its utmost extent; that the condition of the country, and the very being of the Company made such a step absolutely necessary. Mr. Leycester seemed inclined to enter into a debate about the meaning and extent of those powers, but I cut him short, by informing the Board, that

I would not suffer any one to enter into the least discussion about the meaning of those powers; but that the committee alone were absolutely determined to be the sole and only judges; but that they were at liberty to enter upon the face of the consultations any minutes they thought proper, but nothing more. Mr. Johnstone desired that some other paragraphs of the letter might be sent to the different subordinates, &c., as tending, I believe, in his opinion, to invalidate those orders. Upon which I asked him, whether he would dare to dispute our authority? Mr. Johnstone replied, that he never had the least intention of doing such a thing; upon which there was an appearance of very long and pale countenances, and not one of the council uttered another syllable. After despatching the current business, the Board broke up, and to-morrow we sit in committee, when I make no doubt of discovering such a scene as will be shocking to human nature. They have all received immense sums for this new appointment, and are so shameless, as to own it publicly. Hence we can account for the motive of paying so little respect to me and the committee; and, in short, every thing of benefit to themselves they have in this hasty manner concluded, leaving to the committee the getting the covenants signed, which they say is ofsuch consequence, that they cannot think of settling any thing final about them until Lord Clive's arrival.

"Alas! how is the English name sunk! I could not avoid paying the tribute of a few tears to the departed and lost fame of the British nation (irrecoverably so, I fear). However, I do declare, by that Great Being who is the searcher of all hearts, and to whom we must be accountable, if there must be an hereafter, that I am come out with a mind superior to all corruption, and that I am determined to destroy those great and growing evils, or perish in the attempt.

"I hope, when matters are a little settled, to set out for the army; bringing with me full power for you and me to settle every thing for the best."

Bold, imperious, intolerant of contradiction, Clive was the very man to deal with a state of society so demoralized as that on which he had now fallen. It mattered nothing to him that the advocates of corruption pleaded his own example as the groundwork of the system on which they acted. He had arguments at command wherewith to rebut their reasoning, which, whatever weight they might receive from others, appeared perfectly satisfactory to himself. In the first place, he contended that the original conspiracy which broke the line of succession to the throne of Bengal could be considered as nothing more than an experiment. Large gifts were accepted on that occasion from Meer Jaffier, because everybody believed the wealth of the kingdom to be inexhaustible; but experience had demonstrated the fallacy of this opinion, and it became not more unjust than impolitic to burthen the successors of Meer Jaffier with obligations which none knew better than the members of Council, who imposed them, that they could not discharge except at the expense of ruin to the Nabob and incalculable damage to the interests of the Company. In the next place Clive affirmed that the overthrow of Suraj-u-Dowlah, and the elevation of Meer Jaffier, had been the work of the people of Bengal themselves, the English taking part in it as allies and subordinates only. It was not so with the deposition of Meer Jaffier, and still less with the advancement of the reigning Nabob to the throne; and in the case of Cossim Ali, however necessary his removal might have latterly become, he was clearly at the outset rather a sufferer from the wrongs of others than an abuser of the privileges which appertained to his office. The revolution, therefore, which had displaced his own protégé Clive condemned as uncalled for and iniquitous, which was only to be accounted for by looking to the cupidity of those who had been parties to it. But Clive, while he reprobated the whole transaction as a violation of policy and good faith, brought no special charges against the recipients of Cossim Ali's booty. They did what they were not prohibited from doing; they enriched themselves by a process which, however reprehensible, had not yet been condemned by the voice of authority. The case was different with regard to the transactions which accompanied the establishment of the reigning Nabob in his seat. In the face of a Court's order, the representatives of the Company had set up the crown of Bengal for sale, and put the purchase-money into their own pockets. They had hurried forward the transaction, too, with a precipitation which showed that they were aware of its illegality, and feared lest, by the arrival of the Committee, it might be interrupted.   Clive used no measured language in his condemnation of the whole proceeding, and looked anxiously about for means whereby to compel the chief actors in it to disgorge their ill-gotten gains.

Lord Clive had few friends in the Council.   General Carnac was, indeed, attached to him by the ties of old association, and Mr. Verelst, besides that his views were shown to be more sound than those of his colleagues in general, might be expected to go with the select committee, of which he had been nominated a member.   But all the rest, with here and there an exception—in which latter class I must not forget to state that Warren Hastings ranged himself—abhorred the new Governor's principles as much as they dreaded his power.   An attempt was therefore made to get up an opposition to the Committee, of which two members of Council, Messrs. Johnstone and Leycester, put themselves at the head.   It proved imminently unsuccessful.   I have already introduced Lord Clive to the reader's notice as chronicler of the circumstances which attended his first appearance at the Board.   The following portion of a letter, addressed on the 11th of May to Mr. Palk, at that time Governor of Madras, will show that the writer was not disposed to lose, by hesitation or delay, whatever advantages had accrued to him from an energetic commencement of his labours.   His business on the occasion here referred to was to exact from each of the gentlemen present a personal ratification of the covenant, which had been permitted to lie over since the 24th of January, and to send it forth to the out-stations, in order that it might receive the signatures of the chiefs of factories and their subordinates :—

" At the first meeting, the gentlemen began to oppose and treat me in the manner they did Vansittart, by disputing our power, and the meaning of the paragraph in the Company's general letter.   However, I cut that matter short, by telling them they should not be the judges of that power, nor would we allow them to enter into the least discussion about it ; but that they might enter their dissents in writing, upon the face of the consultations.   This brought matters to a conclusion, and spared us the necessity of making use of force, to put the Company's intentions into execution.   We arrived on Tuesday, and effected this on Thursday.   On Friday we held a committee ; and on Monday was read before the council the following resolution from the committee book :—'Resolved, that it is the opinion of this committee, that the covenants be executed immediately by the rest of the Council, and all the Company's servants.' After many idle and evasive arguments, and being given to understand they must either sign or be suspended the service, they executed the covenants upon the spot. From this you will see what I had the honour to inform you of, that I am determined upon an absolute reformation; but here we must act with caution, until a peace is established, which I do not despair of accomplishing during the rains.

"It gives me infinite concern to inform you that Mr. Spencer (of whom I had the highest opinion) is by no means the man of integrity or abilities that I took him to be ; being deeper in the mire than the rest, and who appears to me to have been seduced and led astray by Johnstone and Leycester, having never had any will or opinion of his own, since he came to the chair. Indeed, the dignity of governor is sunk even beyond contempt itself; and the name of Council only heard of in these parts. Would you believe that in his letters to the Nabob and others he has submitted to write, 'I and the Council ?'

"We are waiting the arrival of the Nabob and his ministry, to determine whether we shall suspend them (the obnoxious members) the service, or represent matters in a general light, leaving to the Directors to determine their state ; though I am persuaded they will never wait such a decision, having all of them received large fortunes, which they barefacedly confess, for absolutely and precipitately concluding the late treaty with the young Nabob ; not waiting for our approbation, or leaving it in our power to rectify the least tittle, without being guilty of a breach of faith.

"The large sums of money already received, and obligations given for the rest, on account of this treaty, are so very notorious through the whole town, and they themselves have taken such little pains to conceal them, that we cannot, without forfeiting our honour and reputation, possibly avoid a retrospection as far back as the receipt of the covenants and Meer Jaffier's death. If we should call upon you hereafter for the assistance of Messrs. Broke, Russell, Kelsall, Floyer, and two or three more, we are

persuaded your zeal for the service will not let you hesitate a
moment about sending them by the first conveyance. However,
you will keep the contents of this paragraph to yourself, till you
hear from the committee or me upon the subject."

The sale of the musnud, or throne of Bengal, was an affair
completed. A good deal of mystery, likewise, had been preserved by the chief agents in the transaction regarding the sums
of money which fell to the share of individuals ; and Clive,
though burning with anxiety to punish, and, if possible, strip
the delinquents of their ill-gotten gains, found difficulty in bringing the matter home to them in a moment. It was not so in
reference to the private trade, in which every man professing to
be in the service of the Company, whether white or black, member of council or junior writer, was engaged to an enormous extent. The three articles in which these persons chiefly dealt
were salt, beetle-nuts, and tobacco, of which the value may be
estimated when I state, that out of the duties, by no means im-
moderate, levied upon the two latter, and the monopoly which
they had from time immemorial enjoyed on the former, the Nabobs of Bengal derived no trivial portion of their revenues. To
a share in the profits arising from this trade none of the Company's servants ever thought of admitting the Company itself.
The general commerce was carried on by the exchange of goods
manufactured in Europe for Indian silks, cottons, and other commodities, which might be turned to account in European mar-
kets—or for specie, or specie's worth, which, being conveyed to
China, enabled the masters of ships to lay in their cargoes of
tea, the sale of which in London realized in a great measure their
dividends for the stockholders. The particular or private trade
was in articles of which the consumption went on in the country
itself, and the unfair advantages which they possessed in conducting it, enabled the Company's servants to drive every native
merchant out of the market. I have elsewhere taken occasion
to state, that so long as Clive presided over the affairs of Bengal,
this abuse, if not absolutely repressed, was kept within narrow
limits. But immediately on his departure the very semblance of
moderation was dropped ; and the consequences were such as the
course of this narrative has made apparent.

It is due to the Court of Directors to state that, mistaken in their views as they often were, they gave no countenance, but the reverse, to such proceedings. Many of their letters speak of the system in terms of strong condemnation ; and two in particular, written about this time, are expressed in language so becoming, that they well deserve transcription. But the reader, while he follows these, will do scant justice to the subject if he forget that the Court had made no motion towards raising the salaries of their servants in Bengal from the miserable pittances at which they had hitherto stood. It was manifest, likewise, from their manner of replying to Clive's suggestions on this subject, that the idea of disbursing largely out of their own funds met with little encouragement among them. Now Clive knew, what indeed could not but be known everywhere else, that to expect honesty from ill-paid functionaries, to whom safe opportunities of enriching themselves by underhand means are abundant, is to expect more than the frailty of human nature will sanction. What was he to do? On the one hand, his own sense of right, not less than his duty to the Company, required that at all hazards he should put a stop to the private trade system ; on the other, his knowledge of mankind assured him that all the regulations which he could frame would be snapped like the withes in the hand of the giant, unless the parties affected by them were assured in some other way of earning a competency.

Let me, however, before I go further, put the court in a fair light by transferring to these pages portions of two despatches which Clive received during the first year of what may be called his reform government of Bengal. The former, which is dated the 26th of April, 1765, refers to the arguments of those who endeavoured to defend their right to trade in the three commodities specified above, by reference to the old imperial firman or licence.

" Treaties of commerce are understood to be for the mutual benefit of the contracting parties. Is it then possible to suppose that the Court of Delhi, by conferring the privilege of trading free of customs, could mean an untaxed trade in the commodities of their own country at that period unpractised and unthought of by the English, to the detriment of their revenues and the ruin of their own merchants? We do not find such a construction was ever heard of till our own servants first invented it, and afterwards supported it by violence. Neither could it be claimed by the subsequent treaties with Meer Jaffier, or Cossim Ali, which were never understood to give one additional privilege of trade beyond what the firman expressed. In short, the specious arguments used by those who pretended to set up a right to it convince us they did not want judgment, but virtue to withstand the temptation of suddenly amassing a great fortune, although acquired by means incompatible with the peace of the country, and their duty to the Company.

" Equally blameable were they who, acknowledging they had no right to it, and sensible of the ill consequences resulting from assuming it, have, nevertheless, carried on this trade, and used the authority of the Company to obtain, by a treaty exacted by violence, a sanction for a trade to enrich themselves, without the least regard or advantage to the Company, whose forces they employed to protect them in it.

" Had this short question been put, which their duty ought first to have suggested, ' Is it for the interest of our employers ?' they would not have hesitated one moment about it; but this criterion seems never once to have occurred.

" All barriers being thus broken down between the English and the country government, and everything out of its proper channel, we are at a loss how to prescribe means to restore order from this confusion ; and being deprived of that confidence which we hoped we might have placed in our servants, who appear to have been the actors in these strange scenes, we can only say, that we rely on the zeal and abilities of Lord Clive, and the gentlemen of the Select Committee, to remedy these evils. We hope they will restore our reputation among the country powers, and convince them of our abhorrence of oppression and rapaciousness."

In a second letter, of date 19th of February, 1766, the Court again writes—

" With respect to the treaty with Nujeem-ud-Dowlah, it is proper here to insert, at length, the fifth article, which runs in these words :—' I do ratify and confirm to the English the privilege granted them by their firman, and several husbul-hookums, of carrying on their trade, by means of their own dustucks, free from all duties, taxes, or impositions, in all parts of the country, except in the article of salt, on which the duty of two and a half per cent. is to be levied on the Rowana or Hooghley market price.' This fifth article is totally repugnant to our own order, contained in our general letter, by the Kent and Lapwing, dated the 1st of June, 1764; in which we not only expressed our abhorrence of an article in the treaty with Meer Jaffier, literally corresponding with the present fifth article, but in positive terms directed you, in concert with the Nabob, to form an equitable plan for carrying on the inland trade, and transmit the same to us, accompanied by such explanations and remarks as might enable us to give our sentiments and directions thereupon. We must remind you, too, that in our said general letter we expressly directed, that our orders, in our letter of the 8th of February preceding, which were to put a final and effectual end to the inland trade in salt, beetle-nut, and tobacco, and in all other articles produced and consumed in the country, should remain in force, until an equitable and satisfactory plan could be found and adopted. As, therefore, there is not the least latitude given you for concluding any treaty whatsoever respecting this inland trade, we must and do consider what you have done as an express breach and violation of our orders, and as a detrimental resolution to sacrifice the interest of the Company, and the peace of the country, to lucrative and selfish views.

" This unaccountable behaviour put an end to all confidence in those who made this treaty, and forces us to resolve on measures for the support of our authority, and the preservation of the Company. We do therefore pronounce, that every servant concerned in that trade stands guilty of a breach of his covenants with us and of our orders; and in consequence of this resolution, we positively direct, that if that treaty is now subsisting, you make a formal renunciation, by some solemn act to be entered on your records, of all right under the said treaty, or otherwise, to trade in salt, beetle-nut, and tobacco; and that you transmit this renunciation of that part of the treaty, in form, to the Nabob, in the Persian language. Whatever government may be established, or whatever unforeseen occurrences may arise, it is our resolution to prohibit, and we do absolutely forbid, this trade of salt, beetle-nut, and tobacco, and of all articles that are not for export and import, according to the spirit of the firman, which does not in the least give any latitude whatsoever for carrying on such an inland trade ; and, moreover, we shall deem every European concerned therein, directly or indirectly, guilty of a breach of his covenants, and direct that he be forthwith sent to England, that we may proceed against him accordingly. And every native who shall avail himself of our protection to carry this trade on, without paying all the duties due to the government equally with the rest of the Nabob's subjects, shall forfeit that protection, and be banished the settlement ; we direct, that these resolutions be signified publicly throughout the settlement."

This letter, of the abstract justice of which it is impossible to speak too highly, was written under a misapprehension of the circumstances of the country, and of the end to which Clive's able policy was tending. I have inserted it only for the purpose of showing that, however they might err in regard to the remedies fit to be applied, the Court of Directors were not at this time disposed to sanction the iniquitous proceedings of their servants ; and it is proper that the reader should be fully alive to this fact, otherwise he will fail to notice the true source of the persecutions to which Lord Clive, after his return to England, became exposed. But before it reached Clive's hands he had taken his own course ; and knowing it to be the best which under existing circumstances lay open to him, he declined to be drawn out of it. I will endeavour to explain, in few words, what he desired to do, what he actually did, and what were the consequences, immediate as well as remote, of the arrangements into which he entered.

CHAPTER XIX.

Clive's reforms continued.

IT was Lord Clive's deliberate opinion that no person employed in the service of the East India Company should be permitted, under any circumstances, to embark in trade on his own account. He believed, with Sir Thomas Roe, that the Company would gain far more than individuals by the arrangement. Difficulties would doubtless attend the attempt to eradicate a system which was as old as the existence of the Company itself; but there was needed in his opinion, only firmness, combined with liberality on the part of the Home authorities, to overcome them. In the first place, a revision of salaries would be indispensable. To every youth entering the service, whether as a civilian or a soldier, such pay must be allowed as would enable him to support, with economy, his proper position in India, and assure to him— with the fair chance of promotion which he would be supposed to enjoy—a reasonable prospect of retiring after he should have attained to middle life, with a decent competency to the land of his birth. In the next place, the practice of making promotion depend altogether on seniority ought to be set aside. In ordinary cases men of faithful and long service ought never to be passed over; but to adhere absolutely to the rule of age was to take away all spur to exertion, and to render inevitable a steady supply of mediocrity in places where more than mediocrity might sometimes be required. On the other hand, Clive conceived that excess of remuneration to the junior ranks, whether of the civil or military branch of the Company's service, could not but operate prejudicially; and, if the argument held good where regular pay alone was given, it told with infinitely greater weight against arrangements which threw young men in the way of accumulating, by commerce or otherwise, large fortunes in the course of a few years. Individuals so favoured never found it worth while to hang on, under the pressure of an unhealthy climate, in order that they might ultimately succeed to places of power to which no proportionate emolument was attached. No sooner had they realized as much as promised to support them at home in the style to which their ambition pointed, than they threw up the service; which was thus left to be managed by a succession of raw lads, under the control of functionaries either too rich to care very much about it, or too greedy of gain to withdraw their attention from the management of their own business. But, to counterbalance this clipping at one end, Lord Clive was most desirous of adding largely to the other. As men rose from the rank of junior to that of senior merchant, their pay should be increased. When they went forth as clerks into the remote factories, an increase ought to take place on a still more liberal scale; and finally, as Members of Council and Government secretaries, it was fitting that they should be raised not only above the annoyance of everything like want for the present, but be relieved of all anxiety in regard to the future.

Of the working of this principle as he desired to apply it to the army, I shall take occasion to speak when I come to describe his dealings with that body. My present business is with the civil service exclusively, which he urged the Court of Directors to put upon a proper footing, pointing out to them that their position in India was wholly changed, and that rules which had answered imperfectly for the guidance of commercial establishments were altogether inapplicable to the condition of a substantive and political power. But the time had not yet arrived for the accomplishment of so important a change. Neither the Directors nor the Proprietors were able to realize the fact that they occupied ground in India very different from that which it had entered into their most sanguine anticipations to desire; and while they saw and denounced the wrongs of which their trading representatives were guilty, they refused to close the door of commerce against them by such a process as Lord Clive recommended. How was he, under such circumstances, to proceed? He could not say to Members of Council, " You must live henceforth on your salaries. The Company forbids you to trade. I have no power except to see that their orders are carried into effect. You must therefore do as well as you can with your 300*l.* per annum apiece, or resign the service." And as to the writers, the junior and senior merchants, and so forth, all these were equally secured against the application of so stern a rule by the poverty of the stipends which they drew out of the Company's treasury. Clive pondered the subject carefully, and arrived at the conclusion that, being debarred from doing that which was positively best, he was bound to do the best which under the circumstances might be practicable. He caused an order of Committee to be issued, which took away, at a stroke, all power in individuals to grant dustucks or passes for the transport of goods, and restricted the right of issuing such to certain constituted authorities. By this arrangement the management and control of all private as well as public trade was kept in the hands of the government. A stop was likewise put to the vicious proceedings of those who, calling themselves the native agents of European traders, had been in the habit, without exhibiting any passes at all, of forcing the Nabob's revenue stations; and such a check was imposed upon the entire system of private trade, that, wherever carried on, it could not any longer operate to the serious injury of any one. At the same time as the ordinary sources of the revenues of individuals were thus effectually dried up, Clive found himself obliged to make some compensation for the injury, and he adopted the following expedient to do so.

Of the three branches of private trade to which the mercantile men of Bengal looked as repaying them for exile, and the many privations which attend it, the trade in salt was by far the most important. Clive determined to convert that which had been hitherto a cause of unmixed evil into an instrument of good. With this view he arranged that it should become a monopoly in the hands of the Governor for the time being, and the members of Council and other specified functionaries, and that the profits henceforth should be divided among them in equal shares, according to the stations and rank in the service which those entitled to partake in it might respectively hold. Among these the Governor was to reserve an entire portion to himself; a second portion was to fall to the members of Council collectively; a third took in colonels of the first rank, chiefs of factories, and such like; a fourth became the property of field-officers, chaplains, &c.; and the gross value of the whole may be guessed when I state that Clive estimated a colonel's portion—he being but one out of a numerous body—at not less than 7000*l.* sterling per annum.

Clive, however, was not so careful of the interests of individuals as to be forgetful all this while of the Company's claims. The salt monopoly, be it remembered, had from time immemorial been possessed by the Nabob. So long as the Nabob should continue to collect the revenues, he was entitled to the duty, whatever that might be, which the makers or growers of the commodity had been accustomed to pay. But Clive was already meditating that master-stroke of policy which he soon afterwards completed; and he drew up his regulations so that they might agree rather with what was to be than with what actually existed. For example, he decreed that the Company should receive as its share of the monopoly an *ad valorem* duty of 35 per cent.; which, allowing 10 per cent. as profit on the product, and 5 per cent. to cover losses, would give one half of the gain to the ruling body and the other half to their servants. The letter which I quoted in a previous chapter shows that the Court of Directors were not satisfied with this, to them, most advantageous arrangement; but Clive had scarcely begun to put his own law in force ere he received proof that the individuals whom he desired to serve were prepared to resist both it and him to the uttermost.

Another of Lord Clive's reforms had reference to the constitution of the ruling body, which he looked upon as too numerous in itself for any practical purpose, and which he particularly objected to on account of the manner of disposing of their time, which custom had sanctioned in a large proportion of the members. The old constitution of Bengal required that the government should be carried on by a President and sixteen councillors. The number sixteen Clive held to be preposterously great; and he was fortified in the conviction by observing that most of these left the business of government to be transacted by four or five individuals; while, being appointed to the charge of factories, or becoming supervisors of provinces, they themselves proceeded into the interior that they might devote their energies to the more agreeable occupations of private trade, or the levying of contributions, by a shorter process, on the native princes and nobility. Nor was it the least objectionable feature in this arrangement that the gentlemen thus employed at a distance still kept their seats at the council-board, and were ready, as often as occasion required, to come down and vote in support of the faction to which they belonged. Clive had not been a careless observer of the current of public events under the administration of Mr. Vansittart. He saw how that gentleman was perpetually controlled and thwarted by the votes of persons who had no opportunity of examining the merits of many of the questions which they came from afar to decide; and, looking forward to the time when the extraordinary powers of the select committee would cease, he proposed that the council should hereafter consist of not more than 12 members at the most. The point, however, which he was most anxious to settle in reference to this matter was, that, be the members of council many or few, none of them should be permitted to accept stationary offices in the interior. The Commander-in-chief must of course go with the army whenever it should take the field, but seats in the Council ought not for the future to be tenable by the chiefs of factories or supervisors. As might be expected, innovations such as these were looked at with extreme abhorrence by the parties whose interests they thwarted. Yet the opposition which he met with here was but as a breath of summer air when compared with the hurricane which fell upon him so soon as he began to inquire into past abuses.

I am at a loss how to convey, in words of my own, any idea to the minds of my readers of the state of moral feeling which appears to have held sway at this time among the English residents in Bengal. The Court of Directors have, however, described it so accurately, that in justice to my subject I am constrained to make an extract from one of their letters, written soon after the graver of the abuses had been put down:—" When we look back," they say, " to the system that Lord Clive and the gentlemen of the Select Committee found established, it presents to us a subah (a Nabob) disarmed, with a revenue of almost two millions sterling, (for so much seems to have been left, exclusive of our demands on him,) at the mercy of our servants, who had adopted an unheard-of ruinous principle, of an interest distinct from the Company.   This principle showed itself in laying their hands upon every thing they did not deem the Company's property.

"In the province of Burdwan, the resident and his council took an annual stipend of near 80,000 rupees per annum from the Rajah, in addition to the Company's salary.   This stands on the Burdwan accounts, and we fear was not the whole; for we apprehend it went further, and that they carried this pernicious principle even to the sharing with the Rajah of all he collected beyond the stipulated malguzary, or land revenue, overlooking the point of duty to the Company, to whom, properly, everything belonged that was not necessary for the Rajah's support.   It has been the principle, too, on which our servants have falsely endeavoured to gloss over the crime of their proceedings, on the accession of the present Subah; and we fear would have been soon extended to the grasping the greatest share of that part of the Nabob's revenues which was not allotted to the Company.   In short, this principle was directly undermining the whole fabric; for whilst the Company were sinking under the burden of the war, our servants were enriching themselves from those very funds that ought to have supported the war."

Determined to lay the axe to the root of the tree, and bent upon exposing to public scorn the delinquencies of those high in office, Clive took the bold step at this time of inviting the Nabob, Mahomed Reza Khan his minister, and some of the principal bankers of Moorshedabad, including his ancient comrade Roydullub, to visit him in Calcutta.   They all came, and the disclosures which they made more than confirmed the worst suspicions he had harboured.   Of the Nabob himself Clive saw enough to be convinced that he was in every respect unfitted for his situation.   His ministers, as well as the dependants whom he encouraged to come about him, were equally wanting in talent or integrity; but that which gave to Clive the greatest amount of annoyance was the open way in which this miserable puppet and his satellites brought charges of corruption against the most influential persons in the Company's service, which the latter were unable to refute.   As a specimen of these, the Nabob reported officially to Clive, that since his father's death a distribution had taken place of 20 lacs of rupees by Mahomed Reza Khan, for the purpose of securing such interest as should maintain him in his situation, and that members of the Council had participated in these gifts. This was too serious an accusation to be passed by without a strict investigation; and the matter was accordingly discussed in open Council. The parties implicated sought to defend themselves by accusing Clive and the select committee of acting from the worst motives. " It seems," says Mr. Johnstone, in a minute bearing date the 17th of June, 1765, "the aim of the select committee to render the proceedings of the late President and Council, if possible, obnoxious, instead of striving to promote the cordiality so much to be wished. To what cause must we attribute this temper of the committee? One would almost think they were piqued to find the interest of the Company so well secured before their arrival; only they must know that their coming at all was doubtful, and the gentlemen who had felt the defects of the former treaty were full as well qualified to remedy them in the new one, and have no doubt their masters will approve their services. I have heard that the Governor has expressed much chagrin that the affair of his jaghire has been settled, according to his agreement with the Company, without his interposition, though a better opportunity could not have occurred to get it done. Mr. Spencer, than whose merit none stands in a fairer light with the Company, was, if I may so call him, *the darling of that party—of that party which in England opposed Lord Clive and the gentlemen of the committee.* Any attack of him or his measure is an attack of the party who espoused him; and though I would not assert that any such sentiments influenced any member of the board, yet I cannot help being surprised at the uncommon neglect and disregard shown to Mr. Spencer by Lord Clive."

A more ill-advised species of attack than this upon a man of Lord Clive's iron nerve and strong feelings cannot well be conceived. The allusion to a matter which did disturb him, and on account of which he had just reason to be disturbed—the uncalled—for interference of Mr. Spencer in the matter of his jaghire, which, if Mr. Johnstone spoke true, appeared to have been suggested by Clive's enemies at home—excited his warm indignation. He recorded a minute in reply, which spoke his mind plainly; and, finding that neither that nor anything else short of extreme measures would do, he used the power with which he was invested by suspending Mr. Johnstone, Mr. Spencer, and several others of the senior civil officers, from the service. All these, as a matter of course, became forthwith his personal enemies ; and most of them sailing to England, and purchasing largely of India stock, found an opportunity, as will be shown by and by, of making him feel that they were such. But in the mean while he went forward without faltering in his course of stern but necessary reform. His temper was often ruffled, his mind wearied, his body fatigued, his spirits depressed—yet none of these things could stop him in his honourable career. " Let me but have health sufficient," he says, in a letter to General Carnac, " to go through with the reformation we intend, and I shall die with satisfaction and in peace."

CHAPTER XX.

Treaty with the Nabob—Grant of the Dewannee—Correspondence.

In bringing these several results to bear—in putting a stop to the iniquitous practice in high places of receiving bribes—in striking at the root of the system of private trade, alike fatal to the prosperity of the country and injurious to the Company's interests—in bringing back to the capital a swarm of European adventurers, who, under various denominations, were spread through the interior, and preyed upon the weaknesses of all with whom they came in contact—in checking the insolence of the native agents, and putting the commerce of the country once more upon an intelligible footing,—Clive had accomplished more in two short months than the most sanguine of his admirers ventured to expect from the whole of his administration.   But his views of civil reform did not stop there.   He had long foreseen, and more than once predicted, that the farce of maintaining at the Company's expense a government which was unable either to protect itself from foreign enemies, or to manage its own internal affairs, could not continue long; and, conceiving that the proper moment was come for putting an end to the absurdity, he set himself, with characteristic ardour, to accomplish that important object.   The circumstances under which he acted were these :—

I have abstained from entering into a detailed account of the military operations which ensued upon the massacre of Patna, and the retreat of Cossim Ali into the territories of Oude.   These are not so intimately connected with the subject of the present narrative as to require that I should deviate from this rule further than by stating, that they involved the Bengal government in a very heavy expense, and threatened at one time to become interminable.   The vizier could not, indeed, even after Cossim Ali joined him, keep the field against the English.   He sustained repeated checks, and was at length driven from Lucknow itself. There remained for him, after this, no other course than submission; and having given time to Meer Cossim and a European adventurer named Sumroo, who was supposed to have been the chief instigator of the Nabob's cruelties, to escape into the country of the Rohillas, he opened a communication with General Carnac, and professed himself anxious for peace. There can be no doubt that tidings of Clive's arrival in India helped to hurry forward this consummation. Clive's name among the natives was that of a man irresistible in war. The title which he had received from the Nabob of the Carnatic, in commemoration of his exploits on that side of the peninsula, had followed him to Hindostan; and in Bengal, and indeed as far as the limits of the Mogul Empire extended, Sabat Jung's fame was everywhere spread abroad. But Clive's policy, like that of every other Englishman who has much distinguished himself in the field, was pacific. He knew what war was, and could not desire, except in the last extremity, to incur its hazards and force on its innumerable evils. He therefore wrote to Carnac, advising him to encourage by all means the friendly disposition of the Vizier, and promised to come up in order to assist in the arrangement of a permanent treaty, as soon as the state of affairs in Calcutta would permit. "I hope," he says, in a letter bearing date the 20th of May, 1765, "15 or 20 days will enable me to put affairs in such a channel that the gentlemen may go on with the reformation during my absence, and upon my arrival we must heartily set about a peace; for the expense is now become so enormous (no less than 10 lacs per mensem, civil and military), that the Company must inevitably be undone if the Mahrattas or any other power should invade Bahar and Bengal; for it will then be impossible to raise money sufficient to continue the war. This is a very serious consideration with me, and will, I make no doubt, strike you in the same light."

In pursuance of this resolution, Clive no sooner brought matters into shape at Calcutta than he set out to join Carnac at Benares. He had, however, important business to settle at Moorshedabad, whither the Nabob with his ministers had returned, and he resolved to take that city on his way; for a slight personal acquaintance with Nujeem-ud-Dowlah had sufficed to convince him that the young man was wholly disqualified, both by the natural weakness of his character and the total absence of cultivation from his intellect, to conduct the affairs of government for one day. It was clear that he must always be the tool of somebody. But, indeed, the relations between the Nabob and the Company were become by this time so entangled, that no exercise of ability on the part of the former could cause the machine to go smoothly. Clive conceived that the time had come for applying a decisive remedy to the disease. Considering that the English had already taken upon themselves the military defence of the kingdom, that they were become masters of its trade, and lords to all intents and purposes of its revenues, he came to the conclusion that the surest means of preventing wrong to individuals, as well as guarding against a breach of friendship between the two governments, would be to take all the power into his own hands, leaving to the Nabob only the shadow. To his great satisfaction, perhaps a little to his surprise, he found that there was no indisposition in the Nabob to act upon the suggestion. On the 9th of July he had written from Moorshedabad to inform the select committee that the durbar or administrative council of the Nabob was settled according to their wishes. Mahomed Reza Khan, with two other public men in whom the English had confidence, were accepted by Nujeem-ud-Dowlah as his ministers, and a set of regulations were drawn up and signed, in accordance with which the business of the kingdom should henceforth be conducted. But, even while penning the letter which communicated this intelligence, Clive felt that matters could not stop there. The continued existence of two independent governments in the same country at the same time was impossible; and he, who perfectly understood this, lost no time in getting rid of the difficulty. A second letter to the committee, dated the 11th of July, contains the following statements: —" We have often lamented that the gentlemen of the Council, oy precipitating the late treaty, had lost the most glorious opportunity that could ever happen of settling matters upon that solid and advantageous footing for the Company which no temporary invasion could endanger. The true and only security for our commerce and territorial possessions in this country is, in a manner, always to have it in our power to overawe the very

Nabob we are bound by treaty to support. A maxim contrary to this has of late been much adopted; and from that fundamental error, as I may call it, have sprung the innumerable evils, or at least deficiencies, in our government, which, I have now the pleasure to inform you, are in a fair way of being perfectly removed.

" The Nabob, upon my representation of the great expense of such an army as will be necessary to support him in his government, the large sums due for restitution, and to the navy, together with an annual tribute, which he will be under a necessity of paying to the King, hath consented, and I have agreed, provided it should obtain your approbation, that all the revenues of the country shall be appropriated to those purposes, 50 lacs of rupees excepted. Out of this sum are to be defrayed all his expenses of every nature and denomination. Mahomed Reza Khan, however, being of a disposition extremely timorous, is desirous of having the payment of the cavalry and sepoys pass through his hands, though included in the said 50 lacs. This, I think, will be complied with.

" I am of opinion also, that certain stipends, out of the above-mentioned sum, should be fixed for the Begum, for the Chuta Nabob, and for the rest of the Nabob's brothers and nephews, Miriam's* son included; or else we must be subject to frequent complaints from those quarters; for I am persuaded that the dependants and parasites of the present Nabob will always keep him in distress, be his income what it may. Although the sum proposed to be stipulated for the Nabob, considering the present great expenses and demands, may appear large, yet, by what I now learn, his expense exceeds the sum to be allowed; and although it is certain that neither his education nor abilities will enable him to appear to any advantage at the head of these great and rich provinces, yet, I think, we are bound in honour to support the dignity of his station, so far as is consistent with the true interest of the Company.

" The particulars of this matter may be further adjusted in my absence by Mr. Sykes, to whom I have communicated my ideas,

---

* Miriam or Meeran, the eldest son of Meer Jaffier, had perished, as I have elsewhere described, and his son was in consequence the rival of Nujeem-ud-Dowlah for the throne.

if the plan be approved of by the select committee; and the whole may be finally concluded to our satisfaction, upon the Company's being appointed the King's Duan, who will be empowered, by the nature of their office, as well as by the King's consent, to settle every point."

Of the character of the prince thus pensioned into insignificance, a just estimate will be formed after reading Clive's account of the light in which the projected change was viewed by him:—" He received the proposal of having a sum of money for himself and household at his will with infinite pleasure, and the only remark he made upon leaving me was, ' Thank God, I shall now have as many dancing-girls as I please.' "

So far a large measure of success had attended Clive's endeavours. A stop was put to numerous abuses at Calcutta. The Company's relations with the Nabob were placed upon a more intelligible footing, and both parties had reason to be pleased with the arrangement. The last sentence in his letter of the 11th shows, however, that Clive looked beyond the point to which he had now attained; and he lost no time in seeking to realize the scheme which had long, though indistinctly, been pondered. As a step towards the accomplishment of this scheme, he desired to conclude a peace, on honourable terms, with the Vizier. For this purpose he proceeded to Benares, and on the 2nd of August, he and Sujah-u-Dowlah had their first meeting. It proved eminently satisfactory to both. The Vizier, expecting to be treated as one native power treats another which it may have overcome in war, was as much surprised as delighted at the modest bearing of the conqueror. He gladly consented to surrender the province of Allahabad, of which the annual revenue was estimated at 10 lacs, or 100,000*l.* sterling, and he offered no objection to the loss of Corah likewise, should this further sacrifice be required, though the revenues of Corah came up to 18 lacs. Besides this, he agreed to pay to the Company 600,000*l.* as compensation for expenses incurred in the war, and was grateful for being allowed to make good the payment in two equal instalments. Everything, moreover, appears to have been done in the best spirit. "His expressions of joy and gratitude on the occasion," writes Clive to the select committee, "were many and warm. Such an instance of generosity in a victorious enemy exceeded his most sanguine expectations, and we doubt not will be the foundation of that union and amity which we wish to secure." But Clive's tour of negotiation was not yet ended. After ratifying the treaty with the Vizier, he pushed forward to Allahabad, where the fallen Emperor, the representative of a long and illustrious race of conquerors, waited under the protection of an English brigade to receive him. Clive and Shah Alum met for the first time on the 9th of August, when the demands of the Emperor were innumerable. He required that an arrear of thirty-two lacs of rupees, due to him, as he alleged, from the Nabob of Bengal, should be paid up. This was refused, as well as an extravagant claim on the score of annual tribute; but it was finally settled that his Majesty should receive the annual sum of 26 lacs per annum out of the revenues of Bengal, Bahar, and Orissa; and that the provinces of Corah and Allahabad, yielding between them 28 lacs more, should be made over to him in perpetuity. This done, it became the turn of the representatives of the East India Company to put in their claims. They were acceded to without hesitation, and included firmans or deeds which established the right of holding for ever the lands round Madras and elsewhere which had been assigned to them by the Nabob of the Carnatic, and gave them full possession in proprietary of the Northern Circars. The revenue of Clive's jaghire, also, whenever it should lapse, was secured to the Company. But the most important article of all was that of which Lord Clive, writing to one of his correspondents, thus speaks:—" We then presented the King with two arzies (petitions), desiring he would grant to Nujeem-ud-Dowlah the Nizamut of Bengal, Bahar, and Orissa; and to the Company the Dewannee of the same provinces; to both of which his Majesty has signed his fiat, and the proper instruments for both are now drawing out."

It is impossible to over-estimate the importance to the East India Company, and indeed to the English nation, of this arrangement. The Dewannee, as I have elsewhere taken occasion to explain, included the right of collection and general management of the whole of the province or kingdom over which it extended; and, great as the power of the sword may be, especially in the East, he who holds the purse-strings commands the means of directing the sword in its gyrations. And if this rule held in native states, where the Nizamut retained its original prerogatives, much more stringent was the rule in Bengal, where a previous treaty had reduced the Nabob's influence to the shadow of a shade. The Nizamut, let it be borne in mind, included the right of arming and commanding troops, of managing the police, and administering civil and criminal law throughout the country. Now the treaty of the 11th of July had divested Nujeem-ud-Dowlah of the whole of these prerogatives, and settled him as a pensioner on the bounty of the Company. His name indeed still remained; the English feeling that it might be useful in case circumstances should threaten to bring them into collision with the French or Dutch. But of power not a shred rested with him—none at least beyond that which they in their generosity might be inclined to concede. Moreover, most of the abuses attendant on the commercial operations of the Company's servants were effectually struck at. When the question of payment of duties came to be agitated between individuals on the one hand and the Company on the other, there was little doubt to which side the balance would lean; and private trade, to whatever extent conducted, must, it was agreed, be managed henceforth as the interests of the governing body should require. By many brilliant exploits in the field, by the application of rare administrative talents to the adjustment of their affairs, Clive had often made the Company his debtor; but in this last act he surpassed himself. The signing of the deed which secured to the Company the right of collecting and managing the public revenues of Bengal, Bahar, and Orissa, raised them at once to the condition of a substantive Indian power. It was the first great step in that march of dominion which has since carried them from Cape Comorin to the Indus, and seems destined, sooner or later, to spread the English language and the civilization and the faith of England over the whole of Central Asia; and yet no ceremony was ever performed in the East with less of the parade of circumstance and show. A common bell-tent, pitched in an open field, served for the hall of state, in which the Emperor of Hindostan should admit to an audience the successful English general; and a few cushions laid upon an ordinary dining-table constituted the throne where the Mogul sat, to convey, by a stroke of his pen, to a company of merchants from the west, the sovereignty over a kingdom of which the population did not at that time fall short of 15 millions of souls.

Clive knew that he had wrought a good work. His own vigorous understanding assured him of this, and his chief anxiety was that it should be perpetuated. Neither had his been a war against prejudices. He had smitten down abuses in high places; and though the device by which he accomplished his purpose may appear clumsy to us who live in a world a century older than that which he inhabited, a moment's attentive consideration of the necessities of his case will force from us an acquiescence in its fitness. The pains which he took in his dealings with the native princes to conform on all occasions to the long established customs of the country, marked him for a statesman as prudent as he was bold. Had he chosen to act upon a different principle, the power of gratifying a misplaced vanity was quite within his reach. Bengal, Bahar, and Orissa, and indeed the kingdom of Oude likewise, had been conquered by the sword; and with the sword he might have kept them. But the open assumption of royalty in the name of England, besides that it would have combined against him the whole of the native powers, must have involved England herself in immediate disputes with every other European nation which had a commercial settlement in the provinces. France could hardly be expected to hold Chandernagore, nor Holland Chinchura, at the mere will of the English East India Company; and France and Holland, as allies of the Emperor of Hindostan, might have given great annoyance. Whereas, by adhering strictly to recognised usage, and accepting only such powers as the Emperor had a right to confer,—by observing all the customary forms of vassalage, and maintaining the ostensible Nizamut in the person of the Nabob, he took away ground of complaint from both natives and Europeans, and made himself absolute without appearing to do so. If the device appear clumsy, perhaps ridiculous, when looked at without considering the circumstances which advised it, its wisdom, taking these into account, admits of no question. Nor can his arrangements for the suppression of abuses among European functionaries be spoken of in different terms. Let us not forget that the Company had refused to raise the salaries of their servants to an amount at all corresponding with the exigences of their position, while they required at the same time that these same servants should not, under any circumstances, mix themselves up with the internal trade of the country. Now Clive could not expect members of Council to content themselves with salaries of 300*l.* a-year; nor was it possible to throw back senior and junior merchants, warehousemen, writers, and such like, on the pittances which were doled out to them from Leadenhall-street. But while he compelled these latter classes to be content, with such additions to their pay as a legitimate commerce afforded, he took away from the former every temptation to trade at all, by dividing among them a large portion of the proceeds of the government monopoly in salt. The government share of the profits arising from this branch of trade was, to be sure, on after consideration, commuted for an annual payment of 100,000*l.*; nevertheless, the right to the monopoly remained where from time immemorial it had been—in the government; and Clive, by the manner in which he dealt with it, did injury to no one. But Clive was not content with this. He entertained too mean an opinion of human nature, as it showed itself at least in Bengal, to leave to the principal gainers from this traffic any right of interference in its management. He fixed the places to which the salt should be brought for sale; he settled the price at which, be the season what it might, the article should be sold; and he passed a regulation by which all details of business, the borrowing of money, the raising of capital by subscription, the making of bye-laws, and indeed every other transaction which could be required as pertaining to barter, were intrusted to a sub-committee of four. It was Clive's especial wish that from becoming a member of this sub-committee the Governor should be prohibited. In all his communications, as well with the Court of Directors as with his personal friends belonging to their body, he pressed this point with great earnestness. He saw in it the best preservative that could be devised against a recurrence to practices which, though he had possessed influence enough to put them down, were but too likely to revive under a less energetic successor; and he was the more anxious on this head because, in spite of the weeding which it had undergone, the majority of the old council was still against him. It appears, too, that about this time one member at least of the select Committee began to play fast and loose ; and unfortunately he was the very man to whom, as much at his own suggestion as because of the good opinion generally entertained of him, Clive had been instructed to deliver over the government whenever he should feel inclined to relieve himself of the burthen. But it is best, in such a case, to let the chief actor in the complicated drama speak for himself. I therefore subjoin two letters—one addressed to a Mr. Salvadore, which describes the general results of Clive's negotiations with the native powers ; the other to his friend, Mr. Walsh, wherein the writer's views of the characters of individuals are stated, and suggestions thrown out in regard to measures which in his opinion ought to be adopted if the Company desired to keep the Bengal provinces from falling back into a state of anarchy.

To Mr. Salvadore he writes on the 25th of September, 1765, the following letter :—

" If I was to dwell upon the situation of the Company's affairs in Bengal, both civil and military, a volume would not be sufficient. However, I have the satisfaction of informing you, that I have already made a great progress towards reforming those enormous abuses of power which cry aloud for redress. The inhabitants have been laid under contribution by both civil and military, their goods taken from them at an under price, and presents of money have either been extorted from them, or given for interfering in the affairs of government by insisting on men of high employments being turned out, and others appointed in their room. The gentlemen having the revenues of the country, amounting to upwards of 3,000,000*l.* per annum at their command, were making such hasty strides towards independency, that in two years' time I am persuaded the Company would not have had one servant upon this establishment above the rank of a writer. In short, if the Directors do not behave with spirit and integrity, and the Proprietors lay aside their animosities, they will become answerable to the nation and to Parliament, for being the cause of losing the greatest advantages which ever have happened to England since it has been a nation.

" As for myself, although tempted on all sides by offers of riches without bounds, I have refused everything : and I am the greatest villain upon earth, if either I or any one dependent upon or belonging to me, with my knowledge, either directly or indirectly, benefit ourselves with the value of one farthing, except what shall be specified in an account current which I intend laying before the Directors, upon my arrival in England. Indeed, if I suffered myself to be corrupted, I could not with any face undertake (in conjunction with the Committee who have heartily and unanimously joined me) the reformations which are essentially necessary for the Company's welfare.

" The King has granted to the Company for ever, with the approbation and consent of the Nabob, all the revenues which shall remain after paying him a certain tribute, and allowing a sum sufficient for the dignity and support of the Nabob. The Company's income exceeds 2,000,000*l.* sterling per annum, and their civil and military expenses in future never shall exceed 700,000*l.* per annum, in time of peace, and 1,000,000*l.* in time of war. For further particulars, let me refer you to Mr. Walsh. With regard to the French forces, I shall put those of the Company upon so respectable a footing that all the powers of Europe can have no chance of succeeding, without first landing, and being supported by the powers of the country; and that appears very impracticable, since I have lately acquired a grant from the King of five northern provinces, those the French formerly possessed."

His letter to Mr. Walsh bears date five days subsequently to the preceding. I subjoin an extract from it.

" Had I known Mr. Sumner as well as I do at present, I would never have consented to his being appointed my successor, let the consequences be what they would. I did, indeed, entertain hopes that my example and instructions might furnish that gentleman with a plan of conduct and political knowledge, which would have enabled him to fill the chair with honour, and me to leave it with satisfaction to myself. But I am sorry to inform you that I had been but a short time on board the Kent before I discovered him to be a man no ways fit to be my successor. His ideas of government differ widely indeed from mine; add to this, his judgment is weak, timid, and unsound, and resolution he has none.

" Nor was my opinion of him changed on our arrival here;

for I was frequently mortified with instances of his conduct, which made me look forward with regret to the day on which he was to be intrusted with the government of Bengal.

" When affairs of the utmost consequence to the Company were transacting by me, at the distance of seven hundred miles from the presidency, Mr. Sumner, Governor for the time being, would have yielded up some of the most material privileges of the Committee to Mr. Leycester, Gray, and Burdett, the most factious among the counsellors ; and, if I had not written to him very severely on the subject, and prevailed on Mr. Verelst to hasten down from Burdwan to remonstrate with him on the weakness of his conduct, I verily believe he would have joined with those gentlemen in endeavouring to abolish the power of the Committee.

" Whether his behaviour arose merely from timidity of temper, or from a consideration that his actions formerly, in the Burdwan country, could not bear a scrutiny, if the resentment of those whom he had been obliged to join in condemning should prompt them to retaliate, I cannot say; but it is certain that his attention to those gentlemen, guilty as they had been of the most notorious acts of oppression, was mean and absurd. His conduct, upon the whole, convinces me that, had he been in council during the late transactions, he would have stood next to Mr. Johnstone in the donation list, which I almost wish he had, since the Company and I should, by that means, have been freed from the apprehensions we now labour under, on account of his succeeding me in the government.

" Imagine not that I have exceeded the bounds of truth in this description. A due regard to my own honour, as well as to the advantage of the Company, obliges me to be thus plain ; but it is not my intention to impress you with ideas so far to the disadvantage of Mr. Sumner, as that he may be set aside from the government. I think I cannot go such lengths without hurting my own reputation. I must make a point of his succeeding me according to his appointment ; and I hope affairs will go on very well, as long as he has a good committee or council to watch him.

" If you can prevail upon the Court of Directors to empower me alone, or me in conjunction with the Select Committee, to regulate matters, I will be responsible for his good behaviour; if not, I much fear things will fall into the old channel; and to the advantages arising from salt will be added every other that can be grasped at.

" Remember the oath and penalty bond ·mentioned in my public letter. If, by increasing the Governor's salary, or ordering his proportion of salt to be greater, there was a particular oath for the Governor, whereby he should not be allowed the liberty of private trade at all, but obliged to attend to the affairs of the Company only, leaving trade to the second, &c., I think the plan of government would be much more perfect, as it would be less liable to abuses from the head.

" I have hinted to Dudley only my sentiments of Mr. Sumner, and he knows from me that I have explained myself to you. Consult, therefore, together about the matter; settle it, if possible, in such a manner that I may not be taxed with breach of promise to Mr. Sumner, and I may at the same time resign the government without apprehension for the consequences.

*   *   *   *   *

" It would be endless for me to send you the particulars of every act of extortion and corruption. I had prepared a great many, under the hands and seals of the several zemindars and phousdars, in order to make it impossible for such men to succeed in any of their future designs; but the total overthrow of Sulivan and his party makes such authentic proofs unnecessary, especially as we have sent home sufficient to convince every impartial Director of the general corruption and profligacy of their servants in Bengal."

The language of these letters is stern and uncompromising enough. It cannot be said to belie in any respect the nature of him who made use of it; and yet I think it would be unjust to the memory of a very remarkable man were we to assume that he had not his amiable weaknesses too. Clive seems to have loved as he hated—without stint, and sometimes without much discrimination. We find him often repenting of the predilections which he had been induced to form; and denouncing as idiots men whom for a while he had represented as worthy of a world's admiration. Mr. Sumner is an instance in point; so is Mr. Vansittart; and even General Carnac, as I shall have occasion by and by to show, narrowly escaped being classed in the same category. Neither does his more private correspondence breathe on any occasion that tone of deep domestic feeling which we find in the home communications of many other men hardly less distinguished than he. There are no letters of his extant resembling those which Warren Hastings addressed to his wife; there are none that bear the slightest affinity to the touching passages in which, when writing to Lady Munro, Sir Thomas used to bewail his own solitude. Still Clive had a rude regard for his relatives, as his liberality to them in the shape of money-gifts seems to prove; and he wrote to them familiarly likewise. Let the reader judge from the following specimens of the extent to which he permitted the love of home and its endearments to influence him. On the 25th of September, 1765, he writes to his cousin, as follows:—

" I have received your letter of the 22nd of November, 1764, by which I find you are all in health, though not so happy as when I was among you. I make no doubt of once more contributing towards that happiness, though not quite so soon as I expected, when in England, owing to the length of our passage. I have pitched upon the beginning of December, 1766, for resigning this government; and nothing but my death shall prevent it. General Carnac, myself, and the rest of our family, propose coming most of the way overland; and shall, in all probability, be in London some time in April, 1767.

" I have been seven hundred miles up the country, and have established a firm and lasting peace, I hope, with the Great Mogul and his vizier Shuja Dowlah. I have seen much of his Majesty, and he has appointed me one of his first omrahs, or nobles, of his empire, with an immense title, not worth sixpence in England. Touching all these matters I must refer you to Mr. Walsh.

" I am glad you have put a stop to Styche expenses, they became enormous, and it will be time enough to go on with them upon my arrival in England; but I approve greatly of your repairing Walcot, and making it fit for Lady Clive's reception. The only concern I feel arises from a conviction of what she must suffer from so long an absence.

" With regard to myself, I have full employment, and enjoy

my health rather better than in England, though I find I cannot bear the heat so well as formerly, which makes me determined to quit the country as soon as possible."

" I rejoice," he writes* to his father, " to hear from others, though not from yourself, that, notwithstanding the accident which has happened to one of your eyes, you retain both your spirits, appetite, and health. It is impossible, without a miracle, to enjoy the blessings of life in that perfection in our latter days as in the days of youth: but I really think your temperance and the goodness of your constitution will carry you through life with ease and satisfaction to yourself to an age nearly equal to that of your aunt Judy.

" Although I enjoy better health than in England, India is by no means agreeable to me, separated as I am from my wife, children, and dearest relations. The length of our passage will make my absence one year more than I intended, but this you may be assured of, that nothing shall detain me in Bengal beyond the beginning of December, 1766; and I hope to see you all in good health and spirits some time in April, 1767.

" I have been seven hundred miles up the country, and have been very conversant with his Majesty, the Great Mogul. He has made me one of the first omrahs, or nobles, of his empire. I have concluded a peace for the Company, which I hope will last, and obtained from the King a grant of a revenue of 2,000,000*l.* sterling per annum for them for ever; and, what is more, I have put them on a way of securing this immense revenue, in such a manner that it is almost impossible to deprive the Company of it, at least for some years to come.

" With regard to myself, I have not benefited or added to my fortune one farthing, nor shall I; though I might, by this time, have received 500,000*l.* sterling. What trifling emoluments I cannot avoid receiving shall be bestowed on Maskelyne, Ingham, and Strachey, as a reward for their services and constant attention upon my person. I am much obliged to the Doctor for his care of my health: he is worth about 2000*l.* already. This ship, sent express, will bring the Company the most important news they ever received ; and, if they are not

---

* 24th September, 1765.

satisfied with mine and the Committee's conduct, I will pronounce there is not one grain of honour or integrity remaining in England. The reformation I am making, in both the civil and military branches, will render the acquisition of fortunes not so sudden or certain as formerly. This, added to the shortness of my stay in India, induces me to think Captain Semphill had better stay in England, where we may serve him by our interest at home. Remember me in the most affectionate manner to my mother. She has acted a great part in life. The uniformity of her conduct with regard to her children must, at the same time it affords her the most pleasing reflections, influence them to entertain the highest respect and veneration for so deserving a parent. I will most certainly write to her, and to my brothers and sisters, who have my most affectionate wishes."

CHAPTER XXI.

Commencement of Military Reform—Alarm of Mutiny.

In his struggle with the friends of corruption in civil life, Lord Clive had triumphed. If some abuses still remained, they were few in number and comparatively of slight importance, while the storm of opposition with which he was assailed on his first arrival had died away. Indeed Clive took good care that the political atmosphere immediately about himself should be cleared of the worst elements with which it was charged. Messrs. Johnstone, Leycester, Burdett, and others of less note were summarily dismissed the service and sent home. This left in Bengal, in the regular line of succession, only very young men, on whom, because of their inexperience, Lord Clive could repose little confidence. He therefore applied for leave to bring round from Madras and Bombay, to fill the vacant places, gentlemen accustomed to business, and willing, as he hoped, to take their tone in its management from himself. As was to be expected, a rumour of his intentions in regard to this matter no sooner got abroad than it united in a common feeling of hostility against him almost all who saw in the proposed arrangement a serious hindrance to their personal advancement. These junior malcontents appear, however, to have learned wisdom from the fate of their seniors. Whatever they might feel, they were careful not to make any needless or premature display of indignation ; nor was it until the results of his endeavours to carry the principle of reform into the military establishment of the province became apparent, that the existence of so strong a feeling among the younger civil servants of the Company was suspected. How the truth came to light, and in what manner Clive dealt with it, I now proceed to relate.

The army of the East India Company had arrived at the state in which Lord Clive now found it by a process which could hardly fail of affecting injuriously the moral tone of its European members.　Accidental in its origin, and forced on to maturity against the will of the body which maintained it, there was perhaps no armed force in the world of which the officers were more completely thrown upon the resources of their own ingenuity in order to maintain a respectable station in society.　For more than a century the military defence of the factories had been intrusted to persons armed, like the attendants of native magistrates and princes, with swords and shields and spears.　By and by the European merchants and their clerks enrolled themselves into companies of militia; and when this service proved too severe, they hired runaway seamen from the fleets of all nations, and employed them sometimes as soldiers, and sometimes as labourers in their warehouses, according as the exigences of the moment might seem to require.　Of these people, when under arms, one or more of the Company's factors took the command, for which a slight addition to his regular salary was made, without, however, any restrictions being imposed upon his privileges of private trade, or any exemption afforded from attendance in the Company's counting-house.

In proportion as the current of events swept the Company more and more within the influence of Indian politics, the representatives of that body were compelled to increase their military force.　More deserters were taken into pay; and when this source of recruiting was found to be insufficient, crimps were employed to pick up the scum of London in the streets, and to send out the sweepings of jails and workhouses to swell the ranks of the Indian army.　Such an influx of ragamuffins into their settlements abroad compelled the Court of Directors to set up a corps of military officers as a body distinct from their civil servants.　But the gentlemen of Leadenhall-street could not as yet cease to regard themselves as traders, and nothing more.　They therefore paid their military officers on a scale proportionate to that which had been framed for the remuneration of their civil servants; and being aware that it was inadequate, they applied the same remedy to the evil in one case which had served to counteract, if not to remove it, in the other.　Military officers, like senior and junior merchants, were permitted to improve their fortunes by trading on their own account.

As long as the settlements enjoyed peace, this system worked well enough for individuals. The officer, when not required on parade (and parades were few, and barrack duty marvellously light), worked like any other clerk at his books, or amused himself with cards, horse-racing, cock-fighting, or any other of the sports which were then in fashion. But these sources of emolument and recreation alike failed him when the army took the field. It was necessary, likewise, in order to ensure his efficiency, that he should go forth provided with tents, canteens, baggage-animals of every sort, and horses; and with most of these he could not, while doing garrison duty, be expected to encumber himself. Accordingly he sought and obtained an allowance which, under the head of batta, was supposed to be sufficient to reimburse the first cost of the necessary articles, and to keep them up, as well as to remunerate the native servants who looked after them, and to put a little extra pay in the officer's pocket during the whole season of his absence from the capital or presidency. Prize-money likewise was conceded to him; nor were any objections made to his acceptance of such presents as might be offered by native chiefs. And if he contrived all the while to keep his commercial dealings in activity, the government not only did nothing to interrupt the process, but gave him credit for more than an average share of talent, and rejoiced in the success which attended its exercise.

It was the obvious consequence of such a system to dull the edge of chivalrous honour among the gentlemen brought up in the military service of the Company. Soldiers, like other men, must have enough whereon to live; but the commercial and the military spirit seldom go long together; and the temptations to indulge the one at the expense of the other became at last, especially in the Bengal army, so great, "that flesh and blood," to use one of Lord Clive's expressions, " could not stand it." Moreover, the occurrences of every new day gave to this sordid principle a stronger impulse. When Clive entered into the conspiracy to dethrone Suraj-u-Dowlah, and Meer Jaffier, the better to encourage the English army to be hearty in his cause, promised, out of his own resources, to double the batta, or field-allowance granted by the Company, no one considered it necessary to decline the offer; and, from a precedent of this sort, once set, he would have been a bold Nabob who should have ventured to recede. The consequence was, that from the commencement of the march, which ended in the battle of Plassey down to the date of Clive's return to Calcutta as Governor and President of a Select Committee, double batta had been regularly received by the Bengal army. It is true that the Court of Directors more than once protested against the arrangement. So long, indeed, as the payments came out of the pockets of the Nabob they held their peace. He was pledged to defray the costs of the military force which kept him on the throne ; and if he chose to go to unnecessary expense in doing so, the loss was his—they had nothing whatever to say about it. But as soon as an arrangement was made for transferring the payment of the troops to the Company, the Directors denounced the double batta system as iniquitous. They gave repeated orders to the local government that the abuse should cease ; and more than one feeble, and therefore vain, attempt was made to carry them into execution.

The Court's letter which required an engagement from their civil servants to accept no more presents, and to put the trade of private persons on a reasonable footing, had especially enjoined a cessation in the issue of double batta to the troops. The districts which Cossim Ali had made over being accepted in lieu of all pecuniary contributions to the army, it became a point of importance with the Company to maintain the latter body on a scale as economical as should be consistent with its efficiency ; and as double batta was confessedly an arrangement between the Nabob and the English officers, the Court of Directors decided that there was no obligation on their part to continue the practice. The project of reduction was not, however, taken up with any degree of spirit at Calcutta ; indeed Mr. Vansittart had been early given to understand that any attempt on his part to diminish the customary emoluments of the military classes would lead to consequences more serious than either he or the Directors counted upon. Accordingly, Mr. Vansittart, and the government which succeeded his, both gave way, and double batta continued to be issued to men who, feeling their power, had in more ways than one begun to abuse it. But Clive was made of different materials. He had warned the army at the outset that the indulgence which Meer Jaffier granted to them could not be enjoyed for ever. He had more than once reverted to the subject during his first administration of the affairs of Bengal, and abstained from advising the Nabob to stay his bounty only because he was unwilling to interfere with arrangements which, while they benefited his brother officers, did no injury to the masters whom they served. He had now, however, a specific duty to perform, and he set himself about it. Having redressed the grievances of which the Court complained in the civil branches of the service, he applied himself next to the correction of military abuses, of which one of the most striking had indeed been remedied by the same process which took away from members of council their right of private trade, and divided among them the profits of the salt monopoly.

I have adverted elsewhere to a proposal made by Lord Clive while in England to alter and improve the organization of the troops which the Company kept on foot for the defence of its territories in Bengal. It had already to a certain extent been acted upon ; so that the Bengal army was now told off into regiments of European and native infantry, and had its artillery and cavalry—the latter as yet being an inconsiderable force—distributed into batteries, or, as they were then called, companies of guns,—and squadrons of horse. The whole were, besides, told off in three brigades ; of which the first, under Colonel Sir Robert Fletcher, occupied quarters at Monghir ; the third, under Sir Robert Barker, was cantoned at Bankepore ; while the second, of which Colonel Smith was at the head, lay, in compliance with the united request of the Emperor and the King of Oude, in observation of the Mahrattas at Allahabad.

Such a convenient distribution of the military force of the province concurred with the ratification of a treaty of general peace in affording to Lord Clive as good an opportunity as he could have desired of entering upon the course of military reform which he had made up his mind to pursue. An order accordingly appeared towards the end of September, 1765, which warned the troops that from the 1st of January, 1766, the right of European officers to draw double batta should cease. Forasmuch, however, as the distance from Calcutta to Allahabad was great, and that the officers attached to the brigade doing duty at the latter station were put to heavy charges, the Governor and Council consented to their continuing to draw as heretofore so long as they should remain in the field; but it was provided at the same time that whenever the regiments went into cantonments this privilege should cease, and that the principle of economy which prevailed elsewhere should come into operation at Allahabad likewise. Meanwhile the troops at Patna and Monghir were to receive half-batta, subject to similar restrictions; while those doing duty at the presidency were put upon the same footing with the troops on the Coromandel coast—that is to say, they were to draw no batta at all.

There is no order of persons with whom, under common circumstances, greater liberties may be taken by the governing power than with soldiers. Where the spirit of discipline has been well preserved, soldiers obey, through the force of custom, commands which they feel to be unjust; and submit to wrongs, grumbling perhaps all the while, yet never dreaming that to go beyond a little idle complaint is possible. But the army of Bengal was not at this time in a state of high discipline. Indulged and pampered by the native princes, the officers had learned to regard themselves, rather than the civil power, as supreme; and were confirmed in this idea from finding that the Governor and Council never ventured to enforce obedience to an order against which they or their chiefs protested. A body of men, actuated by such a spirit, and bearing the sword, formidable everywhere, and in India resistless, might have been regarded as not exactly the class of persons on whose forbearance it would be safe to make a rash experiment. Nevertheless Clive, partly perhaps because he scarcely counted on resistance, partly because it was not in his nature to shrink from a contest in whatever source originating, or by whatever adversary offered, published his decree without so much as inquiring how it was likely to be received. It was greeted in every military station throughout the provinces with a howl of condemnation. Remonstrances poured in, as heretofore, to which officers of every rank in the service affixed their names; and the more sanguine flattered themselves that a similar result would attend the present movement which had followed upon others of the same sort. The more thoughtful knew better; and Clive's answer to the protest neither surprised nor disappointed them. The officers of the army were informed that the

Governor and Select Committee had special instructions from the Court of Directors to act as they were doing; and that, not being able to find any loop-hole through which to escape from paying obedience to their superiors, they had only to express a hope that the remonstrants would follow the example which they set. The remonstrants did not act on this wise suggestion. But perceiving that the parties with whom they had to deal were made of less flexible stuff than the governments which they had been accustomed heretofore to overawe at their pleasure, they entered into a regular conspiracy to compel a compliance with their wishes.

Their plan, which seems to have been formed originally at Monghir, and diffused from that station over the rest of the cantonments, amounted simply to this: that on a given day they should all resign their commissions, and steadily refuse to serve any more unless the old allowance of double batta were restored. At first it would appear that the officers of the second brigade, which held, as it were, the outposts at Allahabad, refused to become parties to the conspiracy. They considered themselves, as they stated, in the enemy's presence, and could not, therefore, without sacrificing their personal character, quit the service till relieved. But the feeling of honour, if such it was, which swayed them, soon yielded to the remonstrances of their comrades. Hints were thrown out of men's usual indifference to the wrongs of others so long as they themselves are not sufferers by them; and the gentlemen of the second brigade, rather than be accounted guilty towards their comrades of treason, consented to betray their country. It was accordingly arranged that on the 1st of June the commissions of all should be given up simultaneously to the commandants of their respective brigades, and that till the fifteenth day of the same month the parties thus ceasing to be officers should serve as volunteers. But this respite being granted for the simple purpose of affording time for the Government to relent, it was further resolved that beyond the 15th no inducement short of an absolute concession of the point at issue should keep them to their colours. Moreover, the conspirators bound themselves by oath to secrecy, and came under engagements, which they ratified by a like pledge, to defend with their lives the lives of any of the body who might be condemned to suffer death by sentence of a court-martial. Nor was this all. In order to escape the guilt of mutiny, they resolved to decline accepting the advance of pay which it was the custom of the service to make on the first day of every month. Finally, as if distrustful of their own oaths, each man gave a bond of 500*l.* to another that he would not take back his commission till the double batta was granted ; while all entered into a subscription, in which arrangement several civilians joined them, in order to provide a fund out of which such as should be dismissed the service and sent home might be provided for.

This frightful mutiny, to which, as it afterwards came out, officers of high rank were privy, if they did not positively lend themselves to promote it, was in full operation, when intelligence arrived of the advance of 50,000 or 60,000 Mahrattas towards Corah. The second brigade, being within 100 miles of the point threatened, was ordered to hold itself in readiness for service ; and Colonel Smith, with the sepoy battalions, encamped as far in advance as Serajahpoor. But the European regiment abode still in its quarters at Allahabad—exposure to the intense heat which prevails in that quarter of India in the spring of the year being considered as too severe a risk to be incurred except in case of emergency.

Such was the state of the army of Bengal in the month of March, 1766. Neither Lord Clive nor General Carnac seems to have entertained the slightest suspicion of the truth, when they set out for Calcutta together in order to regulate, with Mr. Sykes, 'the amount of revenue to be collected at Moorshedabad and Patna for the ensuing year, and to receive from the King of Oude the balance of the 50 lacs of rupees which, by the treaty of August, 1765, he had bound himself to pay. They had a further object in view—namely, to form alliances with the princes of the empire against the Mahrattas, whose encroachments threatened evil consequences to all ; and they were all, but especially Clive, who rejoiced in the apparent success of his policy both foreign and domestic, in the highest possible spirits. They reached Moorshedabad in April, and had not been there three weeks ere a despatch arrived from Calcutta which troubled them. It contained a remonstrance from the third brigade, signed by 9 captains, 12 lieutenants, and 20 ensigns, against the reduction of batta, to which, as Mr. Verelst and the Council reported, they did not feel themselves competent, without communication with the Governor, to give any reply. Lord Clive, conceiving that this was a mere repetition of the device which had been concerted some months previously without leading to any serious results, directed that the remonstrance should be sent to Sir R. Barker, by whom the brigade was commanded, and that the gentlemen from whom it came should be informed that the Supreme Council could not take notice of any petition or appeal from officers unless it came to them through the regular channel. At the same time, in order that every possible contingency might be provided against, he communicated his views in detail to the Committee. They were in substance the same with those on which he had acted when the first remonstrance reached him ; and he recommended, in the event of a duplicate document being sent in, through the brigadier, that it should be answered in a like spirit.

Clive's letter was written on the 22nd of April. On the 28th he received a despatch from Sir Robert Fletcher, dated from Monghir on the 25th, which appears to have awakened the earliest suspicion in his mind that the spirit of the army was not good. Indeed, I use an inadequate phrase when I thus express myself. Sir Robert Fletcher's communication stated plainly that the officers, not of his brigade only, but of the whole army, seemed determined to make another attempt for the recovery of the batta ; and that, though they proposed to serve throughout the month of May as volunteers, he had reason to suspect that most of them had bound themselves to one another to send in their commissions to their respective commandants. In corroboration of these statements, Sir Robert begged to enclose copies of a correspondence which had passed between himself and Sir R. Barker, commanding the third brigade. It related to a quarrel among some officers belonging to the latter corps, and to the proceedings of a court of inquiry which had sat to investigate the causes of the difference. Some startling revelations appear to have been made in the course of these proceedings ; but Sir Robert Fletcher affected to treat the whole matter lightly. In his reply to Sir R. Barker, which bore date April 24th, he observes, " that though he had heard for some days that the officers had thoughts of resuming their demands, he could not think it deserved much notice ; and, even if the contrary were the case, he did not see that any great harm would arise. The only result," he continues, " of their proffered resignations will be, that Lord Clive, who is not likely to change a resolution once formed, will find a convenient opportunity of picking out the best officers and getting rid of the bad ones."

CHAPTER XXII.

Progress and suppression of the Mutiny—Letters to various Correspondents.

I HAVE dwelt at some length on the dawn of this remarkable military revolt, partly because, without tracing the progress of the evil from stage to stage, it is impossible to do justice to the individual who quelled it, partly because the full magnitude of the danger will not be understood unless by him who observes to what extent and into what quarters the spirit of disaffection had spread. Here, for example, was Sir Robert Fletcher, an officer of high rank and established reputation, who, on account of former services, had been transferred from Madras to Bengal, and promoted there over the heads of many of his seniors, writing from the brigade of which he was in command, as if, on the 25th of April, he had only for the first time begun to suspect that all was not as it ought to be, yet professing to hold that the evil was of so trifling a nature as to justify him in treating the discontent of his subordinates as a mere matter of raillery. Now, as the progress of my narrative will show, Sir Robert Fletcher had not only been conversant with the plans of the disaffected from the beginning, but he was brought to trial on the charge of encouraging, if he did not positively suggest them ; and, being·found guilty, was dismissed the service. Again, Sir Robert Barker, though exposed to no suspicion of this sort, seems to have been kept so completely in the dark, that of a conspiracy begun in December, 1765, he never heard till towards the end of April, 1766; indeed, his correspondence shows that he might have remained ignorant of the affair till it exploded, but that the conspirators began to quarrel among themselves, and let out by accident that which it was their business to conceal. Nor is this all. It was this quarrel, and nothing else, which, forcing on a premature disclosure of their plot, not only put the supreme government upon its guard, but afforded time to mature plans for counterworking the designs of the mutineers. The scheme, as concocted in the latter days of the past year, had reference to an expected commencement of hostilities, and took into view the straits to which it was probable that, at such a moment, the Government would be reduced. Men calculated that the Mahrattas would be fairly in the field about the beginning of June; and on the 1st of June the commissions of the whole body of European officers were to be thrown up. What could the Government do under such circumstances except yield the point at issue? But the disclosures effected in the course of the proceedings at Bankepore deranged the whole scheme; and now, distrusting one another almost as much as they feared the vigorous interposition of Government, the conspirators resolved that they should strike their blow on the 1st of May. That their confidence as to the result had not, however, abated, was proved by the delivery about this time to Captain Carnac (an officer on Lord Clive's staff) of a letter signed "Full Batta," and dated the 15th of April, in which Captain Carnac was informed of the design in progress, and requested not only to send his own commission to a friend, but to add his name to the list of those who were pledged to provide for the martyrs in the cause. Captain Carnac, as in duty bound, put the letter into Lord Clive's hand. The latter read it, and saw at a glance how the land lay. He was by no means insensible to the danger which threatened; he was alive to the inconvenience—not to call it by a stronger term—which must fall upon every branch of the public service; but he does not seem to have wavered respecting the course which it behoved him to follow. He wrote immediately to the Council at Calcutta, despatching his letter by express; and having informed his colleagues of all that had come to his knowledge, he desired that they would lose no time in sending to Madras and Bombay for as many officers, cadets, and volunteers as could be spared. "Such a spirit as this which pervades the Bengal army," he says, "must be suppressed at all hazards, unless we determine on seeing the government of these provinces pass from the civil into the hands of the military departments." Wherefore it was his deliberate opinion that not one of the 130 individuals, of whose intention to resign he had been made aware, ought, in the event of carrying their resolution into effect, to be re-admitted, under any pretence, into the Company's service. Meanwhile they must fight the Mahrattas, if to fight they were compelled, with such means as were at their disposal ; and, the better to enable them to do so, both the Madras and Bombay authorities were urged to use all convenient despatch in sending on the officers for whom application was about to be made.

Having despatched this letter, Lord Clive proceeded to communicate with Sir R. Fletcher and Sir R. Barker. To both he sent copies of his note to the Supreme Council, and left them at liberty, if they should deem the course expedient, to make the substance of it known to the officers under their respective commands. A lingering hope still, however, cheered him that things might not be in so bad a state as common rumour represented. Sir R. Barker had never made any direct complaint to himself; from Colonel Smith at Allahabad no communications whatever were received. Possibly the contagion might not have spread beyond the circle, wide enough in all conscience, which was known to be infected. But this delusion, if such it may be called, soon gave way to more stern realities. Scarcely were his despatches to the two brigadiers sent off when a letter from Sir Robert Barker informed him that the whole of his command was in a state of dissolution ; that the officers had warned him of their determination to resign on the 1st of May ; and that he entertained serious apprehensious of a mutiny among the men. It appeared, also, that the spirit of disaffection had spread to the civil servants of the Company, among whom a subscription had been got up, to the extent of 16,000l., in order to supply the mutineers with funds, and protect them against the probable consequences of their misconduct. It was impossible, amid such a complication of difficulties, to doubt that the whole army was animated by the same bad spirit, and Clive took his measures accordingly.

It was necessary, in order to save the arms of England from defeat, and the newly-acquired provinces from destruction, that the brigade in advance—in other words, the troops stationed at Allahabad and Serajapoor, should be kept faithful to their colours. Clive therefore sent instructions to Colonel Smith to be much upon his guard ; to yield nothing, to promise nothing, except in the last extremity ; to put down the mutiny, should it break out in his corps, with a strong hand, if possible ; and to come to no terms with the mutineers unless the troops could not be brought by any other means into the field. At the same time he hurried forward to Monghir as many officers as could be collected from Calcutta and elsewhere, and directed them to use their best endeavours, by argument, by persuasion, by the threat of his speedy arrival, to bring back the malcontents to a sense of duty. To Sir Robert Barker, however, and Colonel Smith, in both of whom he appears to have reposed great confidence, he transmitted only general recommendations that they should break the refractory spirit of their mutineers, let the consequences be what they might. Neither Sir Robert Barker nor Colonel Smith failed him at the pinch. The former put in arrest and sent down to Calcutta the field-adjutant or brigade-major of his own brigade, for presuming on the 1st of May to enclose to him the commissions of a large number of officers. To the officers themselves he sent back their commissions, it is true, but he accompanied the gift with a threat that, if they did not immediately return to their duty, the extreme rigour of military law would be enforced against them ; and such was the influence of his well-known character, that, with only three exceptions, the whole of the recusants resumed their places in the ranks. In like manner Colonel Smith justified, by the energy which marked his proceedings, the good opinion entertained of him by his chief. By accepting the resignations of some, and refusing to communicate upon the subject with others, he managed to keep a sufficient number of European officers with his sepoy battalions to ensure their efficiency, and forthwith sent one of these back to the support of the commandant at Allahabad, where the European regiment threatened to break into mutiny. The sepoys, marching a hundred miles in fifty hours, reached the cantonments in good time ; whereupon the mutineers returned to their barracks, and the officers were almost all put in arrest.

Meanwhile Lord Clive proceeded in person to Monghir, where the danger was far more imminent than at either of the other stations. He reached the cantonments on the 15th of May, and was astounded at the tidings which immediately greeted him. The officers whom he had sent forward from Calcutta and Moorshedabad had not, it appeared, been idle. They pointed out to their comrades the folly as well as the moral guilt of their proceeding, and reproached them with acting ungratefully to the Governor, who, instead of appropriating to his own use the legacy left to him in the will of Meer Jaffier, had set aside the whole, amounting to not less than 70,000*l.* sterling, to form a fund out of which pensions to invalids and to the widows of officers and soldiers dying in the service might accrue. The malcontents declared that they had never till that moment heard of Lord Clive's generosity to the service; and when reminded that the circumstance could not but be well known to their brigadier, they replied that, whether well known to him or not, the brigadier had taken care not to make any of their body cognizant of the fact. Indeed they went further; for in direct terms some of them charged Sir Robert Fletcher with giving encouragement to proceedings from which it was now impossible for them to withdraw. Moreover, Lord Clive learned that so recently as the 13th there had been a movement among the European soldiers to support their officers by force, and that they had been diverted from their purpose only by a distribution of money, and the assurance which Sir R. Fletcher gave them, that he was not, as they had been led to believe, about to put himself at their head.

These statements were made to Lord Clive immediately on his arrival at Monghir; and Sir R. Fletcher, being sent for, corroborated them in the main; but he made, during the interview, an admission which sank deep into Clive's mind, though with great self-command he affected at the moment not to notice it. Sir Robert, it came out, had been cognizant of the designs of his officers ever since the month of January. He had sent in no report upon the subject, nor taken any steps to break up the conspiracy, because, as he said, it was desirable that nothing should be done at Bankepore of which he should not possess full knowledge; and he had good ground to believe that premature interference, instead of checking the sedition, would only render the leaders more cautious and their followers more determined. Clive heard, but made no reply to this explanation. He contented himself with ordering the brigade under arms, and explaining to them the nature of the offence of which too many officers had been guilty, and its inevitable consequences, had the conspiracy succeeded, to all classes in the army. This done, he sent down the chief culprits under guard to Calcutta; and, having delayed a day or two to satisfy himself that tranquillity was restored, he pursued his journey to Bankepore.

It would overload these pages were I to describe in detail the measures adopted by Lord Clive at each of the great military stations during this alarming mutiny. They were marked in every instance with the decision and good sense which formed prominent features in his character, and the most perfect success attended them; yet it must not be supposed that a task so Herculean was accomplished without a great deal of mental anxiety and bodily fatigue. Indeed the whole period of Clive's second administration of the affairs of Bengal may be described as little else than a protracted intellectual fever. "Do you think," he asks in a letter to the Governor of Madras, "that history can furnish another instance of a man, with 40,000*l.* per annum, a wife and family, a father and mother, brothers and sisters, cousins and relations in abundance, abandoning his native country, and all the blessings of life, to take charge of a government so corrupt, so headstrong, so lost to all sense of principle and honour as this?" It was a natural question for one to put who found insubordination and misrule everywhere—a civil service corrupt and mercenary to the greatest extent—an army insubordinate, disorganised, and liable at any moment to be swayed by the caprice or ill-humour of its officers into a state of revolt. Nor was there one among the public men with whom he co-operated but in some way or another ruffled his temper by outraging his sense of right. I have taken occasion to point out the degree to which Mr. Sumner disappointed Lord Clive's expectations when acting as President of the committee during his lordship's temporary absence from Calcutta. I have shown that General Carnac himself was the cause to him of uneasiness on more than one occasion. And with respect to the others—the whole of the heads of departments, including Brigadiers Fletcher, Barker, and Smith, incurred in one shape or another his displeasure. They would seem, and especially Sir Robert Fletcher, to have been but indifferent disciplinarians throughout. For example, long before the combination to resist the reduction of batta was entered into, the officers of the Bengal army took deep offence at the introduction of a stranger into their body by a process of purchase which raised him at once to the rank of captain. Clive was no party to the arrangement; indeed in his own breast, and in private conversation, he severely condemned it; but forasmuch as it was the act of the President and Council, he would not sanction anything like rebellion against it. Not so felt and acted the captains and subalterns of the army, or the brigadiers. The former threatened with one accord to resign the service if the appointment were not cancelled; the latter, including General Carnac himself, while they complained of the absence of discipline among their inferiors, showed that they were themselves not more disposed to submit, without repining, to lawful authority. How Lord Clive dealt with these gentlemen under the very delicate circumstances in which their conduct more 'han once placed him, will be best understood by inserting a few extracts from his correspondence, which explain both his sentiments on the important subjects referred to, and his manner of expressing them. Writing to General Carnac after the receipt of a warm remonstrance addressed to the Council, he says :—

"I am concerned at the warmth of your letter to the Board. Although they have used both you and me extremely ill, and, as individuals, deserved our utmost contempt, yet I think there is some indulgence due to their stations. That they have acted unjustly, as well as contrary to the known rules of the army, in the case of Captain Macpherson, cannot be doubted; yet I cannot think the officers ought to carry matters so far as to insist upon a Governor and Council retracting what they have done. There must be an absolute power lodged somewhere, and that certainly is in the hands of the Governor and Council, until the pleasure of the Court of Directors be known. However, if the account of Captain Macpherson is proved true, I will be answerable that he shall act as youngest of the corps he has been introduced to, and take care that no such unjust proceedings shall be countenanced in future. I hope this will prove satisfactory to the officers, who, by their gallant behaviour, are entitled to every mark of attention and distinction from the Company."

This kind and friendly remonstrance, on the part of Lord Clive, had not the desired effect. On the contrary, it appears from the following letter to his friend, General Lawrence, that the anger of the officers was not to be allayed; and that a spirit of insubordination had taken such deep root among them, that nothing short of a mutiny successfully put down could have power to overcome it.

"I should have done myself the pleasure of writing to you sooner, if I had not deferred it from day to day, in hopes of being able to entertain you with some important news from camp. There has, however, but one material circumstance happened, and that I am sure will astonish you. Some time ago, the Governor in Council here permitted Captain Whichcot to dispose of his commission to Captain Macpherson, and appointed the latter to the same rank among the captains that Whichcot held. Upon a representation of this grievance, Macpherson was ordered to take rank as youngest captain ; but the military gentlemen, still dissatisfied, thought fit to remonstrate against his being appointed to any other than that of youngest ensign. Such an unreasonable request could not be granted, and the consequence of the refusal has been, it seems, a general association among the officers, captains as well as subalterns; the former thinking it incumbent on them to support what they are pleased to suppose the rights of the latter. The import of this association is, that all the officers, captains, lieutenants, and ensigns are to resign their commissions, unless Macpherson be degraded to the lowest rank! Civil departments, in every state, will now and then entertain abuses, in spite of the most vigilant magistracy ; but I appeal, my dear General, to your memory, whether, in the long experience you have had in military affairs, a single instance can be given of a corps of officers, in time of actual service and an enemy in the field, uniting in a combination of this nature. To me it appears so repugnant to every regulation of discipline, so destructive of that subordination, without which no army can exist, and above all, so disobedient to the Mutiny Act and Articles of War, that I am determined to refuse them the liberty of resigning (I mean those at least whose contract with the Company is not expired), and break them, or perhaps proceed to greater extremities by a general court-martial. The expediency of my plan of regimenting the forces, and appointing the proper proportion of field officers, appears now, I think, in a stronger light than ever; and in consequence of this mutiny (must I call it ?) I have already ordered all the corps which I brought from Europe to march up to camp, whither I intend to go myself, as soon as the interior policy of affairs will permit. To say truth, every principle of government in this presidency has within these few months past been so debauched, that one can hardly determine upon the branches which ought first to be lopped. Pray tell Mr. Palk that I do not write to him by this post because my politics are not yet ripe for communication, and I consider this as a letter to you both."

Some time before this combination of officers took place, several efforts were made by Clive to enforce the principles of subordination, which, we find from his private letters, had been greatly relaxed in all ranks. He appears to have grounded his chief hopes of restoring and maintaining discipline on his plan, elsewhere referred to, of giving shape to the army, by forming it into corps and brigades, and placing it under officers of rank and reputation; but his difficulty was to keep those in order who had been selected to command others. This is strongly evinced in a letter to Sir R. Fletcher, who, while he recommended the introduction of better discipline, objected to serve under Sir R. Barker.

"I have received your letter," Lord Clive observes, "and agree entirely with you in the necessity of introducing discipline and subordination among the officers and soldiers in the service of the Company, although I see no such difficulty in bringing this about, since those who decline complying with the regulations which are to be made will most certainly be dismissed the service.

"I must confess it gives me much concern, that you, who preach up the necessity of discipline and reformation, should be the first to act in contradiction to your own declared sentiments, by declining to serve under Sir R. Barker; but what surprises me still more is, that you, who have been removed from one settlement to another, and have actually superseded numbers, should object to serve under an officer, who was a captain when you were only an ensign or volunteer on the same establishment. Without disparagement to your merit, which I shall always be ready to acknowledge, it is not in the eyes of the world equal to that of Sir R. Barker, who has had more time and more opportunities than you possibly could of distinguishing himself. You think he should have remained in the artillery. ·That would not have hindered him from commanding you upon all occasions when you were both upon service together. Indeed his rank is so high, that he must always command wherever he is, if Carnac or Smith be not present, which may seldom happen; except, indeed, by being an artillery officer, he should be thought improper to command the whole; and by that means an officer of his rank and merit would be deprived of an opportunity of acting in the field at all. In short, every one who knows Sir R. Barker esteems him equal to any command, both military and artillery; and as a proof of what I affirm, General Lawrence, Mr. Palk, and the Nabob* pressed me, in the strongest terms, to have Sir R. Barker; promising that he should have both rank and command next to Colonel Campbell.

"I am persuaded that when you reflect upon the merits and pretensions which Sir Robert Barker has to the Company's favour, you will not hesitate a moment to give up the point. If you consider that Mr. Sulivan alone sent you out, in that distinguished station which you now possess, and that his interest is at best become a very precarious one, I am sure your own good sense will prevail upon you not to oppose my appointment; for I must frankly tell you, that, though I am really inclined to do you every service in my power, yet, in this instance, you must not expect the same indulgence from me which you have received from General Carnac."

In addition to these there are extant several letters from Lord Clive to Colonel Smith and to Sir R. Barker on the same subject, of which two at least ought not to be omitted in any work which professes to give a history of the life and services of the writer. The former officer, who, after Carnac, stood highest in Lord Clive's estimation in a military point of view, and in point of seniority came next to Carnac in the service, had incurred the personal displeasure of the Governor on a previous occasion, and was treated in consequence with a degree of reserve which greatly distressed him. Being desirous of coming to an explanation, he availed himself of an official correspondence about the re-organization of the army to say—"It remains now in your

* Mahomed Ali, at Madras

breast whether my communications with your lordship in future shall be simply from the Colonel to the Commander-in-chief, or whether I shall go beyond that line, and offer my sentiments on such matters regarding the public service as from time to time may occur." Clive took for a while no notice of this appeal, whereupon it was repeated; and then, and only then, he spoke out, as the following sentences show :—

" I had resolved," he observes, " to give you an answer to your letter of the 31st of August last; but, when I considered that the explanation required could neither afford you pleasure nor be of any service to the Company in your present situation, I determined to remain silent upon so disagreeable a subject. But as you have called upon me a second time, I will answer you with a frankness free from all disguise.

" Your behaviour towards Colonel Peach at the Cape, in re-primanding him for not paying his respects to me through you, was, in my opinion, assuming an authority which did not belong to you; and tended to the lessening of mine. Lieutenant Wen-thorp, after he had obtained my consent for returning to India, because he did not apply to you first, was discouraged in such a manner, that he chose rather to forego all the advantages he might obtain from my promises, than risk the consequences of your displeasure. Such an authority assumed, and resentment expressed, could not but give me great offence. The warmth shown and dissatisfaction expressed (because you were not looked upon as one of the Committee, and allowed to sign the letter of instructions to Captain Abercrombie) by immediately connect-ing yourself with a person whom you had been but very little connected with before, and who had often declared, in the pre-sence of many witnesses, that he would never be connected with you; the continuance of that very extraordinary connexion the rest of the voyage; convinced me at once, I could not be on a footing of intimacy, without subjecting myself to inconveniences which a spirit like mine could never brook. These, Sir, among many other reasons, have occasioned my acting with reserve towards you. Indeed, in the whole course of so long a voyage, I could observe a mind too actuated by ambition,—such a ten-dency in Colonel Smith, to govern and command those who ought to govern and command him, that I could not be unreserved without giving up that authority which I am determined ever to support; and although I do, and always have allowed you many virtues, so long as you continue to give so much general offence by that kind of behaviour, so long will you be exposed to mortification and disappointments."

My next extract shall be from a letter to Sir Robert Barker, which that officer elicited by applying to be made a member of the committee of civil government at Patna, not as an individual, but as the officer commanding the troops stationed in Bahar. Sir Robert Barker, be it observed, was personally an object of great regard to Lord Clive, and this the letter shows:—

" I must confess," he observes, " the receipt of your letter of the 2nd of February has given me infinite concern, because I feel for you as I should for myself, and there is no officer in this part of the world for whom I entertain so strong and true regard, or whom I am so very desirous of serving. I am sure, if it depended upon me, you should, upon Carnac's departure, succeed to his rank and station; so well acquainted am I with your merits as a soldier, your moderation and temper as a man. Your being hurt, therefore, at not having an appointment which is not in my power to obtain for you, cannot but hurt me. I am convinced that, great as my interest is, were I to propose your being joined with Mr. Middleton in directing the collection of the revenues of the Bahar province, I could not carry that point. Consider, Barker, how very separate and distinct the services are; consider how very jealous the Directors are of military men, and how very attentive they will be to every action of mine, whom they look upon in a military more than in a civil light. Recollect that they would not even allow Coote to have a seat at the Board to give his advice, except upon military matters only. I say further, that were I to take such an unprecedented step, I doubt whether it would not add such weight of argument to those counsellors and malcontents, who are gone home with a full design to exclaim against arbitrary and military power, that the Company might be induced to disapprove of everything I have done for them, from an apprehension that I meant to accomplish every measure, by the subversion of civil liberty. Persuaded I am, that the joining with Middleton a man of your steadiness, moderation, and discretion, would be of singular advantage to the Company: notwithstanding which, I dare not attempt to do it.

"But, let us suppose for a moment that I could gratify you in this request, what would be the consequence? Would not every officer commanding a brigade insist upon the like privilege? What use do you imagine the *man* of Allahabad would make of such a concession? Indeed, Barker, if such an appointment were to take place, the letters from this settlement would occasion such an alarm in Leadenhall-street, that I verily believe I should be turned off my government, and all the field-officers ordered home in the first ship. Point out to me, my friend, any method of extending your influence, without prejudice to the service we both wish to promote, and no man shall be readier than I to give the strongest proof of friendship and regard for you. Middleton shall have orders to consult with you upon all occasions where military duties are in agitation; so shall Setabroy and Durge Narain, and be ordered often to wait upon you."

I cannot better conclude the present chapter than by giving a short extract from a letter addressed on the 11th of July, 1765, to Mr. Verelst. It shows what Lord Clive's sentiments were in regard to the tone of mind which is necessarily produced by long habits of command, and deserves to be studied by all military men, some of whom are supposed to be more jealous than is necessary of the subordination of the sword to the toga.

"I have at last received a letter from Carnac, a copy of which has been sent you. However, his silence upon particular subjects convinces me he has too much given way to the warmth of his passions; and much I fear he thinks too highly of the services, dignity, and authority of the military.

"With regard to the first, although a soldier myself, I am of opinion that we imbibe such arbitrary notions, by the absolute power which we are obliged to exercise towards the officers and soldiers, in order to keep up subordination and military discipline, so essentially necessary for the good of the service, that we shall always be endeavouring to encroach upon the civil power, if they do not repeatedly make use of that authority with which they are invested; and I appeal to yourself, whether the commanding officers, whoever they were, since my departure

from India, until my second arrival in this quarter, have not, by
their conduct, endeavoured to impress upon the minds of the
princes of the country, that the power was rather in the commander-in-chief of the army than in the Governor and Council.
Indeed, a few months more of Mr. Spencer's government would
have made them lords paramount "

CHAPTER XXIII.

Trial of Sir Robert Fletcher—Civil Servants implicated in the Conspiracy.

THE reader will collect from the preceding letters, much more accurately than from any statement of mine, how just, upon the whole, were Lord Clive's opinions on all points affecting the government both of a nation and of an army. It is now my business to explain how he followed up the judicious blows which were struck at the advance posts, and with what perfect success he accomplished his object of re-establishing, in every department, the authority of discipline.

Though sincerely attached to the profession of which he was a member, and anxious on all fitting occasions to temper justice with mercy, Lord Clive knew that such a crisis as that which had just been surmounted could be made to work out its proper ends only by making such examples of the more prominent delinquents as should deter others in all time coming from being drawn into a similar vortex. He therefore gave orders that the whole of the captains, with the most conspicuously insubordinate of the subalterns, should be brought to trial, and that those convicted should be sent as prisoners to Calcutta. From various expressions in several of his letters, it appears that he had made up his mind to shoot the ringleaders. But as some doubt existed in the minds of the members of Council in regard to the power of Courts-martial in India to condemn to death, he consented, with some reluctance, to avoid that last extremity. In every instance, however, where the charge of having taken an active part in arranging the conspiracy was brought home to an officer, he was cashiered with disgrace, and transported in the first ship that sailed to England. Nor was justice appeased by dealing thus with persons holding subordinate rank in the service. In the course of the many investigations which took place, it came to light that Sir Robert Fletcher was completely mixed up with

the whole series of in subordinate transactions. Clive's resolution was instantly taken; and Fletcher, being put in arrest at the
head-quarters of his own command, a court was ordered to
assemble for his trial. It was to no purpose that the accused
pleaded his high rank, and demanded to be tried only by the
Governor and council. Clive would not listen to the appeal.
" Your repairing to Calcutta," he says, " in order to be tried by
the President and Council upon an accusation, your exculpation
from which depends mainly upon military law, is totally unprecedented, and therefore improper for me to comply with. That
you may not, however, imagine that I intend to take any other
part upon this occasion than my public station requires, be
assured that the court-martial to be held upon your late conduct
will be assembled by an order from the board, and the sentence
confirmed or approved by them."

The court met; and Sir Robert being found guilty, on the
clearest testimony, of wilfully concealing the treasonable designs
of others during a space of not less than four months, was sen-
tenced to be dismissed the service. Clive gave immediate orders
that the sentence which the Board confirmed should be carried
into effect. And here it may be worth noticing, that both the
individual then deprived of his commission, and the officer, himself implicated in the mutiny, whose evidence went farthest to
bring the charge home, attained, in after years, though by
widely different processes, to eminence in the world. Captain
Goddard, being reinstated in his rank, rose, under Warren Hastings, to command a division of the army, with which he performed one of the most brilliant exploits of which the annals of
Indian warfare make mention. Sir Robert Fletcher returned
to England, degraded and furious; yet, having a powerful interest at the India House, he soon managed to regain his position
in the service, and in due time appeared upon the stage as Commander-in-chief at Madras. Whether or not the disposition to
rebel against established authorities was an instinct with him, I
cannot say; but it is certain that he played successfully at the
latter station a game quite as serious as that in which he had
been interrupted at Bengal. He was the head of the party
which, in 1775, after a long contest with Lord Pigot, placed
him, though governor of the province, in arrest, and kept him a

prisoner at St. Thomas's both in defiance of the protest of the admiral commanding on the station, and the known will of the Court of Directors at home.

It is impossible to speak of Lord Clive's conduct throughout the whole of these most difficult and complicated transactions in terms of exaggerated praise. Calm, collected, resolute, yet just, he faced every danger that presented itself, and met every difficulty as it rose with a perfect self-possession which ensured success. In dealing, likewise, with the guilty, his forbearance won for him as much of admiration as his firmness. They who had abused the influence which they derived from their rank and experience to mislead others had no mercy shown; the young, the thoughtless, the repentant, were pardoned and restored to the service. Moreover, there was manifest in his whole bearing that forgetfulness of self which is the surest test of high principle in the conduct of public men. Of disrespectful words spoken about Lord Clive, when repeated to him, he took no notice. It was the authority of the President and Council, and of the Court of Directors of the East India Company, which he desired to maintain; and on one remarkable occasion he rebuked, by inference, the parties who had endeavoured to mix up this principle with considerations of a different kind. An officer—a Lieutenant Stainsforth—was reported to him as having expressed an intention to put his lordship to death rather than see the conspiracy broken up. Lord Clive refused to take any public notice of the threat, and only once referred to it when, in his address to the troops at Monghir, he spoke of the malcontents as misguided English officers—not as assassins. At the same time, being aware of the publicity which the story had obtained, and not being able to satisfy himself that some threat of the sort had never been uttered, he did not consider that it would be becoming to restore Mr. Stainsforth to the service. The letter from his secretary, however, which conveyed this refusal, was couched in delicate, almost in kind language; and it does not appear that either then or at any subsequent period, Mr. Stainsforth, or indeed any others of those who had gone furthest to mark their hostility to Lord Clive, were treated by him as objects of his resentment.

It was not, however, exclusively by the vigour of his proceed-

ings in putting down this mutiny that Lord Clive set an example
to his contemporaries of what the conduct of military men in
high command ought to be. Certain usages, of some standing,
which, while they bore heavily upon the resources of the private
soldiers, contributed to increase the emoluments of the higher
ranks of the army, came at this time to his knowledge. For
example, it was the practice of commandants of stations to levy
for their own use a trifling duty on every article of consumption
which was sold in the bazar. The impost appears to have been
recognized as a legal perquisite under the euphonious appellation
of Colonel—or Colonel's Gunge; and, when denounced by Clive,
there were not wanting those who threw in his teeth that he was
become zealous for the suppression, where others were affected
by them, of practices which in former days he had not scrupled
to follow for his own benefit. Among others, his friend Sir R.
Barker seems to have made an insinuation of this sort in a letter
which is partly taken up with explanations of the over-lenient
course adopted by the court-martial of which he was president
on the trial of a Lieutenant Vertue. Clive's answer to this communication is too characteristic, as well as too valuable in itself,
to be omitted. It runs thus :—

" I have received your letter of the 3rd of August, and rejoice to find that you have recovered your former state of health.
Orders are sent to the commanding officers to appoint a greater
number of members than thirteen, which, I hope, will prevent
these delays in future.

" I am sorry you should think yourself obliged to defend your
own conduct, as well as that of the members of the general
court-martial appointed to sit upon the trial of Lieutenant Vertue.
When I suggested to you my opinion at Bankepore I addressed
myself to you alone, without mentioning the other members.
The liberty I then took very nearly regarded your honour and
reputation, as well as the welfare of the East India Company, in
which is included the welfare of the nation.

" I must call to your remembrance some particular expressions I made use of that morning at breakfast, as others were
present, and can prove the truth of what I assert. I told you,
that, where conscience was in the case, exclusive of the sacredness of an oath, the world should not bias me to swerve from my

opinion; but where that was not so, and I was convinced in my own mind a man was guilty, neither apprehensions of law, or any deficiency in forms, should influence me to act in favour of those who were not deserving of it. I told you, at the same time, all the general officers in Great Britain would canvass this general court-martial, and that their attention would be more particularly fixed upon you, the President. These were my words, or words to that purpose; this also is my opinion, which I am not ashamed to declare to the whole world. If, therefore, any busy, intermeddling person has represented to you my expressions in another light, he has represented a falsity.

"With regard to the bazar duties, you may be assured from me, that, when I mentioned the circumstance of Sir Robert Fletcher's conduct, I was an utter stranger to any duties whatever being collected by the commanding officers on the necessaries of life. I never received such myself, or knowingly suffered others under me to receive them, either upon the coast or at Bengal; and had Colonel Smith, when he prided himself upon never having received bazar duties, informed me that he had allowed Colonel Peach to receive them, it would have been more consistent with that sincerity which he has always professed.

"No one has shown himself a greater friend to the field officers than myself; yet they seem already to forget the great advantages they enjoy. However, I must remark, that, to an officer whose pay and emoluments amount to 12,000*l.* per annum, the bazar duties can scarce be an object.

"I am surprised to find myself accused of erecting Colonel Gunge at Patna. To speak plainly, Barker, I never established a Gunge in my life, and never will; because I never approved of receiving duties on the necessaries of life; although I do not think those officers much in fault who have done the same from prescription only. Colonel Gunge was created by Colonel Calliaud, and revived by Colonel Cook. The Committee have forbid this custom in future.

"To conclude, the style and diction of this last letter is so contrary to Sir Robert Barker's natural disposition, that I am persuaded some evil-minded persons, who have their own interests more than your reputation at heart, have been the occasion, through misrepresentation. However, since my friendship for you is mistrusted, and the regard and attention which I have shown for your welfare, from the day of your embarkation to this hour, forgotten, I can only lament your misfortune and mine, that there should be men in the world who can make these impressions. For my own part, I am almost weary of the burden. I have found the pride, ambition, resentment, and self-interestedness of individuals so incompatible with the public good, that I should have given up the contest long ago, if I had not set the greatest value upon my own reputation, which is all I must expect to preserve upon my return to England, after so odious and disagreeable an undertaking."

There are two more occurrences connected with the revolt of the Bengal army which I feel that I should not be justified in passing over, though the notice taken of them will necessarily be brief. When the malcontents discovered that Lord Clive was neither to be cajoled nor threatened into concessions, great fear fell upon them; and in the height of their alarm several pondered the wisdom of deserting, and taking refuge either among the country powers, or in the French or Dutch settlements on the Ganges. To prevent the execution of the former of these plans, Clive caused the various roads out of the cantonments to be patroled; and put each officer, as he was arrested, under a guard of sepoys. To obviate all chance of carrying the latter into effect, he wrote to M. Law, now Governor of Chandernagore, and to M. Vernet, the chief of the Dutch settlement at Chinchura, and begged that neither of them would afford an asylum to men who had disgraced their country by insubordination, and proposed to disgrace themselves by deserting their colours. There existed at this time an excellent understanding between the representatives of the French and Dutch East India Companies and the British Government at Calcutta; and as Clive lived personally in habits of familiar intercourse with the two gentlemen just named, his request met with a prompt and favourable reception.

Again, Lord Clive attributed, and with perfect justice, no small measure of his success against the disaffected to the support which was afforded him by the newly-created field-officers, whom, in opposition to a strong party in the Court of Directors, he had succeeded in attaching to the several battalions of the Bengal army. These gentlemen, it appears, were of the same way of thinking, and as soon as order became thoroughly restored, they sent in a memorial praying, as the reward of their services, to be admitted to a share in the profits of the salt trade. Clive pointed out the impropriety of this proceeding, and the memorial was withdrawn. But he could not permit these gentlemen to suppose that any ill feeling towards themselves personally had dictated his opposition to their project. He therefore addressed to them a complimentary letter, from which the following is an extract:—

"Colonel Smith has undoubtedly acquainted you that I declined presenting your memorial to the Board previous to my receipt of your application for withdrawing it; and I conclude that the arguments I urged against the memorial, in my letter to him, have convinced you of my wish to preserve the enjoyment of the present emoluments of the field-officers upon this establishment. The general good of the whole, added to the consideration that every supernumerary Major will succeed, upon vacancies, to a share in the salt trade, will, I hope, prevail upon you to rest satisfied with the present distribution.

"I cannot omit this opportunity of mentioning how sensible I am of the service done by you, and the other field-officers, on the late mutinous combination; as without such assistance the resolution of the President and of the Council must have proved ineffectual. And, perhaps, you will not be displeased upon my assuring you, that, in my letters to the Court of Directors, I have represented your conduct, upon that particular occasion, in the very favourable light it so justly deserved."

And now that I may exempt both myself and the reader from the necessity of referring any more to this memorable page in the history of Lord Clive, it may be well if I permit him to describe, in his own energetic way, both the extent to which the conspiracy had spread, and the feelings with which the contemplation of it affected him. Of the suspicions which were entertained of the co-operation of some of the Company's civil servants with the mutineers in the army, notice has elsewhere been taken. It will be seen that Lord Clive speaks of the matter as a well-ascertained fact, and particularizes certain individuals, one of whom held the responsible office of under-secretary to the supreme council, while the others filled important stations in Calcutta. Against the whole of these, as well as against others of less note, the charges were entirely brought home, and to a man they were dismissed the service. But Lord Clive must tell his own tale He writes to Mr. Verelst on the 28th of May, 1766, in these terms :—

" Enclosed you will receive two letters, one from Mr. Martin, the other, although not signed, I know to be Higginson's handwriting; so that you see we are betrayed even by our own sub-secretary; and I make no doubt but the assistant-secretary is still deeper in the plot.

" You will observe, in the last general letter, the Directors order us to dismiss, not suspend; and I think near all the Company's servants concerned in exciting this mutiny might not only be dismissed, but sent home in the first ship. Such a behaviour in England would be high treason to the state, and every man of them would be hanged.

" I hope the Council will not hesitate one moment about turning out of the office both Stephenson and Higginson, and dismissing them the service, if concerned in fomenting the late mutinous combination. Indeed, very few are to be trusted ; and, in my opinion, the Council should immediately require the assistance of twelve or fourteen junior servants from Madras and Bombay ; for, I am fully persuaded this settlement can never be restored to order, or the honour of the nation or the Company retrieved, until there be a total change in the morals of individuals : and that can only be effected by turning out the most rich and factious, and transplanting others. I have some hopes the Directors will empower me to take such a step in their answer by the Admiral Stevens.

" How shocked must Sulivan and those Directors be, who opposed this appointment of field-officers ! Certain it is that, without their assistance, we must have given way to the mutiny amongst the officers ; and it is equally certain, if we had, Bengal must have been lost, or a civil war carried on to restore to the Company their lost authority, rights, and possessions; for it is beyond a doubt, that men capable of committing such actions as they have lately done would soon have gone such lengths as to have made it impossible ever to return to their native country.

"There was a committee to each brigade, sworn to secrecy; and I have it from undoubted authority, that the officers thought themselves so sure of carrying their point, that a motion was made and agreed to, that the Governor and Council should be directed to release them from their covenants. The next step would, I suppose, have been the turning me and the Committee out of the service. In short, I tremble with horror when I think how near the Company were to the brink of destruction.

"The plot hath been deeply laid, and of four months' standing. I can give a shrewd guess at the first promoters. One of them I have already mentioned to you, who will ere long, I hope, be brought to condign punishment.

"Remember again to act with the greatest spirit; and if the civilians entertain the officers, dismiss them the service; and if the latter behave with insolence, or are refractory, make them all prisoners, and confine them in the new fort. If you have any thing to apprehend, write me word, and I will come down instantly, and bring with me the third brigade, whose officers and men can be depended upon."

CHAPTER XXIV.

IT was now the month of September, 1766, and Lord Clive returned once more to the seat of government at Calcutta, was able to congratulate himself and the Court of Directors on the perfect accomplishment of the very difficult task which he had undertaken to perform. There was peace with all the neighbouring powers, and treaties were in force with some of them which gave as much promise as in those days Indian treaties could give, that the good understanding would continue, at least for a season. With great prudence Clive had resisted the Emperor's overtures to march with him to Delhi. He did not feel that the Company had any commission to settle the government of Hindostan, or to garrison its capital. They acknowledged Shah Alum as the legitimate head of the empire, it is true, paid him a fixed revenue on the provinces over which he had appointed them to act as his receivers, and treated him on every occasion with marks of outward respect. But they were not bound to wage war with the Mahrattas, Affghans, or Jauts on his account; and Clive, as the representative of the Company, declined every invitation and entreaty to do so. At the same time he permitted a brigade of the army to remain at Allahabad, in order to secure the territories of Oude, as well as those of Bahar, from insult.

Again, the corruptions which had so long disfigured both the civil and military services of Bengal were put down. There was no more oppression of the natives by jobmasters and agents; the eagerness of individuals to enrich themselves at the expense of the Company's interests was repressed; order and discipline had come back to the ranks of the army; and hardened offenders from both branches of the service having been removed, new men were brought in from whom better things were to be expected. Moreover, the closer the examination which Clive gave to his plan in regard to the salt trade, the better pleased he was with both its principle and its results. The issues of the first year's experiment had surpassed even his expectations. So large, indeed, were the profits accruing, that the share of the Company received an increase, while that of the society of trade was diminished; yet a commerce which insured to every member o. Council and colonel in the army 7000*l.* per annum, and settled the perquisites of majors and factors—the lowest rank of the officials who shared in it—at 2000*l.*, could not but be satisfactory to the parties embarked in it. At the same time let us not forget that, in a pecuniary point of view, all those persons were losers by the arrangement. The privilege of private trade, as previously claimed and enjoyed, had been far more profitable than these dividends: and they expressed themselves well satisfied with the new arrangement, simply because they had learned from experience that whatever Lord Clive believed to be best for the public service he would do, and compel others to do, whether they approved of his plan of operations or the reverse.

There was yet a third arrangement, more personal, in one sense, to himself, though general too, as concerned the benefits secured by it to the poorer classes of the Company's servants, on which Lord Clive could not but look with satisfaction. I have elsewhere spoken of the legacy bequeathed to him by the late Nabob, Meer Jaffier, and of the uses to which he proposed to apply it. His acceptance of the boon at all did not, of course, escape censure. He who sets himself to correct the frailties of others must lay his account with drawing down upon his own head a large share of odium: he need not expect that any but the worst motives will be attributed to his actions, whatever these may be. It was no sooner noised abroad, for example, in Calcutta that Clive had accepted a sum of money from Meer Jaffier's widow, than the tongue of scandal ran loose. Interested men proclaimed aloud their disbelief in the tale of the dying bequest. It was a present, and nothing else, given with a purpose, and as a consideration received; and the acceptance of it furnished one more proof of the rapacity as well as the tyrannical disposition of the man who did not, in his own person, hesitate to violate the covenant which he compelled others to observe. So spoke and wrote to one another, and to their friends in the Direction, the dregs of the party which Clive had broken up; but the behaviour of the Court was different. On the 8th of April Lord Clive had addressed a note to that body, in which he stated his belief that the Company's order was not intended to apply to the case in point; and that he had in consequence accepted from the Begum an obligation for the sum of five lacs of rupees. His letter went on to say, " that having determined to add nothing to his private resources out of money which might come to him in the form of pay or allowances during his present sojourn in India, he should not appropriate the amount to his own account, but should decree it to be paid into the Company's treasury, in order that a fund might be formed therewith, of which the interest should be dispensed to officers, non-commissioned officers, and private soldiers disqualified by wounds, or disease, or length of service, from further duty; and likewise to their widows who might be left in distressed circumstances." The Council, entertaining no doubt as to the legality of the whole proceeding, replied to this communication by thanking his Lordship for " his generous and well-placed donation ;" and the next packet carried from him a report of all that had been done to the Court of Directors. Here, either because the poison from Calcutta had begun to work, or that there were individuals who entertained honest scruples in the case, considerable hesitation was manifested in regard to the fitness of acceding to Lord Clive's proposal. But a reference to the law-officers of the Crown established, by the opinion which they delivered, the right of the legatee to his deceased friend's bequest, and the Court's misgivings ceased. On the 20th of August, 1767, it was unanimously resolved, " That his Lordship be empowered to accept of the said legacy or donation ; and that the Court do highly approve of his Lordship's generosity in bestowing the said legacy of five lacs in so useful a charity ; and they hereby consent and agree to accept the trust of the said fund, and will give directions that the same be carried into execution in legal and proper form."

The exact sum presented by Lord Clive to the Company's hospital at Poplar was 62,833*l.* To this the Nabob of Bengal added 37,700*l.* ; and the Company allowing interest on the whole to the amount of 24,128*l.*, a fund was raised which was more than sufficient at that time to place above the risk of destitution all who had a just claim to look to it for assistance. It must not, however, be supposed that the hospital itself owes its origin to Lord Clive's munificence. The institution at Poplar was founded so early as the year 1627, as a place of refuge for decayed seamen in the Company's service, and continued, so late as 1768, to provide for that class of persons exclusively ; but this is Clive's glory, in connexion with Poplar Hospital, that he first gave an impulse to that generous regard for the wants of their worn-out military servants which has long distinguished the East India Company above every other governing body in the world. Poplar Hospital is now to the soldiers of India what Chelsea Hospital is to the soldiers of the Crown.

To have accomplished so much in 18 months could not fail of being a proud reflection to Lord Clive. His private letters accordingly show that there was not an act of his brief but successful administration on which, at the period in his history at which we have now arrived, he looked back except with unmixed gratification. No wish to benefit himself, no desire to screen or slur over the faults of others, seems to have been present with him throughout. Whatever he did had been done in obedience to that strong sense of duty which, if we take it as our sole principle of action in private life, may perhaps stiffen rectitude into severity, but which, to public men, is the only guide that can lead them straight to the point which they ought to seek—their country's well-being and their own honour as connected with its advancement. Moreover, Lord Clive had so regulated the expense of his very household, that when the accounts of the government came to be made up, it was found that the pledge given on accepting the government of Bengal had been redeemed even to his own hurt. Clive did not undertake to sacrifice any portion of his private means in striving to benefit the Company. All to which he bound himself was, that, be his sojourn abroad longer or shorter, he would return at the end of it without having made the slightest addition to his private fortune ; and now an exact calculation of receipts and disbursements showed that there was a balance against him of upwards of

5000*l.* The fact is, that he carried no portion of his salary, or of his share in the salt trade, or indeed of any other sums officially paid in, to his private credit. Whatever was not required to cover the unavoidable expenses of his station, he made over in free gift to the gentlemen of his family; and these, being three in number, do not appear to have derived from the act any extravagant addition to their fortunes.

It had been Lord Clive's settled purpose from the outset, as all his letters, public as well as private, show, to resign the government without fail in December, 1766, and to return at once to England. This resolution, prudent in itself, received additional force from the severity of an illness with which he was about this time attacked. The fatigue, both of body and mind, which he had recently endured, and his frequent exposure to the burning suns of a burning climate, told heavily upon a constitution which had never, even in boyhood, been robust, and was now much shattered by past services. Towards the end of October, indeed, he became so alarmingly ill, that for a day or two his life was despaired of; and the effect of the crisis was to leave him enfeebled to such a degree, that he could take no more share in the management of public business. Under these circumstances he retired to a house in the country, where he remained in seclusion, waiting till despatches which were expected from London should arrive, and anticipating with eagerness the day which should relieve him from all further responsibility, and enable him to take his passage for Europe.

Such was Lord Clive's state of body and mind when, in December, the long looked-for packet arrived, bringing two long official communications from the Court of Directors — one addressed to the President and Council, the other to the President alone. They were both written in a spirit of candour which did honour to the feelings of the body which sent them forth; but, being drawn up by one ignorant of the effects of the changes which had recently occurred in Bengal, they conveyed instructions, immediate compliance with which must have resolved society into its elements. The Court entirely disapproved of the plan for remunerating its superior servants out of the profits of the salt monopoly. " In coming to this conclusion, they were not so much influenced by views of the particular merits or de-

merits of the new plan itself, as by a consideration of the mis-
chiefs which had for several years attended the general system of
internal trade carried on by the English gentlemen, with a high
hand, free of duties. Their orders, repeatedly sent out, to pay
the legal duties to the Nabob, and to keep within the meaning
of the Emperor's firman, had been totally neglected or pro-
vokingly evaded. Revolution after revolution had been the consequence, and immense suffering to the country ensued. It was
the deliberate opinion of the Court that no regulations could be
framed of sufficient stringency to prevent a recurrence of such
abuses ; and they saw no other chance of rest for the country
than in the entire withdrawal of their servants from interference
with the trade in articles which it belonged to the natives exclusively to cultivate, or raise, or bring, after the customs of their
forefathers, into the public market. The Court, however, observed, that the usual duties on salt, tobacco, and beetle, as
forming part of the revenues of Bengal, should still be levied ;
but beyond this it was their wish and express command that their
servants should not interfere with the trade in these articles."

I have given the substance of this despatch rather than the
ipsissima verba, because the style of public documents, and especially of Leadenhall-street documents, is sometimes more verbose
than attractive ; but the Court's letter to Lord Clive himself requires that it should be more carefully handled. After expressing
the sense entertained of the many obligations under which his
Lordship had laid the Company, by his penetration in discovering
where its true interests lay—by the rapidity with which he had
restored order to the several branches of the service, and the integrity which had governed all his actions, the Directors go on to say
—" The vast fortunes acquired in the inland trade have been obtained by a series of the most tyrannic and oppressive conduct that
ever was known in any age or country. We have been uniform
in our sentiments and orders on this subject from the first knowledge we had got, and your Lordship will not therefore wonder,
after the fatal experience we had of the violent abuses committed
in this trade, that we could not be brought to approve it, even
in the limited and regulated manner with which it comes to us
in the plan laid down in the committee's proceedings. We agree
in opinion with your Lordship on the propriety of holding out

such advantages to our chief servants, civil and military, as may open to them the means of honourably acquiring a competency in our service; but the difficulties of the subject, in the short time we have to consider it, have obliged us to defer giving our sentiments and directions thereupon until the next despatch."

The Court which ordered these instructions to be drawn out must have overlooked the peculiar position of the parties proposed to be affected by them, if indeed it were not entirely ignorant on the subject. Take away the share in the salt monopoly from the Company's chief servants, and there would be left for them, at this moment, nothing to depend upon but their salaries. The import trade, from which, when Lord Clive first arrived in the country, they derived their main profits, was taken entirely out of their hands. A numerous body of free merchants —that is to say, of Englishmen protected by licence from the Directors, had settled of late at each of the presidencies, who, having nothing to attend to except their private affairs, soon managed to drive the covenanted servants of the Company out of the market. This it was, indeed, which in some measure forced the latter to seek, in a usurpation of the commerce of the Indian traders, those profits of which their own countrymen had deprived them; and the large returns which they derived from the new traffic led them on to turn their undivided attention into this channel. To deprive these gentlemen of their right of traffic first, and then to take away from them the revenues which had been granted as compensation for the loss, was in point of fact to say, that they should have their bare salaries, and nothing else to depend upon. Besides, Clive's plan for the management of the salt trade did no wrong to any one. Salt had been from time immemorial a monopoly in the hands of the native government, and the licences were at stated periods hired out to the best bidder. Clive merely assumed that the Company, as Dewan, had a right to act as the Nabob's Dewans had acted before them; and by making a certain number of senior servants the Company's farmer, he but placed an European corporation in the room of some Indian Zemindar, or, it may be, banker; subjecting his own countrymen, besides, to restrictions more favourable to the native retail dealer than any Nabob or Dewan would have cared to impose on his lessee. His mortification was therefore extreme when he found that both his policy and the reasoning on which it was founded had been misunderstood by the Directors, and that he was commanded, in terms which admitted of no evasion, to reverse it. But Clive was not the man to undo his own work, and to throw a kingdom into confusion merely because those in authority over him required a specific line of proceeding to be followed. He knew that it was to the interest of the Company, much more than to that of individuals, that the Court should have time to revise its judgment and reverse its decree, should the results of further examination point out to them its extreme inexpediency. He therefore directed the Council to make public the wishes of the home authorities. But the same order which conveyed this intelligence to the public of Calcutta contained an act of Council, by which the grant to the society of trade was confirmed for one year, and notice given that on the first of September, 1767, it should terminate.

As the history of this affair, though intimately connected with the history of Lord Clive's public life, stands like a thing apart, and is for many reasons deserving of general notice, it may not be amiss if I endeavour in few words to bring it to an issue. The Court of Directors were not convinced by the arguments of the Supreme Council at Calcutta. They therefore, on the 20th of March, 1767, gave preremptory orders that the society of trade should be broken up, and the salt-pans sold by a public auction, at which no Europeans should be under any pretence permitted to become bidders. At the same time, in order to compensate the senior servants for the loss thereby inflicted upon them, they decreed that an allotment of $2\frac{1}{2}$ per cent. on the net revenues of the Dewannee should be made over to them in specified shares; and that the pay of captains and subalterns of the army should, to a trifling extent, be increased. Meanwhile Mr. Verelst, who had succeeded Lord Clive in the government of Bengal, saw no just reason, when September, 1767, arrived, to act upon the principle laid down in the Order of Council, dated December, 1766. Under the pretext of affording time to wind up accounts and collect debts, he prolonged the existence of the society of trade for another year; nor was it till September, 1768, that the monopoly came to an end. But even then matters were managed very loosely. The local government had received no instructions from home. They only knew that the trade was to be opened, and they threw it open in such a way as should still secure large advantages to themselves. By and by there came a despatch from London, bearing date December, 1769, which declared that all residents within the provinces, whether Europeans or natives, were free to engage in the inland trade in any manner, and to any extent, which might suit their own convenience. And, finally, it was proposed that, for the benefit of the government, a trifling duty should be levied upon salt, which the manufacturer should pay to the excise officers on the spot, leaving the wholesale and retail dealers to make as much profit as they could out of the article after it should have come into their hands.

Lord Clive, having returned, as we shall presently see, to London long before matters took this turn, protested against these arrangements from the beginning. He described the surrender of the Company's share of the monopoly as a gratuitous sacrifice of revenue to the amount of 300,000$l.$ per annum, from which no human being, except the few wealthy individuals engaged in the manufacture and first sale of the salt, would benefit; and he denounced the project of remunerating public servants by a per centage taken out of the public collections, not more because of the loss entailed thereby upon the proprietors, than because it would inevitably lead to the growth of a system of solicitation from which the worst consequences might be anticipated. "If you grant a commission on the revenue," he says in a paper sent in to the Court, " the sum will not only be large, but known to the world : the allowance being publicly ascertained, every man's proportion will at times be the occasion of much discourse, envy, and jealousy, and the great will interfere in your appointments, and noblemen will perpetually solicit you to provide for the younger branches of their families."

It is curious to read these prophetic warnings of Clive, and to compare them with the accomplishment. And it is not less curious to observe the candour with which individuals in the Direction admitted the extent to which the thought of their dividends were mixed up in the minds of the holders of India stock with visions of moral improvement in the newly acquired provinces. Mr. Scrafton, writing to Lord Clive by the same ship which conveyed the Court's disapproval of the plan of the trade society, says—" The proprietors have begun to clamour for an increase of dividend, which the Directors think unsuitable to the situation of the Company's affairs. This has induced the Directors to defer the consideration of the gratification of the servants on abolishing the salt trade. Such considerations could not be but for a vast sum ; and if it had got wind that such gratifications were ordered, the proprietors would be outrageous for an increase of the dividend. Though we cannot open our minds upon it, yet it appears to me an increase of dividend must take place at the quarterly court in June ; and then the court will be under no restraint, but will give a per centage on the revenues, in which the governor will have a great share in lieu of trade ; the rest among the committee, council, colonels, and ten below council, but no lower. * * * Your Lordship may be assured it will take place ; for when the last paragraph was added to the letter to you, the committee declared it was their meaning and intention to do it by the next ship."

CHAPTER XXV.

Clive's parting Address.

IT was the anxious wish of the Court of Directors that Lord Clive should continue yet a little longer in the government of Bengal. Their letter of the 17th of May, 1766, concluded with an earnest request that he would for one year more watch over the developement of his own plans; but the arrangements for his departure were already complete, and the state of his health would not permit that they should be altered. Not only had the digestive organs lost their tone with him, but he suffered from time to time such spasms of acute pain, that a free use of opium, and that alone, had saved him from sinking under it. Still his zeal for the public good never grew dull. He had already weeded out from the civil service its most objectionable members; he still saw with regret that of those who remained, some, from a too exclusive attention to self-interest, others through a laxity of principle, which they may have deceived themselves into regarding as mere easiness of temper, were incapable of doing justice to his arrangements. Besides, men had made their fortunes of late on this side of India with such marvellous rapidity, that the most important offices came to be held by mere boys. To remedy this evil, Lord Clive took it upon himself to call in the aid of civilians from Madras; and gave seats in council to four gentlemen from that presidency very much to the annoyance of the parties over whose heads they passed. But this was not all. The Council, though an important body, had ceased since the late arrangements at home to exercise the powers of government, which were really, if not nominally, vested in the Select Committee. To fill the Committee, therefore, with gentlemen of experience as well as talent, became an object of the first importance, and Lord Clive used his best endeavours, not unsuccessfully, to accomplish it. Not that this was to be done in a moment, or as a matter of course. The acceptance of a place in the select committee, besides implying the necessity of relinquishing all other employment that might have a tendency to withdraw any portion of the individual's care from his public duties, rendered constant residence at or near Fort William inevitable. Now there was nothing about Fort William in those days to bind men's fancy to the place itself, or to the society which frequented it; while the opportunities of saving, if not of making, money were far more abundant at the best stations in the interior than at the capital. But as Clive would not, in his own case, allow private feelings to stand in the way of public duty, so, when he believed that gentlemen were qualified to serve the Company as members of the Select Committee, he did not hesitate to demand from them the same sort of sacrifices which he was willing to make himself. The following extracts from letters to his friend Mr. Sykes and to Mr. Cartier, of whom he entertained a high opinion, will show what his feelings were in regard to this matter. Mr. Sykes was then Resident at Moorshedabad, a position of large emolument. high respectability, and little labour; Mr. Cartier, as chief of a factory, had nothing to gain by being transferred to the Select Committee, and was therefore unwilling to incur the labour and responsibility. To overcome the scruples of the former, Lord Clive wrote as follows :—

" I have received your letter, urging many reasons against your residing at Calcutta, when Mr. Verelst came to the chair. Your intention of declining the government, I must confess, is the only one that seems to carry any weight. Your situation, I believe, is a very agreeable one, and your conduct, I am persuaded, will bring advantage to the Company and honour to yourself. Yet let us not forget, Sykes, the principles upon which you and I have hitherto acted, of sacrificing private convenience to public good. To doubt my friendship, because I cannot carry it to such lengths, is not to know me. I have loved you as a brother; yet a brother cannot alter my sentiments of what is right and wrong. If you are fully convinced that your health will not permit you to live in Calcutta, and for that reason, among others, you mean to decline the government, there may be reasons given in abundance for remaining in your present station; and, among the rest, that of your being the most fit for such an employment. To conclude: this matter must be decided by my successor, Mr. Verelst, after my departure. I have given you my sentiments, which are consistent with my friendship for you, and my duty to the Company."

Mr. Cartier's scruples seem to have been more easily overcome; and Lord Clive wrote immediately to express his gratification at the circumstance. The subjoined letter, bearing date the 22nd of January, 1767, was one of the last to which he ever attached his signature in India :—

" The receipt of your friendly letter and your acceptance of being nominated one of the Select Committee, with so much cordiality, has afforded me more real satisfaction than I have feit for these many months. I can now leave India with satisfaction to myself, because I leave it in tranquillity, and the chief management of these important and extensive concerns in the hands of men of honour and approved probity and abilities.

" Be assured, my good Sir, you will not have to encounter many of those disagreeable circumstances which you seem to apprehend in your letter to Mr. Verelst. That unthankful task has fallen to my lot. The Select Committee, and Committee of Inspection, have already made every regulation for the public good which can be desired or thought of; so that it only rests with you gentlemen to keep matters in the same channel, and not to relax in your authority, or let yourselves down, by declining to support the dignity of your station.

" A gentleman endowed, like Mr. Cartier, with a good capacity and solid judgment, of a generous and disinterested way of thinking, cannot fail of proving a very deserving servant to the Company, and of acquiring honour for himself, if he will but have a little more confidence in himself." After assuring him that, if he finds his new situation at Calcutta agreeable, he will use his interest to have him named Mr. Verelst's successor in the government, he continues :—" The state of my health is such, that I cannot continue in it (the government) another year, with any prospect of doing the Company service; indeed. I do not think I should survive another month; I have therefore determined to resign the government."

It was not, however, exclusively by promoting the best interests of the great body which he served that Clive won for himself a proud name in Indian story. Strange as it may sound, when predicated of one who set up and pulled down princes at his pleasure, no European was ever more desirous than he to preserve in its integrity the framework of native society. While he did his best to realize an adequate revenue for the Company, he deprecated having recourse to measures of which the effect must be to trench on the funds necessary to support, in becoming style, the higher classes of the Indian families. His opinions on this head are stated in a letter to Mr. Palk, in which, bearing date the 25th of April, 1766, he describes, with equal force and truth, the inevitable results to their country should the time ever come when there ceased to be a native gentry in India. I need not quote this document, because the end which Lord Clive so feelingly deprecated has long ago come to pass, and its consequences are felt and lamented in proportion as men look beyond the mere preservation of peace, to the moral and intellectual elevation of 100,000,000 of their fellow creatures.

Another characteristic of Lord Clive's system of government seems to have been this—that, taking no account of personal affection or personal antipathy, he looked out for the fittest men to be employed in the higher service of the state, and placed them where their talents gave the best promise of a prosperous issue. Colonel Richard Smith, as I have elsewhere shown, was certainly not one of his favourites; yet he kept Colonel Smith in high and responsible command, and acknowledged, on every occasion, the services which he performed. On the other hand, it was a matter of principle with him never to thrust unqualified persons into office, nor to spare his dearest friends if, through any error of judgment or principle, they misconducted themselves. Few of the younger servants of the Company stood higher in his personal esteem than Mr. Samuel Middleton; yet, when that gentleman incurred the censure of the Board, Lord Clive, as President, put his name to the letter of reproof, and replied to a private letter from Mr. Middleton in the following terms :—

" I have received your letter of the 19th of September, in which you express your concern at the censure passed upon you by the Board, and imagine you may have done something to forfeit my friendship. To reason in this way is to know but little of the duty of a governor in a public station.

"If the Board were unanimous, which they really were, in thinking you and the other gentlemen had been wanting in diligence and attention to the Company's business, was it in my power to change or alter their sentiments? Or could I attempt such a thing consistently with my duty, or the principles upon which I have hitherto acted? The real truth of the matter is, that the relaxation of government for some years past, has introduced so much luxury, extravagance, independency, and indolence into Bengal, that every effort upon our part to reclaim this settlement is looked upon as a hardship, or an act of injustice; although it be absolutely necessary for the salvation of the whole." After condemning the wrong-headed opposition which had been offered by some of the younger servants, and remarking on the danger which they incurred thereby, he adds :—

" To set aside the Governor, and speak as a friend, I entertain no doubt of the integrity of your intentions, and of your zeal for the service; but you are naturally of an indolent, good-natured, and hospitable disposition, which in private life may make you beloved by all that know you: yet, in a public station, these qualities may subject you to the greatest inconveniences. You become responsible, not only to the public for your want of attention, but for the want of attention of those acting under you, who will perpetually trespass on your good nature. The indulgence shown by you to the young gentlemen of the factory, which I myself was an eye-witness to, must have this consequence—of their becoming very familiar, which in your present station they ought not to be; of being very supine and very neglectful of the Company's business, in which your own reputation is more immediately concerned. And I wish the mischief may only end here. After having led so luxurious, extravagant, and independent a life, there will be much to fear for themselves after your departure.

" The open manner in which you have expressed your sentiments and grievances gives me a right to send you mine in return, which I do assure you proceeds from real friendship and regard for the interests of those who are acting under you.

Perhaps they may not be looked upon in that light by the said young men.   If not, I wish future experience may not convince them to the contrary."

Besides thus watching with jealous care over the conduct of gentlemen employed in the administration of public affairs, Lord Clive did his best to promote among Europeans a study of the native languages, and gave every encouragement to the labours of scientific men, whether they turned their attention to natural history, to botany, or to geology. Mr. Gladwin, one of the earliest, and in those days best, of our Oriental scholars, owed the whole of his success in life to Lord Clive's patronage, who found him a volunteer, and transferred him, on account of his acquirements, to the civil service, where better opportunities of prosecuting his favourite study were afforded.   The celebrated Major Rennell was likewise in the number of his clients.   Clive took him by the hand when a lieutenant of engineers ; and, by employing him in various surveys, and throwing open to him all the maps in store at Fort William, made the way clear before him to future eminence.   Moreover, he caused the mouth of the Ganges, with every channel and creek communicating therewith, to be examined ; and had charts made out, by means of which a navigation heretofore difficult, and not unfrequently dangerous, became as easy as that of any frith or estuary in Europe.   But it is time that I should pass on from this part of my subject, which I shall do after briefly describing the circumstances which attended Clive's final severance from the government and the gentlemen who for 18 months had shared it with him.

On the 16th of January, 1767, Lord Clive for the last time attended a meeting of the Select Committee.   His health, though somewhat renovated, was still very infirm.   He looked as those do who have not long shaken aside an attack of jaundice, and walked with an infirm step to his seat at the head of the Council Board.   He carried a paper in his hand, which, after a few words introductory to the subject, he laid upon the table, and desired the secretary to read.   It was a valedictory letter to the Committee, in which, after explaining that the duty of striving to prolong life alone compelled him to quit the country—that he lamented the necessity, and would have lamented more, but that affairs were in a flourishing state, and in the hands of an upright and able government—he went on to exercise the authority which was vested in him by continuing the Select Committee, filling up vacancies among its members, and laying down general rules for its guidance in time coming. His letter cautions the gentlemen in authority against being too anxious to increase the revenues, especially where this could be effected only by oppressing the landholders and tenants; for that so long as the country remained in peace, the collections would exceed the demands. He points out some difficulties likely to result from the state of the currency, and strongly recommends that all Company's servants and free traders should be recalled from the interior; because till that were done the natives could hardly be said to be masters of their own property. He observes, "that the orders for the abolition of the salt trade being express, there was nothing to be done except to pay obedience to them. But, as I am of opinion," he continues, "that the trade upon its present footing is rather beneficial than injurious to the inhabitants of the country, and that a continuation of this indulgence, or some equivalent, is become absolutely necessary, and would be an honourable incitement to diligence and zeal in the Company's service, I flatter myself the Court of Directors will be induced to settle some plan that will prove agreeable to your wishes."

There seems to have been upon his mind an anxious dread lest the spirit of corruption and insubordination should revive; in which case he observed that the very existence of the empire would be endangered. "It has been too much the custom," he observes, "in this government to make orders and regulations, and thence to suppose the business done. To what end and purpose are they made, if they be not promulgated and enforced? No regulation can be carried into execution, no order obeyed, if you do not make rigorous examples of the disobedient. Upon this point I rest the welfare of the Company in Bengal. The servants are now brought to a proper sense of their duty. If you slacken the reins of government, affairs will soon revert to their former channel; anarchy and corruption will again prevail, and, elate with a new victory, be too headstrong for any future efforts of government. Recall to your memories the many attempts that have been made in the civil and military departments to overcome our authority and to set up a kind of independency against the Court of Directors. Reflect also on the resolute measures we have pursued, and their wholesome effects. Disobedience to legal power is the first step of sedition; and palliative measures effect no cure. Every tender compliance, every condescension on your parts, will only encourage more flagrant attacks, and will daily increase in strength, and be at last in vain resisted. Much of our time has been employed in correcting abuses. The important work has been prosecuted with zeal, diligence, and disinterestedness; and we have had the happiness to see our labours crowned with success. I leave the country in peace. I leave the civil and military departments under discipline and subordination : it is incumbent upon you to keep them so. You have power, you have abilities, you have integrity; let it not be said that you are deficient in resolution. I repeat that you must not fail to exact the most implicit obedience to your orders. Dismiss or suspend from the service any man who shall dare to dispute your authority. If you deviate from the principles upon which you have hitherto acted, and upon which you are conscious you ought to proceed, or if you do not make a proper use of that power with which you are invested, I shall hold myself acquitted, as I do now protest against the consequences."

Such was Lord Clive's parting address to his former colleagues in the government. It was worthy of the man who had raised British India in 18 months from the lowest depth of degradation to the wealth and importance of an empire; and had there been in the body which received it any portion of his genius, it would not have been delivered in vain. But the Select Committee, though composed of men of fair average talent, could not boast of any one commanding intellect among its members. The task, therefore, of completing reforms which Clive himself found considerable difficulty to begin, was too great for it; and the consequences soon began to develope themselves.

CHAPTER XXVI.

Returns to England—Reception.

ON one of the last days of Jan. 1767, Lord Clive, accompanied by the gentlemen of his household, and his old and valued friend General Carnac, embarked on board the Britannia in the Ganges. On the 14th of July he landed at Portsmouth, and the following day reached London. He was admitted almost immediately to private audiences by the King and Queen, both of whom received him most graciously; while the marks of respect shown to him by the Court of Directors appear to have satisfied his wishes. Still the greeting awarded to him by his countrymen in general was not, on the present occasion, what it had formerly been. His old enemies at the India House continued in power and great activity; and their strength had been increased of late by the accession of many new allies, whose violence far exceeded their own. Not only the pilferers and oppressors whom he had removed from the public service in Bengal, but relatives of these men, their friends, and acquaintances, combined to work him harm. Newspapers, more venal then than they are now, had for some time past been hired to run him down; and the tidings of his arrival in his native country seemed to act as a fresh incitement to their malevolence. Stories of his cruelty and rapacity, as incredible as they were hideous, passed current from one extremity of the kingdom to another. Nor was the rancour of his enemies mitigated, far less appeased, by this extended system of persecution. They spent large sums in the purchase of India stock with the view of wielding against him, when a convenient opportunity should offer, the weight of the Court of Proprietors; and left no means untried to obtain an ascendancy in the Court of Directors also. It was unfortunate for Lord Clive, in this state of the public mind, that the party in the Direction which he generally supported should have taken the unpopular side in a controversy which affected men's personal interests more than their abstract opinions. The proprietors of India stock were no sooner informed of the results of Clive's endeavours in Bengal, than they began to clamour for an advance in the dividends from 6 to 10 per cent.; and Clive himself, writing home upon the subject, had recommended that their wish should be complied with. But his friends, either knowing the true state of their pecuniary affairs better than he, or entertaining strong doubts in regard to the future, were not to be persuaded. " Believe the word of a Director," wrote Mr. Scrafton in 1765, " that the Company must have many lacs before they can increase their dividend. Consider, my Lord, what a vast sum of their capital has been locked up without interest in Mahomed Ali's debts, the vast fortifications, the fatal Manilla expedition, and the sum locked up in the support of French prisoners, for which no instalments are yet settled—all form prodigious deductions, which a year's revenue of the whole province of Bengal will barely replace; not to mention the dreadful breach on the Company's capital before the battle of Plassey." In the same spirit another of Clive's warmest admirers, Mr. Dudley, expresses himself. One of his letters, dated the 17th of May, 1766, deprecates every proposal of enlarged dividends, on the ground that the Company had been forced to raise several hundred thousand pounds on loan ; and that demands for repayment were urgent, and of daily occurrence.

The policy of this section of the Court, of which Mr. Rous was at the head, whether prudent or the reverse in itself, offered a favourable *champ de bataille* to Clive's enemies, on which they did not delay to enter. They threw themselves to a man into the opposite scale, and, spending enormous sums in the purchase of shares, succeeded by and by in obtaining a majority among the proprietors. They could not, indeed, command, for a while, strength enough to nominate their own Director. So late as April, 1767, Mr. Rous still kept the chair. But the party which in September, 1766, had forced up the dividend from 6 per cent. to 10, raised it again on the 6th of the following May to 12½, and provoked, by so doing, the immediate interference of the King's government. It would carry me far beyond my proper province, as the biographer of Lord Clive, were I to give an account in detail of the parliamentary proceedings which ensued.

Enough is done when I state that a Cabinet too little confident in itself to act vigorously on any subject, played with the Company's privileges as it did with the claims of the American colonists; and that, lacking courage to transfer the territorial sovereignty to the Crown, it compelled the Company to purchase a continuance of present right by agreeing to pay 400,000*l.* per annum into the exchequer. The dividend likewise was fixed, by an authority more stringent than that of the India House, not to exceed 10 per cent.; and intimation was given that more would be done when a convenient season should arrive.

Meanwhile there had been fierce strife in Leadenhall-street as to the measures which it behoved the Company to adopt in regard to their servants dismissed by the Select Committee, and convicted of having received presents in violation of the order acknowledged to have reached them in January 1764. The Directors, anxious to maintain the authority of their Court, determined to try the result of a prosecution; and were confirmed in their view of the liability of the delinquents by the unanimous opinion of the Crown's and Company's lawyers. The proprietors, dissatisfied with Rous and his friends, and attributing the successful issue of their struggle for an increased dividend to the exertions of the parties threatened, espoused a different side in the controversy. The prosecution which the Upper Court had made preparations to begin, they declared to be uncalled for; and a vote of indemnity being proposed, it was passed by a large majority. A heavier blow on the usefulness of the Court of Directors, and indeed on the power of the Indian government generally, was never inflicted. The decision of the proprietors gave notice that, so long as they had influential friends at home, the Company's servants abroad need not care to what extent they set established regulations at defiance; and the progress of a few years served pretty well to show that the intimation was not lost upon them.

There was no feeling at this time of personal ill-will towards Lord Clive in the great body of proprietors of India stock. On the contrary, their predilections were all in favour of one to whom they justly attributed the flourishing state of their finances; and they were ready to mark the sense which they entertained of his merits by any arrangements which his friends might propose. Enemies he undoubtedly had, both numerous and active, among them; but the mass felt towards him as they had done on the day when they implored him to go out and save from ruin the province which his valour had achieved for them. It would appear too, that Lord Clive's private friends, among whom Mr. Walsh filled a prominent position, took greater pains to conciliate the favour of the proprietors than to carry the Court of Directors with them. The former, anxious for large returns, believed all that was said respecting the money-value of the De-wannee, and perhaps something more. The latter, still averse to increase a rate of interest which could not be paid without adding constantly to the funded debt, sought rather to decry the importance of the acquisition, in a pecuniary point of view, even though by doing so they detracted, as Clive thought, from the importance of his services. Accordingly Mr. Walsh, in bringing forward a proposition that the Company should testify to Lord Clive's merits and to their sense of the obligations under which he had laid them, called upon the proprietors, rather than the Directors, to decree that the feof or jaghire granted by Meer Jaffier should be continued to his lordship and his heirs for a further term of ten years after the current term should have expired. Mr. Walsh carried his first motion by 243 to 170 open votes—a majority which was very little diminished by the result of the ballot; but he provoked, at the same time, a spirit of hostility elsewhere, of which the effects were seen when the final decision came to be taken. The jaghire was confirmed to Lord Clive and his successors according to the spirit of the original proposition, but the majority which settled the point amounted to no more than 29 votes.

Matters were in this state when Lord Clive reached London. Of the entire success of his management of the Company's concerns there could be but one opinion; and the events which characterized the last months of his administration seemed to have put the finishing touch to his glory. It was impossible for the most rancorous of his enemies to get up, under such circumstances, the slightest symptom of hostility towards him. But though their influence was not such as to command a direct display of dissatisfaction, they managed to throw a considerable damp upon the enthusiasm with which he expected to be greeted.

In more than one of their public letters, but especially in that which urged him to abide another year at his post, the Directors, besides expressing themselves in terms of exceeding gratitude and admiration, had spoken of their intention to mark their sense of his eminent services by some appropriate grant; and now that he was come to claim the performance of the promise, the most lukewarm felt that to defer redeeming their pledge would be impossible.   Accordingly, having received him immediately after his audience of the King, and thanked him, through their Chairman, for all that he had done, they summoned a general court to confirm the arrangement previously voted with regard to the Jaghire; and this time, at least, he had the satisfaction of knowing that the proposition was carried without a single vote having been recorded in opposition to it.

Like other men who have done their country good service, Lord Clive was jealous both of his personal renown and of the plans and arrangements which owed their existence to his personal exertions. An apparent reluctance in the Court of Directors, therefore, to take the lead in this question of the jaghire much displeased him.   He treated their excessive care of the Company's finances as a slight offered to himself; and being but little in the habit of disguising his feelings, he made no scruple in giving utterance to his indignation wherever the subject was referred to.   One of his letters, written from Walcot, about three months subsequently to his arrival in England, is so characteristic, that I feel myself constrained to subjoin an extract from it   He had been in correspondence with his friend Mr. Scrafton, himself a Director, at that time, and had not spared the body of which the latter gentleman was a member.   Mr. Scrafton, on the other hand, being anxious that Lord Clive should not hastily withdraw his support from a body of men who had stood by him when at a distance, and were still well disposed in the main, endeavoured to do away with this impression.   "If your lordship," he says, "conceives any resentment on the conduct of the Directors respecting the Jaghire, you will act from misrepresentation.   One or two were cold on the subject, by believing themselves the objects of your resentment in consequence of Whately's story; but the general sense was, 'We cannot, as Directors, recommend so large a grant; the fate the question met with before proves that many thought it too much ; but we will give our votes for it.' To conclude, my lord, I really think it for your own honour and for the interest of the Company to support the present set."

To thwart a man of Lord Clive's temperament upon a subject so nearly touching his self esteem is seldom a prudent measure; and the defence of the Directors by Mr. Scrafton wholly failed of its object. It drew forth a reply to the following effect :—

" I received your letter, and return you many thanks for your congratulations about the jaghire. However, you will scarce believe me when I tell you that I was, before it was confirmed, and am at this time, very indifferent about it. My wish was to have it brought to a conclusion at any rate; for I could not avoid observing all parties at work to suspend coming to a con- clusion; and many were at greater pains, from rank infernal jealousy and envy, to conceal and lessen my services, in order to lessen my influence: but, I thank God, I am now an inde- pendent man, what I was determined to be at all events.

" I cannot but take notice of one paragraph of your letter ; *that the Directors thought the grant too large, and therefore would not recommend it:* I am therefore the more obliged to the Proprietors, who were all of a different way of thinking.

" I am obliged to you for your advice about my conduct towards the Directors, because I am persuaded you mean me well; but know, Scrafton, I have a judgment of my own, which has seldom failed me, in cases of much greater consequence than what you recommend. As to the support which, you say, was given to my government, when abroad, by the Directors, they could not have done otherwise, without suffering in their reputa- tion, and perhaps quitting the Direction. In return, let me ask, whose interest contributed to make them Directors, and keep them so? My conduct wanted no support, it supported itself, because it was disinterested, and tended to nothing but the public good. From the beginning it put all mankind at defiance, as it does at this hour : and had the Court of Directors thought fit to make my conduct more public than they have done, all impartial and disinterested men must have done me justice. However, that remains for myself to make known, when conve- nient and proper.

" After having said thus much, I must tell you (though by your writing you seem to give credit to the report), that what Whately is said to have told Wedderburn is absolutely false, as is everything else said to have been communicated by Mr. Grenville to Mr. Wedderburn ; and I can attribute these mean suspicions of the Directors to nothing but their envy and jealousy. However, as I have often said before, and say now, there is nothing the Directors can do shall make me lose sight of the Company's true interest. Upon principle, I would always stand by the East India Company: I am now farther bound by the ties of gratitude. This is the ground upon which I now stand, and upon which I will risk my reputation. No little, partial considerations shall ever bias me."

The sentiments conveyed in the closing sentences of this letter came from the heart of the writer. The channel into which his earliest interests were turned never ran dry. In spite of his high station in this country, in spite of the influence which he possessed in the House of Commons, to which he returned, including his own seat, seven members, Lord Clive could not withdraw his attention, even in part, from the politics of Leadenhall-street. He regarded India as by far the most important of the dependencies of the British crown ; and entertaining his own views as to the way in which it ought to be managed, he ceased not, by personal interference, by swaying the opinions of others, by splitting votes, and indeed by all other practicable means, short of becoming himself a candidate for the Direction, to prevent any interference with arrangements already made, and to keep those to whom the execution of his plans had been intrusted up to the collar. A remarkable proof of his anxiety on this head is given in a letter which he addressed from Bath on the 7th of November, in this year, to Mr. Verelst, on whom the government of Bengal had devolved. As the document in question is a very valuable one on many accounts, but especially because of the light which it throws on the writer's principle of action, my reader would scarcely thank me were I to withhold it. After apologising for the freedom which he is about to use, and alluding delicately to the share which he had had in raising Mr. Verelst to the high station which he filled, Lord Clive goes on to say :—

" But exclusive of the part I take in your success on my own account, my regard and affection for you lead me to reflect that the reputation, as well as private satisfaction, of your future life in England, must grow out of the honour which you may, and I trust will, acquire by a resolute and unspotted administration of the Company's affairs in Bengal. Your integrity and the goodness of your heart must be acknowledged by all who know you: and it is with pleasure I observe that you have set out with a due attention to other necessary and public qualifications. Continue in the full exertion of that steadiness and resolution with which you began your government. Your judgment is sound. Set a just value, then, upon every opinion of your own, and always entertain a prudent degree of suspicion of the advice of any man who can possibly be biassed by self-interested motives. Before I touch upon particulars, permit me to urge, in general, the necessity there is for you and the whole Council and Committee to join in holding the military under due subordination and subjection. The dangerous consequences which may ensue from the least relaxation of command over a body so numerous as the English officers, should ever be thought of with horror, and the good effects of maintaining an inflexible authority cannot be too often recollected, in the instance of the late association.

" I am glad to find that you are upon your guard against the pride and ambition of the Colonel, who, if there be any merit in the conduct of the military officers, will certainly claim the whole to himself, and write the world to that purpose. His last, I should say his first, dispute, whether the Governor or the Commanding Officer of the troops ought to have the title of Commander-in-Chief, was such an open and audacious attack upon the dignity of your office, that I am surprised you let it pass unnoticed. Had a minute been made of it, he would infallibly have been dismissed the service.

" It is with great concern I observe that you have consented to the increase of the military establishment, by the raising of four regiments of horse, which will be an exorbitant, and yet useless, expense. General Carnac knows, as I do, that black cavalry, instead of being serviceable, are very detrimental to us. I am also sorry that you have augmented the artillery. One independent company at Calcutta, in time of peace, will answer every purpose. To have more, either there or at Ghyrotty, is only sacrificing the lives of so many men without service. The Directors, I fear, will reprimand you on these matters, for they seem much inclined to lessen even the establishment I made for Bengal.

" The sooner you confine the whole of our force within the boundary of the Caramnassa the better. The Abdally's invasion of Bengal must be a mere bugbear. So long a march is next to impossible, and therefore I think he will never attempt it. The Mahratta is the only power we have to manage, as invasions from them must retard our revenues, though they cannot endanger our possessions.

" You certainly did well in persevering not to restore the Monghyr officers ; and I hope you have obliged all, except the young lads, to embark for England.

" You will have heard that all our letters and proceedings have been laid before both Houses of Parliament, and publicly read. Not only the Directors, but every man of consequence from Bengal, have been examined upon oath before the House of Lords ; so that thousands of people are now well acquainted with the revenues, forces, and politics of India, and of Bengal in particular. Permit me here again, my friend, to remind you of the conspicuous situation you are placed in. Consider well the great expectations which this nation entertains of extricating itself out of its present difficulties, by the skill and conduct of the Governor of Bengal. You must therefore exert yourself to the utmost to fulfil its hopes ; for, as I have already observed, hereupon depends, whether you will be a very respectable character, or not, upon your return to England.

" With regard to myself, my health has been very indifferent ever since my arrival ; but I am now following a regimen which has done me much service, and will, I hope, recover me entirely. I have met with the most gracious reception from the King and Queen, and a very respectful and honourable one from the Court of Directors ; nor is there any doubt of my getting an English peerage, whenever I make application for that purpose, which, I understand, is always the custom : but the very unsettled Administration, and my private notions, will not admit of my

applying at present. Hereafter, in all probability, the thing
will come to pass.

· " With regard to the Directors, I tell you frankly, that no
one can entertain a worse opinion of many of them than I do.
They have neither abilities nor resolution to manage such important concerns as are now under their care. Of this the
world in general seem very sensible; and yet what to do I
protest I know not. An attempt to reform may throw matters
into greater confusion.

" You see my jaghire is at last continued to me and my representatives for ten years after the expiration of my present
right. I am more obliged to the Proprietors for this grant than
to the Directors, who threw a great deal of cold water upon it.
Indeed, their whole conduct towards me and my associates in
Committee has shown weakness, or something worse; for they
have upon all occasions endeavoured to lessen the acquisitions
we have obtained for them, and kept everything that might con-
tribute to our reputation as secret as possible; and, if Parliament had not brought our transactions to light, mankind would
have been ignorant of what has been done. In short, they
appear very envious and jealous of my influence, and give ear to
every idle story of my being hostile towards them. Everything
looks as if we were not upon good terms. They have even
asked my opinion upon their affairs in such a mean, sneaking
manner, that I have informed one of them, unless I am applied
to in form, and unless more attention be paid to my advice,
I shall decline giving any whatsoever. Thus stand matters at
present ; but how long they may remain so I know not, nor
what changes may happen at the next election.

" From the manner in which I carried the extension of the
jaghire, I conclude the Directors will pay more attention to my
opinions than they lately did ; but it will be rather through fear
than inclination. They desired, and I consented to a conference with them, and intended going to London from Shropshire
on purpose; but my health has obliged me to come to Bath,
where I daily expect a deputation to consult on many important
points, which the gentlemen themselves cannot readily determine upon."

CHAPTER XXVII.

Lord Clive in Europe—His state of Health—Progress of Public Opinion

Lord Clive's health was quite broken down before he quitted
India. The sea-voyage appeared, indeed, somewhat to recruit
his strength : but he had not been many weeks in England ere
the unfavourable symptoms returned with such violence that his
physicians were induced to order an immediate and entire withdrawal from business. Doubtless the advice was good in the
abstract, for maladies of the nature of those with which Clive
was affected admit of no cure so long as the mind is at work, or
in agitation. Yet in this particular instance it may be doubted
whether both mind and body would not have better recovered
their tone had there been found for the former some subject agreeable to its tastes, on which to occupy itself in
moderation. Men who have passed their youth and the best
years of their maturity in the turmoil of public life take but ill
with absolute idleness ; and Clive, though he had achieved a
European reputation for himself, and conquered kingdoms, was
yet barely in the 43rd year of his age. There was no refusing,
however, to act as the faculty advised, and Clive retired, first to
his house of Walcot, in Shropshire, and next to Bath, where he
drank the waters. But neither the air of Walcot nor the
mineral springs of Bath produced the effect which had been
expected from them. He could not be prevailed upon to lay
aside his interest in public affairs ; and the medical men, looking
partly to that circumstance, and partly hoping something from
an entire change of climate and scene, ordered him to go
abroad. He set out, attended by Lady Clive and Mr. Latham,
a relative of Lady Clive, by Mr. Maskelyne, her brother, Mr.
Strachey, and his own physician Mr. Langham ; and so entirely
was the experiment successful at the outset, that sanguine hopes
were entertained in regard to the future. The opium which he

was accustomed to take in large doses was gradually diminished; and, though never absolutely laid aside, its distressing effects upon the moral being of the man became continually less perceptible. The party proceeded to Paris, where, a few days after his arrival, Lord Clive wrote in excellent spirits to Mr. Verelst. " I am certain it will give you infinite pleasure," he says, " to hear of my safe arrival at this place, and of my recovery beyond what either my friends or myself could have expected in so short a time. The remedy, I believe, was found out before I left England; but the travelling and climate have undoubtedly done me much good. In short, by the time I have spent a few months in the south of France, and drank the waters of Spa, I doubt not of enjoying a better state of health than I have done for some years.

" I cannot but acknowledge that my recovery gives me a more particular pleasure from the prospect I have of exerting myself in favour of the Company next winter, a time very critical for them indeed, since it will then be finally determined upon what footing they are to be in future; whether a part, or the whole, or none of the power be lodged in them hereafter. Let me tell you in secret, that I have the King's command to lay before him my ideas of the Company's affairs both at home and abroad, with a promise of his countenance and protection in everything I might attempt for the good of the nation and the Company. Mr. Grenville also, who, I think, must be minister at last, paid me a visit at Berkeley Square, two days before I left London, and did me the honour to say, that, in his opinion, it was the duty of the Court of Directors to let no steps whatever be taken, either at home or abroad, without my advice : and to assure me that either in ministry or out of it, he would preach that doctrine in the House of Commons."

It will be seen from this letter that Lord Clive's friendship for Mr. George Grenville had not grown cold. Though far inferior in every respect as a statesman to Lord Chatham, and filling a less important place as the leader of a party than Lord Rockingham, George Grenville, through the influence of personal character and an engaging manner, was still the nucleus round which a considerable section of the House of Commons rallied ; and Clive, won by the attentions which, while yet com-

paratively obscure, he had received from Mr. Grenville, continued to the hour of his friend's death to support him with every
vote which he could command. The general election, which
took place in the spring of this year, enabled him to strengthen
Mr. Grenville's hands considerably; for by great exertion he
added another seat to the number of which he had already obtained the command. But the excitement thence arising, as well
as the anticipation of an Indian discussion in the approaching
session, rendered him impatient of a longer continuance abroad.
He had proceeded from Paris to Lyons, and from Lyons to
Montpelier, where he resided some time. He afterwards returned to Paris, and going on to Spa drank the waters with
advantage. But the listlessness attending an existence such as
this became by degrees intolerable to him. Though earnestly
entreated to abide where he was till the rigour of the winter
should have passed, he would not listen to the suggestion.
He desired to take his seat in Parliament. He was quite
equal to business; he considered that life itself was not worth
having if the attempt to prolong it must entail the necessity
of doing nothing. He therefore gave orders for preparations
to be made for an immediate departure; and in the month either
of August or September he and his party returned to England.
He plunged at once into the vortex of public life, and suffered
for doing so. The violence of party in the Court of Proprietors,
from which he could not be prevailed upon to stand aloof, chafed
him exceedingly. He delivered his sentiments in language which,
without gratifying his friends, neither conciliated nor controlled
an enemy. His views were for the most part masterly and comprehensive; but, accustomed to give the law abroad, his irritable
temper could not be brought to sustain the wear and tear of argument and persuasion at home. His friend, Mr. Grenville, deprecated such a needless waste both of energy and influence; and
the power which he possessed over the mind of Lord Clive was
never more clearly shown than by the result which attended this
remonstrance. The question before the Court had reference to a
projected bill in Parliament for the better regulation of the
Company's affairs, and the settlement of the part which the
Crown should take in their management. It was agitated with
all the warmth which comes rather of personal attachments and

antipathies than from a regard to the general good; and Lord Clive, than whom no man ever loved or hated more in extremes, threw himself unreservedly into the struggle. He was cautioned against the process by Mr. Grenville with a delicacy and good sense which carried the point. "The account which you have sent to me of what passed at the last Court," he writes on the 29th December, 1768, "is of itself a sufficient reason, in my opinion, for your declining to attend at the next, while things are in the state of uncertainty and irregularity in which they appear to me; and therefore, even if your health would allow it (the establishment of which must be with me and all your friends superior to every other consideration), yet I should not advise you to interfere in these questions till they come nearer to an issue. If these disputes shall be carried to greater lengths, your opinion will have still greater weight both within doors and without; if, on the contrary, they shall all be agreed and settled before the next meeting, I do not see that your interposition will be attended with any credit to you or advantage to the public. If this great question is to be brought before the Parliament, with everything in a state of uncertainty, as it was last year, as you truly observe that it may be necessary to take some part there, it seems to me that it would be more desirable for you to keep yourself at liberty in that case, and not to pledge yourself beforehand to no purpose at a General Court."

Lord Clive so far acted upon this advice, that his personal attendance in the Court of Proprietors became rare; but the politics of India filled his mind; and to think continually on any subject, yet to deal with it in the spirit of a philosopher, was not in his nature. He bestirred himself, therefore, to retain a preponderating influence in the Court and elsewhere, and gave back the blows which Mr. Sulivan and his adherents dealt forth on every occasion with interest. The consequence was, that through the columns of the newspapers, and by means of innumerable pamphlets, the public had received impressions of a great national subject which were as unjust as they were illiberal. Men fighting for supremacy in the management of the Company's affairs, scrupled not to blacken and defame one another before a wider audience; till by and by the very name of a Nabob—and such was the generic title bestowed at this time on all persons who had made fortunes in India and returned to spend them in England—came to be associated with images of oppression and cruelty abroad, and intolerable insolence and the most unscrupulous corruption at home.

There was little need, on the part of these gentlemen, to raise up a feeling in society unfriendly to themselves; causes enough were already at work to bring them into general disrepute, which, had they been less under the guidance of passion, and more swayed by reason, they would have laboured rather to assuage than to aggravate; for the Nabob of the last century was a very different sort of person from his representative in our own days.　Now, the young man who goes to India, whether in the civil or military service of the Company, may consider himself fortunate if he return at the end of 20 or 30 years master of a moderate competency. You find him, in this case, either settled near some country town in Scotland, or it may be in Devonshire or Cornwall; or else seeking out his kind in the recesses of Portman-street or St. John's Wood, where he may share his curry and his claret with such friends as have escaped, like himself, the ravages of fever and cholera, and varying the scene by occasional visits to the Oriental Club.　Here and there, indeed, an individual more fortunate than the rest may bring back with him some 80 or 100,000*l.*, the result of 40 years' savings; but 100,000*l.*, though amply sufficient for all the comforts and many of the elegancies of life, do not supply, in this country at least, the means of extravagant display.　The case was widely different 80 or 90 years ago.　Then London was astonished by finding men thrown day after day upon its surface of whom nothing more was known than that they had gone out to India a few years previously as writers or volunteers, and were now rich enough to outshine both Lord Mayor and Prime Minister.　Moreover, nobody could tell either their lineage or their personal merit.　Their wealth was indeed as notorious as their manner of using it was offensive; for they bought up the country houses and estates of a decayed nobility, and became, as a matter of course, the objects of dislike and envy to their neighbours.　But how they had acquired the means of thus supplanting their betters nobody could tell.　Their manners, also, and many of their habits, offended the more delicate tastes of the aristocracy. They

strove to command admission into a class of society which re-
pelled them, perhaps the more carefully, because it was felt that
in point of expenditure they were far ahead of it. They were
slighted, and they repaid the slight by more and more endeavouring to outvie the parties which affected to look down upon
them. Indeed they did more. They disputed the representation
of counties with families which had been accustomed time out of
mind to name the members, and bought up boroughs to an extent
which put the landed interests, long accustomed to a monopoly
in that species of traffic, to their wits' end. People of yesterday
—mere successful adventurers, whom nobody knew, whom everybody envied—were pretty sure, in an age so entirely aristocratic,
to draw down upon themselves a tolerable load of unpopularity ;
and when they began mutually to charge one another with the
commission of enormous crimes, unpopularity soon deepened into
general execration. Mr. Macaulay, in one of his collected es-
says, has well described the progress of the social hurricane :—

" The Nabobs," he says, " soon became a most unpopular
class of men. Some of them had in the East displayed eminent
talents, and rendered great services to the state; but at home
their talents were not shown to advantage, and their services
were little known. That they had sprung from obscurity, that
they had acquired great wealth, that they exhibited it insolently,
that they spent it extravagantly, that they raised the price of
everything in their neighbourhood, from fresh eggs to rotten
boroughs ; that their liveries outshone those of dukes, that their
coaches were finer than that of the Lord Mayor, that the examples of their large and ill-governed households corrupted half
the servants in the country ; that some of them, with all their
magnificence, could not catch the tone of good society, but, in
spite of the stud and the crowd of menials, of the plate and the
Dresden china, of the venison and the Burgundy, were still low
men ;—these were things which excited, both in the class from
which they had sprung and in that into which they attempted to
force themselves, the bitter aversion which is the effect of mingled
envy and contempt. But when it was also rumoured that the
fortune which had enabled its possessor to eclipse the Lord-Lieutenant on the race-ground, or to carry the county against the
head of a house as old as ' Domesday Book,' had been accumu-

lated by violating public faith—by deposing legitimate princes, by reducing whole provinces to beggary—all the higher and better as well as all the low and evil parts of human nature were stirred against the wretch who had obtained, by guilt and dishonour, the riches which he now lavished with arrogant and inelegant profusion. The unfortunate Nabob seemed to be made up of those foibles against which comedy has pointed the most merciless ridicule, and of those crimes which have thrown the deepest gloom over tragedy—of Turcaret and Nero, of Monsieur Jourdain and Richard the Third. A tempest of execration and derision, such as can be compared only to that outbreak of public feeling against the Puritans which took place at the time of the Restoration, burst on the servants of the Company. The humane man was horror-struck at the way in which they had got their money, the thrifty man at the way in which they spent it. The dilettante sneered at their want of taste. The maccaroni black-balled them as vulgar fellows. Writers the most unlike in sentiment and style—Methodists and libertines, philosophers and buffoons—were for once on the same side. It is hardly too much to say, that, during a space of about thirty years, the whole lighter literature of England was coloured by the feelings which we have described. Foote brought on the stage an Anglo-Indian chief, dissolute, ungenerous, and tyrannical, ashamed of the humble friends of his youth, hating the aristocracy, yet childishly eager to be numbered among them, squandering his wealth on pandars and flatterers, tricking out his chairmen with the most costly hot-house flowers, and astounding the ignorant with jargon about rupees, lacs, and jaghires. Mackenzie, with more delicate humour, depicted a plain country family raised by the Indian acquisitions of one of its members to sudden opulence, and exciting derision by an awkward mimicry of the manners of the great. Cowper, in that lofty expostulation which glows with the very spirit of the Hebrew poets, placed the oppression of India foremost in the list of those national crimes for which God had punished England with years of disastrous war, with discomfiture in her own seas, and with the loss of her transatlantic empire. If any of our readers will take the trouble to search in the dusty recesses of circulating libraries for some novel published sixty years ago, the chance is that the villain or sub-villain of the story will prove to be a savage old Nabob, with an immense fortune, a tawny complexion, a bad liver, and a worse heart."

In the feeling thus raised against his class Clive shared to a more than ordinary extent. He was by far the most conspicuous of his order—the ablest, the most celebrated, the wealthiest, the highest in rank. In the boundless expense of his style of living he outshone them all. He dispensed the hospitality of a prince at his mansion in Berkeley Square. He had built one palace on his estate in Shropshire; and having recently purchased Claremont of the Duchess of Newcastle, he began forthwith to erect another there. His family residence at Styche, enlarged and beautified, was generally occupied by some of his relatives; and now, as if a man of his consequence could not, without degradation, occupy lodgings in a watering place, he obtained at an enormous price the lease of Lord Chatham's house in Bath. His munificence, likewise, to relatives, and even to friends, offended because of the scale on which it was dispensed. It was natural, perhaps, that he should desire to draw up brothers, sisters, and cousins into his own sphere; and if the possession of ample means had been sufficient to give them place and weight in society, they might have secured both. But defects of manner which society might have overlooked in Lord Clive were sneered at and censured in his relatives; and the sneer glanced off, as it is apt in such cases to do, most unfairly upon his lordship. To Mr. Wedderburn, afterwards Lord Chancellor Loughborough, of his connexion with whom I shall have occasion to speak by and by, he made a present of a mansion and the grounds attached to it in Surrey; in order, as he said, that he might, when residing at Claremont, have an agreeable neighbour near him. Now the world is not very tolerant, under any circumstances, either of the wealth which enables an individual thus to heap favours upon others, or of the disposition which urges him so to use it; and if, as in this instance, the man be the founder of his own fortunes, he becomes a ready butt for the shafts of the envious to hit against. Accordingly there is no end to the frightful and incredible tales of atrocities committed in distant lands which soon began to circulate concerning Clive.

Not the aristocracy alone, but all classes of people drank them in; and to such a height was the prejudice carried, that the very helpers in his own stables, and the labouring people who worked at his houses and on his farms, came at last to look upon him with terror. Mr. Macaulay, quoting Boswell's 'Life of Johnson,' tells us that Brown, the celebrated landscape-gardener of that day, whom "Clive employed to lay out his pleasure-grounds, was amazed to see in his house a chest which had once been filled with gold from the treasury of Moorshedabad, and could not understand how the conscience of the criminal could suffer him to sleep with such an object so near to his bed-chamber." From the same authority we learn that " the peasantry of Surrey looked with mysterious horror on the stately house which was rising at Claremont, and whispered that the great wicked lord had ordered the walls to be made so thick in order to keep out the devil, who would one day carry him away bodily." And it is well known that William Huntingdon, one of the most successful of the impostors who have from time to time abused the credulity of the lower orders in this country, made Lord Clive the frequent subject of his revelations. Clive never heard of many of the rumours that circulated concerning him, and would have treated them with contempt had they been chronicled in his presence ; nevertheless he could scarcely be ignorant that beyond the circle of his immediate relatives and connexions he was the reverse of popular ; and to feel that we are not esteemed in society has little tendency to soften our manners or enlarge our sympathies. Lord Clive lived with much ostentation. His entertainments were sumptuous, his equipages brilliant, his style of dress extravagantly rich ; yet somehow or another they failed to win the favour even of those to whom they were most freely exhibited. The truth is, that his lordship's manner and personal appearance were both against him. Generally reserved, often silent, and, as it appeared, absorbed in thought, he impressed the casual observer with an idea that some load lay on his mind from which he could not shake himself free ; while even in his lighter moments there was an awkwardness about his mirth which rendered it the reverse of infectious. *We* know that these were in a great measure the results of a physical malady to which from boyhood he had been more or less subject; but the world, which grudged him his wealth, and hated him on account of his glory, took a different view of the subject. However, events were already in progress which should call once more into active operation his talent and energies; and of these it has become my business to give a brief account.

CHAPTER XXVIII.

**Clive's position in Parliament and at the India House—Bad news from
India.**

IN the month of October, 1768, Lord Chatham resigned his
office of privy seal. A reconciliation immediately took place
between him and Lord Temple ; and Lord Rockingham and Mr.
George Grenville sinking in like manner their differences, the
opposition, which had heretofore been powerless on account of
intestine divisions, became very formidable. A great deal of
shifting and jobbing occurred, as it usually does, in such cases ;
and amid the heats of debate the hangers-on for place hardly
knew to what party it might be prudent to attach themselves.
Of this class was Mr. Wedderburn, a gentleman of a good
border family, and more than respectable talents, whom motives of ambition had urged to exchange the Scotch for the
English bar, where he attained to considerable eminence. Attached originally to Lord Bute, and passing over by and by to
Mr. Pitt, he had been one of the most noisy of the advocates of
John Wilkes, and subsided, as the stir on account of that dema-
gogue grew slack, into an adherent of the Grenville section of
the opposition. Amid the confusion incident to the breaking up
of parties in 1768, Mr. Wedderburn was required by his patron
Lord Bute to relinquish his seat for the Rothesay boroughs. In
this emergency Lord Clive, who was aware of Mr. Wedderburn's
value, wrote to Mr. Grenville, and proposed, if agreeable to his
friend, that he would return him to Parliament. The offer was
accepted with gratitude both by Mr. Grenville and Mr. Wedderburn ; and from that day forth there grew up between the
patron and the client a firm union. That the former dealt with
the latter in a liberal spirit throughout, is shown by the tenor of
their whole correspondence. He appears to have left him at
liberty, on all subjects and on every occasion, to speak and to

vote as his own judgment might direct; and Wedderburn, to do him justice, continued a steady supporter of the Grenville party as long as George Grenville lived. But the death of this latter gentleman in November, 1770, appeared to free Mr. Wedderburn from all ties except those which a regard to his own interests might create; and he began immediately to coquet with the minister, under whom he eventually accepted office as Solicitor-General. The letters which passed between him and Lord Clive at the commencement of this change of view on his part are too characteristic to be omitted. On the 14th of November, 1770, Mr. Wedderburn having just learned that their mutual friend Mr. Grenville was dead, wrote as follows:—

"My dear Lord,—The misfortune we dreaded has at last happened. I could not prevail upon myself to send you the first account of it, knowing from my own experience how much you would feel upon such an occasion. I had it immediately in my view for three days together, and yet I was shocked with the event that I had expected.

"I am not able to send you any distinct account of the opening of the Parliament, for I have not yet been in the House of Commons; and if people would impute my absence to its true cause, a real indifference to all that passes there at present, I should continue for some time in the same ignorance. Mr. Woodfall has done me the honour of making me refuse an office that never was offered to me. If it had, your lordship will do me the justice to believe, that you would not have received the first intimation of it from a newspaper. Whatever part I may take in this conjuncture will never be decided without the fullest communication with you; and I am persuaded your lordship's sentiments upon the present unfortunate occasion are so similar to those I feel, that no circumstance is likely to make us think differently. It is possible, I believe, even in these times, for a man to acquire some degree of credit without being enlisted in any party; and if it is, the situation, I am sure, is more eligible than any other that either a court or an opposition have to bestow.

"If Bath agrees with your lordship, as I trust it does, I should not wish to see you in town; but I very much wish that it were in my power to make you a visit at Bath : I should then have the pleasure of hearing your sentiments upon the present state of affairs, which I assure you, without any sort of compliment, but in the plainest sincerity, will always have more weight with me than perhaps you will wish them to have; and I should likewise have the good fortune to escape hearing the sentiments of people who, in this town, have no other employment than to speculate for their neighbours.

" Lincoln's Inn Fields,
" 14th November, 1770."

To this communication Lord Clive replied in the following terms:—

" Bath, 18th November, 1770.

" Dear Sir,—If the receipt of your very obliging and confidential letter had not roused me, I doubt much whether I should have prevailed upon myself to put pen to paper, though there is something within that tells me I shall at last overcome a disorder so very distressing both to the mind (and to the body). Although the waters agree with me better than any place I have yet tried, yet by my feelings a journey abroad, I fear, must be undertaken before I can obtain a perfect recovery of my health.

" Mr. Grenville's death, though long expected, could not but affect me very severely. Gratitude first bound me to him: a more intimate connexion afterwards gave an opportunity of admiring his abilities, and respecting his worth and integrity. The dissolution of our valuable friend has shipwrecked all our hopes for the present; and my indisposition hath not only made me indifferent [to the world of politics], but to the world in general. What effect returning health may have I cannot answer for; but if I can judge for myself in my present situation, I wish to support that independency which will be approved of by my friends in particular, and by the public in general. My sentiments are the same as yours, with regard to our conduct in the present times.

" Your delicacy towards me serves only to convince me of the propriety of my conduct in leaving you the absolute master of your own conduct in Parliament, free from all control but that of your own judgment, and I am happy in this opportunity. Your great and uncommon abilities must sooner or later place you in one of the first posts of this kingdom ; and you may be

assured no man on earth wishes to see your honour and your independency firmly established more than I."

The tone of the preceding letter sufficiently indicates that, in
regard to the general politics of the empire, Lord Clive had
never become in any sense a party man. Views of his own
he doubtless entertained as to the wisdom of the measures which
were in progress to restrain the colonies; and his letter, elsewhere quoted, on the subject of the defences of Brazil, shows
that even the foreign relations of the country were not indifferent
to him. But it was in India, and the manner of its administration, that his interest wholly centered. Amid the disruption of
parties, therefore, he thought only of the effect which the
ascendency of one or the other was likely to have upon the
Company's affairs; and nowise doubting that Mr. Wedderburn
would on this question of questions speak and vote as he wished,
he left him free on every other, either to serve in the ranks of
the opposition, as heretofore, or to pass over to the minister.
It was one of Clive's greatest misfortunes to have thus surrendered up his energies to a single subject. The importance of
India to the British nation is but imperfectly understood even
now; at the period when Lord Clive lived and took the lead in
Indian discussions, it was not understood at all. Hence he, who
stood aloof watching the course which events might take, and
ready to support whatever party should do justice, according to
his view of the case, to India and its rulers, found himself, in the
hour of difficulty or need, without any party at all to support
him. Had Mr. Grenville lived, the chances are, that of Clive's
persecution in the House of Commons I should have had no tale
to tell. The occurrence of that misfortune left him to sustain
single-handed the attacks of enemies as unscrupulous as they
were implacable; and the results of the struggle, though in the
main honourable to his character, he never entirely overcame.

Of the agreement to which, in 1767, the Court of Directors
had come with the King's Government, Lord Clive never approved. He was averse to all half measures; and though it is by
no means impossible that a well-digested plan for transferring
the territorial sovereignty of British India to the Crown would
have met with his support, of the sort of compromise to which
the Court assented he always spoke as a discreditable arrange-

ment. He was still more averse to the proposed measure of
1768-9, and spoke against it in the House of Commons, as he himself says, " with some applause, but all to no purpose." Now, it was
an object with the Government, pressed on every side for money,
to secure for a term of five years an annual subsidy of 400,000*l.*
or 500,000*l.* from the Company. They therefore resented Lord
Clive's opposition exceedingly, and threw the whole weight of
their influence into the scale of his rival, Mr. Sulivan. In
April, 1769, an election of Directors took place. The same
measures for securing a majority of votes which Clive had on a
former occasion adopted were now used without stint on the
opposite side; and the result was the triumphant return of Mr.
Sulivan and a majority of his friends to the Direction. To describe the events that followed belongs rather to the historian
of the East India Company than to the biographer of Clive.
Whatever the Government sought was conceded; and the
attempt to invest Mr. Vansittart with the authority of Governor-
General having failed, a new commission was created, of which
he became a member, and of which the powers were without
limits. Nor indeed were Lord Clive's enemies in the Direction
without a plausible excuse for the decided step thus taken. The
reports received from India by every ship continued to be less
and less favourable; and they who hated Clive were glad at the
opportunity of alleging that the root of the evil lay in the
arrangements which he had effected for its government. Hence
a commission of supervisors was made out, with power to inquire
on the spot into every department of public affairs as well as
into the conduct of all public officers; to suspend, if necessary,
even the Presidents and Councils of the different settlements,
and to frame such regulations as should to them appear suitable
to the exigences of each. It is well known that the gentlemen
nominated to act on this important commission never reached
the scene of their proposed labours. The ship in which they
took their passage, the " Aurora " frigate, was last heard of as
touching at the Cape of Good Hope. She spoke no vessel afterwards, nor visited any port either in South America or Asia, and
doubtless foundered at sea.

Lord Clive was greatly annoyed by the issues of this controversy in the India House. His vexation received no salve

from the renewed strife of 1770 and 1771; for Mr. Sulivan's party continued in the ascendant; and public prejudice, guided by the exertions of that cunning individual, ran with increased violence against his Lordship. The tidings from India likewise became daily more alarming. Hyder Ali laid the Carnatic waste; and in Bengal Sujah Dowlah, the Viceroy of Oude, was become an object of great alarm. Besides, the framework of internal administration was falling to pieces. Mr. Verelst, too good-natured to keep the curb on his subordinates as he ought to have done, retired in January, 1770, and was succeeded by Mr. Cartier, from whose feeble hands the reins of government may be said to have fallen altogether. Both these gentlemen permitted the expenses of their local establishments to increase to such an extent that, instead of being able to remit the surplus of the revenues of the provinces to London, they were forced to draw heavy bills upon the Court of Directors, and even then declared that the country could not support itself. Of course they did not stop to explain that all these fresh outlays—that all this absurd interference of individuals with the internal trade of the provinces—was in direct violation of the rules of government which Lord Clive had laid down. On the contrary, they alluded to them either as necessary precautions, or as mere matters of routine, while they dwelt with greater show of reason on the effects of the terrible famine which began about this time to desolate the whole valley of the Ganges. It was hard upon Lord Clive that to him should be attributed the blame not only of blunders which he neither committed nor sanctioned, but of the consequences of that failure of rain against which no human forethought could have provided; nevertheless such was his fate. The newspapers, which teemed with accounts of the sufferings of the Bengalese, which told of the earth parched up—of lakes empty—of rivers dried in their beds—and people dying by thousands—seldom failed to conclude their most exciting sketches by references to the tyranny and rapacity of the man who had drained a kingdom in order to fill his own coffers, and was now insulting the British people by the ostentatious display of wealth stained by the blood of thousands. These wicked insinuations were not thrown away either upon the friends or the enemies of him who was the subject of them. The former affected to treat them lightly ; the latter cherished them up; and by and by, when they conceived that the public mind was ripe for the movement, they did their best to make use of them.

Meanwhile, though there was general corruption in Bengal, individuals were to be found there, high in office, who deprecated the abuses which they lacked authority to restrain. Among these Mr. Sykes deserves to be particularized. He early saw and lamented the unfitness of Lord Clive's successors for the trust which had been reposed in them, and has the merit of having been one of the first of Indian statesmen to urge the advancement of Mr. Hastings to high station. He wrote to Lord Clive on this subject so early as March, 1768. But Hastings had attached himself to that party in the Direction of which Mr. Sulivan and Mr. Vansittart were the chiefs; and Clive, however ready he might be to bear testimony to the great ability of the candidate, could not bring himself directly to support the friend of his personal enemies. He seems, however, to have offered no opposition to Mr. Hastings's appointment to be second in Council at Madras; and consented, after the loss of the " Aurora," to his removal, in 1771, as Governor to Bengal. I cannot deny to my readers the satisfaction of perusing the letter which Lord Clive addressed on this occasion to the statesman whose merits, as the conservator of British India, must be considered as only second—if indeed they be second—to those of the soldier who acquired it.

" Berkeley-Square, 1st August, 1771.

" Dear Sir,—" The despatch of the ' Lapwing ' gives me an early opportunity of congratulating with you on your removal to Bengal ; and as my zeal for the service actuated me to take the share I did in your appointment, the same principle prevails upon me to offer you a few of my ideas upon the important Government in which you now preside.

" Two or three months ago, when the plan of Supervisors was renewed, Sir George Colebrooke and Mr. Purling desired my opinion. My advice was, that, as the prosperity of the Company was now become a matter of very serious national concern, it behoved them to show that, in appointments of this nature, they were guided, not by the view of particular friends, but merely by that zeal which the duty of their station demanded, for preserving and rendering permanent our possessions in India: and that, therefore, they should turn their thoughts towards men who stood high in public character and reputation. I proposed Mr. Wedderburn, Mr. Cornwall, and Sir Jeffrey Amherst, together with you, as Governor, and one of the Council; and that these five should be invested with all the powers civil and military. Sir Jeffrey Amherst, however, declined. As to the two former, they might be prevailed upon; but the Directors do not seem ready to embrace any great comprehensive plan of supervisorship, so as to make it an object for men of such consequence. My last proposition was, that the Company should revert to the plan of my Government, viz. that a Committee of five should be appointed out of the best and ablest men in Bengal, of whom the Governor should be the head; and this, I imagine, will be adopted.

" The situation of affairs requires that you should be very circumspect and active. You are appointed Governor at a very critical time, when things are suspected to be almost at the worst, and when a general apprehension prevails of the mismanagement of the Company's affairs. The last Parliamentary inquiry has thrown the whole state of India before the public, and every man sees clearly, that as matters are now conducted abroad, the Company will not long be able to pay the 400,000*l.* to Government. The late dreadful famine, or a war, either with Sujah-u-Dowlah or the Mahrattas, will plunge us into still deeper distress. A discontented nation and disappointed Minister will then call to account a weak and pusillanimous Court of Directors, who will turn the blow from themselves upon their agents abroad; and the consequences must be ruinous both to the Company and the servants. In this situation you see the necessity of exerting yourself in time, provided the Directors give you proper powers, without which, I confess, you can do nothing; for self-interest or ignorance will obstruct every plan you can form for the public good.

" You are upon the spot, and will learn my conduct from disinterested persons; and I wish your government to be attended, as mine was, with success to the Company, and with the consciousness of having discharged every duty with firmness and fidelity. Be impartial and just to the public, regardless of the interests of individuals, where the honour of the nation and the real advantage of the Company are at stake, and resolute in carrying into execution your determination, which I hope will at all times be rather founded upon your own opinion than that of others.

" The business of politics and finance being so extensive, the Committee should not be embarrassed with private concerns. They ought not, therefore, to be allowed to trade. But their emoluments ought to be so large as to render trade unnecessary to the attainment of a competent fortune. For this purpose I am confident the salt will prove very sufficient. The Society should be formed upon an improvement of the plan which was not perfected in my time. The price to the natives was too great, and so was the advantage to the servants. Reduce both, and I am persuaded there will be no complaint of oppression on the one hand, or want of emolument on the other.

" The Company's servants should all have a subsistence, but every idea of raising a fortune, till they are entitled to it by some years' service, ought to be suppressed. If a general system of economy could be introduced, it would be happy for individuals as well as for the public. The expenses of the Company in Bengal are hardly to be supported. Great savings, I am certain, may be made. Bills for fortifications, cantonments, contracts, &c. must be abolished, together with every extravagant charge for travelling, diet, parade, and pomp of subordinates. In short, by economy alone the Company may yet preserve its credit and affluence.

" With regard to political measures, they are to be taken according to the occasion. When danger arises, every precaution must be made use of, but at the same time you must be prepared to meet and encounter it. This you must do with cheerfulness and confidence, never entertaining a thought of miscarrying till the misfortune actually happens; and even then you are not to despair, but be constantly contriving and carrying into execution schemes for retrieving affairs; always flattering yourself with an opinion that time and perseverance will get the better of every thing.

" From the little knowledge I have of you I am convinced that you have not only abilities and personal resolution, but integrity, and moderation with regard to riches; but I thought I discovered in you a diffidence in your own judgment, and too great an easiness of disposition, which may subject you insensibly to be *led* where you ought to *guide*. Another evil which may arise from it is, that you may pay too great an attention to the reports of the natives, and be inclined to look upon things in the worst, instead of the best, light. A proper confidence in yourself, and never-failing hope of success, will be a bar to this and every other ill that your situation is liable to; and, as I am sure that you are not wanting in abilities for the great office or Governor, I must add that an opportunity is now given you of making yourself one of the most distinguished characters of this country.

" I perceive I have been very free in delivering my sentiments; but to make an apology were to contradict the opinion I profess to have of your understanding, and to doubt whether you would receive this as a token of my esteem.

" It is, perhaps, unnecessary to add, that this letter, which I have written in the fullest confidence, should be kept entirely to yourself. If a reciprocal communication of our sentiments on India affairs be agreeable to you, you may depend upon my continuing the correspondence in such manner as to show that I am, with the sincerest wishes for your honour and success,

" Dear Sir,

" Your very faithful humble servant,

" CLIVE."

No man could be more sensible of the worth of praise from such a quarter than Mr. Hastings. No man was ever more disposed to put value upon Lord Clive's advice. But Hastings, like Clive, lived in times when it was difficult, consistently with men's received notions of duty to their employers, to walk within the exact line of Christian, or even of European integrity. It would be a libel to say of either that he ever swerved from the path of integrity for the mere purpose of advancing his own selfish interests. Clive became rich, but won his wealth by a process of which the fitness was then acknowledged. Hastings returned home after long years of sovereignty a poor man, and died a beggar. Yet there are events in the lives of both on which we cannot look back without regretting that they should have occurred, even while we acknowledge that they show but as spots upon the sun or as a few passing clouds on a summer's sky. It is certain that the men themselves entertained great respect the one for the other, and that each played the part on the stage of Indian life for which nature seemed especially to have fitted him.

CHAPTER XXIX.

Confusion in the Company's Affairs—Parliamentary Proceedings.

Up to this moment the Crown and the Parliament had evinced little disposition to interfere in a decided manner in the management of the Company's affairs. Since the death of George the Second a series of feeble administrations had followed one another, each of which was in its turn cast aside by the King. Intrigues in their own bodies, riots in the country, and insurrectionary movements among the American colonists, had left them no leisure to investigate the politics of India, or deal with the subject as it deserved. As has elsewhere been explained, their interference, when it occurred at all, was irresolute, and therefore injurious; and the mind to direct, as well as the energy to accomplish, a comprehensive plan seemed to be wanting. No doubt Lord Chatham, during his brief season of power, meditated a bold and sweeping measure in regard to the Company's possessions. And to this Lord Clive seems to have given his adhesion, if indeed he may not with truth be said to have been the author of it. But, just as his arrangements were understood to be completed, that dark cloud passed over the minister's judgment which compelled him to withdraw from public life, and out of the shadow of which he never afterwards escaped, except for a brief interval. The time, however, was come when, in the policy of procrastination, no Cabinet could venture to persevere; and arrangements were made for bringing before Parliament a complete view of the state of the Company's affairs, as well as a permanent scheme for their future management both at home and abroad.

It was out of the question that any minister of the Crown should ponder such a design, and entertain serious thoughts of acting upon it, without consulting Lord Clive. To be sure, between Lord Clive and the head of the existing Cabinet there had never been any intimate connexion; but Lord North, whatever his private sentiments might be, knew too well the worth of Clive's opinion to overlook it, and employed his Solicitor-General, Mr. Wedderburn, to bring him and the Indian Colossus together. Mr. Wedderburn conducted this delicate negotiation with his usual skill. He first proposed that Lord Rochfort should communicate with his patron, to which the latter at once assented ; and by and by acted as the mutual friend of Lord Clive and the Prime Minister. Proceedings of this sort could not be kept secret from the dominant party in the India House; and their fears for the consequences, operating upon a harsher feeling, urged them to lay aside the mask, and to attack their great opponent himself. On the 7th of January, 1772, just a fortnight previously to the day fixed for the meeting of Parliament, Lord Clive received from the secretary a dry official letter, informing him that papers had reached the Court of Directors in which his Lordship was charged with being a party to the mismanagement of the Company's affairs in Bengal ; and that if his Lordship had any observations to make upon such papers—of which copies were transmitted to him—the Court of Directors would be glad to receive the same as expeditiously as might suit his Lordship's convenience. Lord Clive's answer being both short and very dignified, I think that I am bound to give it in his own words :—

" You have not been pleased," he says, " to inform me from whom you received these papers, to what end they were laid before you, what resolution you have come to concerning them, nor for what purpose you expect my observations upon them. I shall, however, observe to you, that upon the public records of the Company, where the whole of my conduct is stated, you may find a sufficient confutation of the charges which you have transmitted to me ; and I cannot but suppose that if any part of my conduct had been injurious to the service, contradictory to my arrangements with the Company, or even mysterious to you, four years and a half since my arrival in England would not have elapsed before your duty would have impelled you to call me to account."

Parliament met on the 22nd of January; and the King's speech contained a clause which indicated the intention of the Minister to propose some measure in the course of the session which should put upon a better footing the general administration of the Company's affairs both at home and abroad. There was nothing in the Royal speech itself to indicate a bias on the mind of the Minister one way or another. Clive, in all his statements on the subject, had never hesitated to lay the chief blame of Indian misgovernment on the home authorities. He charged the Directors with interfering incessantly in matters which they did not understand ; and was not less indignant with the Proprietors for sheltering delinquents whom the Bengal government had sent home, and employing them again in places of trust. Mr. Sulivan and his allies, on the contrary, attributed the whole of the misfortunes under which the Company laboured to the misconduct of their servants abroad. The tone of the gentleman who seconded the address in the House of Commons indicated pretty accurately to which side in this dispute the Cabinet leaned. He was eloquent on the delinquencies of the servants to whom the Company had entrusted the management of its affairs in India, and loud in his demands that enlarged powers for restraining and punishing them should be given to the Directors. Lord Clive heard this speech with amazement. Still, as the Government kept quiet, and no member connected with it stirred in the business, he held aloof; and so matters remained, as the calm precedes a storm, till the 30th of March. But on that day Mr. Sulivan, who, besides being Deputy-Chairman of the Court of Directors, had a seat in Parliament, brought in a bill " For the better regulation of the affairs of the East India Company, and of their servants in India, and for the due administration of justice in Bengal;" and Lord Clive, after listening to the speech which was directed ostensibly to enforce the adoption of the measure, felt that in point of fact he was upon his trial before the great council of the nation.

I cannot pretend, within the limits of a work like this, to give the details either of the Deputy-Chairman's address or of Lord Clive's answer to it. The former, professing to deal in general charges, was yet so constructed as to direct the attention of the House to the principal events in Lord Clive's public life. The latter, assuming that such was the real object of the speaker, met him upon his own ground, and overthrew him sentence by sentence. With regard to the general object of the bill, it had Lord Clive's hearty approval. Many of the most important

changes proposed to be effected by it he had himself suggested to
the Company long before; but of the minute details on which
they were grounded he in numerous instances disapproved, and
he condemned throughout the spirit in which they seemed to have
been brought forward. No account of his own career, coming
from Clive, would have been genuine had it failed to partake
largely of the grandiloquent; nevertheless, being just in the
main, the present narrative told; and its effect would have been
greater, but for the strong and unguarded terms in which the
speaker censured every other individual and party who had
taken any share whatever in the management of the Company's
affairs. His own successor in Bengal—the Courts of Directors
and of Proprietors—the ill-disposed persons who, by bribery
and otherwise, had achieved an ascendancy in both—nay, the
King's ministers themselves, on account of the hard bargains
they had driven with the Company, and their repeated neglect
of the advice which he had given—all came in for a portion of
his censure. It was remarked by his best friends, on this occasion, that he had never spoken with greater eloquence, or with
a more evil tendency as regarded himself. Though the answer
of Governor Johnstone, the brother of that Mr. Johnstone
whom Lord Clive had removed from the service of the Company at Bengal, and who was now one of the most active of
his enemies in the India House, was as feeble as it was rancorous,
a considerable portion of the House listened to it with favour;
and inferences were drawn from the circumstance, as the event
proved, not without reason, that the debate would, before it
closed, take a turn more decidedly hostile to Lord Clive than
the nature of the motion on which it was grounded seemed at
the outset to promise.

Leave being granted to introduce the bill, it was laid upon the
table of the House on the 13th of April; upon which occasion
Colonel Burgoyne moved, " That a Select Committee be appointed to inquire into the nature, state, and condition of the
East India Company, and of the British affairs in the East Indies." Colonel Burgoyne was known, at this time, as a man of
wit, and the author of some dramatic pieces which had obtained
a certain degree of popularity. He had served in Portugal with
some distinction; and, being free of speech, and of showy parts,

contrived to impress society with a belief that his military talents were of a high order. In politics he seems to have been a mere adventurer, who, being anxious to bring himself into notice, was not very scrupulous in regard to the means. By what process Mr. Sulivan and his party contrived to enlist him under their banner does not appear ; but he played their game, as long as it suited his purposes, with considerable skill, and did not hesitate, when the proper moment arrived, to throw them overboard. Colonel Burgoyne carried his motion, though not without a struggle ; and Mr. Sulivan's bill was dropped after the second reading. Moreover, Burgoyne took care that to the constitution of his committee no overt objections should be raised. Lord Clive and Mr. Strachey were both appointed members of it, as indeed their well-known acquaintance with the subjects to be brought under discussion rendered indispensable. But the committee was scarcely constituted ere the spirit in which it was designed to act became manifest. Governor Johnstone brought forward a plan of operations, of which it was the tendency to put Lord Clive upon his trial. He proposed that inquiry should be made into the conduct of individuals who, whether in the civil or military service of the Company, had amassed great wealth in India ; and by skilfully dating his researches from the period of the dethronement of Suraj-u-Dowlah, he brought the object of his own and his brother's hatred at once upon the stage. Accordingly, the two first reports of the Select Committee contained only the evidence of well-informed witnesses in regard to the revolutions of 1757 and 1760 ; the former dwelling especially on the presents which were received, and the grant of the jaghire or feof to Lord Clive : the latter embodying a list of details, wherein were set forth the evil results of the inland trade, under the government of Mr. Verelst. These being hurried on, and presented to Parliament on the 26th of May, were forthwith printed, and circulated from one extremity of the kingdom to another, with the scarcely concealed purpose of aggravating as much as possible the prejudices which were known already to exist against the parties chiefly affected by them. But the authors of the scheme had somewhat undercalculated its effects. The names of Clive and of the rest who had taken money, or were assumed to have done so, as the price of making and unmaking Nabobs, were indeed greeted with execration ; but the Company itself fell likewise into disrepute ; and the confusion of its pecuniary arrangements, which could no longer be concealed, instead of awakening sympathy, served but to deepen the feeling. It was with extreme difficulty that the Directors managed to ward off the blows which from every side were struck at them during the remainder of the session ; and when at length Parliament adjourned, the boldest went away with a conviction on his mind that a crisis could not be very distant.

In the course of the inquiries which led to the reports of which I have just spoken, Lord Clive had been subjected to the most minute and ungenerous cross-examination. He was questioned not merely in regard to what he had done, but to the motives which swayed him, and the purposes which he desired to accomplish; while by insinuation—where ground for direct attack seemed wanting—the committee did its best to resolve every act of public duty into a selfish or a mercenary endeavour. He bore himself throughout the whole process with the same unbending firmness which characterised his proceedings on the stage of more active life. He denied nothing that he had ever done or said ; he sought neither to extenuate nor to explain it away. When charged with the acts whereby he had deceived Omichund, and accused of forging Admiral Watson's name, he replied that what he had done occasioned him neither shame nor regret, for, under precisely the same circumstances, he was prepared to do it all over again. He admitted that he had received enormous sums from Meer Jaffier ; but protested that no obligation either of morality or public faith had been violated by the proceeding. " Am I not rather," he exclaimed, " deserving of praise for the moderation which marked my proceedings? Consider the situation in which the victory at Plassey placed me. A great prince was dependent on my pleasure ; an opulent city lay at my mercy ; its richest bankers bid against each other for my smiles ; I walked through vaults which were thrown open to me alone, piled on either hand with gold and jewels ! Mr. Chairman," cried he, warming with his subject, and striking his hand against his brow, " this moment I stand astonished at my own moderation."

This high tone of rebuke—this vindication rather than defence of a line of conduct which, though long previously marked by the approval both of the Crown and of the Company—it was now the object of the Committee to hold up to public odium—stood Lord Clive in good stead out of doors. The multitude cried him down, it is true; but the recess was yet young when he received intimations from more than one quarter that his name stood as high in the palace as it had ever done. His installation as a Knight of the Bath, which took place on the 15th of June, was honoured by the presence of Royalty; and on the death of Earl Powis, which occurred in September of the same year, a way was opened for him to obtain the lieutenancy of the county of Salop. His friends wished him to apply directly to the King; for they, as well as he, were dissatisfied with the conduct of the minister during the past session; but Clive was too prudent to act on the suggestion. "I cannot," he writes to Mr. Strachey, on this subject, "be of your opinion, because I think that things are not yet ripe for an open rupture. Until my conduct in Parliament is decided upon, I do not desire the King and his Ministers to be my declared enemies. In such a situation I should certainly not meet with much applause from the House for my conduct in the East Indies; and I wish at least that the members of the House, when they come to decide, may have no other motive for an unfavourable decision than envy: that, indeed, is too strongly implanted in the human breast to be removed." His own desire was to wait till the dignity should be offered; but such a course being represented on all sides as unprecedented, he was with some difficulty persuaded to depart from it. Lord Rochfort, it appeared, in the first instance, and by and by Lord North, threw out hints that, provided they were assured the office would be agreeable to Lord Clive, they should have much pleasure in bringing his name under the King's notice. The result was, that, after a little coquetting, Clive did make a formal application to the Minister; and he kissed hands on the 9th of October for the Lieutenancy of Salop, to which, in the month of December following, the Lieutenancy of Montgomeryshire was added.

It was natural that the readiness shown by Lord North to meet the personal wishes of the new lord-lieutenant should lead to a revival of friendly offices between them. I find, accordingly, that Clive was in communication this winter with the Cabinet; and that he laid before it the outlines of a plan for the management of the affairs of India, which included a transfer of the territorial sovereignty to the Crown. The Directors, on the other hand, were busy negotiating loans in all quarters; and finding that neither the Bank nor the Government was disposed to accede to the terms of their request, they had recourse to a fresh Commission of Supervisors, on which they found some difficulty in persuading six gentlemen to serve. But before the commission had embarked, the session of 1773 opened, and a new turn was given to the course of Indian affairs. The Minister asked for and obtained a Committee of Secrecy, with power to examine the Company's books, and to report to the House upon the state of debts and credits set forth therein, as well as on the system of management generally; and forasmuch as it was not considered desirable that pending such examination any change of system should be introduced, the Committee was directed to state whether or not, in their judgment, the Company ought to be allowed to send out the Commission of Supervisors to India.

To detail, one by one, the memorable events which followed, belongs rather to the writer of English history than to me. The Committee of Secrecy met, much to the chagrin of the Select Committee; and both pursued their labours—sometimes in directions widely apart, sometimes by travelling over the self-same ground. The Committee of Secrecy affected to deal with abstract questions of financial and mercantile management. The Select Committee put the public career of individuals to the torture, till in due time the reports of both threw the Administration before which they were laid into a fever of uncertainty. At last the papers were handed over to the then Attorney-General, Thurlow, who undertook to sift them during the Easter recess, and make a proposition. He did so, and it was as curious as it was sweeping. Having called a meeting of the members of the Administration, from which, however, the Solicitor-General, being Lord Clive's friend, was excluded, Mr. Attorney-General Thurlow informed them that the affairs of the Company were involved beyond the reach of cure, and that he saw nothing for it except to confiscate, by act of Parliament, all the sums acquired

by English public servants, under the head of gifts, grants, or
bequests, from Indian princes. It was clear, he said, that the
Company could never discharge the obligations under which it
had come to the public, and the public had therefore no alternative except to act upon the principle which determined that;
whatever was obtained of land, treasure, or any thing else by
the military force of the country, belonged in law to the state.
The Attorney-General's proposal seems to have confounded his
colleagues. Some of them objected to it on the ground that,
when the obnoxious presents were received, there was no law or
regulation in force against them ; others reminded him that it
was too late to stretch the law to its extreme limits now, seeing
that the conduct of those whom his bill would consign to ruin
had been approved and rewarded by the Sovereign. The Attorney-General declared that, after mature deliberation, he had no
better plan to bring forward ; and so the Ministerial conference
broke up.

CHAPTER XXX.

Charges brought against Clive in the House of Commons—They are
rejected.

NEITHER the objects nor the issues of this conference of Ministers
appear to have been communicated to Lord Clive. Colonel Burgoyne, however, seems to have been in some way or another made
acquainted with both; and the proceedings of the committee over
which he presided, as well as of the Ministerial Committee of
Secrecy, took forthwith a turn more decidedly hostile than before.
Charges were brought against Lord Clive on the authority of the
Company's accounts, which bore upon the face of them such a
show of plausibility, that nothing short of the clearest proof of their
groundlessness could have saved the accused party from disgrace.
For example, the Secret Committee, in one of its reports, stated,
that Lord Clive and his Council had paid away a large sum to
individuals, under the head of donation money, though an order
from the Court of Directors forbidding such payments had been
issued, and was in force at the time. It was fortunate for Clive
that he was able to show that no such order had reached him till
long after the payments were made; for the packet-ship Fal-
mouth, in which the original document was transmitted, had
been lost at sea, and the duplicate copy, received many
months subsequently, came too late. Again, in reply to some
observations from Lord North, which seemed to rest on
certain statements put forward in a Select Committee's report,
Lord Clive, after severely handling the Minister, went on
to expose the spirit in which the report in question had been
drawn up. In the course of this speech he stated " that one
gentleman, a member of that House, who had long been the
principal manager of the affairs of the East India Company, had,
on the 7th day of November last, in a private conversation with
Mr. Hoole, the Auditor-General, told that functionary that he
desired his assistance in a matter which would be particularly

serviceable, and requested him to draw up a complete state of the civil and military charges of Bengal, and likewise of the revenues since Lord Clive's arrival in Bengal in 1765; and directed him to refer to all the letters, plans, or regulations of Lord Clive, noting how far the charges, revenues, &c. agreed with them; to trace out the causes of any increase or decrease; to draw up the whole historically and progressively, making *all the accounts his own*—and, as the individual to whom he alluded expressed himself—*to mark the man;* for, continued he, it is my wish to show that all the distresses of the Company arise from him. " Sir," exclaimed Clive, " let me remind the House that a report drawn up in such a spirit, and materials drawn from such a source, must be received with exceeding caution; for against an engine of such great power no man's reputation is safe."

It is painful to go on with such a subject. It is humiliating to observe, turn whither we may, and deal with whom we can, that every question connected with Indian politics—whether the point mooted be the conquest of a province, or the establishment of machinery for the due administration of law—resolves itself, sooner or later, into a matter of pounds, shillings, and pence. If the object be to crush an Indian statesman, he is accused of falsifying accounts, or selling justice to the best bidder. If a soldier acquire wealth by a course of successful warfare, he is questioned, not regarding his manner of wielding the sword, but in respect to the property which he may have acquired by it. And so completely interwoven with the nature of Indian politics does this idolatry of gold seem to be, that where materials for a real charge of peculation are wanting, enemy seeks to undermine enemy by inventing them. Mr. Sulivan— for to him it was that Lord Clive on the present occasion alluded —made no attempt to refute this accusation. He admitted that it was substantially correct, and justified his own conduct by stating that, forasmuch as his lordship in a former session had imputed the Company's distresses to mismanagement on the part of the Directors, so he, as a Director, conceived that he had a perfect right to turn the tables, and to lay the blame upon his lord-ship, as, with Mr. Hoole's assistance, he hoped that he might have been able to do. " But to show," continued he, " that the enmity which has long been between us has never prevailed with me to work his lordship wrong, I will now make a disclosure which, through delicacy towards him, I have hitherto refrained from doing." Mr. Sulivan then proceeded to state, that in the correspondence of Lord Clive with the native powers, during his first administration of Bengal, a gap of not fewer than sixteen months was to be found; that the Directors, suspecting that it related to the grant of the feof, had repeatedly applied for copies of the same to no purpose; and that not even now, when the non-production of these documents might be said seriously to involve his lordship's honour, were they forthcoming. This was not the first occasion on which Lord Clive had been compelled to notice insinuations of the same sort. In 1763, when driven to bring an action against the Court of Directors, they had applied to him for copies of the missing letters, stating their reasons ; and he had told them then, as he now told the House, that these letters had nothing whatever to do with the grant of the feof. The fact was, that he had lent the letters in 1760 to a Mr. Campbell, who was engaged in drawing up a memorial on Dutch affairs for the purpose of having it laid before Mr. Pitt; and from that day to this, in spite of frequent inquiries, he had never been able to ascertain whither Mr. Campbell had betaken himself, nor, as a necessary consequence, what had become of his correspondence.

A story such as this was not likely to be received with implicit faith by the personal enemies of the narrator; and the members of the House of Commons could hardly be blamed if they gave to it no more credit than it seemed to deserve. Yet its truth was made manifest in the course of a few days; for Mr Campbell, reading in the newspapers an account of all that had passed, communicated with Lord Clive immediately, and the whole of the missing letters were restored to him first, and eventually to the Court of Directors. They were found, on careful examination, to be complete, and to agree literally with the description which Lord Clive had given of them.

Thus far, it will be seen, that out of every contest into which his enemies drew him, Clive came forth, if not scatheless, at least triumphant. He had skirmished well against their light troops; it was now to be seen how he could sustain the weight of a general action; for the wrath of the adverse party in the India House seemed to grow more violent after each repulse, and nothing short of a great effort to crush him would content them. Accordingly, Colonel Burgoyne, who on the 8th and 29th of April had brought up the 3rd and 4th reports of the Select Committee on Indian Affairs, called the attention of the House on the 10th of May to the subjects embraced by them, and proposed three resolutions, on which, if the House should approve of them, he gave notice of his intention, at an early period of the session, to found a motion. The resolutions in question were these :—

" 1. That all acquisitions made under the influence of a military force, or by treaty with foreign princes, did of right belong to the state.

" 2 That to appropriate acquisitions so made to the private emolument of persons intrusted with any civil or military power of the state is illegal.

" 3. That very great sums of money and other valuable property had been acquired in Bengal from princes and others of that country by persons intrusted with the civil and military powers of the state by means of such powers ; which sums of money and valuable property have been appropriated to the private use of such persons."

Colonel Burgoyne's resolutions were prefaced by a speech in which all the delinquencies, real and imaginary, of all the civil and military servants of the Company were set forth. Lord Clive's dealings in particular with Suraj-u-Dowlah and Meer Jaffier—his treachery to Omichund—his abuse of Admiral Watson's confidence, were painted in the blackest colours, as were the proceedings of the Select Committee, out of which, as the speaker asserted, all the ills which had subsequently oppressed Bengal and the Company arose. The same line of argument was followed by Sir William Meredith, by whom Burgoyne's motion was seconded. And though Mr. Wedderburn spoke well on the opposite side, and Clive himself vindicated his own character with dignity, the feeling of the House ran so strongly in favour of the oppressed, that the two former of the resolutions were carried without a division, and the last by a large majority. It was not so when the motion which Colonel Burgoyne had undertaken to found upon them came to be discussed. The House seemed then to feel that it had gone far enough to vindi-

cate the national honour. Clive might have been guilty—and
he surely had been—of some acts which would admit of no
justification. The authority of all the most sacred of the laws
which regulate the intercourse of states and of individuals
must be set aside were they to acquit him of blame. But, on
the other hand, it was certain that he had displayed great talents,
and exercised great virtues; that he had rendered eminent services both to his country and the people of India; and that it
was not for his dealings with Meer Jaffier or with Omichund
that he was now called in question, but for his determined resistance to avarice and tyranny. Under these circumstances they
came to the discussion of the last point in the argument with
minds perfectly free from that bias which it was the object of the
prime movers in the business to create against him whom they
described as " the great delinquent." Colonel Burgoyne's speech,
therefore, though able of its kind, and ably supported by that of
his original seconder, Sir W. Meredith, fell comparatively
pointless on the House; and when first Mr. Wedderburn, then
Mr. Fuller, and last of all Clive himself, had spoken in reply,
there was no room to doubt how the matter would end. Colonel
Burgoyne had proposed a resolution to this effect:—" That it
appears to this House that the Right Hon. Robert Lord Clive,
Baron of Plassey in the kingdom of Ireland, about the time of
the deposition of Suraj-u-Dowlah, and the establishment of
Meer Jaffier on the musnud, through the influence of the powers
with which he was intrusted as a member of the Select Committee and Commander-in-chief of the British forces, did obtain
and possess himself of two lacs of rupees as Commander-in-chief,
a further sum of two lacs and 80,000 rupees as member of the Select Committee, and a further sum of 16 lacs or more under the
denomination of a private donation; which sums, amounting together to 20 lacs and 80,000 rupees, were of the value, in English
money, of 234,000*l.* ; and that, in so doing, the said Robert
Lord Clive abused the power with which he was intrusted, to
the evil example of the servants of the public, and to the dishonour and detriment of the State."

Lord Clive's friends denounced the proposition as both illo-
gical and iniquitous. Lord Clive himself did more. After mi-

nutely recapitulating the services which he had rendered to the country, and calling the attention of his auditors to the acknowledgments of his merits which had over and over again been made,—after adverting to the motives in which this prosecution originated, and dealing out some hard blows to all, whether in the Cabinet or elsewhere, who suffered themselves to be made parties to it, Lord Clive spoke at large of the circumstances under which his last administration of Bengal had been forced upon him, and of the special Courts which met to thank him on his return, and to express their regret that he had not continued longer at his post.　He then burst forth into the following apostrophe, of which the effect upon the House is described in the publications of the day to have been electrical :—

"These, Sir, were circumstances certainly that gave me a full satisfaction, and a ground to think that my conduct in every instance was approved of.　After such certificates as these, Sir, am I to be brought here like a criminal, and the very best parts of my conduct construed into crimes against the state?　Is this the reward that is now held out to persons who have performed such important services to their country?　If it is, Sir, the future consequences that will attend the execution of any important trust committed to the persons who have the care of it will be fatal indeed; and I am sure the noble Lord upon the Treasury bench, whose great humanity I revere, would never have consented to the resolutions that passed the other night, if he had thought on the dreadful consequences that would attend them. Sir, I cannot say that I either sit or rest easy when I find, by that extensive resolution, that all I have in the world is confiscated, and that no one will take my security for a shilling. These, Sir, are dreadful apprehensions to remain under; and I cannot look upon myself but as a bankrupt.　I have not anything left that I can call my own, except my paternal fortune of 500l. per annum, and which has been in the family for ages past.　But upon this I am content to live; and perhaps I shall find more real content of mind and happiness than in the trembling affluence of an unsettled fortune.　But, Sir, I must make one more observation,—that if the definition of the honourable gentleman (Colonel Burgoyne), and of this House, that the state, as expressed in these resolutions, is, *quoad hoc*, the Company, then, Sir, every farthing I enjoy is granted to me. But to be called upon, after sixteen years have elapsed, to account for my conduct in this manner, and, after an uninterrupted enjoyment of my property, to be questioned, and considered as obtaining it unwarrantably, is hard indeed ! and a treatment I should not think the British Senate capable of. But, if such should be the case, I have a conscious innocence within me that tells me my conduct is irreproachable. *Frangas, non flectes.* My enemies may take from me what I have ; they may, as they think, make me poor, but I will be happy ! I mean not this as my defence, though I have done for the present. My defence will be heard at that bar ; but, before I sit down, I have one request to make to the House,—that, when they come to decide upon my honour, they will not forget their own."

The immediate effect of this appeal was to cause an adjournment of the debate ; its ultimate consequence, to rob Colonel Burgoyne's resolution of all power to hurt either the honour or the fortune of Lord Clive. On the 21st of May the subject was again taken up by the examination of a few witnesses and the reading of the evidence which Lord Clive had given before the Select Committee. A second debate followed, which was scarcely less animated, and more prolonged than the former, and on the 22nd the House decided, by a majority of 155 to 95, that, admitting all to be true which was stated in regard to the moneys acquired, " Robert Lord Clive did at the same time render great and meritorious services to his country." As the whole spirit of the motion was changed, on the motion of Mr. Stanley and Mr. Fuller, not merely by the substitution of a new for the original clause at the end, but by the omission of certain words from the body of the second clause, I cannot better conclude the present chapter than by transferring it entire to my own pages. It stands on the records of the Commons' House of Parliament thus :—

" That it appears to this House, that the Right Hon. Robert Lord Clive, Baron of Plassey in the kingdom of Ireland, about the time of the deposition of Suraj-u-Dowlah, and the establishment of Meer Jaffier on the musnud, did obtain and possess himself of two lacs of rupees as Commander-in-Chief, a further sum of

two lacs and 80,000 rupees as member of the Select Committee,
and a further sum of 16 lacs or more under the denomination of
a private donation ; which sums, amounting together to 20 lacs
and 80,000 rupees, were of the value, in English money, of
234,000*l.* ; and that Lord Clive did at the same time render
great and meritorious services to his country."

CHAPTER XXXI.

Death of Lord Clive—His Character

In the subsequent proceedings, which ended in the granting of a
new charter to the Company, and established Mr. Hastings as
Governor-General of India, with a Council nominated, as it
seemed, for the express purpose of thwarting him in everything which he might desire to accomplish, Lord Clive took no
part. The persecutions to which he had been subjected appear
to have weighed heavily upon his spirits, and he withdrew in
gloom and undisguised mortification from public life. It is said,
though I cannot find that the anecdote rests upon any sound
authority, that the Government, finding war with the colonies to
be inevitable, pressed him to undertake the command of the
army which they were preparing to send to America. But such
a proposal, if made at all, was declined ; for the state of his
health entirely unfitted him for continuous exertion either of body
or of mind.   Probably, too, it was the same sad cause which operated to restrain him from supplying Voltaire, then in the meri-
dian of his literary renown, with materials out of which to
compile a history of the Conquest of Bengal. We know, at
least, that the French philosopher applied through Dr. Moore,
the ingenious author of ' Zeluco,' to be put in possession of his
lordship's papers, and that the application was not attended to.
Be this, however, as it may, the events which gave a character
to the remainder of Lord Clive's existence were not of a nature
to admit of minute description ; and I shall therefore content
myself with adverting to them in general terms.

As long as the Parliament sat, Clive continued to reside in
Berkeley Square. Immediately on its rising—that is, on the
17th of June—he proceeded to Bath, whence, after a short residence, he removed to Walcot. There he saw his more intimate
and familiar acquaintances as heretofore, and corresponded occa-

siona.ly with friends at a distance; but the paroxysms of pain under which he suffered became continually greater, and he more and more had recourse to the frightful palliative of opium, under the continued use of which his whole nervous system gave way. Some fragments of letters from him are preserved, which show that he never ceased to take an interest in those to whom through life he had been attached. It is said, also, that he had occasional conferences with Lord North on the subject of Indian affairs; and one, at least, of his communications with that minister, written about six weeks previously to his decease, remains. But the sword, which had been throughout too sharp for the scabbard, was rapidly cutting its way through. I do not know why I should shrink from describing the circumstances under which he died. The world knows that he committed suicide; and according as men have thought of the " self-murderer " while he lived, they are wont in every case, to blame or to pity, or to do both, after the deed is done. Now, Clive's manner of perpetrating the stern act seems to be but in keeping with the whole tenor of his existence; and I therefore tell the tale as it has been told to me.

A female friend, it appears, was on a visit at his house. He had suffered extremely throughout the whole of the 21st of November, and was driven more than was usual with him to seek relief in strong doses of laudanum. The same process continued during the early part of the 22nd; but that his reason was not clouded, nor his self-possession taken away, the following fact seems to prove. About noon on the 22nd, or a little later, the lady came into his room, and said,—" Lord Clive, I cannot find a good pen; will you be so good as make me one?" " To be sure," replied he; and, taking a penknife from his waistcoat pocket, he moved towards one of the windows, and mended the pen. The lady received it back with thanks, and withdrew. In a short time afterwards, a servant, entering, found Lord Clive dead; and the instrument with which he had destroyed himself proved, on examination, to be the same small knife with which he had mended his friend's pen.

It was not to be expected, that a termination so awful to a career of glory and success well-nigh unexampled in English history should fail of affecting with deep and painful impressions the minds of all to whom the event was made known. Many, I

regret to say, received the tidings in a spirit which testified as
little to their sagacity as to their Christian temper ; many more
—and I confess that I belong to the number—accepted them as
proof that there may be intolerable world-weariness in the heart
of him into whose lap the world seems to have poured its richest
treasures.   At all events, the event itself vouches for something amiss, either in the moral or in the physical organization
of the individual, or in both.   For the line which separates genius from eccentricity is often so narrow, that, unless there be
some principle of action more elevated than the world can supply, the chances are equal that the one will sooner or later
merge in the other.   Now, whatever Clive's excellences of character may have been, I confess myself unable to detect in him
any trace of the sort of principle of which I am now speaking.
His honour, in the commonly received acceptation of the term—
west of the tropical line—is admitted ; and his generosity to
friends and relatives has never been called in question.   But I
have not succeeded in bringing home to him a solitary act—I
cannot discover in those portions of his correspondence which I
have perused a single expression—which can be so interpreted as
to lead to the belief that there was any spring or motive of conduct within, apart from the prospect of immediate advantage to
his country, or to himself, or to the authorities whom he served.
Hence life ceased to have an aim for him as soon as the excitement of enterprise was taken away ; and the fatal remedies to
which he had recourse, while striving to blunt the pressure of
bodily suffering, quite broke him down, through the nervous
exhaustion of which they were at once the cause and the effect.

Looking, on the other hand, to his public proceedings, it
seems impossible to refuse to his name a place in the list of those
who have done their country eminent service.   To him belongs
the merit of having restored, being yet a boy, the tarnished
honour of the English arms, while he saved an important settlement from destruction.   The foundations of English political
ascendancy in the East were laid by him during the first stage of
his manhood ; and, finally, the wisdom of his more matured
counsels, and the energy with which he acted upon them, overcame all abuses in the management of the Company's affairs, and
brought order and system out of their very opposites.   " From

Clive's first visit to India," writes Mr. Macaulay with perfect truth, "dates the renown of the English arms in the East; from his second visit to India dates the political ascendancy of the English in that country; from his third visit to India dates the purity of the administration of our Eastern Empire."

The individual who, with the means at Clive's disposal, could accomplish all this—who could boast that between the twenty-fourth and forty-fourth years of his age he had saved a province, conquered a kingdom, and substituted in the management of its affairs order for anarchy, and justice for violence and wrong, deserves to be ranked among the most remarkable men of his generation. No doubt the qualities which made him what he was belong rather to the man of action than to the philosopher. He was brave, firm of purpose, full of self-reliance, indifferent to responsibility, and not over-scrupulous in regard to the morality of his measures so long as important and successful results promised to be obtained by them. He was as indifferent, likewise, to the feelings of others, as heroes are usually supposed to be, though certainly not more so. At the same time it would be unjust to deny, that, if the philosophy of statesmanship be in any measure based upon a knowledge of human nature, Clive in his own peculiar sphere of action had his share of such philosophy too. There never lived a European who more thoroughly mastered than he all the tricks and artifices of Oriental diplomacy. This it was which so eminently qualified him to govern where the will of the ruler is law; for he permitted no tyranny to be exercised except his own, and tyranny on his part proved to be in the main only a stern and uncompromising ministration of justice. The same turn of mind, however, rendered him incapable of dealing aright with the passions and prejudices of a free people. Whatever he sought to accomplish he sought to accomplish by force; he had neither the temper nor the talent that are needed to battle with preconceived opinion, or to surmount the obstacles of party. Accordingly, his intrigues at the India House were mere efforts to outbuy his rivals, as on another field he would have ridden them down, or swept them aside by the fire of his artillery. And in the House of Commons he never became influential, because he could not bring himself to give and take, to yield a point, it may be of slight importance, in order to ensure the accomplishment of a great end.

Considered as a politican, Clive was essentially oriental; considered as a military man, circumstances render the task of classifying him very difficult. On the whole, however, I am inclined to think that, on any theatre of operations, whether in Europe or America, he would have proved a great commander. No doubt the field on which he played his part was peculiar. He waged war at the head of a handful of disciplined troops against hordes of undisciplined warriors, and defeated them; but he waged it in such a way as to prove that the principles on which he acted were those which are applicable to every combination of circumstances, and against every description of enemy. I have elsewhere alluded to the supposed wish of the Minister to employ him against the North American colonists, already in a state of incipient revolt. I cannot tell what truth there may be in the story; but of this I have little doubt, that, had the state of his health and the temper of his mind permitted him to embark upon the enterprise, the dependence of the United States on the mother-country would have been continued for at least another half-century.

Lord Clive's reading was not extensive, and his learning a mere blank. He never acquired even of the languages of India knowledge enough to be able to correspond or even to converse in any of them except imperfectly. His general manner in society was silent and reserved. Still, when a subject was broached in which he took an interest, that harsh and heavy countenance of his would light up, and he spoke with a degree of animation which appears to have told powerfully. Boswell, in his 'Life of Johnson,' has placed on record the substance of a brief dialogue between the moralist and Robertson the historian, which, because it illustrates two of the statements hazarded in this *résumé* of the great man's character, I may be permitted to transcribe. "Dr. Robertson," says the biographer, "expatiated on the character of a certain nobleman, that he was one of the strongest-minded men that ever lived; that he would sit in company quite sluggish while there was nothing to call forth his intellectual vigour; but the moment that any important subject was started—for instance, how this country is to be defended

from a French invasion—he would rouse himself and show his
extraordinary talents with the most powerful ability and animation." *Johnson,*—" Yet this man cut his own throat! The
true strong and sound mind can embrace equally great things
and small."

Johnson might have expressed himself with more delicacy,
but in the main his argument is sound ; for I cannot agree with
Mr. Macaulay in laying any portion of the blame of Lord
Clive's death " on the pangs of wounded honour " arising out of
the Parliamentary persecution to which he had been subjected.
The sad event appears to me to have been the result of that
want of balance in the arrangement of mind with matter which,
if not produced by a disordered intellect, comes of satiety,
which is itself a disease in the moral nature of the man, if,
indeed, a total absence of the religious principle may, without
the misuse of terms, be so spoken of.

Lord Clive's personal appearance was not prepossessing. To
a countenance which was saved from vulgarity only by the expression of decision and natural intelligence which pervaded it,
he added a figure without symmetry or grace, which he rendered doubly conspicuous by the elaborate care with which it
was his custom to adorn it. His social habits were hospitable
and sumptuous in the extreme. He loaded with presents all to
whom he took a fancy, and kept open table both in London and
in the country. Yet he never succeeded in achieving even a
moderate share of popularity, and with a large acquaintance
could boast but of few friends. He was a great man ; and in
tracing his career I have felt that I was following the footsteps
of a giant. I regret that I am not able to add, that I can
think of him likewise as an object of love and personal admiration.

Lord Clive was buried in the church of Moreton Say, the
parish in which he was born. He left a family of two sons and
three daughters to inherit his fortune and his name.

THE END.

LONDON: PRINTED BY WILLIAM CLOWES AND SONS, LIMITED, STAMFORD STREET
AND CHARING CROSS.